Praise for #1 *New York Times* bestselling author Susan Wiggs

Also by Susan Wiggs

CONTEMPORARY ROMANCES

Home Before Dark
The Ocean Between Us
Lakeside Cottage
Summer by the Sea
Table for Five
Just Breathe
The Goodbye Quilt

The Lakeshore Chronicles

Summer at Willow Lake
The Winter Lodge
Dockside
Snowfall at Willow Lake
Fireside
Lakeshore Christmas
The Summer Hideaway
Marrying Daisy Bellamy
Return to Willow Lake
Starlight on Willow Lake

The Bella Vista Chronicles

The Apple Orchard
The Beekeeper's Ball

HISTORICAL ROMANCES

The Lightkeeper
The Drifter
The Mistress of Normandy
The Maiden of Ireland

Tudor Rose

At the King's Command
The Maiden's Hand
At the Queen's Summons

Chicago Fire Trilogy

The Hostage
The Mistress
The Firebrand

Calhoun Chronicles

The Charm School
The Horsemaster's Daughter
Halfway to Heaven
Enchanted Afternoon
A Summer Affair

Look for Susan Wiggs's new novel,
THE OYSTERVILLE SEWING CIRCLE,
available now!

SUSAN WIGGS

Snowfall
IN THE CITY

mira

mira

Recycling programs
for this product may
not exist in your area.

ISBN-13: 978-0-7783-1019-8

Snowfall in the City

Copyright © 2019 by Harlequin Books S.A.

The St. James Affair
Copyright © 2003 by Susan Wiggs

Candlelight Christmas
Copyright © 2013 by Susan Wiggs

For questions and comments about the quality of this book, please contact us at
CustomerService@Harlequin.com.

BookClubbish.com

Printed in U.S.A.

CONTENTS

For dreamers everywhere.
May the spark of your imagination take you wherever you wish to go.

THE ST. JAMES AFFAIR

CHAPTER ONE

❖◆❖⸱⸱◆⸱⸱❖◆❖

Elaine St. James hurried along Fifth Avenue, trying to out-
run Christmas, but it was gaining on her. She was only
a few steps ahead of a troop of apple-cheeked carolers belting
out "Hark the Herald Angels Sing" and collecting donations
from shoppers and tourists. She dodged to avoid a Santa reeling in the crosswalk, his breath smelling of too much holiday
cheer too early in the day.

Although she had a cell phone glued to her ear, Elaine could
barely hear Byron, her boyfriend. Still, she'd heard enough to
know the news was not good.

"A bra model?" she yelled into the tiny daisy-decorated
phone.

His response was a garbled remark ending in "Huh?"

And so she yelled even louder, "You're dumping me for a
bra model?"

Too late, she realized the heralds had stopped harking, and the stoplight had brought traffic to a halt. Everyone within half a city block had heard her.

Caught in the glare of dozens of curious looks, Elaine dropped her hand to her side and hitched her purse strap up on her shoulder. Byron's mosquito-voiced reply squawked faintly from the receiver, but she didn't want to hear another word. Belying the flames of humiliated color in her cheeks, she held her head high and said to no one in particular, "Whatever."

Then she clicked off her Star-Tac, turned on her kitten-heeled boot and headed up the street. Behind her, traffic started up as the light changed. The carolers struck up "Silver Bells," and the city sidewalks became busy sidewalks again.

Okay, so it's Christmas, Elaine told herself, appalled to feel a sudden sting of tears in her eyes. *Tears*. Not for Byron, she realized. But for yet another dream gone, just like that. It was hard to say goodbye to a dream, hard to close the door on hope.

Elaine squared her shoulders and soldiered on down the avenue. The fact was, she had enormous reserves of self-discipline. She'd been raised to do what was expected of her, and she was extremely good at it. She just had to get through the day. How hard could that be?

She tried to get into the spirit of children laughing, people passing. She saw smile after smile and even made a valiant attempt at smiling herself, but it felt more like gritting her teeth.

Why was Christmas so easy for some people, but so impossible for Elaine? Where had she been when they were passing out Christmas spirit?

She knew where she'd been—in the chill confines of the right boarding school, the right summer camp, the right college. She'd been so busy training herself to do what was expected of her that she'd forgotten to ask herself what the point of all her efforts was.

At the next crosswalk, a woman laden with glossy bags and beribboned parcels shoved herself in Elaine's way like a barge pushing into port. Elaine bit her lip to keep from making some smart remark, but she couldn't help scowling. She was later than ever for her lunch, and in no mood. Given her current situation, a slight edge of crankiness was justifiable.

There had been a time, long ago, when the bustle and noise of the season had filled her with a sense of magic. She missed her former self, but had no idea how to revive that breathless, boundless feeling. Clearly Byron was not the answer. Of course, she should have known that from the start, but in spite of all the ways life had disappointed her, deep down, she still had this secret, frisky inner self that wanted to believe in magic.

Someone had a set of real silver bells. She heard them chiming like a windup alarm clock.

A moment later, she found herself confronted by an elf holding out a collection jar with a picture of a grinning orphan. Clenching her teeth, she merely stared straight ahead, pretending she hadn't seen him. If she didn't make eye contact, she might be able to shake him off. Elaine was pretty successful at avoiding contact. It had kept her safe for years.

These street singers for charity were bogus, she reminded herself, thinking of the reeling Santa. The donations went into the collectors' pockets, to be spent later at the pool hall or package store. Falling for that game merely encouraged more panhandlers.

"Soon it will beeee Christmas day," sang the elf.

Duh, thought Elaine, eyeing the swags of plastic greenery and twinkling lights that had infested the city since the day after Halloween. The season seemed to descend earlier every year. Yet every year, Elaine couldn't help feeling a little secret jolt of excitement. And hope. *Maybe this year will be different,* she always thought. But nothing ever changed, and she grew more cynical and brittle as time went on.

"Come on, lady, gimme a break. Bestow a trifle." The elf rattled the collection jar at her. He had a sing-along songbook and a stick-on name tag that said, "Hi! My Name Is Larry." He wore a bright red muffler and an unjustifiably cheerful grin.

The light changed and she joined the surge of pedestrians in the crosswalk, but the persistent caroler kept stalking her.

"Just a little something for Westside Children's Charities." He flashed an official-looking permit.

It was probably forged, Elaine thought.

"Do it for the kids, lady." Jingle bells bobbed from his pointy cap.

She scowled at him. "Go away."

He gave her a puppy-dog look.

Be strong, she told herself. If she gave in to this one, another would take his place, and the next thing she knew, half the city would be wanting something from her. Pointing her face into the icy wind, she strode on.

"Away in a Manger" swept through the marauding carolers. The elf bobbed along at her side. "Look," he said, "it's not my fault the guy dumped you for some bimbo. Don't take it out on the kids."

Finally she could hold her tongue no longer. "This is not endearing you to me."

"Think of the kids, then. There's magic in giving, don't you know that?"

"I don't believe in magic." There. Saying so aloud made it as real as the pitted, frozen sidewalk beneath her fashionably clad feet.

"That won't keep it from happening. But you have to make a donation. Come on. What's five bucks to someone wearing thousand-dollar Manolo boots?"

An elf who knew footwear. This was getting stranger by the moment.

"Five bucks, and the magic starts happening," he said. "Guaranteed."

"What, I pay you, and you disappear?"

He winked, and sent her a gladsome look. "Trust me, you won't be sorry. Help us out, and the world will start helping you."

"What makes you think I need help?"

"You can't keep edging your way along the crowded paths of life, warning all human sympathy to keep its distance," he pointed out.

Great. Not only did he know shoes, he quoted Dickens. *I live in a world of fools*, thought Elaine.

"Make it a ten, and I'll throw in a miracle," Larry offered.

"Oh, for Pete's sake." As the last threads of her patience unraveled, she reached into her purse, then shoved a twenty at him.

"Merry Christmas, Elaine," he called cheerfully.

"Whatever."

Then it struck her that he'd called her by name. She stopped, causing a businessman to slam into her from behind, then walk around her with only the gruffest of apologies. She searched the bustling crowd, but Larry the elf was nowhere in sight. How had he known her name? A lucky guess? No, he'd probably seen something with her name on it when she'd whipped out the twenty.

Dismissing the incident with a shrug, she continued up the avenue. The herd of carolers brayed, "We Wish You a Merry Christmas."

Christmas didn't mean merriment of any sort to Elaine. It hadn't for a long time. These days, the holiday meant more meetings to schedule, more events to plan, more clients demanding her time.

Without Byron, it meant one less gift to buy this afternoon. The only discomfort his defection would create was a pained and awkward explanation to her parents, who had given Byron the St. James stamp of approval. The only fallout would be invisible to the world and felt only by Elaine. And she was getting awfully good at covering up her pain.

She ducked down a side street, mercifully uncongested except for a panhandler in an army surplus jacket and his scruffy dog. They watched her from a stoop next to Fezzywig's Bar and Grill.

In her haste, she dropped her handbag and half the contents spilled across the dirty, rock-salted sidewalk. Gritting her teeth in irritation, she squatted down and scooped up the spillage— her cell phone, a tin of breath mints, her Coach leather agenda, a lipstick and assorted other gear—and stood up.

"Miss, you forgot something." The panhandler held out a cluster of keys, strung on a ring attached to a silver skate.

"Thanks." She grabbed the keys, stuffed them in her bag. She started to walk away, then hesitated and fished a bill from her wallet. Elaine was no pushover when it came to money, but she expected to pay for services rendered. Besides, the panhandler had given her back her silver skate key ring and for that he deserved a reward.

That key ring had a special purpose for Elaine. She kept it as a reminder of the price of giving her heart.

CHAPTER TWO

Elaine hurried under the awning leading to Fezzywig's, a supertrendy spot that had recently become the hottest in the city. Thanks to Elaine's publicity firm, the upscale place was currently the favorite midday rendezvous of the twenty-somethings whose names graced the society pages and celebrity columns.

She dashed inside, and was immediately enveloped by the sleek, dimly lit decor of chrome and leather, the cheerful clink of glassware, and—mercifully—no piped-in Christmas Muzak. Instead, sinuous strains of vintage Coltrane provided a tasteful sound track for the ultrachic crowd. Gratefully, she shrugged out of coat, hat and gloves and handed them to the coat-check girl.

She ducked into the ladies' room. Her ivory cashmere slacks and sweater looked fine—particularly with the buttery-soft

Manolos, she thought—but her hair and makeup were a disaster. Yet another thing she hated about Christmas—the rough winds, not to mention the brutal cold and the icy streets.

She fluffed her hair back into a shining blond bob, then took out her compact and went to work, restoring order to her face with practiced strokes. Her mind worked furiously as she performed the damage control.

So Byron had dumped her. She had to decide the best way to play it. On the one hand, she could assume the role of the wounded party, fragile and in desperate need of support. That would allow her to bask in her friends' soothing platitudes about how the jerk didn't deserve her, how he'd never been good enough for her in the first place, how he'd grow old and bitterly regretful, thinking of the opportunity he'd passed up with her.

Leaning toward the mirror, she used an eyelash comb to de-clump her mascara. On the other hand, she could mask her humiliation and disappointment behind sarcasm, turning Byron Witherspoon into the joke of the day among their crowd. In throwing her over for a grade-A bimbo, he'd certainly given her adequate material.

Okay, she thought, holstering her lip-gloss wand and pasting on a smile. It's Christmas Eve. The perfect time for amusement. She'd breeze through this, pretending the loss of her boyfriend was nothing.

Except she didn't have to pretend. Her brow puckering a little, she studied her image in the mirror. Not bad, with that tousle-haired, cashmere-sweater, gold-earring thing going on. She hardly looked like a woman scorned.

Searching her feelings, she discovered she'd suffered no emotional breakdown over this. The only twinge of regret she felt was that losing Byron now meant showing up at her parents' party dateless tonight. How terribly inconvenient. She'd never hear the end of it.

She was actually a little disappointed in herself. Where were the pain, the trauma, the weeping and the wailing? The wallowing? Wasn't this supposed to be a personal train wreck rather than the emotional equivalent of a broken nail? At least if she wept and carried on, even for a few minutes, it would mean that she hadn't wasted the past six months dating a guy she didn't care about. But she had no urge to cry and carry on. She felt like getting some work done.

Although it was still early, a good crowd had gathered to fuel themselves for the last day of shopping and tonight's round of parties. Elaine greeted, waved and air-kissed her way across the room, her practiced smile untroubled by Byron's betrayal. She loved this crowd of socialites and actors and trendsetters, and they loved her. She was in her element here, in the spotlight as she made her way to meet with her partners, who also happened to be her best friends.

Yet Elaine had a problem. And it had nothing to do with her recent, very public conversation with Byron.

She wasn't sure why it happened, but sometimes, at the least convenient of moments, she felt something a person in her position wasn't ever supposed to feel. Loneliness.

It was absurd, given the full, busy life she led, but she couldn't help it. No matter how much she tried to deny the truth, she often found herself gripped by a sense of futility and the bone-deep ache of emptiness.

That emptiness was the enemy. She battled it with direct action. Land that account, grab that media spot, get out there in the glitzy world of fashion and entertainment and make a name for yourself. A willful, determined nature had compelled her to turn herself, in just a few short years, into one of the busiest, most influential publicists in the city.

Bolstering herself with the thought, she strode across the bar to the high-backed booth where her friends waited, nursing Seven-and-Skyy cocktails and chattering at warp speed.

"There you are, Elaine." Melanie paddled her hand in the air. "You're late."

"Sorry." Elaine slid into the horseshoe-shaped booth next to Bobbi, who was not just her best friend, but her very best friend. "I had a lot of calls to make from the office." She felt mildly annoyed at her partners. Just because it was Christmas, they thought they could take time off and neglect important business. They were supposed to know better. Public relations opportunities didn't disappear just because the calendar declared a holiday. In fact, that was even more reason to get busy.

Larry the elf was dead wrong. The magic of the season wasn't the spirit of giving. It was that Christmas added an extra media hook to their press releases.

Since it was past noon, she ordered a kir royale, slipped her purse strap off her shoulder and made a conscious effort to smile. Jenny P (her last name was Pinkwater but she'd dropped it long ago) looked perfect and polished in Kajal lipstick, black merino and knee-high suede boots. Melanie Benz, affectionately known as Bitchcakes by her adoring clients, laid out her Day Timer and Palm Pilot on the table. She was chopstick-thin. Her white-blond hair was spiked, her eyebrows pared into arches of perpetual surprise. Bobbi, graced with the looks of a supermodel, was a walking billboard for their clients in a T. Gallagher sweater and leather skirt, Chez Moi makeup and a hairstyle by Iago.

Elaine had handpicked Bobbi, a nobody from a North Carolina mill town looking to break into show business or modeling. Elaine and her partners had other plans. Through the magic of their power over the press, they turned Bobbi into the city's latest girl-about-town. They gave her the right look, posed her with the right stars and socialites, dropped her name in the right ears. And it had worked. She appeared in all the magazines that mattered—*W, Vogue* and *Quest.* Within days, the phone had begun to ring, invitations rolled in. Within weeks, *Cosmo* was calling to get her take on the best spot-reducing exercise for summer. Bobbi's launch was a ringing success.

There was an unexpected bonus in Elaine's project to create a media darling. As bubbly and refreshing as a split of Moët, Bobbi had become her best friend and confidant, the sister she'd never had. She was someone to share secrets and dreams with, someone to whom Elaine might even dare to admit that breaking up with Byron didn't actually hurt, but had frightened her by making her doubt her ability to sustain any sort of relationship.

No. She wouldn't go that far. Even her soul sister would not be privy to that fact.

Tonight Bobbi would play a key part in moving their firm up the food chain. It was going to be her job to beguile the mysterious and ambitious Axel, a hip Swiss parfumier they were trying to lure as a client. Everything important rode on landing this account. Axel would be proof at last to her parents that she was capable of doing something that mattered, of making a life for herself and standing on her own two feet. They'd always believed she was dabbling, their Upper East Side princess, playing at being a publicist to pass the time until she settled down and married someone with the right credentials, someone like Byron Witherspoon.

Now Elaine needed Axel more than ever. Acquiring the business of the Swiss billionaire would lessen the humiliation and soften the betrayal of losing Byron.

"If we manage to sign him, he'll open the door to major accounts in Europe," Elaine said as they went over the final details of tonight's event, known for decades in the society pages as the St. James affair. Each year, as her grandparents had before them, her parents invited everyone who was anyone to their annual Christmas Eve bash. Unlike past years, however, this time they'd allowed Elaine's firm to handle the planning. She didn't want to screw up.

"What's he like?" asked Bobbi. "I'm ninety-seven-percent sure I've never done it with a billionaire."

"He's perfect."

"What, you've done it with him?" asked Mel.

"Of course not. But Axel and I go way back. Boarding school days, actually. Looks that good should be banned from boarding school. You'll see." Elaine felt a surge of ambition. Playing the power matching game and teaching someone else the ropes were what she did best. She never stopped playing or thinking of the next move. It was what kept her going, how she made sense of the world.

Melanie and Jenny put their heads together like a couple of battle commanders, mapping out a seating strategy for the party.

"I guess I'll find out tonight." Bobbi lowered her voice. "Um, Elaine …do you think I could get a teeny weeny advance on my check? I'm a little strapped."

Elaine gritted her teeth. "Your advances are already taking you into the summer," she said.

"I know, but it's so expensive to keep up this lifestyle. Everything just piles up. My credit cards are totally maxed out. Tomorrow's Christmas, Elaine. What do you say, honey?"

She forced her jaw to relax. Honestly, some people had no self-control or work ethic. "Stop by the office in the morning and I'll write you a check."

"Actually, I wasn't planning on coming in tomorrow."

"It's our busiest time of year, Bobbi."

"It's Christmas."

"I rest my case. Busy." Elaine took a gulp of her drink.

"It's only once a year." Bobbi's tone wheedled. "I was hoping to fly home to see my family. My sister Jimmi just had another baby. Oh, Elaine. What could be sweeter than a baby at Christmas?"

"A contract with a Swiss billionaire," Jenny said.

Melanie ran a shiny-tipped finger down a list in her planner. "By the way, Elaine, your mom's a peach to work with."

Elaine forced a smile over the rim of her glass. "Isn't she just?" In fact, Freddie St. James had given only the most grudging approval to Elaine's list of suggestions. Despite her skepticism of the edgy menu items and trendy guest list, her appreciation of Elaine's handling of the press had persuaded her.

To Freddie, the only thing more important than putting on a successful affair was having the papers report that she'd put on a successful affair. Perversely, having this goal in common had brought Elaine closer to her mother than she'd ever been. Now they were merely oceans apart instead of galaxies.

"You look nervous," Jenny commented, tilting her head to one side to study Elaine. "You're never nervous. What's up with that?"

"It's my parents' party, for heaven's sake."

"So? We do parties all the time. We're the best in town. People are still talking about the Helpline Foundation fundraiser we did last Thanksgiving in Bridgehampton. What's really eating you?"

Elaine took a deep breath. She might as well spill. "I hate Christmas. I hate my life. Byron dumped me for a bra model."

The announcement fell into a collective, stunned silence.

"But you were supposed to marry him," Jenny said after a horrified pause. "His father practically owns a broadcasting empire. You two were going to be the ultimate media power couple."

Bobbi leaned in close to give her a hug. Her forgiving nature made Elaine feel small. "Oh, honey," Bobbi said in her delightful Southern accent, "We're so sorry."

"Don't be. I'm more annoyed by his timing than anything else."

"It's not too late to find another plus-one for tonight." Mel started a search on her Palm. "It's Christmas. You can't be dateless."

Elaine bit her tongue. The truth was, she didn't want a date. Or even Christmas, for that matter. She just wanted to make it through the holiday rush and get back to work.

"Tonight will be perfect," Jenny declared, raising her glass. "Your parents will be blown away, we'll have Axel eating out of our hands and everyone will live happily ever after."

Elaine's smile felt stiff as she lifted her champagne flute to her friends' highball glasses. "To happily ever after."

The bright sound of clinking glasses penetrated the din of piped-in music and high-octane conversation. She would get past this, Elaine told herself. Loneliness and yearning were for losers. Tonight would be perfect.

She watched the bubbles in her champagne cocktail. Through the half-empty glass, she spied something—someone—that made her freeze. She forgot to breathe, to move, to think.

Everything receded into a blur of color and sound, everything except him. He came into sharp focus, each detail about him familiar despite the passage of—she counted quickly in her head—seven years. Seven years this very day, in fact.

She felt trapped, yet at the same time helplessly enchanted, as though she were drowning in honey. All the intensity of first love came roaring back at her, possessing her, waking up feelings she had thought long dead.

It was, she discovered, physically impossible to tear her gaze from that broad-shouldered stance and easy smile, that air of assurance and electric sex appeal. Time had only deepened and sharpened the attributes that still sometimes haunted her dreams.

A classic Bob Marley tune filled the air.

"Elaine, what's the matter?" asked Jenny. "You look as though you've seen a ghost."

Ducking her head to hide the flush in her cheeks, she set down her glass. "The ghost of Christmas past."

CHAPTER THREE

"Whose past?" Jenny demanded.

"My past." Shaken, Elaine propped her chin in her hand and continued to gaze across the room at the tall, unforgettable silhouette, outlined by frosty winter light streaming in through the wide window.

Memories flooded her, of a brief time when Christmas had meant more to her than juggling a social schedule with a business plan. Against her will, she remembered those nostalgic days when the softest, most vulnerable part of her had felt safe with an unexpected stranger.

They never should have met in the first place. She belonged to a social class governed by strict but invisible rules. One of those rules prohibited her from fraternizing with guys like Tony Fiore. He came from a different world entirely, and that world had rules of its own. He'd been raised in a large Italian-

American family in Brooklyn that believed, as much as the St. Jameses did, in sticking to its own kind.

At eighteen, she was only just discovering the world outside her privileged, insulated life. He was definitely a major discovery.

Now an older, possibly even more interesting, Tony Fiore stopped at a crowded table across the room. He started talking to the well-dressed patrons there. Every face at the table turned toward him as he spoke.

Elaine's friends followed the direction of her rapt stare. "Holy mistletoe," Mel said. "That guy?"

"Who is he?" asked Jen.

Bobbi patted Elaine's arm. "Whoever he is, he'll make Byron seem like a bad dream."

"His name's Tony Fiore. We met a long time ago, when we were in college." Their lives had intersected for the first time at the ice rink at Rockefeller Center during Christmas break. Tony was attending Notre Dame on a hockey scholarship. She'd never forget her first glimpse of him. Crowds of tourists and regulars had jammed the ice, yet Tony Fiore had glided effortlessly between couples and children and daredevil teenagers. His imposing profile and swift athletic strokes across the ice had caught her attention.

"Fiore." Jenny studied him, her expression that of a jeweler inspecting a flawless gem. Elaine followed her gaze. Pale daylight flickered on his thick indigo hair, which lay in glossy, unruly waves that defied a conservative haircut. "I've never heard of him," Jen continued. "How can that be?"

Elaine struggled to act blasé. She reminded herself of the way things had ended between them—or failed to end, depending on how you looked at it. They'd been Romeo and Juliet without the messy final act.

Hardening her heart, she said, "You wouldn't have. He's

nobody." Even as she said the words, her throat went tight. Nobody but the only guy who had ever convinced her that magic was real. Nobody but the guy who, on the night she'd gone to offer her heart to him, had stood her up.

"He looks like somebody to me," Melanie said. "I can't quite place him."

"Maybe he's a movie star," Bobbi suggested, reaching across the table to snatch the cherry from Mel's drink.

"If he was a star, we'd know who he is."

"What's he doing?" asked Bobbi.

Holding a clipboard with a pen attached, Tony Fiore moved to another table and greeted the people seated there. Again, everyone turned to him, and their faces lit up as though he'd flipped a switch.

"Maybe collecting pledges or donations," said Jenny. "Who cares? Look at him."

He set down the clipboard, bracing his hands on the table and bending slightly to lend someone a pen. They could now see the reflective lettering on the back of his bulky parka.

"Well, how about that," said Melanie. "He's a cop."

Elaine stared at him. A cop? He was supposed to be a hockey star. That was the only way she'd made sense of what had happened to them. She'd assumed he'd realized he wouldn't be able to juggle a professional athlete's career with falling in love. Now she was forced to consider the idea that he'd thrown her over for the dubious glories of being a cop.

Bobbi shifted in the booth and fussed with the pashmina bunching in her lap. "He's coming this way, isn't he?"

Before anyone could reply, he approached their table.

Oh, that smile, Elaine thought, suppressing a groan. Those eyes, the color of melted chocolate. This man, she realized, had a face she couldn't seem to stop dreaming about no matter how many Christmases had passed.

"Afternoon, ladies," he said. That voice was another haunting memory that wouldn't leave her alone. It was deep and self-assured, faintly brushed with the real-world tones of his native Brooklyn.

Elaine fixed a smile on her face, though everything from the neck down froze in panic. "Tony Fiore. It's been a long time." She wondered if he realized that tonight was the anniversary of their doom.

"Six years tonight," he said, staring down at her with appreciation.

Well, thank God, she thought. If he'd failed to remember her, she would have died, right in the middle of Fezzywig's. But the warmth in his eyes, the extra layer of color in his face, confirmed that he had not forgotten her.

She wondered if he recalled the feeling of holding hands, gliding across the ice, if he could never listen to Christmas music without thinking of her, if he lay awake nights and wondered what his life would be like if only he had dared …

"Seven," she corrected him, not at all surprised he'd gotten it wrong. "But who's counting?"

He smiled, his generous, sensual lips forming a dangerous curve. Yet, like the young, unpretentious man she'd known, he appeared to be completely unconscious of his devastating effect on women. There was nothing so sexy as a guy who didn't realize he was sexy. His gaze frisked her from head to toe. "You look good, Elaine."

"You, too." She glanced questioningly at his clipboard. What she was really doing was looking for the expected wedding band. Surely a guy like this had a plump, happy wife and a couple of bambinos. Long ago, he'd told her he wanted exactly that, along with his NHL career. But to Elaine's surprise, she saw no ring. "What's up with that?" she asked.

"Fund drive," he said unapologetically, nodding to greet her companions.

Aha, she thought. He was just like Larry the elf. Only taller. Darker. Handsomer.

Then he did the grinning thing she remembered so well. His eyes, with their thick, criminally long lashes, took possession of everyone around the table. Elaine's friends opened to him like budding flowers to warm sunshine.

She had never been able to figure out how he did it, but he had a mesmerizing effect on people. Maybe it was the way he leaned forward a little, the warmth in his expression reaching out to everyone. It was like ...magic. She flashed on another memory of the elf, promising her miracles.

Even Melanie, who was so cool she made ice cubes shiver, sighed audibly.

Elaine felt curiously exposed, running into Tony again like this. The past was behind her for a reason—so she wouldn't have to look at it. Straightening her shoulders, she was determined to hide her vulnerability and brazen it out.

She made the introductions in the smooth, polished way she had perfected over the years, and with a little laugh that completely covered everything she was feeling, she said, "This is Tony Fiore, who broke my heart back when we were in college."

"Yeah?" Jenny aimed a blatant invitation at him. "He's breaking mine now."

"I broke your heart?" He grinned, incredulous. "Very funny, Elaine. I did you a favor."

She gulped down the rest of her drink. Could he really believe that?

"So spill," Mel said. "You two were an item?"

"We dated like ...three times," Elaine said blithely.

Jenny gave a low whistle. "For most guys, that's a long-term relationship."

"So what are you collecting for?" asked Bobbi, squirming in her seat.

"Kids' hockey league," Tony said. "It's a pet project of my division. We fund coaching and ice time in all five boroughs."

Elaine wasn't surprised. Hockey used to be his life. It was supposed to be his future, his career. She couldn't help wondering about him as she studied this new, different Tony who hadn't changed a bit, who still set her heart on fire. What was his life now? Expired licences and shoplifters?

"What can we do for you?" Melanie asked.

That entrancing smile never wavered. "Anything you can spare. It's Christmas Eve," he reminded them needlessly.

"That's great that you're helping out inner-city kids," Jen said.

"It's an outstanding idea," Elaine announced.

"Thanks. I'm sorry to say, funds are low this year. We're going to need a miracle to keep the league going."

"You ought to have a gala." Jenny beamed at him. "Trust me, we know about this stuff. We're publicists."

He looked blank.

"We are responsible for getting our clients' faces in front of the press, or getting their products mentioned in magazines as the hot new must-have. That sort of thing," Elaine said. "I've never heard of your organization. You should do some PR for exposure. It would increase your contributions tremendously. Trust me, I know the benefits of PR."

"Yeah? What do you charge?" When she didn't answer, he grinned. "I can't afford you. Anyway, the time I put in is just as important."

Everyone went for their bags. It struck Elaine that she hadn't always hated Christmas. Sure, her self-disciplined approach to life had never allowed her to indulge too freely in the frivolities of the season. But, now that she thought about it, she once loved the warmth and joy of the season, the sentimental music and the spirit of generosity that took over even the most miserly of individuals. When had that hardened into annoyance and exasperation?

Watching Tony, she knew precisely when. It began the night he'd let her down. Right then had begun a slow erosion of the spirit. Hope had deflated, giving way to bleak reality. She'd begun to view the world through the eyes of a cynic. In the most holy of seasons, she saw greed instead of generosity, phoniness instead of sincerity. She'd learned to expect the worst of people and she was never disappointed.

Hiding her troubled thoughts, she rummaged deep in her handbag, sifting through gear she toted everywhere but the shower.

No wallet.

She frowned and rummaged some more, searching for the smooth leather case stuffed with plastic cards and folded bills.

No wallet.

"Something's wrong here," she muttered. She dumped the contents of her purse on the table, then put them back one by one. She felt Tony watching, and realized he had focused on her key chain, the one with the silver skate. It had been a gift from him, years ago, the only thing he'd ever given her. So what? she thought. Let him make what he would of it. She knew why she carried it.

As she sifted through the clutter on the table, a sinking feeling plummeted through her. "Somebody stole my wallet."

CHAPTER FOUR

"You're in luck," Melanie said, gesturing at Tony. "We got a professional right here."

"It was the elf, or maybe the panhandler," Elaine said, jumping up.

"You were with an elf and a panhandler?" asked Jenny. "Honey, you really do need to take some time off."

"I dropped everything right in front of him and he must have grabbed it." Elaine headed for the door.

A hand on her shoulder stopped her. "Don't be in such a hurry." Tony's voice was the same slow, intimate murmur that used to melt her knees.

"What do you mean?"

"Your friend's got it." He nodded in Bobbi's direction.

"Bobbi?" Confused, Elaine turned back to the table.

Bobbi's face hardened, and suddenly she looked like a

stranger, not the sister Elaine had brought into her heart. "I don't know what you're talking about," Bobbi said.

"That spare wallet you're holding," said Tony.

"You've got to be kidding." Melanie grabbed Bobbi's pashmina, which had pooled in her lap, and there lay Elaine's red leather wallet.

"What is this, a joke?" asked Jenny.

"Harsh," Melanie muttered under her breath.

"I was only kidding," Bobbi said, her voice a nervous octave higher than normal.

Elaine felt as though she had been punched. This was Bobbi, whom she'd rescued from sandwich-cart-girl obscurity; Bobbi, who was her best friend in the world. "How could you?"

Bobbi shot to her feet. "How could I what? Wear your stupid clothes and go to your stupid parties in places I can't afford? Kiss up to your stupid clients?"

"I thought we were friends," Elaine said, her senses growing numb from shock—but not numb enough.

"Just because you put me in a pair of Pradas and gave me a cell phone doesn't make me your friend. What gives you the idea that any of us are friends? My salary barely covers the rent on my crummy downtown walkup. For that I should be grateful? Ha. For that, I should go drown myself in the East River."

"Well, that'd save you on the rent," Jenny pointed out.

"Hush up. You just want to marry someone important, and Melanie snorts everything she earns up her nose." As her voice rose, the genteel Southern accent turned twangy and raucous. She turned on Elaine. "They only keep you around because you grew up on the Upper East Side and you have connections. Don't ever mistake that for liking you. They're using you every bit as much as they're using me."

"Don't listen to her, Elaine," Melanie said. "She's obviously a nutcake."

"No, maybe I've finally had enough," Bobbi snapped. "You think this has been a picnic for me?"

"Actually, yes," said Elaine, thinking of yesterday's shopping excursion to BCBG.

"You would," Bobbi said, dramatically tossing her pashmina over her head and around her shoulders, Mary-in-the-manger style. "I wish I were dead."

"Be careful what you wish for," said Jenny, but Bobbi was already walking away, leaving a wreckage of hurt and confusion in her wake.

"She's toast," Melanie sputtered. "She'll never work in this business again."

"She'll never get so much as a dinner reservation again," Jenny swore. "She'd better go back to Bubba Mills, Carolina, or wherever she came from."

"I have no idea what came over her," Elaine said. "I told her I'd give her an advance tomorrow." But she wanted to fly home tonight, she reminded herself.

Tony still stood there, watching impassively. As a cop, he probably witnessed meltdowns and exploding relationships all the time.

"Forget her. Forget what she said." Melanie handed over the purloined wallet. "She has no class."

Elaine forced herself to seem calm as she extracted a bill from her wallet and pushed it across the table toward Tony. "For your cause. And thanks for ...getting my wallet back."

He recorded the donations on the clipboard while the Marley tune wailed from the speakers.

Elaine withered inside. How had her life turned out this way? How had she wound up getting dropped by her so-called boyfriend on Christmas Eve, and getting stolen from by her best friend? Not to mention the Christmas Eve Tony had stood her up. Truly, this night was her own personal Bermuda triangle.

Could this sort of lousy luck somehow be her fault? Elaine forced herself to consider it. Bobbi was trash. She was disloyal, and yet Bobbi's tirade lingered in Elaine's mind like a morning-after hangover. To Elaine's horror, her ex-friend's words held an eerie ring of truth. Were Jenny and Melanie her friends, or did they just act that way because they needed Elaine for them to get ahead in business?

Her hand shook a little as she tucked the wallet away.

"Sorry about your friend," Tony said with genuine sympathy. Those brown eyes, so sincere, penetrated all the sturdy barriers she'd constructed around her heart. With just one look, he could remind her that life didn't have to be this way. "Really, I'm sorry. I saw her lift the wallet from across the room."

So he'd seen her first. He'd been watching her. Elaine tried to figure out how she felt about that. "Um, thanks again," she said. Suddenly she found herself terrified of him walking away. But he would, of course. That's what everyone had been doing all her life. There had been a time when she'd thought he was different, but that had only been wishful thinking. Oh, she wanted him to stay. She wanted him to sit down and tell her that her life wasn't as awful as it seemed, that she'd just hit a speed bump. She wanted him to explain why he'd filled her head with dreams, then disappeared.

He stepped back as though to move on to the next table, but Elaine put out her hand to stop him. "Hey, not so fast." She scooted over in the booth. "Join us, Tony. We're not letting you leave."

"Thanks," he said. "I'm about ready to turn in my numbers at the ice rink for the day, anyway. Thanks to you ladies, I'm looking fine. I'm just sorry your friend's not so fine."

"Yeah. Are you okay?" Melanie asked Elaine. "I know you thought the world of Bobbi."

Elaine burned with self-loathing over her foolishness. She was supposed to know better than to give her heart. Hadn't she learned that lesson? "I guess I should associate with a better class of people." She could hear echoes of her mother in the statement and cringed inwardly.

"Don't beat yourself up," Melanie said. "She had us all fooled, every one of us. What a day you're having, Elaine. First Byron, now this." She turned to Tony. "We usually have a sense of humor about these things. With a clientele like ours, we need it."

He leaned toward Elaine with genuine interest. Just as he had years ago, he managed to make her feel as though she mattered. "So she was a client?"

"No, we invented her," Jenny said. "It was Elaine's idea."

"She started out as a transplant from a mill town in the South," Elaine explained, "selling sandwiches from a cart in our office building while trying to get an agent. We fixed her up, and before you knew it, she was clubbing with the Fixtures and Jade, wearing stuff from boutiques no ordinary human can afford, featured in magazines, that sort of thing. Everyone wanted her. She was the new cover girl on the block."

Melanie whirled a candy-cane swizzle stick in her drink. "It was a pure display of power."

"Just call us the three Dr. Frankensteins," Elaine said.

"Scary," said Tony.

Elaine tried to figure out why her career seemed so trivial as she explained it to him. Maybe it was because she'd had such big dreams back when she had known him. She'd wanted to travel the world, report on matters of international importance, make a difference in people's lives. Yet now her world consisted of high-end power shopping, over-the-top event planning and puff-piece press releases. Making a difference meant changing the color of her manicure.

"So anyway, we were counting on her tonight," Melanie was explaining to Tony. "We needed her to land a big account."

"On Christmas Eve?"

"That's what's so great about this job. Work is as much fun as play," Elaine said with forced brightness. But her comment rang hollow as apprehension clutched at her stomach.

"I have a brilliant idea." Jenny covered Tony's hand with hers. "You have to come tonight. It's a fabulous event put on by Elaine's family. The—"

"St. James affair," Tony finished for her, then grinned at her surprised expression. "I live in Brooklyn, not in a cave." As he slowly and charmingly removed his hand, the message was clear. He would not be condescended to.

"I'm sure Tony has plans," Elaine felt obligated to say. And why wouldn't he? Just because he didn't wear a ring didn't mean he wasn't married. She arranged her mouth into a lighthearted smile. "I bet you have some sweet Italian girl waiting for you at home. Toys to put together for your kids."

He lifted the corner of his mouth in a half grin. "Hey, if I had that, I wouldn't be out in the cold today."

"I always figured you'd marry young and have a big family," she said. Even if he was still single, he was definitely a family man. She'd always known that about him.

"I'm not so old, and I still plan to have kids. You know how much family means to the Fiores."

She still remembered the warmth in his voice when he'd told her about his family. They were a loud, unwieldy Italian bunch that had lived in the same brownstone neighborhood for generations. She'd never met them, of course, but in her mind she carried a picture of Mama Fiore in a ruffled apron,

THE ST. JAMES AFFAIR

stirring a kettle of puttanesca sauce on an old-fashioned kitchen range. She was definitely not the sort of woman who would leave her youngest son unaccounted for on Christmas Eve.

"So what do you say, Officer Friendly?" Jenny prodded.

Say yes, Elaine caught herself silently urging. How strange that she could still believe, even after all that had happened, that there was something special about Christmas Eve.

"I guess I could stop by for a while," he said.

Her heart took a leap before she could remind herself not to let it matter. But the fact was, it mattered a lot. She had the absurd feeling that he was rescuing her. She'd never liked her parents' annual affair. Overdressed people eating tiny hors d'oeuvres and talking about nothing while jockeying for position in front of the society column photographers.

This year, the event would improve somewhat, given the infusion of youthful energy and imagination of her partners. But to Elaine, it would always be excruciating. Having Tony present could not possibly make the night any worse. In fact, he might just make it better.

CHAPTER FIVE

Elaine began to doubt her naive sense of hope a short time later, when she stood on the curb, nearly turning into a Popsicle while trying to flag a taxi. At the same time she talked on her cell phone, trying to fill the void left by Bobbi. Axel liked supermodels, but, so far, all the SMs she knew were busy tonight. Maybe he'd bring his own, she thought, stabbing another number into the keypad.

The marauding carolers had migrated to the other side of the street, but she could still hear happy strains of "Joy to the World" above the throaty sound of traffic and the distant chimes of an old-fashioned church. Larry the elf was a liar. He'd promised magic and miracles, but things had only gone from bad to worse. And into the middle of everything had walked Tony Fiore, stirring up emotions she'd worked years to bury.

The number was busy. Exasperated, she hung up and scanned the avenue. Through a thickening curtain of snowfall, not a single available cab appeared.

Christmas was for the birds, she thought, scowling at a moon-eyed young couple walking arm in arm past glowing shop windows. Christmas was nothing but a commercialized excuse for people to knock off work early and overeat. Who needed that?

Spying a taxi half a block away, she made a desperate bid for it. Relief flooded her when it pulled alongside the curb. She pulled open the door, welcoming a waft of heat from the interior of the car.

Then, seemingly out of nowhere, a woman and a boy on crutches appeared. Some unthinking impulse nearly made her ignore them and get in. At the last second, she realized what that would make her and backed off.

The boy glanced in her direction, his sweet round face lit with a smile, before carefully folding himself and his crutches into the taxi.

"Thanks," said his mother, a harried woman in a plain cloth coat. She carried one of those humiliating clear plastic purses the retailers made clerks carry in order to control employee theft.

Elaine called herself a pushover as she handed the driver a bill to cover the fare.

"Thank you," the woman called. "Merry Christmas, and God bless."

Elaine gave a nod, then stepped from the curb and scanned the roadway for another taxi. There was none in sight. She envisioned herself standing here, freezing to death, while everyone else hurried away to celebrations and family gatherings and chestnuts roasting on an open fire. Who would miss her? she wondered forlornly. Who would even notice she wasn't around anymore, that she had turned into a curbside ice sculpture for the pigeons to land on?

Irritated, she tried to get Zora on the phone. Zora was the hardest-working modeling agent in town, but her voice mail picked up. What was wrong with everyone? You'd think a national holiday had been declared.

A black sedan pulled alongside the curb and the tinted window slid down. "Need a lift?" asked Tony Fiore.

Her heart did it again—sped up with excitement even though she cautioned herself to get a grip. "Thanks," she said, hurrying to open the passenger-side door. The car smelled of baby-powder-scented air freshener. The console was covered in electronic gear she couldn't fathom. It felt strangely intimate to ride with him, giving her a glimpse into his life. There was an official ID card and a bank of permits affixed to the console, a pad of sticky notes with a scrawled reminder: Pick up Nona's ham, buy duct tape, WD-40.

He pulled into the logjam of traffic. The windshield wipers slapped at the thick, soft flakes. The snow turned the bustling city into a sparkling world of color and light. Tony glanced over at her. She felt that glance as though they'd parted only yesterday. No man had ever looked at her the way he did, with so much interest and caring and frank desire.

"So. Where to?" he asked.

"You guessed right when you headed north."

"The Upper East Side."

"You've got it."

"Didn't fall far from the tree, eh, Elaine?"

The remark was friendly but pointed, marking off the boundaries between them. They'd never really had a chance, thanks to their different backgrounds. People liked to say such things didn't matter in this day and age, but, the fact was, it absolutely did. Especially to Elaine, whose parents' approval meant everything. And to Tony, whose sense of duty to his family dominated all his choices.

She felt unaccountably defensive, as though it was all her fault she'd grown up in the rarefied world of the Gold Coast. The proper address was everything to the St. Jameses. Her parents had a park-view apartment, and a summer house on the Sound in the Hamptons. They'd sent her to Marymount and Bennington, and she now lived in a perfect, elegantly restored pre-war luxury building in the east nineties. She led, from all perspectives, a charmed existence. On paper, everything looked peachy. In truth, she rarely had time to sit back and think about the things that were missing from her life.

"How about you?" she asked, mildly annoyed.

"I didn't fall far, either. I got a place in Park Slope."

She didn't know much about the neighborhood, except that it was in Brooklyn. And she didn't know much about Brooklyn, except that it was the destination of the creaky, local F train she would never take.

He drove the next few blocks in silence, and she thought about how weird it was to be with him after all this time. Her phone chirped, and she hurried to answer it, but it was only Jenny saying they were still scouting for arm candy for Axel.

As though he felt her stare, he turned and glanced at her. "It's good to see you, Elaine. You look great."

"Thanks. So do you." Elaine was usually good at small talk. It was her stock-in-trade, a power tool in her arsenal. Yet the customary name-dropping and light witticisms would not work in this situation, with this man. He didn't want to be impressed by her or entertained by her. As he had so many years before, he simply wanted to know her.

And what she feared was that he could already see all there was to know, that she was all surface. Peeled away, there was nothing of substance inside.

Unanswered questions and old business hung in the air between them. He reached down and flicked on the radio, and Christmas music eased through the car. He hummed along with chestnuts roasting.

"I meant what I said earlier. I'm sorry about your friend," he remarked.

She had to think for a moment about which friend he meant. They were all sorry in different ways. "Oh, Bobbi. I don't know what to say. It's a little embarrassing."

"Unfortunately, one of the things I've learned in my line of work is that people are betrayed all the time by people they trust."

"That's a cheerful thought for Christmas Eve." She concentrated on the view through the windshield. Throngs of pedestrians, hurrying and hunched against the thickening snowfall, streamed past brightly lit windows of busy shops. Twinkling fairy lights held every available tree in a choke hold.

Again, the silent questions hovered. Where were you that night? Why didn't you keep your promise? How come we didn't fall in love and live happily ever after?

"So who's Byron?" Tony asked, seemingly out of the blue.

She'd been hoping he wouldn't mention her ex, but no such luck. He must have developed a cop's instincts.

"Some guy I was dating." She downplayed it, of course. Byron was really supposed to be the one. His credentials were perfect. He came from the right family, had gone to the right schools, lived at the right address. Her parents adored him, and his parents admired her. Freddie St. James was already picking out china patterns. Elaine had almost convinced herself that he was going to be her first husband.

In reality he was a single woman's nightmare. He was self-centered, irresponsible and sometimes even faintly, subtly cruel.

"*Was* dating." Tony navigated the traffic with infinite patience.

She nodded. "He threw me over just before lunch today."

"Yeah? Tough break."

"For a bra model."

"Even tougher."

"I announced it to everyone on Fifth Avenue." She explained about the phone call and the carolers, and turned sideways on the seat to watch him. He had such a great face, saved from being too pretty by a slightly crooked nose caused by an old hockey injury. His mouth was the sort you kept staring at, helplessly, as though it were a Godiva chocolate truffle.

"You'd better not be laughing," she warned him.

"I would never do that. Why would I laugh about something that's hurting you?"

She shifted her gaze forward and concentrated on counting the evergreen swags strung from the streetlight poles. This was a particular talent of his—saying something sweet and sincere just when she needed it.

"So, did you love him?" Tony asked.

"I've never been in love," she blurted out, then covered her honesty with a laugh. "Look, I'm all right. Byron wasn't that …special. I suppose I tried to make him seem that way, but the two of us simply didn't have it." She despised the way that made her sound. Superficial. Shallow. Heartless.

Honestly, what must he think of her? Dumped on Christmas Eve, robbed by her latest best friend, and here she was behaving as though she had missed a hair appointment. The fact was, she had put such thick layers of insulation around her emotions that nothing could penetrate anymore. Not the hurt—but not the joy, either.

"You don't have to downplay this, Elaine," he said. "You're entitled to feel like crap, at least for a while."

"That's a total waste of energy, and it's not going to fix anything."

He draped his wrist over the arch of the steering wheel. "How much of a hurry are you in?"

She glanced at her Gucci watch, a little token of appreciation from a client. Then she glared at the silent phone. Well, here was a choice. She could spend the afternoon fretting about the St. James affair. Or she could surrender control for once in her life. She felt a glimmer of ...something. Possibility?

"Actually, none. Everything is under control for tonight. Thanks to Byron, I have no last-minute gifts to buy. Why do you ask?"

"I need to make a stop." He swung into a spot marked Official Vehicles Only and came around to the passenger side. He held the door open for her as she stepped out, batting her eyelashes against snow flurries. The giant, gaudy Prometheus sculpture, aglow in floodlights and drowning in the blare of Christmas carols, marked the entrance to the ice rink at Rockefeller Center.

"What is this?" she asked with a laugh that sounded phony even to her own ears. "A trip down memory lane?"

"You got a problem with that?"

She forced herself to look him square in the eye. "Not if you don't."

CHAPTER SIX

"Good. I need to drop off this stuff." Holding the clipboard and a flat, zippered bag, Tony led the way across the jammed concrete labyrinth.

The chill in the air, the echoing music and the unanticipated breathlessness Elaine felt stirred recollections of their first meeting. Every detail still lived in her heart, though no one knew that about her. She kept her most cherished memories a secret, like a delicious dream that would be ruined by the telling. Even the painful aftermath of her encounter with Tony Fiore did not dim the power of the memories. Instead, it turned them brittle and delicate, brushed with the bittersweet shadows of what might have been.

Elaine had never been the shy type. The first time she'd seen Tony on that fateful Christmas Eve, she hadn't hesitated to make her interest known. A privileged upbringing had given her an unearned sense of self-confidence and the conviction that she would never be rejected. Eighteen years old and unafraid, she'd approached him and said, "Hi. I'm Elaine. I've been watching you skate."

His cocky grin had melted her bones, at the same time assuring her that bashfulness was not an issue with him, either. "Tony. I've been watching you, too."

It wasn't exactly a date, but an encounter like a chemical reaction—brief and unexpected, leaving them both forever changed. At the end of the evening, they'd gone their separate ways, he to his family's traditional celebration followed by midnight mass, she to her parents' gala affair. The day after Christmas, he'd left for Indiana to resume the hockey season, and she'd gone skiing in St. Moritz. She'd thought of him all during the rest of Christmas break that year, wishing she'd given him her phone number, or at least her last name.

Drawn back to the present, she followed him down the concrete steps to the main office, where he handed in his clipboard. "I only wish it was more," he said as they left. "Every kid should love hockey the way I do. It kept me out of trouble more times than I can count." He offered his arm. "Let's go put on some skates."

She balked. "Aren't you supposed to be out chasing muggers or car thieves?"

"I'm off duty. Come on, Elaine. For old time's sake." He kept walking, pulling her along with him through the passageway to the ice level.

"Why would I want to remember old times?" she asked.

He stopped walking but kept hold of her arm as he turned to her. "Because they were good times," he said in a soft tone. "Mostly."

Before she could reply, he started walking again, bringing her to the rental kiosk.

"It's too crowded," she said. "No one can get ice time on Christmas Eve."

"A cop can."

"I haven't skated since …you know."

"You've got to be kidding," he said. "What, did you have an injury?"

She almost laughed at his assumption. "No, I had a life. A career. Who has time for skating?"

"Don't tell me you've been all work and no play the whole time."

"My work *is* my play. But ice skating is just not something I normally do."

"All the more reason to skate now. It's like riding a bike— you never forget."

She narrowed her gaze and took refuge in a lie. "I'm very good at forgetting things."

Unexpectedly, he took her gloved hand in his and squeezed. "I'm good at reminding people of things."

Despite her conflicted feelings about being with this man, Elaine found herself lacing up a pair of gamey-smelling size-seven rental skates and worrying about the way the attendant had eyed her designer boots. It felt strange, wobbling along on the rubber matting toward the entrance to the rink, grabbing Tony's arm for support. This was not at all how she had planned to spend her afternoon. She'd intended to visit Bergdorf's or Saks to buy Byron another designer sweater. Instead, fate had thrown her a singing elf, an old flame and a break from those parts of her life that were all too real.

When Tony led her to the ice, reality fell away. The piped-in music, blaring from speakers mounted on lightpoles, should have annoyed her but instead made her wistful. The huge Christmas tree, alive with thousands of twinkling lights, took on a diffuse, fairy-tale beauty in the flurrying snow. Even goldchrome Prometheus and the parade of international flags surrounding the center seemed as charming and friendly as a scene inside a snow globe.

With a wink and a nod at the attendant, Tony stepped through the low gate and stood aside, motioning her onto the white expanse of ice, gouged by thousands of skate marks per hour. She pushed off and her legs immediately bowed out, blades heading in different directions until her knees started to scream. Sheer determination gave her the strength to reel her feet back in, and a moment later, she was gliding.

"You're doing great," Tony said, flashing the grin she'd never quite forgotten.

She lurched, then found her balance, and, in spite of everything—the terrible day she'd had, the stressful night ahead—she found herself grinning back at him. With exaggerated gallantry, he held out his hand, and she remembered something she'd learned the first night she'd met him—it was impossible to skate and not smile.

Clinging to Tony's hand, she raced around the ice, feeling the wind in her hair and the snow on her face. He skated with the power and grace she remembered. He darted effortlessly through the milling throng, bringing her along on a ride that made her feel as though she were flying.

Just for these few moments, she touched the sort of joy that used to be so abundant in her life. Where had that gone? Like an uninvited guest slinking off to avoid being ejected, it had slipped away when she wasn't looking. Now the feelings of hope and possibility returned and she refused to examine the reason for the change. Post-Byron euphoria, she told herself.

But a little inner voice whispered that her ex had nothing to do with the way she was feeling right now.

She soared over the ice with a man she'd never thought to see again. She even hummed along with the music. She had no idea who Wenceslas was, but she'd known his song forever, and she believed in his goodness. The crowd parted before them, some slowing down to watch—Tony, of course, not her. He was the pro, after all. Together, they probably looked like a Porsche towing a Volkswagen.

Tony matched his pace to hers, giving only a hint of the speed and aggression that had propelled him to the top of his sport, winning him scholarships and offers from the NHL. Now he swung along with an easy glide. He didn't even seem to be watching where he was going. He was watching her.

And she couldn't help but watch him. He had a face filled with character, a marked contrast to the conventional, vacuous good looks of the male models and socialites of her world. That was what had attracted her in the first place—that he was so different from the boys she knew. Through prep school and the early months of college, she'd dated slender blond young men with blasé attitudes of noblesse oblige and Roman numerals after their names. Unlike those pale, pampered boys, Tony Fiore had an unabashed appetite for life, a fiercely competitive spirit and something no one else had ever given her— genuine interest in Elaine herself, in her hopes and dreams, not her social connections and bank account.

As they skated, the edges of the rink elongated to streaks of color and light, and the smeared, surreal images revived all the sensations she'd felt years ago. She'd been giddy, filled with a sense of promise. Even though the first meeting was a chance encounter and they'd gone their separate ways, a part of her had believed it was the start of something special. How could it not be, when he gazed at her with magic in his eyes?

Yet the sturdy barriers between them had remained in place.

"We should date," he'd said.

"How?" she'd asked. "By phone? E-mail? No, thanks."

He had kissed her just once that night, but it had made every subsequent kiss thereafter pale in comparison. And then, only half joking, he had said, "Same time next year?"

Despite the futility of a romance between them, they'd both kept their promise. Christmas Eve, sophomore year. Elaine stealing away from the St. James affair, Tony making himself late for midnight mass. They spotted each other across the ice and met in the middle. Both of them knew that whatever spark they'd initially felt hadn't dimmed.

"So we're starting this forbidden Romeo-and-Juliet thing, eh?" he'd said, and then when he'd laughed and kissed her again, she'd had the strong and undeniable conviction that their attraction was something rare and not easily dismissed. But she was leaving for St. Kitts the next day, he had to go back to hockey, and it was all completely impossible. They'd even joked about the way the world was conspiring to keep them apart.

They'd indulged in a brief fantasy. She would transfer to Notre Dame, live in the sorority house across the street from his frat... The very idea had made her laugh.

"What's funny?" he asked.

"The thought of my father paying for me to go to a Catholic college in the midwest."

"Hey, it's Notre Dame. People respect Domers."

"But they don't send their daughters to school with them."

Yet their lives had crossed a third time the following Christmas Eve. Elaine could still picture how he'd looked after waiting for her in the cold. Ears and nose red, eyes aglow with pleasure at the sight of her. This time, there was no pretense of surprise or coy declaration of "I was just passing by ..." Each admitted that they'd come looking for the other, that the past year had been endless, the urge to track the other down almost irresistible. But they hadn't wanted to disturb the magic that happened each Christmas Eve. Meeting in between was like knowing what your presents were early. They were young. It was a game. But they both knew it was turning into something more.

Naturally, they'd discussed meeting between Christmases—but they never actually did it. There was magic at work. They hadn't understood it. They were almost afraid to mess with it. Until that third year, when Tony had news. He was going pro. He had an agent, he'd told her with an endearing sense of wonder. The New York Rangers wanted him, offering the chance of a lifetime, a shot at a life he'd only dreamed about. For the sake of his proud, adoring parents, he would stay in school and finish his degree, because no Fiore had yet earned a college degree. They wanted Tony to be the first. The wait would be excruciating, but he owed it to them. He wouldn't think of doing it any other way.

That night, he'd given her a gift—a key chain attached to a silver skate. Elaine, accustomed to receiving tokens from Tiffany and Harry Winston from other boys, was reduced to tears. At the gift kiosk, she'd bought a little snow globe with two tiny figures skating arm in arm, and told him to think of her every time he looked at it.

She became obsessed with Tony. His new status as rising professional sports star had changed everything. He was becoming someone her parents would adore. She'd dreamed about him, fantasized about him. He would be the next Wayne Gretzky. They would keep a condo in the city and a summer place on Long Island, maybe one with an ice rink.

By the time the fourth Christmas had rolled around, she'd been convinced. After only three encounters, she knew she was going to fall in love with him. Never mind that he was an Italian-American from a working-class family, that he had attended public school and worked summers for the sanitation department to earn extra money. Never mind that her parents would immediately enroll her in therapy sessions and try to convince her she was delusional. She was falling in love with Tony Fiore. She'd never been in love before. That fourth year, she showed up early at the ice rink.

Even now, she felt flushed with embarrassment as she recalled how long she'd waited for him. How many times she'd paid for ice time, how many wobbly ovals she'd skated around the rink, how cold she'd gotten from being outside for so long. When she could no longer feel her feet, she'd turned in her skates, trudged out to the street and flagged a taxi. At her parents' annual affair, she drank too much champagne and danced with too many men she didn't care about. The very next day, she'd embarked on the annual vacation with her family.

When she returned, she called her college counselor to accept an overseas internship that had been offered to her. Numb with disillusionment, she went to London to work for a prestigious magazine and embark on a fabulous life. Whether or not she'd succeeded at the latter depended on whose yardstick was used.

For the next year, she became an avid browser of the sports pages, seeking news of the NHL. She dug for information about rookie players but found nothing on Tony Fiore, only that he'd graduated with distinction from Notre Dame. She refused to let herself dwell on him, though she burned with curiosity. What had happened to his dreams? His big plans to become a star on ice?

What did it matter if his plans didn't include her? Eventually she'd forced herself to stop wondering. Stop caring.

A musical chiming noise, like the sound of silver bells, startled Elaine, drawing her back to the present. Apparently the bells signaled the skaters to clear the ice for grooming. The blocky Zamboni machine emerged from its tunnel and pushed out onto the oval to methodically smooth out the ice that had been chopped up by the blades of the skaters. Perched like a toy high on the seat, the driver wore a bright red muffler that streaked like a banner down his back.

Elaine did a double take.

"What's wrong?" asked Tony.

"I'm being stalked by an elf."

"Come on." Laughing, he grabbed her hand. "I'll buy you a hot chocolate."

It was lousy hot chocolate from a machine, but the watery sweetness had a strange, simple appeal. "So you became a cop," she said. "How did that happen?"

"It was my backup plan, in case hockey didn't work out."

"I take it hockey didn't work out."

He took a gulp from his white cardboard cup. She waited, but he didn't address her comment. Instead, he asked, "So what about you? I figured you'd be an ace reporter or something. Didn't you study journalism in college?"

She had a fleeting recollection of her idealism. By becoming a reporter, she'd wanted to make a difference in people's lives, digging out the facts and holding up a mirror to society. Instead, she made dinner reservations and threw parties and pushed luxury products. She convinced women who couldn't afford subway fare that they must not be without a certain seventeen-dollar brand of lipstick. As the writer of overwrought press releases, she practiced a strange, hybrid form of reporting and publicity.

Tony's question was still hanging in the air.

She sipped her drink. "So I became a publicist, okay? Maybe I don't protect and serve, but it's a living. Look, Tony, you caught me on a bad day."

"So tell me what a good day is like."

She hesitated. "When my clients are all happy and the firm bills them for hours well spent, I have fun at my job," she said, feeling a bit defensive. "That's no crime. Working in my field is like going out on dates and to parties. People pay me to attend movie premieres and celebrity galas. How bad is that?"

"Doesn't sound bad at all. Unless it makes real dates and real parties feel like work."

Ouch, she thought. She stared down at the table, trying to talk herself out of asking what she knew she would ask. But she couldn't stand it a moment longer, couldn't keep in the bitter accusation that had been pressing at the back of her throat from the first moment she'd spied him today. "You didn't show up that last night."

He didn't even ask which night she referred to. "I'm here now."

CHAPTER SEVEN

The Zamboni driver had worked on the ice forever, it seemed. More than an ice tech or maintenance drone, he was a vital part of the skating operation, practically a celebrity in his own right. Sometimes kids even asked for his autograph, which he obligingly gave. He even put up with the tedious "Zamboni Song," which some smart aleck invariably belted out now and then.

When his big Lego block of a machine chugged out onto the ice to enact the hourly ritual of renewal, he attracted as much attention as the amateur figure skaters practicing their double axels. The sight of the surface being groomed satisfied on a deep level; rough imperfections disappeared almost instantly. There was a mesmeric, Zen-like appeal in watching the resurfacing of the ice. In perfect, overlapping oval swaths, the machine scraped off the gouged and pitted epidermis of the rink, washed the shavings and then laid down a slick, smooth mirror of perfect ice in its wake.

Reaching a top speed of nine miles per hour, the Zamboni crept along so slowly that the driver had plenty of time to study the crowd, studying him. This was what kept him in his heated vinyl seat each winter, year after year—the opportunity to watch people. He had all the time in the world to observe the way they looked at the world, weathered storms, slammed into walls and picked themselves up after a fall, the way they raced out to embrace life.

He'd seen all sorts of people come and go. The crowd here was made up mostly of tourists and occasional regulars. Every once in awhile, someone interesting was swept up in emotional turmoil—that sort of thing always caught his attention. He'd never tire of watching a mother arguing with her almost-grown daughter. A newly divorced man working up the courage to ask a woman out. A young couple on the brink of falling in love.

They were tantalizing, those glimpses of lives, flickering across his ice. Some disappeared forever, leaving their resolution to his thoughtful imagination. Others came back, their stories deepening, darkening or sometimes turning out all right.

He had one hard-and-fast rule. Never meddle. He was here to smooth out the ice, not mess up people's lives. But it was tempting sometimes, like right now.

There was no forgetting Tony Fiore and the girl he loved, some society debutante named Elaine. Some years back, Fiore had been a hot prospect in hockey, maybe the best ever to cross the ice here. His explosive speed and unfailing coordination had made him a good bet for any team. But it was his love of skating, that rare and genuine feel for the ice beneath his blades, that sharpened his edge. The overcrowded tourist mecca wasn't his usual place to skate, of course, but one Christmas Eve long ago, he'd stopped in on a lark. And so had the girl named Elaine. Maybe they'd been lonely that day, possibly frustrated by last-minute shopping or needing to kill time before some engagement, yet they'd both shown up within minutes of one another.

It happened all the time, but these two, they were something. From the first moment they saw each other, they practically melted the ice beneath their feet. They were youth and spirit and hope personified, and anyone watching them could tell they were seeing something special.

When the hour was up, they went their separate ways, of course. The Zamboni driver hadn't been surprised to see them back the next year, and then the year after that, their interest and passion deepening perceptibly each time. They'd changed, as all young folk do. But there was something about this pair that had never wavered. They'd looked at each other as though they were the first to discover the true meaning of love. It was all there in those young, good-looking faces, those glowing smiles, those hands clasped tight.

And then ...nothing. It was no big deal and certainly none of his business, but the ice groomer had taken their disappearance as a personal failure. Deep down, he knew what had happened, and he always wanted to believe he was wrong, but he wasn't. Life had interfered with these two, and they'd been foolish enough to allow it.

Now they were back, and he was anxious to see if they'd finally figured out what he already knew—that they belonged together, not just once a year, but always. After finishing his rounds, he parked the machine and headed over to the concessions area, which consisted of a few tables and benches arranged on a large mat of interlocking rubber squares. At a cheap metal table, they sat across from each other, hands cradling paper cups of thin hot chocolate, gazes anxious with everything the years had done to them.

"Well, if it ain't the lovebirds," he said. "So what is it with you two?"

Elaine glared up at him. "Do you mind?"

"Not at all." He had a seat at their table, unsnapped the top buttons of his coveralls and let his red scarf hang loose. The name Larry was embroidered on his shirt pocket.

She gasped, then pruned up her face into a frown. Probably trying to figure out if he was the same Larry from the carolers, not that he'd care to enlighten her. "You don't remember me, do you?"

"You're the Zamboni driver," Tony said.

"The question is," Elaine said, "why are you behaving as though you remember us?"

"Because I do."

She laughed a little nervously. She was even prettier than she'd been years before—more sophisticated, sure of herself. Yet there was something about her, something a little wistful.

"Right," she said.

"Three years in a row I see the two of you meeting like you invented love at first sight, and then the fourth year—"

"He didn't show," Elaine said, and Larry heard the sudden spike of hurt in her voice. Then she looked a little queasy, probably regretting that she'd said exactly what was on her mind. He sometimes had that effect on people. He wasn't surprised when she left her hot chocolate on the table and headed off to the rental kiosk.

"Sure, he did," Larry called out after her.

She froze like an ice sculpture, then pivoted slowly back to face him.

He winked at Tony, who shot him a look of fury. "I guess you got some explaining to do."

CHAPTER EIGHT

"Thanks a lot, pal." Tony glared at the Zamboni driver. "You don't have time to thank me." Larry jerked his thumb at the rental booth. He was compact and spry, a blunt, friendly man of indeterminate age. He had a froth of white hair, but the light in his eyes sparkled with an ageless mingling of wisdom and merriment. "So, what are you waiting for? An engraved invitation?"

Tony followed Elaine, who barely looked at him as she put on her boots, then stood there tapping her toe in impatience. Okay, he thought. Party's over even before it started. He led her back to the car and held open the door for her, catching a whiff of sweet cold air in her hair as she got in.

"You want to explain that?" asked Elaine, clipping on her seatbelt.

No. He really didn't.

He slid a glance at her, then concentrated on his driving. The car surged into the string of taxis, limos and private cars. Tony stole another look at her.

Elaine St. James. He couldn't believe he was seeing her again after all this time. He'd never forgotten her. How could he? All that cool blond beauty, that smart-alecky sense of humor, and the almost-hidden sweet vulnerability he noticed when she didn't know he was watching. The passage of time had added polish and sophistication to a woman who had been polished and sophisticated to begin with. And in spite of all the ways he'd reasoned with himself over the years, he still wanted her. Bad.

She was the reason he had never married and settled down. Thanks to her, he would never be happy with any other woman. She didn't know that, and he wasn't about to tell her. Yet what he had done—rather, what he'd failed to do—the last time he'd seen her had had ramifications he never could have predicted. Because of that moment of decision, just that one moment, his heart had been stuck in the same place. He was beginning to think maybe this was true for Elaine, too.

As he navigated the flow of traffic, he could feel her watching him. Waiting for his answer. "I got no idea what that guy was talking about," he said.

"Simple. He knew we met there every year on Christmas Eve—"

"Every year, Elaine?"

"Okay, for three years. There was a pattern. Even the Zamboni driver realized that."

He said nothing for a few minutes. A crooner on the radio made "Little Drummer Boy" sound like a timeless love ballad. "Okay," he said at last. "I showed up that night."

A small intake of breath. "I didn't see you."

"I changed my mind." He figured she was too proud to

ask why, but the question shouted through the silence. "I couldn't even get down to the rink level. I was just out of the hospital, recovering from surgery. I had to use a wheelchair to get around."

"A wheelchair?" She leaned forward to get a closer look at his legs. "What happened?"

"Wrecked my knee and couldn't skate. I was looking at months of physical therapy, and then God knew what."

Incredulous silence pulsed through the car.

He had not wrecked just his knee. He'd wrecked his shot at the pros, his plans for the future and his chance to offer something to a girl who had everything. He still remembered sitting at the rail above the rink, his knee throbbing, his eyes smarting as he watched her circling the rink below. He'd tried to imagine what was going through her mind. Or did skating blank everything out as it did for him? Even now, he remembered everything he had seen and felt while she'd skated around the ice, alone, a slender figure moving in and out of the skaters. Anger. Grief. Frustration. Shame. *Love.*

"I watched you for a while," he said. "You were wearing a long white scarf."

"Let me get this straight. You showed up after knee surgery and you couldn't be bothered to speak to me?"

"We were brand new. I didn't want to blow it."

"Well, you did."

"No excuse." Except stupid male pride. The shattering realization that everything he'd worked for all his life was gone. "I didn't even know what I was going to say to you. I was still trying to figure out what to say to myself. I had to figure out what to do with the rest of my life. I was a little preoccupied with that. I told myself I'd get in touch with you later, when my head was in a better place—"

"Your head? What about mine? I was frantic with worry."

"I figured you'd move on."

"How could you figure that? You didn't know me at all. I would have understood." She almost admitted that she'd been heartbroken, but she was too angry to give him that.

"So tell me this, Elaine, and be honest. If I'd come rolling up to you in a wheelchair and said, 'Gee, I may be on permanent disability and I might not even walk again, but how about we plan a future together?' What would your reaction have been? Would you have stood by me in rehab and helped me learn to walk again?"

She blanched, but didn't look away. "You'll never know, because you made up my mind for me."

He couldn't dispute that. He hesitated, then opted for honesty. "I made a big mistake that night. I don't want to make it again."

"Tell me one reason why I should give you another chance."

He pulled up to the curb in front of the address she'd given him. It was a luxury building from the 1930s, complete with a liveried doorman.

This was nuts, he thought, eyeing a career dog walker following a pedigreed pack up the tree-lined street. He and Elaine were from different worlds. They ought to forget the whole thing. Instead, he slid his arm along the seat behind her. "Because," he said, "you've never been in love."

"I never said that."

"Sure you did."

"What's that got to do with us?"

"Maybe nothing," he said. "Maybe everything."

She parted her lips a little, and he thought about kissing her. He didn't let himself act on it. Later, he told himself. Definitely later.

"Thanks for the skating," she said, then studied him for a few seconds. "Would you like to come up?"

CHAPTER NINE

As she greeted the doorman, Elaine felt a beat of unease. Maybe it wasn't such a good idea, letting Tony Fiore into her life. They'd only had three dates, after all, and they hadn't really been dates as much as accidents. They barely knew each other. It was probably best to leave it that way.

Yet what he had just revealed to her could change everything between them—if she let it. She hated that he hadn't told her about his injury. But what she hated even more was a deeply shameful realization. If he'd told her, she would have wept for him. She would have raged with him at the injustice, mourned the loss of his lifelong dream with him. But then she would have slunk away in fear. That was the sort of person she was, back then. And it struck her that she didn't want to be that sort of person anymore.

"Some building," he said.

"Thanks. It's a co-op."

"Places like this are tough to find," he said.

"The Board knows more about me than my gynecologist, my therapist and the IRS." She gritted her teeth, wishing she hadn't admitted she was seeing a therapist. She opened the door to her apartment and led the way inside. The answering machine had a welcome message—Jenny had arranged for some talent to take Bobbi's place tonight. That was something, at least.

Her apartment was exquisite. The spare white-on-white decor imparted a mood of space and cool elegance. She found herself wishing it was a little more …whimsical, maybe. Some colorful throw pillows on the designer sofa, or artwork that actually represented something recognizable. She turned to see Tony studying an array of silver-framed black-and-white photos on a glass-and-chrome étagère. Maybe the pictures conveyed a personal touch, Elaine thought. But no. There were no warm portraits of a laughing family, but merely souvenirs—pictures of her with celebrities, socialites, rock stars, company executives.

As though feeling her stare, he smiled at her. "Nice—"

"Please don't say nice place."

"Why not?"

"It's not nice."

"It's not?" He picked up a small Baccarat bowl and carefully set it down. "So why do you live here?"

She blinked. "No one ever asked me that before." She'd never even asked herself that question. She lived here because it was on the Upper East Side. The brushed-steel-framed Italian sofa was there because the designer had chosen it for style, of course. Not for comfort. The Venetian glass-top coffee table was there because it matched the sofa. Everything in her apartment went together perfectly. Her designer wouldn't have it any other way.

The only thing out of place at the moment was Tony Fiore himself. He was too earthy, too real.

"It's a great apartment. People wait for years to find an apartment like this." She gestured at the tree-framed view out the window. The snow had rendered the world more brilliantly white than her stark interior.

"You didn't answer the question, Elaine."

"Can I offer you something to drink?" She went into the gleaming kitchen and he followed. She swung open the fridge. "Soda? Beer?"

"Thanks." He helped himself to a soda.

She tried to put herself in his place that night, the night she'd stopped believing in Christmas.

He'd lost something, too. What must it be like to have a dream as powerful as the dream he'd had, and then to have that taken away? She pictured him watching her from the upper level, trying to figure out what to do now that his entire life plan had shattered to pieces. The horrible truth was, she was afraid to contemplate what her reaction might have been if he'd come rolling toward her in a wheelchair. She'd been young and self-centered and focused on glamour and success. She'd built up such fantasies around the sort of life they would have together, with Tony as a famous hockey player, and she as an international journalist. Maybe, just maybe, he had made the right choice, turning his back on her that night. The person she was back then could not have dealt with him. She'd simply had no resources to love a man who didn't fit her idealized view of what the future would be. Now, years later, she knew the problem of living a life that looked perfect on paper. It was as one-dimensional as the piece of paper itself.

It felt so strange having him here, where she lived. Where

she slept and showered and talked on the phone. He was seeing her in a different context, and she desperately wanted him to like what he saw. But how could he, when *she* didn't even like it?

"Look," she said. "About tonight ...you don't have to—"

"Are you kidding?" He set his soda on the counter and turned to her, and when he smiled, it was like glimpsing a dream she thought she'd forgotten. "You think I'd pass up another chance to spend Christmas Eve with you?"

CHAPTER TEN

"Ma, it's not the end of the world," Tony said, wedging the phone under his jaw as he stood back and surveyed the contents of his closet. If he didn't have a clean shirt, he was going to shoot himself. "It's just a change of plans."

"Change of plans, he says. You hear that, Salvatore? He abandons his family on Christmas Eve, and he calls it a change of plans." Gina Fiore always had two-way conversations with people—one on the phone, the other in her warm, yeasty-smelling kitchen.

Tony's father, Sal, mumbled something indistinct. He was used to the fact that his wife thrived on drama and, like Tony, secretly found her entertaining.

"Tell you what …" Tony said. He spotted a crisp white shirt, still in the cleaner's cellophane, and pounced. "I'll try to get back in time for midnight mass."

"Mass, he says."

"It's the reason for the season, Ma."

"What about supper, eh? You're going to miss the *torta di spinaci*, the *bauletti di maiale*, the *pandoro*."

He dragged five different ties from the rack on the back of the closet door. "I'll live, Ma. I'll eat the *pandoro* for breakfast tomorrow morning."

"Oh, so now we don't see you until breakfast. What's going on, eh, Tony?"

He took a deep breath, then said, "Well, there's this girl—"

"I knew it! *Ringrazi il cielo*, did you hear that, Sal? Tony's got a girl. A Christmas Eve girl."

He grinned, shaking his head. "Look, Ma, don't get too exci—"

"Ha. Don't you tell me. I know what it means when a man spends Christmas Eve with a girl. Didn't your father and I get engaged on Christmas Eve, eh? Didn't we?" She paused to blow her nose. "It's just like when you were in college, and you kept promising to bring someone to meet us. It always broke my heart that you never brought her home, Tony."

He knew he should explain that this was a casual date that happened to fall on Christmas Eve. He knew he should explain that Elaine St. James was out of his league, that they'd probably go their separate ways after tonight, that she was no more cut out to be a cop's wife than he was to be a society husband. He should tell his mother that he'd stood in the middle of Elaine's designer apartment today and felt like an alien life-form.

But he didn't say any of that. Because there was something stubborn about his heart, something that made him think that maybe, just maybe, he and Elaine could get it right this time.

"Are your shoes polished?" she demanded, businesslike now.

"Huh?"

"Your shoes, your shoes. You shine them until you see your teeth reflected, you hear me?"

Grinning again, he excavated his dress shoes. "No problem, Ma."

"And your suit—the one you bought for Uncle Rico's funeral, yes?"

"An excellent choice."

She rattled off a string of instructions while he held up each tie, looking for the perfect match.

"I got to get in the shower, Ma," he said after a while. "I don't want to be late."

"Go, go," she urged him. "But ... Tony?"

"Yeah?"

"Bring her home this time, eh?"

He ripped the cellophane off the white shirt. "I'll do my best, Ma."

CHAPTER ELEVEN

❖◆✦✦◆◆❖✦✦◆◆❖

Elaine's work on the St. James affair had long been finished. What she was supposed to do, at this point, was relax, enjoy the party and make sure everyone had a fabulous time.

But tonight was different. It was Christmas Eve, the clients were her parents and she was getting a shot at her biggest account to date. In the midst of all this, she was supposed to forget her troubles, forget that her best friend had betrayed her, forget that her boyfriend had dropped her.

But that wasn't what was making her nerves jangle on the swift, thirty-one-story rise to the St. James apartment. Smiling tautly at the elevator man, she admitted to herself that the source of her apprehension was something—someone—altogether different.

There was no denying it. Just being near Tony Fiore, even the very thought of him, made her tingle with an awareness that was actually embarrassing in its intensity. She wasn't a naive girl anymore, yet with Tony, she felt young and light and full of feelings she had long thought lost to her.

Catching a glimpse of herself in the smoke-tinted elevator mirror, she detected a splotchy blush on her neck. It was like a red map of the former Soviet Union rising up from the décolletage of her perfect cocktail dress. She hadn't blushed like this in ages, though it used to be a common and embarrassing trait of hers. The red rash of rapture, she had once jokingly called it when her college roommate had asked her if she had a fever. Agitated, she raised the collar of her coat.

As they arrived at the thirty-first floor, the elevator man tipped his cap. "Merry Christmas, Miss St. James."

"What? Uh, thanks. Same to you."

Flustered, she stepped out of the elevator and into the place where she'd spent her over-privileged childhood. It was gorgeous as always, in the gleaming-marble, sleekly chic way of the city's finest old money roosts. It had a special holiday sparkle imparted by the subtle, elegant touches of the floral designer she'd engaged for the event.

Graceful and minimalist, the seasonal decor avoided the usual swags of holly and mistletoe in favor of simple elegance. In the foyer, a pair of beeswax tapers flanked a single calla lily in a crystal vase, artfully displayed atop the Louis XVI side table. The living room had been arranged for conversation and dancing. She and the designer had talked her mother out of putting up the traditional twelve-foot tree because it would take up too much space. Instead, the designer had insisted that the "suggestion" of a tree—an abstract stainless-steel sculpture of a branch over the mantel—would suffice.

Elaine found herself wishing she had argued more with the designer.

Sinbad, who had no last name and whose talents were

booked for years in advance, was warming up on the white Steinway. Elaine surrendered her coat to one of the caterer's uniformed staffers, who bore it away to the guest room that tonight would serve as a cloakroom.

Elaine took a few moments for a quick tour. In the vast, well-equipped kitchen, Armand orchestrated the preparations like an air traffic controller. He paused only long enough to greet Elaine, assure her that everything was perfect and on time, and insist that she sample the tamarind-perfumed ceviche.

"Outstanding," she assured him, savoring the lime-cured raw fish. Secretly, she yearned for Chex Mix and little cubes of cheese.

The familiar tap-tapping of her mother's footsteps drew her back to the huge, beautiful living room, which had been designed by Mongiardino. But the room itself faded to obscurity when Elaine's mother walked in.

The press had always been especially kind to Freddie St. James, and for good reason. She had married Banner St. James, whose roots and wealth were sunk deep into the mythos of the city, and she was everything the media wanted from a woman like her: graceful, educated and generous. She was admired by everyone from her bookkeeper's assistant to the attorney general.

Tonight she wore a Vera Wang original and Cartier jewels. An invisible fog of Gucci Rush surrounded her.

"Wow," said Elaine. "If I didn't know better, I'd swear you were from central casting. You look perfect, Mom."

Freddie smiled and held out both hands. "Hello, sweetheart. Merry Christmas."

They leaned toward each other but didn't touch except for their hands. Both were conscious of not wanting to disturb the other's porcelain-perfect makeup. Freddie stepped away from

Elaine and subjected her to a shrewd study. "Wow, yourself," she said with genuine admiration. "That dress is fabulous."

Elaine had thought so when she'd first put it on. Over a long-sleeved tunic of black Sea Isle cotton, the designer had draped a shimmery mesh of babyfine gold cord.

"You think?" she asked, realizing how much she had always sought her mother's good opinion by trying to appear just right. "It reminds me of chains. Didn't Marley's ghost wear chains?"

"Merry Christmas," called a jovial voice. Banner St. James joined them, timelessly handsome in his crisp Armani tux.

Elaine greeted her father with cordial warmth, and regarded both her parents with a certain diffuse wistfulness. Despite that she was an only child, they weren't really a close family. Her most cherished Christmas memory was the year of the biggest blizzard in the history of the city. Socked in by a record snowfall and extended power outage, the three of them had slept together under duvets in the living room around the fireplace. They'd fixed canned soup and crackers for supper, then played board games by candlelight. Something about the slow rhythm of that magical day had fulfilled her more than any international ski trip or luxury cruise.

She did not doubt that her parents loved her, or she them, but they had never shared the sort of easy, natural affection she sometimes observed in families that were less busy, less self-conscious, less preoccupied with appearances.

As she smiled with confidence and assured them that the party was going to be wonderful, there was so much she wished for. She wished she could tell them about Bobbi and Byron. She wished she could explain that she'd run into Tony Fiore and was totally confused by him. She wished they could spend Christmas doing something quiet and cozy rather than over-the-top entertaining. But, of course, she couldn't say those things to them.

Melanie and Jenny arrived, setting off a chain reaction of preparatory events, followed by the arrival of the guests in convivial clusters. Within a short while, the St. James affair was underway. With Sinbad's expert playing as a sound track, the party burst into a flurry of celebration that seemed to Elaine to be as staged and visually busy as a music video.

When Tony Fiore walked into the room, there seemed to be a subtle pause, like a collective intake of breath. Even as Elaine hurried to welcome him, the speculation started, an insistent current of whispers flowing beneath the surface small talk. He was a rising young star, a socialite's lover, an Olympic athlete.

As he removed his parka and gloves, he was either oblivious or took the attention in stride, focusing solely on Elaine. He looked wonderful in a dark suit and white shirt that set off a burgundy-colored tie.

She took his hand, grimacing a little. "You're freezing."

"My hands are always cold. Even when I remember my gloves." He handed the gloves, along with his jacket, to an attendant.

Elaine's parents greeted him with their usual poise, but also silent questions they couldn't quite conceal.

"Byron's not coming," Elaine said, taking the coward's way out and breaking the news in the safety of the public eye. "Tony's my plus-one tonight."

"It's very nice to meet you," Freddie said, her voice perfectly modulated.

"He's an ex-hockey star," Elaine added, easing into the familiar phony party patter she'd developed into an art. She was an expert spin doctor, adept at making people and products seem larger-than-life. With a simple verbal twist, she changed out-of-work actors into rising stars, has-been artists into cutting-edge visionaries.

But the trouble was, Tony seemed amused by her spin. When she said, "He's in law enforcement—"

He burst out laughing and said, "I better get you out on the dance floor before I find out I'm a Kennedy cousin." He offered her parents a jovial smile, and led Elaine into the midst of the milling couples.

"I get it now," he said.

"Get what?"

"The reason it wouldn't have worked out for us."

"Really. And why is that?"

"Your folks. I'm sure they're great people but I'm not exactly their idea of the perfect guy for their daughter."

"Back then, maybe."

"And now?"

"Now that so-called perfect daughter has a mind of her own."

"I was counting on that, Elaine."

She found herself swept against him, and something incredible came over her, as it had when he'd taken her skating. He moved with the grace of an athlete, his hand firm and secure at her waist. There was magic in his embrace, in the hard bulk of his body and the soft smile that curved his full lips. She was engulfed by his nearness, his warmth, the heady essence of his masculinity.

As the music filled her, so did memory and emotion, warmed by a contentment deeper and more real than anything she'd felt in years. She'd been out in the cold too long and had gone numb in vital places. Now she was thawing out and she welcomed the surging tingles of pain that reminded her she was alive.

When was the last time she had danced just for the pleasure of it? Just for the feel of a man's arms around her and the mindless delight of moving to the rhythm of the music? She couldn't remember, because these days when she danced in a man's arms, it was to entertain or conduct business or impress someone. Tony Fiore couldn't know it, but this was such a gift, to simply be with him for no other reason than to dance. She wasn't stupid. She knew the reason for this newfound sense of fun and freedom was Tony. He had that effect on her. That was why she'd fallen for him the first night they skated together, and why she'd kept coming back.

She tilted back her chin to gaze up at him. And to her astonishment, a tear slipped from her eye. She prayed he wouldn't notice. He did, of course.

"Hey, what's this?"

What the heck, she thought. He already knew far too much about her. He always had. She saw no point in hiding her feelings. "This is fun," she said. "I love dancing with you. It's sort of like skating, but *I'm* better at it."

He grinned. "If this is your idea of fun, I guess I don't want to see you depressed." With infinite gentleness, he brushed his thumb over the crest of her cheekbone, wiping away the tear. His smile softened, and she was startled to discern a hint of genuine, uncomplicated affection in his regard. It was so different from the way others looked at her. With interest, perhaps. Ambition, undoubtedly. Wariness or respect, occasionally. But straightforward, no-strings-attached caring was something she rarely encountered. He made her feel important and valued, not for her social pedigree but simply for being in the world.

"The women in my family get all choked up over Christmas, too," he said, misinterpreting her tears. "My Aunt Flo can't even look at a manger scene without turning into a leaky faucet."

Elaine decided to leave it at that. Her unexpected reaction was too complicated to explain. Nor did she want to try explaining that she didn't like Christmas because she was afraid to let it mean something to her. She couldn't bring herself to confess that the last time she'd tried to let someone into her heart, she'd been so hurt that she'd simply stopped trying. And she would never admit that the someone had been him.

"He's here," Jenny hissed, breaking in on their dance without apology. "It's showtime."

"We're in the middle of a dance here," Tony said, his voice neutral but firm.

"Sorry, but we're in the middle of a deal here," Jenny said, flashing a smile designed to dazzle.

He wasn't dazzled. Elaine could see that immediately. "Give us a minute, Jen."

"Half a minute," she said curtly.

Elaine pretended to be amused as Jen hurried away. "So you've got thirty seconds, and then it really is showtime."

"Elaine, even I'm not working on Christmas."

She tried to forget how much it meant to dance with him, how it had felt when he'd wiped away her tears. She reminded herself of the importance of landing this account. And not just to her. Jenny and Melanie needed it, too. The three of them had built the business and rose or fell with the firm's success or failure. And her partners didn't have room to fail. Unlike her, they had no trust fund spread out like a safety net below them, ready to cushion them when they failed or simply got bored and walked away.

"Look," she whispered to Tony, "I gave my word I'd help out with this guy. And we're shorthanded tonight." The thought of Bobbi tugged at her spirits. She pictured her former friend alone in her tiny walkup, fretting over unpaid bills, wishing she'd gone home for Christmas. The image of Bobbi's misery gave Elaine no sense of justice or moral victory. It was merely depressing.

"Okay," Tony said good-naturedly. "I'll go help myself to more of those liverwurst sandwiches."

She couldn't help smiling as he headed for a waiter holding out a tray of *pâté de foie gras en croute*. For the next hour or so, Tony mingled effortlessly with the glittering company, his friendly, genuine manner endearing him to everyone, from the bartender to the ambassador of Uruguay.

There was an artful pause in the music and conversation when Axel entered the room. The subtle hush was different and more dramatic than it had been for Tony, because Melanie had arranged for Sinbad to pause dramatically in his playing. Axel and his Euro-chic entourage were so cutting-edge sharp that they resembled fashion mannequins. Their close-cut hair was slick and glossy, their black suits glovelike around starving bodies that probably subsisted on Campari and Dunhill cigarettes.

"So there he is," Melanie murmured in her ear, "the holy grail of accounts. Let's hope you can snag him without Bobbi's help. Get going."

Elaine turned on the charm with no more effort than flipping a switch. She made introductions and drew the somber Swiss man into the center of the action. He was stunningly handsome, his slender body impeccably clad in an Italian suit, his face as perfectly smooth and gleaming as carved and polished wood. He had a reputation as a fabulous but demanding lover, and was nearly always found draped in supermodels. That was where Bobbi came in. Without her, they'd have to improvise. Jenny came forward with the hired escorts, a pair of bony, bright-eyed actresses in borrowed designer dresses.

Axel was suave and low-key, greeting everyone with continental panache. Elaine's parents were as taken with him now as they had been at Parents' Day at school in Lugano. He was precisely their type. Despite the trendy moniker, he had a family tree hung with European royalty. Anyone who could call Prince Rainier "Uncle" was certainly welcome in their home.

She felt his attention on her like a beam of cold light.

"Your daughter has always charmed me until I cannot see straight," he declared in an accent more delicious than melted chocolate.

It was all Elaine could do to keep from rolling her eyes. Although just thinking about Tony could summon up a blush, blatant flattery from a Swiss billionaire blew past her like dust bunnies.

She caught Tony's eye and motioned him over. The moment he joined their group, she saw the contrast between them. Side-by-side, they were almost comical, with Tony the picture of the all-American male, big and brawny, exuding self-confidence and a tangible amount of testosterone. By contrast, Axel was a svelte and polished European import, his sculpted mouth taut with a condescending smile. Clearly they both sensed an undeclared rivalry afoot.

"May I have this dance?" Axel said to Elaine, offering his hand. The nails gleamed from a Japanese manicure. His laser-whitened teeth flashed as he smiled.

Winning his business was the sole purpose of the night, she reminded herself. She said, "Of course," then turned to Tony. "Jenny and Melanie will take good care of you."

"That's okay. I need to get going anyway."

She felt a stab of panic. How could he leave her when she'd only just found him again? "But—"

"I always go to midnight mass with my family. 'Night, Elaine. Thanks for having me." He gave her a brief peck on the cheek and then turned away. "I'll see you around, okay?"

Before she could say another word, he was gone and she

was dancing with the holy grail, unthinkingly maneuvering him in front of the photographer from *W*, insincerely offering a blissful smile for the camera. Old habits died hard. It was pointless to think she could spend a successful Christmas Eve with Tony Fiore. She'd tried that in the past and it had never turned out well for her.

She heard herself chatting blithely with Axel, heard him laugh with sensual appreciation as he led her around the dance floor. He was a flawless dancer, she conceded. But he didn't sweep her away. He didn't make her feel glad she was alive. He didn't make her wish she could love Christmas again.

At the end of the dance, he handed her a white business-size envelope. "This is for you."

The envelope contained a printed travel itinerary.

"I want you to come skiing with me," he said. "Just give your passport information to my service, and they'll take care of the reservations and tickets."

Skiing. In Gstaad. With European royalty. It was a moment, Elaine had to admit that. So why did she feel so underwhelmed?

She glanced at the departure date. "This is for tomorrow."

"Yes."

She shoved the paper into the envelope. "This is so unexpected—I don't quite know what to say."

He sent her a practiced smile. "Come now. You expected it. I'm sure your parents will be delighted. If we're going to do business together, we might as well have fun doing it, yes?"

He was all but offering her his business. It should have been the biggest moment in her career—her life, maybe. But it wasn't.

She smiled brightly, falsely, spying her reflection in the slick black glass of the picture window. "I'll let you know."

Without another glance at him, she headed for the foyer.

Jenny and Melanie hissed questions and protests in an undertone. "What are you doing?" Jen demanded.

Elaine filled them in on Axel's invitation.

"Don't tick him off," Melanie warned.

"Are your passports current?" Elaine asked them both.

"Mine is," Melanie said. "But what—"

"I'll tell you what." With a little laugh, Elaine handed over the envelope. "It's your lucky day. You're going skiing in Switzerland tomorrow. Staying at the Hotel Grande Suisse. Just contact this agency, and they'll take care of the paperwork."

Leaving them gasping and sputtering—Melanie with a broad grin breaking through her surprise—she headed for the cloakroom. "The Gallignani," she said, indicating her coat, which hung from a portable rack set up in the guest room. She felt light and free. "The gentleman who left a short while ago—did he mention where he was going?"

"No."

Well, of course he hadn't. But he lived in Brooklyn. That narrowed it down.

"He forgot his gloves," the girl added, holding out a large, lived-in pair.

Elaine shoved them in her purse. "Then I'd better take them to him."

On her way out, she found her parents to say good-night.

Startled, her mother studied her. "Are you ill?"

"I've never felt better." Elaine leaned forward for the customary makeup-preserving air kiss, then impulsively hugged her mother close and embraced her father. "Merry Christmas," she said to them both, and realized it was the first time she'd said those words in years.

CHAPTER TWELVE

Outside, the world had gone white; the streets and side-walks were smooth and clean. Sable, the doorman, who was actually a woman, phoned for a taxi and they waited together in the gleaming, midcentury-era lobby.

"So, the man who just left—Mr. Fiore—didn't take a taxi?" Elaine asked.

"No. He had his own car." Sable studied the thick fall of snow on the pavement outside. "Bad night for driving."

"Did you see which way he went?"

"Toward Roosevelt, I guess."

Nervous, Elaine studied Sable. The unflattering double-breasted uniform had not changed in generations, and on a young woman, it looked particularly absurd. At least in winter, the traditional warm coachman's cloak helped conceal the two-toned fashion crime. "Do you have plans for tonight?" Elaine asked her suddenly.

Sable glanced behind her to see who Elaine was talking to. "Me?" She put a hand to her chest. "I got to play Santa Claus to my two kids."

Until now, Elaine had never realized Sable had kids. "Sounds like fun."

"Oh, it is." Her glance crept almost imperceptibly to the lobby clock. "This year, there's a bike and a dollhouse to put together. I imagine my husband made a good start on the bike, but he doesn't know the first thing about dollhouses." She smiled, and there was a special quality to her smile, a softness made of love and pride and wistfulness. "He'll have his hands full getting them to bed."

"Then you should go home and help him," Elaine said, surprising herself with the words.

Sable glanced at the lobby clock. "Ravi doesn't come in for another hour."

Despite her urgency to find Tony, Elaine felt a keen sense of sympathy. She hesitated, the dilemma weighing heavily on her.

She'd lost Tony for a long time. Now she knew where to find him. Yet here was a woman who was working rather than tucking her babies in on Christmas Eve. How could anything in the world be more important than that? True giving meant sacrifice, didn't it? "I'll cover for you."

Sable laughed. "I don't think so, Ms. St. James. I could lose my job if someone found out."

"Oh, for heaven's sake. Things like that don't happen to good people on Christmas. Now, hand over the cloak and hat and whistle."

Sable looked torn to the point of breaking. Elaine put a hand on her arm. "Please. This is as much for me as it is for you." She gestured outside. "Look, your cab's here." Seizing the doorman's accessories, she pushed and bullied Sable out through the cold night and into the waiting taxi. Then she prepaid the driver and stood on the sidewalk, watching the yellow car pull away. Sable turned and waved through the rear window until the snowy night swallowed her up. The woman's smile was the last thing Elaine saw, like the grin of the Cheshire cat before he disappeared.

As she returned to the lobby, Elaine felt the satisfying weight of her mission. Maybe Christmas was a disaster for her, but that was no reason for anyone else to give up on it. Christmas really meant something to women like Sable, who worked hard all year and deserved to spend time making their kids happy.

With a dramatic flourish, Elaine flung on the crimson and dove-gray cloak, fastening the ornate frog closures down the front. Turning to the gilt-framed lobby mirror, she donned a matching flat cap, angling the patent leather bill jauntily down over her eye. She looked ridiculous. An overgrown organ grinder's monkey. What were the building managers thinking, making the doorman work in this getup?

They were thinking residents like the St. Jameses wanted it that way.

A movement outside caught her eye. A party of well-dressed couples emerged from a Town Car at the curb. Clients! She hurried to let them in, holding the brass-and-glass door wide for three couples. It was on the tip of her tongue to greet the Wyndhams, the Blantons and the McQuiggs, old friends of her parents. Over the years, she had attended school and summer camp with some of their kids.

They swept past her in a laughing, babbling mass. No one looked at Elaine. No one greeted her. She didn't feel hurt, but mystified. Was it just this group of guests or did everyone treat the doorman this way? *Everyone*, she thought, answering her own question. In her world, the help was invisible, and friends were chosen for their social value as much as for their personal qualities.

After the next group swept through, she realized it was no fluke. They ignored her, too, even though she'd sent one couple a Tiffany bowl as a wedding present not so long ago. Then a man she recognized, a famous orchestra conductor who had come to dinner several times while she was growing up, alighted from a taxi. Certain he would be delighted to see her, she arranged her face in a smile. But his eyes barely flickered in her direction as he gave a curt, dismissive nod and headed for the elevator. These people, Elaine realized, treated the doorman with no more regard than a potted fern.

As she stood watching the polished-steel elevator doors closing, Elaine made an even more disturbing realization. She was one of "these people."

When Ravi arrived for his shift, she made a hasty explanation he clearly didn't understand, then called a cab for herself. She slid into the back seat, shivering as her thighs touched the hard plastic upholstery. She tucked her warm designer coat more securely around her and thought for a moment. The fact was, she had no clue where she wanted to go.

She wanted to find Tony. She wanted to tell him that seeing him again had caused her to step back and take a hard, painful look at her life. She'd left the best party in town and put her career in jeopardy to work for an hour as a doorman. All because she'd seen him again and realized the dream was still there, hiding, waiting for the right moment. So she was either losing her marbles or turning into a different person.

She felt the driver eyeing her in the rearview mirror. "Brooklyn," she said. Ordinarily, even an hour ago, she wouldn't have given a second glance at a cabbie. Now she frowned as she detected something—a flicker of recognition?—in his glance.

"Got it." He turned south on Roosevelt Drive. "You probably want to be more specific."

She thought hard. "Do you know of a Catholic church in Brooklyn? One that holds midnight mass?"

He narrowed his eyes in the mirror. "That'd narrow it down to a couple dozen."

"Maybe I'll think of the name on the way over."

As it turned out, she had plenty of time to think because traffic came to a standstill a few blocks north of the bridge.

"Great," Elaine said. "I'm going to throw myself at a man for the second time in my life, and I get stuck in a traffic jam."

"The second time in your life? What happened the first time?"

"He didn't show." The chime of bells shimmered from the radio speaker. There was a silvery quality to the chimes that made her shiver.

"I thought he explained all that." Something in his voice caught her attention, and she studied him with more than passing interest. He was just a cabbie, she told herself. He wore a cap with earflaps and a bright red muffler.

The back of her neck prickled. Clutching the back of the seat, she leaned forward to read the driver ID affixed to the meter box. Lawrence E. Simms.

"Larry?" she said.

At last, they reached the bridge. The normally busy span was oddly deserted. "That's me."

"Larry the elf? Larry the Zamboni driver?"

The cabbie seemed not to hear her as he cranked down his window and stuck his head out. "Hey, lady. Do you see what I see? Oh, man."

She craned her neck and squinted, straining to see through the foggy curtain of snow lit by the headlamps of the taxi. "What?" she asked.

"There's someone on the bridge."

"What do you mean?"

He slowed and pulled over. "There. Isn't that a jumper?"

A woman stood alone on the wrong side of the bridge rail. She had somehow gone around the protective chain-link fencing and was facing out over the river. She wore no coat, and the wind whipped her hair around her face.

Chills zipped down Elaine's spine. "What's going on? Is that woman …" She stopped, unable to voice her fear.

"They say this is the time of year for it."

She wrenched open the door of the taxi and got out. Eerily, there was no one in sight—only the taxi …and the woman on the bridge rail.

Elaine walked through the snowy night, feeling the cold feathers of snowflakes on her face. She headed toward the woman, no longer intent on finding Tony but on trying to help.

It was absurd, of course. What could she possibly do to help? She whipped a glance around, but still no cars emerged from the storm. "This is the busiest bridge in the city," she muttered through chattering teeth. "How can it be deserted?"

Down on the river, the heartbeat rhythm of a boat motor pulsed into the ghostly stillness of the night. The winter wind off the water smelled cold and harsh. Shuddering with apprehension, Elaine approached the woman. The misty glow of a sodium vapor light illuminated the slender form, the delicate profile, her features seemingly frozen by the wind off the water. She wore nothing but a suede skirt and cashmere sweater—no coat, no hat, no gloves.

An icy sense of recognition raced over Elaine. Her heart jolted. Numbed by dread, she stepped to the chain-link fence and clutched at the cold wires. "Bobbi," she said, obeying an instinct to keep her voice low. "It's me, Elaine."

Bobbi didn't seem startled, so that was something. Nor did she seem in the least surprised to encounter Elaine. As fragile and brittle as a snowflake, Bobbi did not move. She simply stood there, like a figurehead at the prow of a ship.

"Go away," she said simply, her voice clear and firm.

"Not on your li—not in a million years. I'm so glad I'm here," she said. "Please don't hurt yourself, Bobbi. Please."

"What does it matter to you?"

"Well, for one thing, I didn't get a chance to tell you how sorry I am about today."

"Oh, that's great, Elaine. Let's make this about you."

Elaine was slightly encouraged by Bobbi's anger. "That's not what I'm doing."

"Then what are you doing, Elaine? Trying to improve my life for fun and profit?"

Elaine was wracked by guilt, as well as fear. In the frigid night, she was forced to truly see her relationship with Bobbi. They'd made friends for all the wrong reasons—Elaine had "created" a media figure, nothing more. Their friendship had never had any depth or genuine intimacy. It had been, like all of Elaine's other relationships, a business arrangement.

"I was wrong," said Elaine. "I was awful to you. Bobbi, please. Think what you will of me, but don't hurt yourself. For heaven's sake, it's Christmas."

"Another work day, as far as you're concerned. What's suddenly so special about Christmas?"

"Well, there's …" Elaine's voice trailed off. Suddenly, at the very worst possible moment, she had absolutely no idea what to say.

"There's what?"

"The Christmas tree," Elaine said. "What other time of year can you put such a large home fashion accessory in your living room and actually feel good about it?"

"That's only because you know you're going to take it down. And if that's supposed to give me a reason for living, you'll have to do better. You wouldn't know the true meaning of Christmas if it slapped you upside the head."

"Then maybe I'm the one who should be out there on the bridge," Elaine snapped. She was still terrified, but keeping Bobbi engaged in conversation was at least stopping her from doing a swan dive into the East River. "And I do, too, know the meaning of Christmas. It's to celebrate the birth of Christ. Everybody knows that."

"Actually, Christmas is not the birthday of Christ," Bobbi contradicted her. "He wasn't born in the middle of winter."

"How do you know that?"

"Well, for one thing, the sheep were out in the fields. It would have been very cold at night in the hills of Judea, and shepherds in that area never keep sheep in the fields after the end of October."

"What's that got to do with—" Elaine shut her mouth.

"Besides," Bobbi went on, "Herod never would have ordered people to travel to their hometowns for tax registration in the middle of winter."

"I can believe that," Elaine said. "Everyone knows you pay taxes in the spring." This was nuts. She was supposed to be convincing Bobbi of the true meaning of Christmas so she wouldn't take a flying leap off the bridge. Keep her talking, Elaine told herself. That was the key. "But listen," she said, "December twenty-fifth is as good a time as any to honor Christmas."

Bobbi hugged herself against the cold. "Jesus wouldn't have celebrated his own birthday because it wasn't a Jewish custom to do so."

"Anyone with half a brain ignores birthdays," Elaine said. "Look, Christmas is not just a time for people to be extra nice to each other, to make ourselves feel good by giving gifts. Christmas is to celebrate the fact that we don't have to shoulder our own burdens alone, that a humble child can be our salvation. It's a joyful thing, Bobbi, and what better way to show joy than to share it? I'm not doing such a good job giving you a reason to come down off this bridge, but here's something I know. I've been awful. I need to learn kindness and generosity again. I'm learning it from people like you, Bobbi. The world needs you in it."

"What, more thieves?" Bobbi's voice broke.

"More people like you to show people like me what desperation really is. You were desperate, and I didn't let myself see that."

For the first time, Bobbi turned her head to look directly at Elaine. "That's a little more like it. But it's still about you." She turned back to stare at the river. "This isn't the life I wanted for myself. I need to be with people I love, with family. I need for my life to mean something more than a media opportunity. You didn't give me anything, Elaine, except the chance to live a phony life. Today I finally woke up to that."

"Fine, then let's get you home for Christmas. Your mother wants to see you on Christmas, honey. She needs you. We can get you to the airport and on the next flight to Raleigh Durham. You'll be home by Christmas morning."

"All right," said Bobbi softly, and a ripple of relief moved through Elaine.

"Perfect." Elaine rummaged in her purse. "I'll call my service. There's someone on 24/7." As she took out the phone, her key ring came with it. Her special key ring, the one with the silver skate. Before she could catch it, the trinket fell through the iron grating, disappearing into deep blackness.

She imagined the small splash as it hit the water. She shut her eyes briefly, telling herself it didn't matter, it wasn't a portent of bad luck. Then she speed-dialed her twenty-four-hour travel service and secured a seat on the next flight out. "You're all set," she said to Bobbi. "It's time you headed for the airport."

Bobbi stared down at the river, seemingly fascinated by the

descent of the key ring. Finally in a tiny, pathetic voice, she said, "I'm scared."

Somewhere behind her, Elaine heard traffic sounds. A car, coming from the other direction, she thought. She was terrified Bobbi would panic and fall.

Bobbi's designer boots wobbled on the slippery narrow ledge of steel. How on earth would she ever turn around?

Elaine heard a car stop but didn't dare turn to look.

"I got her." A tall, swift-moving man strode past her.

Elaine nearly melted into a puddle of relief. "Tony."

He barely glanced at her as he approached Bobbi. He was totally focused on saving her. He squeezed through an opening that had been bent in the fence, then climbed over the rail and edged toward her.

"We're both going to fall," Bobbi wailed.

"No, we won't. Don't even say that."

Elaine held her breath. The shiny cold steel framework was encased in ice. Tony wrapped one arm around the pole and reached out with the other. "Take my hand," he said. "There you go. I got you."

Trembling with panic, she reached back blindly. Tony took hold with his bare hand. "It's okay," he said quietly. "You're okay now." Safe in his grip, Bobbi turned and let him coax her along the pipe, feet scraping along. She slipped, and her arms flailed. Elaine crushed her knuckles to her mouth to keep from screaming. Tony grabbed Bobbi and tugged, until she pitched forward into his arms.

Elaine rushed forward and hugged Bobbi. Heartsore, she took off her coat and settled it around Bobbi's shoulders. "I'm so sorry," Bobbi said. "What I did was wrong."

"But I was wrong, too," Elaine admitted. "I didn't listen to you."

Bobbi shivered uncontrollably. "No kidding."

Elaine remembered looking at the glossy black window in her parents' apartment. She'd seen a reflection of herself at the party, with her perfect career and perfect clothes and perfect jewelry—and a loneliness in her eyes that reminded her of two empty bowls.

The cabbie tapped the car horn. "Let's go already," he called. "It's another fifteen minutes to the airport."

Elaine bundled Bobbi into the cab and pressed a wad of cash into her hand. "Should I come to the airport with you?"

"No. I'll be all right," Bobbi said with a sniff.

As the taxi pulled away, Tony scratched his head. "That cabdriver. Isn't he the guy—"

"Don't ask," Elaine said. "He's magic."

Traffic started up again. Tony settled his jacket around Elaine's shoulders and held it in place with a firm embrace. She could have stayed like that all night, warm and safe and protected.

"How did you know?" she asked. "How did you know to find me?"

"I was driving to church, and a dispatch came over the radio."

The cabdriver, she realized.

"What are you doing here, Elaine?" he asked.

"You left your gloves." She fished them out of her purse and handed them over.

"You were coming all the way over to Brooklyn on Christmas Eve to give me my gloves?"

She nodded.

With a laugh that was deep and pure, he brought her to his car and turned on the heater full blast. "So I guess you need a ride home."

She started to nod her head, then looked him in the eye. "I don't want to go home."

CHAPTER THIRTEEN

Elaine St. James was the last person Tony thought he'd be spending Christmas Eve with. At the same time, she was the only person he wanted to spend Christmas Eve with. He led the way out of the underground parking and up the block to his building, situated on a quiet Park Slope street. He glanced at the silent woman beside him. She was coming into his home, into his life. He hoped he hadn't left the place too much of a mess.

The old brownstone wore garlands of holly on the stair rail and around the door. In the foyer, someone had suspended a sprig of mistletoe over the mailboxes. There was a Santa hat on the newel post. The scent of bayberry candles spiced the air. It was late, so they didn't speak until they were inside his third-floor apartment.

He let her in and watched her, trying to gauge her reaction.

At some point in his life he had figured out how not to be a slob. The place didn't look too bad or smell like a hamster cage.

But it also didn't look like the kind of place Elaine St. James belonged in. She was like some exotic flower standing there, completely out of her element. But then she smiled.

She took off his parka and handed it over. "Thanks," she said. "I would have frozen without it."

The fancy coat she'd given her friend was probably worth a month's rent.

"So ...am I keeping you from something?" she asked, surprising him by seeming a little nervous.

"I skipped mass tonight," he said. "But I suppose that can be forgiven, seeing as how we had to help out your friend."

She nodded and gave a little shudder. "I hope she's going to be all right."

"Helluva thing, seeing your friend like that."

"I'm not sure she was ever my friend, but I'd never want to see her hurt herself."

"That's up to her. You did a good thing, Elaine."

"Did I? What about at lunch, when she asked me for an advance and I turned her down? That's what started this whole mess."

"You don't always get it right the first time. Nobody does. How about you have a seat?" He indicated the brown corduroy sofa. His scrawny Christmas tree was set up on a table in the window, a little lopsided thing sagging with too many colored lights.

He left a message on his parents' answering machine as he poured two glasses of wine—he hoped she liked red—and handed one to her. "So, are you all right?" he asked.

"I guess." She wandered through the apartment, much as he had hers. When she studied his collection of framed photos, the expression on her face broke his heart. Glancing up, she saw him watching her. "Pictures of friends and family," she said wistfully, sitting on his rumpled sofa. "It's nice."

She deserved friends and family of her own, Tony thought. She was a good person. Yet, somehow, she'd wound up stuck in a life that was less than she deserved and more than she wanted.

He wasn't to blame for that, but he'd played a part. Years ago, he'd abandoned her because he felt that, without a pro hockey career, he didn't measure up to her standards. He'd really believed that. But then he'd come to terms with the end of his dream and made a new life for himself.

It occurred to him that Elaine was still rich and sophisticated. But he no longer considered her out of his league. Life had sent him a bum shot, and he'd made his peace with that. Now life was giving him a second chance.

He watched the way her throat moved as she took a swallow of wine. She had the kind of face that would always be beautiful, at any age, glowing with youth or softened and lined by years. He knew he wanted to be there for that transformation, no matter how crazy it seemed and how different their worlds were. And he wanted it all to start now.

The air between them was hot, electric. Some things never changed.

"Elaine." He took her glass and set it with his on the coffee table. "What are you doing here?"

CHAPTER FOURTEEN

Elaine wasn't sure how to answer him. She clenched and unclenched her hands as she watched him, his attention focused wholly on her. Even though they weren't touching, she could feel his warmth; he glowed with it. She wasn't sure how to answer his question. *What are you doing here?*

She wanted nothing. She wanted everything. And he would never understand.

Silently, deliberately, she slid toward him on the sofa, pressed her hands to his chest. He took in a quick breath, then grabbed her wrists. At first she feared he was going to push her away, but he gripped her hand and lifted it to his lips. Then his mouth lowered over hers, brushing lightly and finally pressing, exploring. It was the kind of kiss she didn't experience anymore. It was fierce and deeply honest, sharing emotions that could not be shaped into words.

She felt as though someone had touched a flame to a fast-burning fuse. Everything welled up inside her and spilled over, as though all her longing and desires converged in this single desperate moment.

She clung to him, her hands smoothing the big shoulders, fingers tangling in the thick hair curling against his collar. She had not realized she could feel this way anymore. She was young and giddy and hopeful again, filled with the knowledge that she was, finally, in the right place with the right man.

He stood and drew her up with him, holding her by the upper arms and gazing intently down into her face. "Just so you know," he whispered, "I don't do one-night stands."

"That's not what this is," she said.

"So what is it?"

Oh, she needed him. Not just in her arms, but in her life. Not just for tonight, but forever. She needed soft searching kisses and warm flesh against warm flesh. Endless conversations about things only they understood. The simple joy of building a life together, moment by moment. It was amazing, the way she and Tony seemed to know and crave each other. They were intimate strangers who had been dreaming of this meeting for years, moving toward it without knowing it.

"It's what should have happened years ago."

He smiled. "That's what I thought, too." He kissed her again, keeping their mouths joined even as he walked her slowly backward. The hardwood floor changed to carpet under her feet, and she pulled back briefly to gather fleeting impressions of his bedroom. King-size bed. Old-fashioned dresser with a framed photo of his family. A shoeshine kit left out. Several neckties draped over the back of a chair.

He grinned sheepishly. "I wasn't sure what to wear tonight. I was a little nervous."

She took his hand, held it over her thumping heart. She was so glad he'd admitted it. "I'm nervous now."

"Yeah," he said, his thumb tracing the line of her collarbone. "Me, too. I've been thinking about this for a long time." He plucked ineffectually at her dress. "I didn't picture you wearing chain mail, though. Geez, Elaine, you got a chastity belt under this?"

She laughed softly and reached back to unclasp the mesh overdress, letting it slide down her torso and pool like fallen coins around her feet. She stepped toward him, into his arms, and when she looked into his eyes, she saw herself reflected there, and the love and wonder on her face was startling.

After that, there were no more awkward moments between them, not even as they undressed. She felt only a searing anticipation and breath-held awe at the realization that finally, unexpectedly, she had rediscovered something real, something to give depth and resonance to her life, to fill the empty spaces where cold loneliness had taken up residence, to make her matter in a way she had never mattered before.

He turned back the covers and brought her against him. Shivery heat coursed through her. She reached out and caressed him, discovering the shape and texture and warmth she had only imagined before. He returned the caresses with exquisite tenderness, wringing wonder and emotion from her as her lips formed a wordless cry of startled joy. She couldn't believe how deeply she felt each intimate stroke of his hands, his mouth, how profound it seemed with him. Her heart was engaged, hopelessly tangled, and it made all the difference. When their bodies joined, she clasped him tighter, wishing for a way to bring him closer still. And then she found it, whispering love words into his ear while ecstasy lifted her up, transported her and held her high and light in some exalted place she thought she would never have reached. When after long blissful moments she returned to herself, Elaine knew she was a different person.

She felt the change deep in her bones. After this night, she knew, nothing would ever be the same.

CHAPTER FIFTEEN

The smell of freshly brewed coffee teased Tony awake by small degrees of awareness. *Elaine.* The thought came to him like the last precious shred of an almost forgotten dream, and for a second he thought maybe he *had* dreamed her. But no. She'd been with him. Her presence was still there, a faint warmth in the hollow in the bed next to him where she had slept in his arms all night. The smell of her hair lingered on his pillow.

And in his heart lived the feeling that no morning in the history of the world could ever be as good as this one.

Elaine St. James. Finding her again was a small miracle, like coming across a diamond glittering in the snow.

She stood in the kitchen, seemingly mesmerized by the fragrant drip of the coffeemaker. She wore a pair of his socks and an ancient hockey practice jersey. Her makeup was gone and her hair was a mess. She looked like a goddess.

"Merry Christmas," he said, coming up behind her. He slipped his hands around her waist and kissed the side of her neck.

"It is," she said softly, pressing herself back against him. "I was going to find some Christmas carols on the radio."

He reached across the counter and clicked it on, then fiddled with the dial. "God Rest Ye Merry Gentlemen," drifted through the room.

"Good idea," he said, turning her in his arms and pulling her back toward the bedroom, where the bed was still warm and inviting. His heart soared, because he knew exactly what he was going to do—in the next few moments, and for the rest of his life. He had never been more sure of anything.

"I was trying to make coffee," she protested.

"That thing takes forever."

She started to protest again, but then her face softened, and she looked up at him with her heart in her eyes. "Good."

"Do you think it's ready now?"

"What's ready?" Elaine felt a smile spread across her face. It simply would not go away. It was as though she had been born this way and would live the rest of her life this way.

"The coffee."

"I think it must be. I started it over an hour ago."

He rolled to one side, offering a tantalizing glimpse of all of him, and grabbed the clock from the bedside table. "Oh, man."

"What's the matter?"

"I'm supposed to be at my folks."

She deflated a little but hid her disappointment by looking away, shaking her hair across her face. Just because everything had changed for her didn't mean it had for the rest of humanity. One of the painful discoveries she'd made as an adult was that the world did not revolve around her. And, this morning, reality lay in wait, ready to spring like a predator on her happiness.

"You'd better head for the shower," she said, being practical. "I'll phone for a taxi."

"It's walking distance."

"For you. I've got to get going."

He turned back to her, pulling her against him. "Going where?"

She hesitated. Her family usually slept late on Christmas, exchanged tasteful gifts, had a champagne brunch and then took off on vacation, to ski or sun themselves somewhere exotic. They liked to travel on Christmas Day, because it was less crowded than just before or just after the holiday. This logical program did not appeal to her in the least and hadn't for a long time. She simply went along with it because there was nothing else to do.

"To my parents' apartment, I suppose," she felt obliged to say.

"Call them and say you can't make it."

"Why can't I make it?" she asked, eyeing Tony.

"You're coming with me," he announced. "You're going to love my family. They're going to love you." His face, shadowed by the night's growth of beard, wore a lopsided smile that took all her willpower to resist.

"No way," she said, getting up from the bed. One by one, she retrieved articles of clothing, feeling tingles of remembered pleasure as she picked up each discarded piece.

"Remember what I said." He stood and pulled her against him. "I don't do one-night stands."

"I remember." She shuddered in his arms, now feeling the burden of her decision to change her life. She was different. She was brand-new, she reminded herself.

"So," said Tony, "that's what it'll turn into if you leave now."

★ ★ ★

A half hour later, in her couture dress minus the chain mail, and a shapeless borrowed coat from Tony's hall closet, Elaine stepped out into Christmas morning. Church bells clanged with joyous abandon and, somewhere in the distance, carolers sang. The snowstorm was over, and the sun peeked through a crack in the clouds. A sparkling carpet of dazzling white lay over everything, turning parked cars to anonymous giant marshmallows, heaps of garbage to glistening ivory sculptures. Laughing children played in the streets while their parents, cradling steaming mugs in their hands, looked on from stairways and stoops. Kids tried out new sleds and skis and radio-controlled trucks.

They encountered a dark-eyed girl with a shy smile who carried a large box as she walked along with her mother. "Tony," she said, "look what Santa brought." She lifted the lid to show off a brand-new pair of hockey skates. He winked at her mom and tugged at the end of her stocking cap. "You must have been extra good this year, kiddo."

"We're going to Prospect Park to try them out right away."

He waved at them as they headed for the bus stop. "She's one of my best left wings," he said.

"So she's in your hockey league?"

"Yeah. For the time being." A troubled crease appeared on his brow.

"The lack of funds is a big problem, isn't it?" She watched the girl and her mother at the bus stop, their faces glowing with excitement. "It doesn't have to be that way."

"I know. Better PR, bigger donations. But we can't afford better PR."

"You can if it's free."

He lifted an eyebrow. "Yeah? When are you going to have time for that?"

She smiled, suddenly sure of herself, more sure than she'd ever been in her life. "From now on, I'm going to make time. My firm's going to open a nonprofit PR division and take on some pro bono clients."

He grinned and put his arm around her. "It's good to be the boss."

As she walked at his side, she felt lighter than air. She felt as though she'd been roused from a long sleep of numbness and was finally waking up to life. This was Tony's world, this colorful, noisy, imperfect place, and it made more sense to her than her own. He was a part of this neighborhood, this tree-lined street filled with families and laughter.

There was a quality of belonging here, and as she walked through the winter morning with him, it encompassed her like a vast embrace. She heard herself singing along with the carolers and laughing at a family playing with a frisky new puppy with a bow around its neck. Everything warm and real bubbled up inside her and spilled over and, at last, after the long, strange night, she knew what it was. And it was so simple, so very simple. It was happiness, pure and unpretentious and more real than the fresh snow squeaking beneath her feet.

"'I am as merry as a schoolboy'," she said with a laugh, quoting half-remembered lines from Dickens. "'As giddy as a drunken man!'"

Tony laughed with her and pulled her close. "Good thing you smell better."

The sweet yearning she had felt for him all those years ago had never gone away. It had only grown, nurtured in the dark, secret places of her heart. The things that truly mattered had

been buried under the smothering press of ambition and ex-
pectation and all the other business that had taken over her
life when she wasn't paying attention. But she was free now,
and she could tell her joy shone in her face when she looked
up at him, because she could see an answering joy reflected
in his eyes.

They didn't speak as they walked the next few blocks to the
classic Prospect Park West townhouse where he'd grown up.
Finally, as they stood on the sidewalk in front of the handsome, blocky building, she couldn't stay silent any longer.
"You wouldn't believe how nervous I am."

He stopped walking and turned to face her, seemingly
oblivious to the pedestrians who had to go around them.
"Hey, do you know how long my family's been waiting for
me to bring home the love of my life?"

She couldn't breathe, couldn't think. She had never, ever
felt this way before, but somehow she recognized the emotion.
It was the feeling of a dream coming to life. Her dream. The
time stretching out before her was her own. It was up to her
to decide how to spend it. She could forge ahead, fueled by
ambition, toward the shadowy fate she'd glimpsed in Bobbi's
desperate eyes as she'd hovered on the edge of the bridge. Or
she could choose a different path to a new and unexpected
destination.

"About as long," she said, "as I've been waiting to meet
them."

Tony's smile turned slightly shy. "Before we go in, I need
to give you something."

She frowned. "What?"

He rummaged in his pocket. "I meant to give it to you
last night."

Her heart quickened. "So why don't you give it to me now?"

Right in the middle of the snowy sidewalk, he went down on one knee and handed her a small box. "Elaine St. James, this means more than you think it means." Passersby were trying to be polite and not stare but they did anyway, grinning and whispering and nudging each other. But it didn't matter. Nothing mattered but this moment, the two of them, the warmth flowing between them.

Her hands trembled as she opened the box. She gasped, taking out a key ring with a silver skate. "How on earth did you get this?"

"Don't ask," he said with a grin. "It's magic."

She stared at him and her heart started to sing every carol and love song she'd ever heard.

"One of these days," he promised her, "this is going to be a different kind of ring," he added, getting to his feet. "And you're going to say yes, Elaine. Because, well, I love you," he said. "I always have."

A warm wash of tears fell down her cheeks, and a hush of reverence gripped her. "I know," she whispered. "I know that. Tony, I love you. I'll love you forever."

She clasped the silver skate in her hand, knowing the real gift was something she hadn't expected and maybe didn't even deserve—a chance to change her life.

She buried her face against his shoulder and inhaled. A thousand hopes and dreams gave birth to a thousand more, and all the cares in the world slipped away. *I promise*, she thought. *I promise I won't blow it this time.*

They stood like that for a long time, with Christmas exploding all around them, and finally Tony pulled away and walked up to the blocky brownstone.

He opened the door to a big, loud, cluttered kitchen that smelled of baking bread and rang with laughter and conversation. Everyone turned to them when they stepped inside.

"This is Elaine," Tony said, drawing her into the room with him. "We're home."

★ ★ ★ ★ ★

CANDLELIGHT CHRISTMAS

PART ONE

Christmas Pickles

The origin of the Christmas pickle is steeped in mystery. It seems no one knows the real truth. The handblown glass pickle ornaments from Lauscha in Germany can date back as far as 1847, and are treasured by families everywhere. The first child to spy the ornament on the tree Christmas morning gets an extra gift from Santa, and the first adult enjoys good luck all the year through. It's probably just a marketing hook, but who doesn't like presents and good luck?

The pickle prize inspired this recipe for jars of colorful pickles. Since these are no-process pickles, they are a) easy and b) perishable.

Much like a woman's heart.

No-Process-Pickles

1 cup water
1 cup white vinegar
2 teaspoons salt
1 tablespoon sugar
Handful of fresh dill
Whole peppercorns and peeled garlic cloves
Kirby cucumbers (or regular cucumbers, cut into quarters lengthwise)
Red radishes, sliced thin

Fill clear glass jars with the pickles and radishes, creating a nice color palette of red and green. Add the herbs and spices. Combine the water, vinegar, sugar and salt in a jar with a lid, and shake to dissolve. Pour over pickles in the jars. Seal and refrigerate. These will be ready the next morning and can last up to a month—after that, please discard for safety's sake. The longer the cucumbers pickle, the softer they will get, and if you don't grasp *that* metaphor, I can't help you. Anyway, if you like things fresh and crisp, don't wait too long to eat these.

[Source: Original; adapted from Ohio State University Extension guidelines, 2009]

PROLOGUE

Christmas Past

There were worse things than spending Christmas with your ex-husband, thought Darcy Fitzgerald as she pulled up in front of the house.

A root canal without novocaine, for example. That was probably worse. A crash landing in a small aircraft, perhaps. Reading *Silas Marner* in ninth grade. Frostbite, a crocodile attack, eating a bad oyster. Head lice.

She enumerated the many ways things could be worse, all the while bracing herself for the hours to come. The car tires churned up last night's melting snow as she jockeyed her Volkswagen into the small space.

She'd dressed with special care, determined for Huntley to see that he'd lost something special. Deep down, she knew the notion was ridiculous; Huntley Collins had not truly seen her in a very long time.

While pulling the bag of gifts from the trunk, she stepped into the ankle-deep grimy slush. As it flooded her favorite kitten-heel suede shoes, the bone-freezing ice took her breath away. She reared back, slipping on the crusty ice, and landed butt-first in a dirty snowbank. The bag of parcels broke open, and her festively wrapped packages littered the ground.

"Awesome," she muttered, pulling herself up and trying to brush the filth off her skirt.

Perhaps the most hellish part of the day was the knowledge that she had agreed to this travesty. Huntley had convinced her to get through the holidays together so they wouldn't ruin things for everyone else.

The Fitzgeralds and the Collinses had been best friends and neighbors for decades. The two Collins boys and the five Fitzgerald girls had grown up together, playing hide-and-seek on summer nights, surfing at Cupsogue Beach, pulling pranks on one another, sneaking beer from the fridge for liquid courage before a school dance, telling each other secrets...and lies. Huntley's older brother was married to Darcy's older sister. The families' fortunes were meant to be entwined forever.

Unfortunately, Huntley's notion of forever spanned approximately five years. Darcy had found out about his affair—with his ex-wife, just to make things even worse—before Thanksgiving. Yet she had come today out of regard for her stepkids, Amy and Orion, though she expected little from the sullen, resentful teenagers.

She'd been part of their lives for five years, and she had selected their gifts with care. In a weak moment, she'd bought a little something for Huntley, so he'd have something under the tree from his kids, who were too self-absorbed and, at the moment, confused, to shop for him.

She found the smallest of the scattered packages in the ditch—the yodeling plastic pickle. There was a tradition that the first to find the pickle on the tree would get a special surprise. She moved the switch on the back of the pickle. It made a brief gurgling sound and then died.

"Surprise," she muttered, and trudged grimly up the stairs to the front door.

PART TWO

Just because you're a single dad is no excuse for feeding your kid junk food. At some point you have to suck it up and learn to cook like a man.

Massive Spaghetti Feed

Never underestimate the power of the fantastic bowl of spaghetti.

1 15-ounce can of San Marzano tomatoes, crushed
1 stick of butter
1 onion about the size of your fist, cut up
Parmesan cheese
1 pound of spaghetti, cooked al dente

Simmer the first three ingredients together for 45 minutes, and then blend with an immersion blender or food processor. Pour over hot spaghetti and pass the parm.

[Source: San Marzano tomato label]

CHAPTER ONE

◆◆▥◈▥◆◆

Summer's End

Logan O'Donnell stood on a platform one hundred feet in the air, preparing to shove his ten-year-old son off the edge. A light breeze shimmered through the canopy of trees, scattering leaves on the forest floor far below. A zip line cable, slender as a thread in a spider's web, hung between the tree platforms, waiting. Below, Meerskill Falls crashed down a rocky gorge.

"There's no way I'm going off this." Logan's son, Charlie, drew his shoulders up until they practically touched the edge of his helmet.

"Come on," Logan said. "You told me you'd do it. The other kids had a ball. They're all waiting for you on the other side, and I heard a rumor about a bag of Cheetos being passed around."

"I changed my mind." Charlie set his jaw in a way that was all too familiar to Logan. "No way. No W-A-Y-F."

Logan knew the shtick, but he went along with it. "There's no *F* in way, dude."

"That's right. There's no effin' way I'm going off this thing."

"Aw, Charlie. It's almost like flying. You like to fly, right?" Of course he did. Charlie's stepfather was a pilot, after all. Logan crushed the thought. There were few things more depressing than thinking about the fact that your kid had a stepfather, even if the stepfather was an okay guy. Fortunately for Charlie, he'd ended up with a good one. But it was still depressing.

Charlie spent every summer with Logan. During the school year, he lived with his mom and stepfather in Oklahoma, a million miles away from Logan's home in upstate New York. It sucked, living that far from his kid. Being without Charlie was like missing a limb.

When he did have his son with him, Logan tried to make the most of their time together. He planned the entire season around Charlie, and that included working as a volunteer counselor at Camp Kioga, helping out with the summer program for local kids and inner-city kids on scholarship. The zip line over Meerskill Falls was a new installation, and had already become everyone's favorite feature. Nearly everyone.

"Hey, it's the last day of camp. Your last chance to try the zip line."

Charlie dragged in a shaky breath. He eyed the harness, made of stout webbing and metal buckles. "It looked really fun until I started thinking about actually doing it."

"Remember how you used to be scared to jump off the dock into Willow Lake? And then you did it and it was awesome."

"Hel-*lo*. The landing was a lot different," Charlie pointed out.

"You're going to love it. Trust me on this." Logan patted

the top of Charlie's helmet. "Look at all the safety features on this thing. The harness, the clips, the secondary ropes. There's not one thing that can go wrong."

"Yo, Charlie," shouted a kid on the opposite platform. "Go for it!"

The encouragement came from André, Charlie's best friend. The two had been inseparable all summer long, and if anyone could talk Charlie into something, it was André. He was one of the city kids in the program. He lived in a low-income project in the Bronx, and for André, it had been a summer of firsts—his first train trip, his first visit upstate to Ulster County, where Camp Kioga nestled on the north shore of Willow Lake. His first time to sleep in a cabin, see wildlife up close, swim and paddle in a pristine lake…and tell ghost stories around a campfire with his buddies. Logan liked the fact that at camp, all the kids were equal, no matter what their background.

"I kind of want to do it," Charlie said.

"Up to you, buddy. You saw how it's done. You just stand on the edge and take one step forward."

Charlie fell silent. He stared at the waterfall cascading down the rocky gorge. The fine spray from the rushing cataract cooled the air.

"Hey, buddy," Logan said, wondering about his son's far-away expression. "What's on your mind?"

"I miss Blake," he said, his voice barely audible over the rush of the falls. "When I go back to Mom's, Blake won't be there anymore."

Logan's heart went out to the kid. Blake had been Charlie's beloved dog, a little brown terrier who had lived to a ripe old age. At the start of summer, she'd passed away. Apparently Charlie was dreading his return to his mom's dogless house.

"I don't blame you," Logan said, "but you were lucky to have Blake as your best friend for a long time."

Charlie stared at the planks of the platform. "Yeah." He didn't sound convinced.

"It sucks, losing a dog," Logan admitted. "No way around it. That's why we're not getting one. Hurts too bad when you have to say goodbye."

"Yeah," Charlie said again. "But I still like having a dog."

"Tell me something nice about Blake," Logan said.

"I never needed an alarm to get up for school in the morning. She'd just come into my room and burrow under the covers, like a rabbit, and she'd squirm until I got up." He smiled, just a little. "She got old and quiet and gentle. And then she couldn't jump up on the bed anymore, so I had to lift her."

"I bet you were really gentle with her."

He nodded. After another silence, he said, "Dad?"

"Yeah, bud?"

"I kinda want another dog."

Aw, jeez. Logan patted him on the shoulder. "You can talk to your mom about it tomorrow, when you see her." *Yeah,* he thought. *Let Charlie's mom deal with the mess and inconvenience of a dog.*

"Okay," said Charlie. "But, Dad?"

"Yeah, buddy?"

"Kids were telling ghost stories in the cabin last night," he said, picking at a thread in the webbing of his harness.

"You're at summer camp. Kids are supposed to tell ghost stories."

"André told the one about these people who committed suicide by jumping off a cliff above the falls."

"I've heard that story. Goes way back to the 1920s."

"Yeah, well, the ghosts are still around."

"They won't mess with the zip line."

"How do you know?"

Logan pointed to the group of kids and counselors on the distant platform. "They all got across, no problem. You saw them." The other campers appeared to be having the time of their lives, eating Cheetos and acting like Tarzan.

"Show me again, Dad," said Charlie. "I want to see you do it."

"Sure, buddy." Logan clipped Charlie to the safety cable and himself to the pulleys. "You're gonna love it." With a grin, he stepped off the platform into thin air, giving Charlie the thumbs-up sign with his free hand.

His son stood on the platform, his arms folded, his face screwed into an expression of skepticism. Logan tipped himself upside down, a crazy perspective for watching the waterfall below, crashing against the rocks. How could any kid not like this?

When Logan was young, he would have loved having a dad who would take him zip-lining, a dad who knew the difference between fun and frivolity, a dad who encouraged rather than demanded.

He landed with an exaggerated flourish on the opposite platform. Paige Albertson, cocounselor of the group, pointed at Charlie. "Aren't you forgetting something?"

"Oh yeah, my only son. Oops."

"Why is he staying over there?" asked Rufus, one of the kids.

"I bet he's scared," said another kid.

Logan ignored them. On the opposite platform, Charlie looked very small and alone. Vulnerable.

"Everything all right?" Paige put her hand on Logan's arm.

Paige had a crush on him. Logan knew this. He even wished he felt the same way, because she was great. She was a kindergarten teacher during the school year and a Camp Kioga

SUSAN WIGGS

volunteer during the summer. She had the all-American cheer-leader looks, the bubbly, uncomplicated personality that most guys couldn't resist. She was exactly the kind of girl his parents would want for him—pretty, stable, from a good family.

Could be that was the reason he wasn't feeling it for her.

"He's balking," said Logan. "And he feels really bad about it. I thought he'd love zip-lining."

"It's not for everybody," Paige pointed out. "And remember, if he doesn't go for it, the world won't come to an end."

"Good point." Logan saluted her and jumped off, crossing back to the platform on the other side, where Charlie waited. The zipping sound of the pulley and cable sang in his ears. Damn, this never got old.

"Just like Spider-Man," he said as he came in for a landing. "I swear, it's the coolest thing ever."

Charlie shuffled across the wooden planks of the platform. Logan reached for the clips to attach him to the pulley. "That's gonna be one small step for Charlie," he intoned, "one giant leap for—"

"Dad, hang on a second," Charlie said, shrinking back. "I changed my mind again."

Logan studied his son's posture: the hunched shoulders, the knees that were literally shaking. "Seriously?"

"Unhook me." Beneath the helmet, Charlie's face was pale, his green eyes haunted and wide.

"It's okay to change your mind," Logan said, "but I don't want you to have any regrets. Remember, we talked about regrets."

"When you have a chance to do something and then you don't do it and later on you wish you had," Charlie muttered.

Which pretty much summed up Logan's assessment of his marriage. "Yep," he said. "At the farewell dinner tonight, are you going to wish you'd done the zip line?"

Logan unhitched himself. Charlie studied the cables and pulleys with a look of yearning on his face. Okay, Logan admitted to himself, it bugged him that Charlie had conquered the jump off the dock with his mom, but Logan couldn't get him to push past his fear of the zip line. He had a flashing urge to grab the kid, strap him in and shove him off the platform, just to get him past his hesitation.

Then he remembered his own pushy father: *get in there and fight. Don't be a chickenshit.* Al O'Donnell had been a blustering, bossy, demanding dad. Logan had grown up resenting the hell out of him in a tense relationship that even now was full of turmoil.

The moment Charlie was born, Logan had made a vow. He would never be that dad.

"All right, buddy," he said, forcing cheerfulness into his tone. "Maybe another time. Let's climb down together."

The final dinner of summer at Camp Kioga was served banquet-style in the massive dining hall of the main pavilion. There was a spaghetti feed with all the trimmings—garlic bread, a salad bar, watermelon, ice cream. Awards would be given, songs sung, jokes told, tributes offered and farewells spoken.

The families of the campers were invited to the event. Parents arrived, eager to reunite with their kids and hear about their summer.

A sense of tradition hung like the painted paddles and colorful woven blankets on the walls. The old Catskills camp had been in operation since the 1920s. People as far back as Logan's grandparents remembered with nostalgia the childhood summers they'd spent in the draughty timber-and-stone cabins, swimming in the clear, cold waters of Willow Lake, boating in the summer sun each day, sitting around the campfire and telling stories at night. In a hundred years, the traditions had scarcely changed.

But the kids had. Back in the era of the Great Camps, places like Camp Kioga had been a playground for the ultrawealthy—Vanderbilts, Asters, Roosevelts. These days, the campers were a more diverse bunch. This summer's group included kids of Hollywood power brokers and Manhattan tycoons, recording artists and star athletes, alongside kids from the projects of the inner city and downriver industrial towns.

The organizers of the city kids program, Sonnet and Zach Alger, pulled out all the stops for the end of summer party. In addition to the banquet, there would be a performance by Jezebel, a hip-hop artist who had starred in a hit reality TV series. The show had been filmed at Camp Kioga, chronicling the efforts of the outspoken star to work with youngsters in the program.

Tonight, the only cameras present belonged to proud parents and grandparents.

Charlie was practically bouncing up and down with excitement, because he knew he was getting a swimming award. André was next to him as they took their seats at their assigned banquet table.

Paige, who stood nearby, handing out table assignments, leaned over and said, "Those two are such a great pair. I bet they're going to miss each other now that summer's over."

"Yeah, it'd be nice if they could stay in touch. Tricky, though, with André in the city and Charlie off to an air force base in Oklahoma."

"Must be hard for you, too."

"I can't even tell you. But...we deal. I'll see him at Thanksgiving, and he's mine—all mine—for Christmas."

At the moment, Christmas seemed light-years away. Logan wondered how the hell he'd keep himself busy after Charlie left.

He had his work, a thriving insurance business he'd founded in the nearby town of Avalon. If he was being honest with himself, he was bored stiff with the work, even though he liked helping friends and neighbors and made a good living at it.

Initially, the whole point of setting up a business in Avalon had been to enable him to live close to Charlie. Now that Charlie's mom had remarried and moved away, Logan was starting to think about making a change. A big change.

His sister India arrived to join in the festivities, and Logan excused himself to say hi. Her twin boys, Fisher and Goose, had spent the summer here. Charlie had had a great time with his two cousins, who lived on Long Island, where India and her husband ran an art gallery.

Red-haired like Logan and Charlie both, and dressed in flowing silks unlike *anybody,* India rushed over to her twin sons, practically in tears.

"I missed you guys so much," she said, gathering them against her. "Did you have a good time at camp?"

"The best," said Fisher.

"We made you some stuff," said Goose.

"Real ugly jewelry, and we're gonna make you wear it," Fisher told her.

"If you made it, then I'm sure it's beautiful," she said.

"Uncle Logan taught us how to light farts."

"That's my baby brother," India said. "Now, you need no introduction, but I'll introduce you, anyway." She indicated the woman behind her. "Darcy, this is my brother, who probably needs to be sent to the naughty corner, but instead, he's a volunteer counselor."

"And head fart lighter," said the woman, sticking out her hand. "I'm Darcy Fitzgerald."

He took her hand, liking her straightforward expression. She had dark hair done in a messy ponytail and a direct, brown-eyed gaze. Her hand felt small but firm, and she had a quirky smile. For no reason Logan could name, he felt a subtle nudge of interest.

"Are you here to pick up a kid?" he asked her. "Which one belongs to you?"

"None, thank God," she said with a shudder.

"Allergies?" Logan asked.

"Something like that."

"Then you came to the wrong place." He gestured around the dining hall, swarming with excited, hungry kids. To him, it was a vision of paradise. He liked kids. He liked big, loud, loving families. It was the tragedy of his life that he was restricted to summers and holidays with his only child.

"Except for one thing," said Darcy, turning toward the dais where the band was setting up. "I'm a huge Jezebel fan."

"You must be. We're a long way from anywhere."

She nodded. "I came along for the ride with India when she invited me to pick up her boys. Thought it would be nice to get out to the countryside for a weekend."

"So you live in the city?" he asked.

"In SoHo. I didn't have anything else going on this weekend. Yes, I'm that pathetic friend everybody feels sorry for, all alone and getting over a broken heart." She spoke lightly, but he detected a serious note in her tone.

"Oh, sorry. About the broken heart. Glad to hear you're getting over it."

"Thanks," she said. "It takes time. That's what people keep telling me. I keep looking for distractions. But hearts are funny that way. They don't let you lie, even to yourself."

"Not for long, anyway. Anything I can do to help?" He instantly regretted the offer. He had no idea what to do about someone else's broken heart.

"I'll spare you the details."

Good.

She scanned the big, noisy room. "Where can a girl get a drink around here?"

"It's not that kind of party."

"Oops. Of course." She set down her bag and peeled off her jacket. Underneath, she wore a shapeless T-shirt commemorating Jezebel in Madison Square Garden. "I guess we'd better have a seat," she said, glancing around. "Looks like India found a table." His nephews, along with Charlie and André, had already visited the buffet and were chowing down.

"Right this way," he said, unconsciously touching the small of her back as he steered her through the dining hall.

She glanced up at him, and he noticed something in her stare. Startlement? Recognition? And he noticed something in himself. Attraction? No, couldn't be. She was not his type. Like Paige, she was the type his family would want him to date, only unlike Paige, she wasn't girl-next-door cute. She was...funny and ironic, and she spoke with a boarding school accent that somehow didn't sound affected. He had no idea why he would suddenly find this interesting.

They went through the buffet line on opposite sides of the long table. "This doesn't look like the camp food we had when I was a kid," she said.

"Where'd you go to camp?"

"Walden, in Maine."

Further evidence that she was the "right" sort of girl, in his parents' eyes. But Logan told himself not to let that prejudice him. "I've got an idea," he said. "How about we—"

"Hey, Dad!" Charlie piped up, motioning him over to the table. "Check it out. I'm Mr. Potato Head."

Charlie had decked himself out at the salad bar, with rings of green pepper for eyeglasses, a cherry tomato nose, carrot sticks for vampire teeth.

"Oh, that's brilliant," Logan said. "And so appetizing." He turned to Darcy as she set her plate down at an empty place. "My son, Charlie, the boy genius. Charlie, this is Darcy."

"Nice to meet you." With the firm, direct manner Logan had drilled into him, Charlie made eye contact and stuck out his hand. The effect was ruined by the stickiness of his hand.

Logan felt Darcy stiffen as she briefly took the grubby little hand. "Hiya, Charlie," she said. "Who's your friend?"

"This is André," said Charlie. "He's got a frog in his pocket, so watch out."

"You weren't supposed to tell," André said, though he was clearly proud of his find.

"André and Charlie have been buddies this summer," Logan told Darcy.

"BFFs," Charlie said. "We made a blood oath."

"Not with real blood," André said. "With ketchup."

"Sounds tasty." Darcy discreetly wiped her hands with a napkin. "So, are your parents here, André?"

"My mom's coming up tomorrow. I wish I didn't have to go back to the city."

André's mother, Maya, worked as a nanny in Manhattan. André claimed she spent more time with her employer's kids than she did with her own.

Logan could relate to the situation from a different perspective. He'd been the employer's kid, once upon a time. His parents, busy with work and social obligations, had been distant yet powerful figures in his world, a dynamic he was determined *not* to pass on to his own son.

"They look like a great pair," Darcy said, watching André and Charlie fencing with their forks.

He nodded. "They're going to miss each other after this summer. Last night I signed them both up for a Skype account so they can talk to each other on the phone."

"That's nice."

"I'm nice. Didn't my sister tell you?"

"She didn't need to. You just did. Seriously, that's a kind thing to do."

During the banquet, the speeches were mercifully brief. Olivia and Connor Davis, who managed Camp Kioga, gave a quick welcome before handing the mic to Sonnet Alger. Sparkling with enthusiasm, Sonnet welcomed the families and friends of the campers.

Sonnet was Charlie's aunt by marriage, stepsister to Charlie's mom, Daisy. Right out of college, she'd been an intense, driven young woman, fierce in her quest for career success. But it was only recently, now that she was a newlywed making a life with her husband, Zach, that she seemed truly happy. She glowed with that inner light of joy of a woman in love. And Zach was watching from the wings, camera in hand, regarding her with a goofy, smitten expression.

Logan was happy for them. The pair hadn't had an easy road. Logan knew that. Maybe this was how love worked; it had to be tested and proved, over and over again. There had been a time when Logan thought he knew what true love was. Then he looked at couples like Sonnet and Zach Alger, and realized he didn't know shit. It was nice, seeing the two of them so happy together, but at the same time, it accentuated the giant, hollowed-out ache Logan felt in his own life.

Jezebel performed some of her hit songs, PG-rated ones. The kids and even some of the parents went nuts, clapping and stomping. During a particularly angry rendition of "Put Back the Things You Stole," he glanced at Darcy, who had stopped eating to simply stare in admiration.

Logan found himself wishing he wasn't so intrigued by her. She seemed complicated, and he wasn't so good with complicated women.

★ ★ ★

After the music, everyone went outside for a bonfire on the beach. "Our last night here," Sonnet told the group. "We hope you'll carry a bit of Camp Kioga home with you—the beautiful places you've seen, the new skills you've learned, the adventures you've had. Right now I have a little assignment."

Groans erupted, but she ignored them. "It's simple. I want you each to take one of these envelopes and write yourself a Christmas card."

"A Christmas card? In summer?"

"To yourself." She passed around a container of pens. "Put your home address on the envelope. Quit looking at me like that. As least this way, you know you'll get one card this year. I'm going to collect them all and mail them the week before Christmas. On the card, I want you to write a Christmas wish. Keep it to yourself. This is just for you. Friends and parents, you can do the same thing."

Balancing the small card on his knee, Charlie began writing diligently, without hesitating. Logan paused, noticing Darcy Fitzgerald writing swiftly, as well. Logan wished for a lot of things, but the only wish that really mattered was the one he couldn't have—more time with Charlie. All he could do was make sure the time they did have together was perfect.

And that was what he ended up writing on his card—*Make Christmas awesome for Charlie.*

Charlie sealed his envelope and wrote his address, then tossed it into the basket. Darcy followed suit, then tilted back her head, gazing up at the starry sky. "Hard to think about winter on a night like this," she said.

"True. What's your Christmas like?"

She stiffened and brought her gaze level with his. "Ridiculous," she said. "I have four sisters. Christmas is always chaos. And this year..." Her voice trailed off.

"What about this year?"

"I don't think I'll be up for all the madness."

"There's an alternative?"

"I could go to an ashram. How about you? Is there a typical O'Donnell family Christmas?"

"My folks like to spend the winter in Paradise Cove, Florida. We usually rendezvous down there. Charlie loves getting together with all his cousins."

"And how about you? What do you like?"

The question took him by surprise. It had been a long while since someone had asked him that.

"What do I like? Family. Friends and food. I want to be with Charlie," he said. "Actually, I'd love to take him snowboarding, but that's tough to do in Florida."

"Snowboarding sounds fun. Is there a ski resort nearby?"

"Saddle Mountain," he said. "It's a twenty-minute drive, tops. Some of my best memories with Charlie were made there. I hope it can stay open."

"Financial troubles?"

"Not that I know of. It's been privately owned by one family for years. Now the owner's retiring, so he's looking for a buyer."

"You should buy it."

He turned slightly to face her. "You're a mind reader. I had the same thought, and it's not out of the realm of possibility if I could get a group of investors together. Most people think it's a crazy idea."

"Some of the best ideas are the crazy ones."

He grinned. "I like the way you think."

Bags of marshmallows were being passed around. Logan found a stick for himself and one for Darcy. "So, how long have you known India?" he asked.

"Freshman year of college. Glee club and ski club."

Bennington girl, then. He tried not to generalize, but it was hard not to do when every single Bennington girl he met came from the same cookie-cutter mold. "So you sing and ski."

"More like a squawk and snowboard."

"You like snowboarding?"

"Yeah. Especially on a bluebird day. Or any day, really. I love to ride the way other people love to breathe."

A jock, he thought. Dang. He loved girl jocks. "And after college?" he asked, more and more interested.

"I took a few wrong turns," she said, her gaze sliding away. "So... Avalon. Gorgeous. But tiny. How did you end up here?"

"Charlie's mom." He gestured at his pride and joy, who was currently jamming several marshmallows on the end of his stick. "I moved here to be near him. The irony is, his mother remarried and moved away. Now I'm still here and I only get Charlie for summers and holidays. It's tough."

"Sorry to hear it. Kids are life's biggest complication, aren't they?"

"And its biggest perk."

She chuckled. "I'll take your word for it."

He tried to toast the marshmallows slowly, but they burst into flame. He blew on them and offered the end of the stick to Darcy. "Crispy critter?"

"Don't mind if I do." She took a whole marshmallow into her mouth in a motion he found ridiculously sexy. "Delicious," she said.

He liked talking to her. There was something easy about her, something genuine. "Tell me about life in SoHo."

"It's all right," she said. "I moved recently, to a little walk-up—emphasis on little—and I work on Madison Avenue."

"Advertising?" He ate the rest of the melting marshmallows, liking the burned sweetness.

"Good guess. And you're right."

Their shoulders brushed. He felt it again, that pleasant sting of attraction.

She looked up at him, her expression slightly quizzical.

"So, listen," he suggested, "after the kids are all tucked in for lights out, you want to go paddling?"

She laughed. "In the dark?"

"A moonlight paddle on Willow Lake. Since it's your first time here, you don't want to miss the lake by the light of the moon."

"Just the two of us?"

"Up to you. We could invite India along, or not…if you're sufficiently over your broken heart."

"Sounds like fun," she said easily. "*You* sound like fun, Logan. And as for my heart…" She sighed. "Do we ever get over it? Or just through it?"

"Good question."

"And?" She gazed at him in a way that made him glad he'd suggested the after-hours paddle.

"And I don't know."

Wow, he thought. There was definitely some potential here. "I'm glad India brought you to see the place," he said. "My family's always trying to fix me up."

"Do you need fixing?"

"Depends on who you ask. You're not afraid of the dark, are you?"

She laughed. "I'm not afraid of anything. Except maybe—"

"Dad. Hey, Dad, check it out." Charlie burst between them, brandishing a long stick with a marshmallow on the end. "Me and André are having a marshmallow war."

"With *flaming* marshmallows," André declared, bending back his stick, with a burning marshmallow on the end.

"Cripes, you can't be doing that." Logan grabbed the stick. "This stuff burns like napalm."

"We'll aim for the water," Charlie said. "Da-*ad*." He'd started a movement. Now a whole group of kids were catapulting marshmallows.

"Damn it," said Logan, "I swear, Charlie... Excuse me," he said to Darcy, and went to confiscate the weapons. By the time he finished and had the kids marching off to their cabins, Darcy had stood up, her shoulder bag in hand.

"I'm just going to call it a night," she said. "Thanks for the offer, though. Maybe some other time."

Great, thought Logan. Just great. "Say, the Pavilion bar is open for adults after lights out. How about we get a drink after—"

"Dad, guess what?" Charlie came running over. "Eugene wants to tell ghost stories again in the cabin tonight. Really gory ones."

"You hate ghost stories."

"Right. That's why I need you to pull cabin duty tonight."

"No can do," said Logan.

"Dad, it's my last night with you." Charlie played his trump card early.

Logan felt torn—a familiar sensation. When you were a single dad, you felt pulled in a lot of different directions. "You and André can hang out. You don't have to listen to the ghost stories."

"Dad—"

"Hey, Logan," said Darcy, "I'd better get going. We're heading back to the city in the morning."

No, don't let her go. "Then how about we—"

"It was nice to meet you," she said. "You, too, Charlie. See you around."

Logan watched her go, then swung back to face Charlie. "Dude, couldn't you see I was busy?"

"Hitting on some lady? Yeah, I could see that."

"And still you interrupted."

"I'm worried about the ghost stories."

"I'm worried about your manners."

Charlie gazed at the ground. "Sorry, Dad. I just really want you in the cabin tonight."

Logan was a sucker for his kid. He hoped like hell he wasn't a pushover. Hoped he wasn't spoiling Charlie. The truth was, Charlie had a true horror of ghost stories ever since his cousin Bernie had told him the tale of the bloody toe last summer. The kid had suffered from nightmares for weeks afterward, and to this day still slept with his socks on.

Turning, Logan watched Darcy Fitzgerald as she walked along a lighted path toward the parking lot. For the first time in ages, he'd actually felt something strong and true, just talking with her. But one of the first things she'd told him was that she wasn't into kids. It was just as well they hadn't started anything, he told himself.

CHAPTER TWO

"You are in such trouble," Darcy said to India as they drove away from Camp Kioga to their hotel in the nearby town of Avalon.

"What?" India offered an elaborate look of innocence.

"You know perfectly well what. Your brother, that's what. You couldn't be more obvious if you tried."

"Darce. I *am* trying."

"And you're totally obvious. This was supposed to be a relaxing, forget-all-your-troubles girlfriends' weekend. You turned it into a setup."

"I introduced you to my kid brother, that's all."

"He's no kid." She couldn't get the image of Logan O'Donnell out of her head. Tall, athletic build. Blaze of red hair—not the dorky kind of red hair, but deep glossy waves of auburn, which she found ridiculously sexy. And his smile.

He had an easy smile that made her forget, if only briefly, that she'd ever been hurt by a man. "He *has* a kid," she added.

"That would be my adorable nephew, Charlie," India said. "Thank you for reminding me."

"Listen, because I don't think you heard me the first time," said Darcy. "The only thing I want less than a guy is a guy with a kid."

"All men are not all like Huntley Collins," India pointed out.

"I realize that. One day, I will embrace that truth. But I'm not ready to meet anyone."

"You've been divorced a year."

Divorced. *Destroyed* was a more apt word for it.

She had married a man who had seemed perfect for her in every way. Huntley was a single dad, sharing custody of Amy and Orion with his ex. Darcy had fallen for the three of them, opening her heart to a ready-made family.

Yet the children, dear as they had been to her, had also taken a hand in the demise of her marriage. As they grew older, they distanced themselves from Darcy, and eventually convinced themselves—or let their mother convince them—that their parents wanted to get back together.

Darcy still recalled the day her marriage had unraveled, though the memory no longer made her cringe. Huntley's daughter, Amy, had come to her with a bright smile on her face, false as sunshine in November. Darcy had learned to recognize that hollow smile. It was hard at the edges, the grin of a not-very-skilled actress who knew her range was limited, and didn't care.

"He's cheating on you," Amy had said. "With *our mom*."

Darcy's heart had stumbled. Then, clinging to well-honed denial, she had dismissed the notion out of hand. "Your mom and dad are just friends."

"Nope, they're back together. Check his email," Amy said, a clean blade of triumph sharpening her tone. "In the drafts folder. That's how they communicate. They never hit Send, just log in to the same account and read the drafts. They're so stupid about it, though. They don't delete correctly, so the notes still are all there."

"Nonsense," Darcy said. Yet the moment Amy had said those words—*He's cheating on you*—her body was telling her to pay attention for once, to listen. Her heart knew the truth before her mind caught on to the situation. The blood in her veins congealed into ice. In that moment, she had felt weirdly detached from her own life, as though entering a different reality. "You shouldn't be looking at your dad's email," she scolded. Classic nagging stepmom, as ineffective as a barkless Chihuahua.

"Neither should you," Amy shot back. Then the girl had burst into tears and collapsed, sobbing, into Darcy's lap.

And that, Darcy had realized, had been the first undeniable sign of her failing marriage—not the drafts folder, which of course completely confirmed Amy's accusation, but the fact that, months earlier, Darcy herself had begun monitoring Huntley's messages.

He was both careless and unsophisticated about computers. She hadn't been looking for anything specific. Just…looking. For answers. For the reason she couldn't feel the love from him anymore. For the reason he had emotionally left the building, like a traveler checking out of a motel he never planned to return to.

It was said that there are no winners in a divorce, but Darcy discovered that wasn't true in her case. She had lost a husband, a family, a way of life. She had lost half her assets, her home and her belief in her own judgment when it came to men. Huntley had lost, too; the fling with his ex had flamed out, and these days, as far as she knew, he was alone. But there were winners—the crafty Amy and her brother, Orion. They had not wanted a stepmother, and now she was gone, vanished from their lives.

And here was a surprise. She missed them. She had managed to stop loving Huntley. That was easy enough, crushing her feelings for someone who had crushed her heart with the most intimate of betrayals. She couldn't simply turn off her feelings for the kids, though. When she'd married Huntley, they were eight and ten, filling her with joy. Five years later, they were teenagers, challenging her at every turn. Yet even at their most manipulative and obnoxious, they were children to whom she had given herself entirely. Even now she couldn't stop remembering how it felt to be a family, swept up in the busy days of their lives together. Knowing she couldn't see them, could never hold or touch them again was a special kind of hell.

In the Fitzgerald family, Darcy herself had been the daughter most likely to procreate. After all, she had married a man with children, and she'd made no secret of wanting more. She'd loved being a stepmom to Amy and Orion—until everything had changed. The special, knife-sharp hurt of their campaign against her had caused a fundamental shift deep inside Darcy. She'd gone from being a woman who thought she could have it all to a woman who wanted none of it.

"I'm not ready to meet anyone," she said to India. "It seems like only yesterday, I considered myself a happily married woman."

"Now you'll be happily single."

"And determined to stay that way. Not only do I want to stay away from guys, but I want to stay away from guys with kids. So quit trying to throw me together with your yummy brother."

"You think he's yummy?"

"Don't you dare tell him I said that."

"I was just going to send him a text. Jeez, what do you take me for? The idea of 'brother' and 'yummy' do not compute in my mind. Ew."

"Spoken like a true sister."

"I'm trying to help here, Darcy. Look at it this way—you got your starter marriage over early."

"It was supposed to be forever."

"The next one will be. Just you wait."

"Exactly. I'm *waiting*. Forever is worth waiting for. So don't be trying to fix me up with your brother."

They rounded a bend in the road, and the main square of Avalon came into view. Gilded by sunset, the little lakeside village had the kind of charm seen in tourist brochures, touting the wonders of the Catskills—glorious rolling hills clad in end-of-summer excess, colorful painted cottages along the lake, catboats flying their white sails on the water, out for an evening sail. The sight was so pretty, it took her breath away for a moment—the deep purple of twilight reflected in the still water, the stars sprinkled above the distant hills, the fairy lights of the town.

The bucolic allure of scenery and serenity tugged at her heart. She'd been living in Manhattan for too long. It was good to get out into nature for a while, to see the sky above and the scenery all around her.

"Okay," Darcy said, "you're forgiven. It's beautiful here. A nice change from the sock warehouse out my window in the city."

"Agreed. We should come up to see Logan more often."

"He said he moved here to be near Charlie."

"That's right. Charlie was born the summer after they got out of high school."

"So young," Darcy mused.

"Never underestimate the power of a teenager to do dumb things. I worry constantly about my boys. Logan definitely had a wild streak in high school. Daisy—that's Charlie's mom—came here to be with her family. She thought she'd be raising the baby alone, but Logan surprised everyone, including our parents. He got his act together, moved up here to be near Charlie, and turned himself into an awesome dad. Put himself through college and started a solid business. I adore him for turning his life around, but the path he took still makes our parents mental."

"You can't be serious. Aren't they proud of him?"

"Yes, but they had other plans for him. He was supposed to go to an Ivy League school like all good O'Donnells, and then he was supposed to take over the reins of the family business. Instead, he wound up here, running an insurance office and being Charlie's dad. I guess our folks have made their peace with it, but they still think he took a wrong turn."

"Parents," Darcy mused, gazing out the window at the play of light on the water. "What is it with parents, projecting all their expectations on their kids? I've been in violation of my folks' expectations since the moment I was born a girl instead of a boy."

"Yes, how dare you?" said India.

"Such a burden, having five daughters," said Darcy. "And now only one of us is decently married. Lydia and the oh-so-perfect Badgley Collins."

"Huntley's older brother. How is everyone handling that?" asked India.

"We're all so terribly civilized about it. My folks and the Collinses go way back to their college days. We are meant to get along no matter what."

Darcy had not been able to bring herself to tell her family

about the cheating. They had no idea how hard it was for her to simply grit her teeth and pretend she had smoothly moved on with her life, to pretend that the Collinses' son Huntley had not shredded her heart into irreparable bits. "I'm already dreading the holidays," she confessed. "Our families have been swapping host duties for decades. My mom and Rachel Collins are already planning the usual joint celebration at Thanksgiving."

"You could spend the holidays with us," India said.

Darcy imagined her family's horror at the prospect of her defection. Their holiday traditions were chiseled in stone. The season always started off with a Thanksgiving feast that would make Martha Stewart green as collectible glass with envy. After that, the holidays kicked into high gear—the plans, the shopping, the food, the music. The previous year, she had made the mistake of trying to join in, and the stress had nearly wrecked her. The prospect of enduring even a salmon mousse canapé in the presence of her ex-husband made her nauseated.

"What do you say?" asked India. "I swear, my family would love to have you."

"Seriously?"

"Sure. We usually all go to my folks' place in Florida, at Paradise Cove. The house is huge, and located right on a private beach, a surfer's mecca. You can sit on the sugar-fine sand, sipping a fruity drink, and let your ex deal with the mess he made."

"Surfing? Do you know how tempting that sounds?"

"That's the idea—to tempt you."

"I might take you up on it. Wait a second. Is your brother going to be there?"

"Yep."

Darcy couldn't stop herself from flashing on an image of

Logan O'Donnell in board shorts and flip-flops, on a sugar-sand Florida beach.

"I'll think about it," she said. She probably wouldn't be able to *stop* thinking about it.

India peered at the shady street ahead and switched on the headlamps. "Hey, do me a favor and see if the hotel brochure has directions. We're staying at the Inn at Willow Lake."

Darcy found a colorful flyer and angled it toward the light. "There's an annex in the middle of town, and the main location is on the lake."

"We're staying at the one on the lake."

"It's easy to find, then. Just stay on the Lakeshore Road and we'll come right to it. Looks gorgeous in the brochure."

"I'm sure it is. Just as an aside—the owners, Nina and Greg Bellamy, are Logan's former in-laws."

"Wait, what? His ex is their daughter?"

"Hazard of life in a small town—eventually, everyone is connected."

"So, was he married to Charlie's mother for long?"

"No. They tried to make it work for Charlie's sake, but they realized it wasn't right and never would be. It was hard, watching him struggle to hold them together. There was... drama. Maybe someday Logan will tell you all about it."

"Assuming I want him to tell me. Assuming he wants to."

"Ah, Darce. I know you're still raw, but I promise, things will get better. After his breakup, Logan was kind of a mess for a while, but he came out of the fog."

"Meaning he climbed right back on the horse, so to speak."

"I think it's a guy thing. They tend to start dating right away. He hasn't had a serious relationship yet, though. Just a string of...distractions, I guess you'd call them. Daisy, his ex, is remarried now, living in Oklahoma with her new husband.

That's why Logan's time with Charlie is so precious—he has to split custody with Charlie's mom."

Darcy pictured the little boy, an adorable mixture of sweetness and mischief, his wavy red hair matching his father's. "Just so you know, Charlie is one of the many reasons I'm not interested in hooking up with your brother. I'm sure he's a nice little kid, but I've been with a man who has children, and I'm not going there again. I intend to remain happily childless for all of my days."

CHAPTER THREE

Saying goodbye to Charlie had become steeped in ritual. First Logan took him to the house and they arranged his room so that when he returned, he'd find everything in place. Then they packed his duffel bag and drove to the center of town for a snack and to say goodbye to friends and neighbors.

Signs of autumn and back-to-school were already popping up. Suzanne Bailey of Zuzu's Petals boutique was on the sidewalk in front of her shop, arguing with Adam Bellamy, a newcomer to town who happened to be from an old Avalon family. He'd recently moved to Avalon and worked as a fireman. He and Logan were buddies, both of them fans of outdoor sports—mountain biking, snowboarding, white-water kayaking, rock and ice-climbing. Suzanne's husband, Jeff, was also a firefighter, probably on duty at the moment. She and Adam were like oil and water; at the moment they appeared to be bickering about the placement of her sidewalk sale racks.

"Sorry to interrupt the fun," said Logan, "but I brought Charlie to say goodbye."

Adam turned, his scowl at Suzanne turning to a grin for Charlie. "Hate to see you go, my brother. I'll keep an eye on your old man while you're away."

"Cool," said Charlie. "Don't let him give you any trouble."

"He's always trouble, but I think I can handle him." Adam looked like the kind of guy who could handle anything. Built like a linebacker, he was a three-time winner of a seventy-story stair-running marathon in the city.

Suzanne gave Charlie a quick hug. "I remember when you got all your back-to-school clothes from me. I miss that."

Something must have shown on Charlie's face, because she added hastily, "Here's a little something for you." She handed him a small solar-powered reading light, something she sold in her shop. "For your travels."

"Wow, thanks," said Charlie.

"Will you be back for Thanksgiving?" she asked.

"We always go to Florida."

"That's rough," Adam said, patting him on the shoulder.

"Christmas, then?" Suzanne asked. "Or will you be basking in the Florida sun then, too?"

"Unless we get a better offer," Logan said.

Charlie tugged at his sleeve. "Bakery next, Dad?"

"Bakery next."

"Cool, I'll get a table." Charlie headed down the block toward the Sky River Bakery for his last visit to the beloved place for the holy grail of pastries, the iced maple bar.

"He's really grown this summer," said Suzanne. "He acts more grown-up, too."

Logan nodded. "I guess having to shuttle back and forth between parents is making him grow up fast."

"Charlie's an awesome kid," said Adam. "If I ever have kids, I'm coming to you for advice."

"Thanks. I'm trying to get used to the part-time parenting thing, but it sucks. Love that little guy, and I miss him so damn much when he's not around."

"Dive into work," Suzanne suggested. "That's what I do."

"What, to escape your humdrum existence?" Adam asked. "I'll be sure to tell Jeff that."

"Hey." She swatted him with a coat hanger.

"Diving into my work isn't exactly an escape," said Logan.

"You're a good businessman," Adam pointed out. "That must feel good, right? Everybody I know uses you."

"'For all your insurance needs,'" Logan finished, quoting his own slogan. "I'm so freaking bored with my business, I can't even tell you. I got into it because I wanted to be near Charlie. It's a stable, predictable racket with regular hours. But since he moved away with his mom, it's just a job."

"Then find a job you like," Adam said simply. "That's what I did." He'd been an executive for a big multinational corporation, but seemed a lot more content these days as a firefighter and an arson investigator.

"I'm thinking about taking over Saddle Mountain," said Logan. Every time he thought about it, the idea fixed itself more firmly in his mind.

"The ski resort?" asked Suzanne. "You're joking."

"Maybe not."

"You're crazy," she said.

"I bet people told you that when you said you were opening your shop," Adam pointed out.

"You'd lose," she retorted, though she seemed to like his teasing.

"I'd better catch up with Charlie," said Logan.

"I'll join you," Adam said. "Hungry again. And I want to hear more about your new plan."

They found Charlie waiting at the bakery, seated at a painted enamel table and eyeing the fragrant, glistening contents in the display case. The café seating area was busy with its morning crowd of locals and tourists. The walls featured a series of stunning photographs by Daisy Bellamy—Logan's ex. Even though she'd moved away, reminders of her lingered everywhere. She was a Bellamy, after all; in Avalon, they were ubiquitous.

As he studied the beautifully photographed nature scenes, Logan felt a curious detachment. He didn't miss her. He didn't still love her. But he missed the life of the family they'd made, the day-to-day routines, the companionship, the fun they'd had with Charlie.

Adam went to the counter and ordered coffee and kolaches, and Charlie's usual—an iced maple bar and a mug of hot chocolate. "So, when are you going to set this new plan in motion?" he asked Logan.

"New plan doing what?" Charlie asked, then took a big bite of the soft pastry.

Logan gave a slight shake of his head. *Not now.*

"His new plan to be as awesome as me," Adam said, clinking cups with Charlie. "Your dad says he needs a cooler job." He consumed half a kolache in one bite.

"Yeah, like a time traveler or a shape-shifter," Charlie suggested.

"I already do that," said Logan. "But don't tell anybody."

"Really?"

"You don't think I sit at a desk all day studying actuary tables, do you? That's just a cover for my true identity."

"What's your true identity?"

"The Silver Snowboarder."

"You like snowboarding with your dad?" Adam asked him.

Charlie nodded. "It's the best."

"Better than that maple bar?"

"Well...almost."

Adam finished his coffee. "I need to roll, my brothers." He bumped knuckles with Charlie, then gravely shook his hand. "You take care, now. Work hard in school, and I'll see you when you come back around."

"Okay, Adam. Don't let the place burn down while I'm gone."

"Never happen." He left a tip on the table. "MTB later?" he asked Logan.

"Indubitably." Mountain-biking was exactly what he'd need later in the day, when Charlie's departure for Oklahoma hurt like a fresh, gaping wound in his chest. He and Adam had begun a tradition of tearing up the trails in the hills above Avalon after work, in all kinds of weather.

Charlie dawdled over finishing his snack, and Logan didn't rush him. Though neither had mentioned it, they both knew they were only minutes away from the dreaded long goodbye.

As soon as they left the bakery, the inevitable process would begin. Charlie's mom was waiting for him at the Inn at Willow Lake, which was owned by her folks. Daisy always stayed there when she came to town. Logan's duty was to hand the kid over and pretend it was great, a big adventure for Charlie. "Coparenting" was one of those terms that sounded like a good idea until it was actually put into practice. In actual fact, every time he said goodbye to Charlie, it ripped out a piece of his heart.

His phone vibrated, signaling a text message. Daisy's ID came up. We're hoping to make the noon train to the city. Possible?

Shit.

"We need to go, buddy." Logan added to the tip on the table. "Don't forget your stuff."

Charlie grabbed his Camp Kioga baseball cap and put it on. "Ready," he said.

They got in the car. Logan drove a banana-yellow Jeep, good for getting around when the winter snows came.

Avalon looked like one of his ex-wife's flawless photos today, the leaves just starting to turn, the lake placid and flat, the covered bridge over the Schuyler River drawing the last of the summer tourists. It would still be hot in Oklahoma, flat and scrubby around the air force base.

"Excited about fifth grade?" Logan asked.

"Oh yeah. Can't wait."

"I know, buddy. School's your job. You'll do great. You're going out for soccer this fall?"

"Sure. Soccer's cool."

Soccer had been Logan's life when he was a kid, right up through high school. He still remembered the rush of a good play, the euphoria of drilling a goal home. His father rarely missed a game. It was the one thing that kept them close. Ultimately, though, the sport had become *too* important. Logan's need to perform superseded common sense. In high school, his determination to impress his father had pushed him to play injured, and that had led to a ripped-up knee, multiple surgeries and a dangerous dependence on painkillers.

Logan resigned himself to missing all of Charlie's games. Maybe that wasn't such a bad thing. He would find other activities to do with Charlie. Kioga in the summer, snowboarding or Florida in winter, daily phone calls, being there for his son whenever he could. He hoped like hell their time together would be enough.

They pulled up at the inn, a historic property in a grand mansion by the lake. The main building, with its wraparound porch and belvedere tower, was reflected in the glassy water. Hiding the heaviness in his heart, Logan grabbed Charlie's duffel bag and backpack and went up the walk. Charlie's mom came out the door.

Daisy looked amazing, no surprise. She'd always been smoking hot, even in high school, and she'd been as reckless and rebellious as Logan, which had led to the unplanned pregnancy in the first place. She wore her blond hair short, and her face was wreathed in smiles. Now, however, there was something new about her. The angry, reckless girl had turned into a woman—a mom. She was holding a baby on her hip. Behind her was her husband, Air Force Captain Julian Gastineaux, tall and dark, casual in civilian clothes today.

"Charlie boy!" Daisy flung her free arm around Charlie and hugged him close to both her and the baby.

Logan stood back, watching. An outsider.

"Look at your sister," Daisy said. "She's grown so much."

Charlie grinned and kissed the down-fuzz head. "Hiya, Princess Caroline," he said, then looked back at Logan. "Dad, check it out, she's really cute."

"Totally cute," Logan agreed.

Charlie broke away to give Julian a hug. "Hi, Daddy-boy." His nickname for Julian had always been Daddy-boy. Logan hated that.

"Man, look at you," Julian said. "You're tall, my man."

Logan and Julian acknowledged each other with a nod. The two of them were not exactly friends, but they shared a mutual respect and a love for Charlie.

"Congratulations," Logan said. "Your baby's really cute."

"Thanks."

Charlie took command of his sister, holding her with care. He showed her and Julian the paddle he'd painted and all the campers had autographed. Each camper went home with one.

"So, his stuff is here," Logan said to Daisy. "He's all set."

"Thanks." She gazed up at him, her blue eyes a stranger's eyes now. "How are you?"

"Good." It still felt surreal, talking to this person who had once been his whole world. He used to be on intimate terms with her not just physically, but with her every thought, her every dream and desire. Now she was just someone he didn't really know anymore. She had truly moved on. The baby was stark evidence of that. Daisy had made a new life for herself.

Logan couldn't say for certain that he'd done the same. He still lived in the house he and Daisy had bought together and remodeled, dreaming of the future. He still had the same job. Same friends. Same life—minus the family.

"You look good," she said. "Summer camp agrees with you and Charlie both."

That, at least, was gratifying. Toward the end of his marriage, Logan had let himself go, not bothering to pay attention to his diet, forgetting to exercise. Once he emerged from the fog of divorce, he'd taken out his frustration by mountain-biking, rowing on the lake, scrambling up rocks and mountainsides. He'd embraced single fatherhood with a vengeance, studying nutrition and cooking as if his son's life depended on it. Cool that Daisy had noticed the improvement.

"Charlie had a great time at Camp Kioga. Be sure he tells you about all his adventures."

"I will."

Julian was already loading things into the car. Daisy's stepmother, Nina, came out on the porch and gave Logan a wave. She had a baby of her own, a little boy about a year old. *One big happy family.* Logan felt like a chump, standing there, a complete outsider, his connection to the Bellamys now so tenuous. There had been a time when he'd come here for holiday gatherings, dinners and picnics on the lawn. Now his only role was to hand over Charlie and walk away.

"Um, so Julian got new orders," Daisy said. Her gaze shifted from side to side, then to the ground.

Logan still knew her well enough to read nervousness in her manner. "What's that mean?"

"We're moving."

"Why do I sense this is not good news?"

"The new assignment's Yokota Air Force Base."

He narrowed his eyes. "Where the hell is that?"

She swallowed visibly. "It's in Fussa. Er, that's in Japan."

"Fuck."

She winced, and he didn't even bother to apologize for the profanity. To Logan, the real profanity was losing his son.

"The custody arrangement will still work the same," she hurriedly stated. "He's with you holidays and summers. It's just...the travel time will be longer."

"That's great, Daze. Just freaking great."

"There are daily nonstops from Tokyo to the States. I checked. We'll make it work, Logan. I swear we will."

He shot a glare in Julian's direction. As an officer in the air force, he had an exciting career. Good for him. But not so good for Logan and Charlie. "When?" he demanded.

"Right after Christmas break. Charlie will go to school on base. He'll learn a new culture, a new language. I've already found him a tutor to give him Japanese lessons. He'll see a whole new world over there. It's an amazing opportunity for him." She spoke hurriedly, enumerating the advantages as if she'd memorized them, one by one.

"More amazing than spending time with his dad?"

"You'll still have him for the same number of days."

"Have you told him yet?"

"No. We will today."

Logan raked a hand through his hair. "Jesus."

"We need to make this a positive thing for Charlie."

"Right." Composing himself with an effort, he went to say goodbye to his son. He walked over to Charlie and sank down on one knee. "I sure had a great time with you," he said. "What an awesome summer."

"Yep. Um, can you keep my paddle? There's no room to take it with me."

The kid had no idea that he was destined to move half a world away. He'd probably have to leave a lot more behind. "Sure. I'll keep it safe for you, buddy."

Charlie stared down at the ground. His chin trembled. "Thanks, Dad."

Goodbyes were always the hardest. Logan's job was to assure his son that everything was perfectly fine—even if it wasn't. "You're going to have the time of your life in fifth grade, buddy. And you've got a new little sister to play with."

"I guess."

"We'll talk every day," he said. "Just like always."

"And I'll see you at Thanksgiving." Charlie's effort at being positive was heartbreaking.

"Indubitably."

"And then we'll be together at Christmas."

"That's right. Maybe we'll have Christmas in Avalon instead of Florida this year. I could get us season passes at Saddle Mountain. Maybe I'll just get us the whole resort."

"Okay." A tremulous smile curved Charlie's mouth.

Logan took the little boy in his arms. Despite everyone's exclamations over how he'd grown, Charlie felt so small and fragile. He was being taken away to the other side of the world, where Logan couldn't see him or touch him, inhale the little boy smell of him, lie next to him while he fell asleep at night. "I'll miss you, buddy."

"Me, too."

"Okay. One more kiss and a hug."

A big squeeze. Logan pressed his lips to his son's warm, silky red hair. "So long, pal." He pasted on a smile and pretended a piece of his heart was not being torn out. Then he stood up and headed for his car. At the edge of the parking lot, he turned and watched Charlie and his other family bustling around. Just for a moment, Charlie paused and looked back. He offered a big smile, and then their special salute, index finger and pinky in the air as if at a rock concert. Then Charlie turned back to the family and was swept into the business of leaving.

The hole in Logan's chest felt as big and jagged as the Grand Canyon.

"Fuck," he said again, and without thinking, broke the painted paddle in two.

"You look as if you could use a friend," said a voice behind him.

He swung around. Darcy Fitzgerald was walking toward him, carrying an overnight bag. "Or an anger-management class," she added, eyeing the broken paddle.

"Just handed my son off to his mom," Logan said. "Never the best start to the day."

"I'm sorry. I know it's hard."

Hell no, she had no idea. He wasn't going to argue with her, though. "I'll deal," he said, picking up the pieces of Charlie's paddle, the paddle he'd promised to safeguard. To change the subject, he asked, "You're going back to the city?"

"That's right." She tilted her face to the sun. "Hard to leave on a day like today."

He kind of hated it that Darcy had come upon him in such a vulnerable moment, his emotions raw from having Charlie ripped from him.

"India said Charlie lives part-time in Oklahoma."

"That's right."

"Must be so challenging for you."

"Every time I say goodbye to Charlie, it kills me a little bit."

"I'm sorry."

"I need to get going," he said.

"Back to work?"

"That's right."

"So, your sister said you're in business for yourself?"

She was probably just making polite conversation. But her question annoyed him. Maybe she was fishing for information on him. Did he have a steady, stable job? Was he a good prospect? A catch?

Some devil made him reply, "As a matter of fact, I'm just about to change jobs. That local ski area I mentioned? I'll be taking it over."

He had no idea where those words had come from. Probably the idea had been simmering on the back burner of his mind for a long time. But all of a sudden it was the truest thing he'd said since telling Daisy Bellamy, "Let's have the baby and raise it together," eleven years ago.

Hearing a guy declare he was going to take on such a risky enterprise was bound to send a woman running for cover. Trying to make a living by running a ski resort was like betting on horses or playing the lottery.

Darcy's reaction was the last thing he'd expected. "That's awesome," she said.

"Awesome as in a wise investment, or awesome as in bat-shit crazy?"

She laughed. "Depends on who you ask."

"I'm asking you."

"Why? Does my opinion matter?"

Not really, he thought. There had been a time, long ago,

when he'd put great stock in opinions—of parents, teachers, coaches. There had been a time when his father's opinion had mattered so much that Logan had lost himself. He could admit that now. He had been lost in some mythic quest for perfect—on the soccer field, in school, in business.

Then out of the worst thing to happen in his life had come the best thing he'd ever done—Charlie. Since he became a dad, every move he made had been for Charlie's sake.

Telling Darcy about the ski resort made Logan feel a spark of...something. That touch or spike that happened when an idea struck a chord. He hadn't felt it in a long time. Since Charlie had left, Logan had tried to do the right thing—take care of his business and his life, contribute to his 401(k), go to the dentist for regular checkups. He'd done everything by the book and look what it had brought him. Charlie was moving farther away—proof that doing the right thing did not automatically cause the right thing to happen. For all of his efforts, he had nothing but routine predictability. It was time to shake things up. He'd been good long enough.

"I'm ready to take the risk," he told Darcy. "Are you a risk taker?"

"I have been." She touched her bottom lip with her finger, an absent gesture. "Not lately, though. I used to be a frequent flier when it comes to taking risks. But sometimes that means you come crashing down. Still, I think I liked myself better when I was a risk taker."

Odd thing to say. He found himself wanting to hear more. He needed to have a normal conversation right now. He needed to escape the torn-up feeling inside. "How about we—"

"Oh, good, you're here," said India, hurrying toward them. "I was wondering if I was going to see my baby brother before we left."

"Lucky you," he said, giving her a hug.

"The baby of the family," India said to Darcy. "You'd never know it by his height, though." She stepped back and beamed at them both. "It's good to see you two getting along. I knew you'd hit it off. Mom and Dad are crazy about Darcy."

Shoot. The last thing he wanted was matchmaking by his family. "Is that what we're doing?" Logan asked. "Hitting it off?"

Darcy shrugged. "Nobody's hitting anything. Hey, India, did you know your baby brother's buying a ski resort?"

"Right," India said, "very funny."

"She doesn't believe you," Darcy pointed out.

"She will."

"I'm telling Dad," said India.

"She's always been the family snitch," he told Darcy. For a split second, he pictured his father turning purple, with steam coming out of his ears. "What the hell are you thinking? Are you out of your fool mind?" Al O'Donnell would demand.

Yeah, Dad, maybe I am.

India gave him a hug. "We have to go. Don't do anything crazy, okay?"

"Right." He stepped away and there was an awkward moment when he faced Darcy. "Nice meeting you," he said.

"Likewise." She hiked her bag up on her shoulder.

"See you at Thanksgiving, yes?" India said.

Logan had one more goodbye to say—to Charlie's friend André. The boy's mom had come up on the train, and he saw them both off at the station. Maya Martin was stunningly beautiful, with caramel-colored skin, abundant dark hair and slender gorgeous legs. Yet she had a fragile look about her, harried and worn. Logan knew she'd endured a lot of trouble in her life, and he knew it wasn't easy being a single parent. But beyond that, he didn't know much about her.

So when Maya faced him with a troubled quirk on her brow, he braced himself to find out more.

"Do you have a minute?" She seemed nervous. He had the sense that she was on edge, expecting disaster at any moment. André was on the station platform, hanging out with some of the other departing campers.

"First off, I wanted to say thanks for giving André such an amazing summer." She spoke with a slight Caribbean accent.

"It was great having him. I'm going to miss him almost as much as I miss Charlie."

"It's hard, isn't it, being away from your kids? Makes it easier to know he's having a good time, with good people. His sister was so jealous. Angelica had to spend all her days at the Y day camp in Tribeca. She's excited that next year she'll be old enough to come to Camp Kioga, too."

"I look forward to meeting her."

"Charlie and André get along great," Maya said. "There's nothing quite like a best friend, is there?"

Logan nodded in agreement. "When I was a kid, my best friend was named Doug. Doug Tarski. Someone to share adventures with, secrets, getting in trouble together, thinking up ideas, making things. Did André tell you about the fort they made?"

"Yes, they had so much fun. They..." Without warning, her voice broke.

"Maya? Hey, you okay?"

She visibly gathered herself together, inhaling deeply. Her hands flexed and unflexed. "I... Thanks for asking. Actually, I had some trouble this summer."

"Anything I can help with?"

"I... Maybe. Yes." She glanced over at André as if to make

sure he was out of earshot. "Look, I'll try to sum it up. André's dad is not a good guy. He's one of my dumbest mistakes, in fact. He sells drugs, and when I found out, I made him leave. Last year, he swore he'd gone straight, and even though I suspected he was lying, I went to see him. That's when he told me he was in trouble, bad trouble, and all he needed was one tiny favor, and then everything would be all right. I was so stupid, I hate myself. I delivered a parcel for him. That's all. And then the next thing I knew, I was under arrest. I couldn't afford a defense attorney, but a guy at a legal clinic represented me. He got…he made a deal, but I'm going to have to do time." Her eyes were filled with panic and tears.

Logan's gut pounded. "Oh man."

"I'm not a bad person," she said. "Stupid, maybe, but not bad. I just hate myself for what I did, and now I can't undo it."

"So…what's next for you?"

She swallowed hard, turned away from where André was playing and dabbed at her eyes. "The courts are backed up, so my sentencing date doesn't come up until December. The guy at the legal clinic said since I don't have any priors, I might get parole only. That's what I'm praying for. But there's a risk. The maximum sentence is twenty-one months." She practically choked on the words.

The back of Logan's neck prickled, but he kept his face neutral. "If you're… If you have to go away, what happens to the kids?"

"That's what I'm getting to. I don't have anyone. My family's in Haiti. I don't have a plan. I'm going to throw myself on the mercy of the court. I'm going to beg to stay out of jail for the sake of my kids. But there's no guarantee. So if… if the worst happens, they'll go into the foster care system." She shook with sobs now, looking broken as if the pieces of her would fall to the ground at any moment.

He put his arms around her, feeling her misery lashing at his chest. "I'm really sorry. I've never had to deal with something like this, but I do know it sucks to be separated from your kid."

She gently pulled back, visibly gathering herself back together. "I'm sorry, too. It's just... I don't have a lot of friends. The people I work for... I've managed to keep it from them, but I know when I tell them, they won't offer to help with André and Angelica." She dabbed at her eyes with her sleeve and gave a short, humorless laugh. "Their dad's mother lives in Jersey. But I can't ask her. I don't want anyone from that family looking after my kids," she said. "My lawyer said foster care is good these days. Lots of enrichment opportunities for the kids. But it's..."

"Foster care," he finished for her. And then, from a place inside himself he did not know existed, he said, "I'll take care of them, if it turns out you need someone."

She fell utterly still. She even seemed to stop breathing. "You don't mean it."

"I do," he said, "completely." The surprise was not the offer he'd made. The surprise was how clear he was on this decision. He did intend to help her. "Look, you're probably not going to need my help," he said, "but if you do, I'm here."

"Really?" she whispered, still not moving. "Seriously?"

"Seriously. If your kids need to stay with someone, I'm here."

"An angel, that's what you are." Tears rolled slowly down her cheeks. "You're a flesh-and-blood angel."

He laughed, trying to lighten the moment. "Don't lay that on me. Believe me, I'm nobody's angel."

PART THREE

Man Food

◆·•◆••◆··◆

A lot of business is done over beer and food. It helps a man think better.

Beer-Cheese-Spread

1 (2-pound) block sharp Cheddar cheese, shredded
1 small onion, minced
2 garlic cloves, minced
½ teaspoon hot sauce
¼ teaspoon ground red pepper
1 (12-ounce) bottle amber beer, at room temperature
Salt and pepper to taste
Garnish: thyme sprig

Beat together first 5 ingredients at low speed with a heavy-duty electric stand mixer until blended. Gradually add beer, beating until blended. Beat at medium-high speed until blended and creamy. Season with salt and pepper to taste. Cover and chill. Garnish with a thyme sprig. Store in refrigerator up to two weeks. Serve with crackers, or use to make grilled cheese sandwiches.

[Source: Adapted from *Southern Living*, 2007]

CHAPTER FOUR

Following through on a crazy impulse was often the right thing to do.

As soon as the workweek started, Logan got together with his two best buddies, Adam Bellamy and Jeff Bailey, Suzanne's husband. They hooked their mountain bikes on the back of his Jeep and headed up the winding road that curved around the mountain.

"Hope you're up for a screaming ride," Logan said. "And then a business meeting." He'd told them about his idea of taking on the resort at Saddle Mountain. In the bright sun of a September morning, the wild hills around Willow Lake were clad in a crazy quilt of colors. The drive up to the ski resort filled Logan with nostalgia, for the boy he'd once been, and for Charlie, the boy he'd raised.

The boy who was moving half a world away.

Logan had worked nonstop on the new enterprise, meeting with the retiring owner and sketching out a detailed business plan. There was only one glitch—money. He needed lots of money, more than any one guy had. He needed investors. He'd been on the phone and email constantly, talking with bankers, brokers, private investors. Thanks to his business in town, he knew a lot of people, and there was serious interest. He was working with an expert in ski resort financing, who told him the preliminary financials looked good. There was a lot more work to do, but Logan was determined.

He'd told his father his plan, and had received the predictable wet blanket treatment. Still, he did want his dad to see the place, and had persuaded him to drive up to the mountain today for a meeting about the idea. He'd even offered Al a stake in the enterprise. Al, of course, had assumed he was joking, but he'd agree to pay a visit, just to see.

But first—the ride. He, Jeff and Adam spent an hour careening along the trails that, when the snows came, would be ski runs. As he churned over the bumpy terrain, his mind went into overdrive. Once he took over, this was going to be a year-round resort. The trails would be waymarked and graded for mountain biking, and they'd modify the main chairlift to take riders to the top. This new direction felt, to Logan, kind of like falling in love. He woke up each morning thinking about it, fantasizing, knowing in the deepest part of his gut that he could make it work. He'd heard people talk about finding their life's passion. This, he was fast discovering, was his.

The runs were swaths of green, veined by forest and rock. Streams cut through some of the runs; in winter they would be frozen over and buried by several feet of snow. Pedals churning, he climbed and descended, sweat and dust mingling on his forearms. The hour they'd allotted themselves before the meeting went by quickly, and they reluctantly concluded the ride at the resort's main lodge.

"Awesome," said Jeff, brushing the dust off his shorts. "Excellent way to start the day."

"I thought you'd like it. There's going to be a lot more going on up here in the off-season next year." Logan unclasped his helmet and sucked down half a bottle of water. He used the rest of the water and a hand towel to get the sweat and grime off his face.

The resort's owner walked down from the on-site residence, a big, rambling place that had been the original lodge in the 1950s and had been converted into a bed-and-breakfast and owner's lodgings.

Logan already knew that if they made a deal, he'd be selling his house in town and moving to the residence. It was huge, way too much house for him, but it made sense to be on-site, especially when he was in the process of taking over.

In jeans and a plaid shirt, and a graying beard that needed a trim, Karsten Berger looked like one of the workmen. "You guys are crazy," he said, indicating the bikes.

"Mountain-biking kicks ass," said Adam. "You ought to try it sometime."

"I just might, at that. The lodge is open if you need more water or something to eat."

Just then, a shiny black vehicle turned off the road into the parking lot and came to a stop in front of the lodge.

"Holy crap," murmured Adam, watching Al exit the sleek black Escalade, his bespoke suit catching dust from the wind blowing across the parking lot. "You never told me your father was Darth Vader."

"Yeah, he's kind of got that whole evil empire thing down pat." When Logan was a kid, he used to greet his father with a mixture of apprehension and excitement.

Now Al O'Donnell arrived at the resort like the pontiff making a papal visit. He traveled with a small entourage—the driver of his sleek black SUV, his personal assistant, a humorless stick figure of a woman named Miss Teasdale, and two others who looked like bodyguards but were more likely in charge of guarding Al's wealth.

"Thanks for coming, Dad," Logan said. "This is Karsten Berger. His family has owned Saddle Mountain since 1949."

"Nice to meet you," said Karsten.

"That's a hell of a long time to keep a business in the family."

Karsten chuckled. "Some would say I'm a slow learner. Should have ditched the place decades ago."

"So why are you ditching it now?"

Logan had explained the situation to his father numerous times over the phone. But his father didn't believe Logan should make a financial move without checking out every angle—repeatedly. Saddle Mountain had been teetering on the brink of closure for several years. Karsten was ready to retire, and hadn't put as much money into the place as he probably should have. He'd told Logan he had interest from a big corporation that was in the real estate development business. The downside was that the developer would simply do a cookie-cutter rehabilitation, creating mediocre ski terrain in order to drive condo sales.

The alternative was for someone local to take over the resort and focus on its best and most unique assets. That was where Logan came in.

"I'm older than these hills you see around us," said Karsten. "None of my kids or grandkids wants to take it on."

"I know what that's like," said Al. "You spend your life building something to last, but there's nobody to carry on."

"Hell, Dad, why be subtle when you can make your point

with a sledgehammer?" asked Logan. He was already starting to regret inviting his father up for the day. "Tell you what. Let's take a look around."

It was a cozy resort complex designed like an old Tyrolean place in the Alps of Austria. The centerpiece was the big brown-and-orange Austrian-style chalet, set squarely in the middle of everything. Five chairlifts radiated up the mountain in different directions.

Some of Logan's best memories with Charlie had been made right here on the mountain. They came here together every year, reveling in the snow and the scenery, savoring the rush of speed as they rode down the mountain on their snowboards. It was the one time Logan could simply be with his kid and escape everything else—the tedium of running his firm, a marriage that wasn't working, the everyday challenges of parenthood.

"It's a diamond in the rough," said Logan.

"Emphasis on rough," said Al, shading his eyes and checking out the old lodge.

"It's got the second-highest vertical drop in the state," said Logan. "Three thousand three hundred feet."

"Could be this is one of those ideas that's just crazy enough to work," said Adam, never one to hold back his opinion.

"How's that?" Logan's father's scowl darkened.

Logan used to be afraid of that scowl. Not anymore. "The idea's not crazy at all. This resort is just a few hours from the city. The financials are going to be a challenge, but I can make it work." Looking out over the vast property, he could picture a vibrant family place, alive with skiers and snowboarders in winter, mountain bikers, hikers and climbers in summer. With or without his father's approval, he'd find a way to bring his vision to life.

"Why this?" Al demanded. "Why now?"

"This place means something to me. It's unique in the world, and I know exactly what I want to do. I practically raise Charlie here in the winter."

"I didn't know you were so keen on skiing," said Al.

You wouldn't, thought Logan. As a kid, when he wasn't playing soccer, Logan had barely been a blip on his father's radar. "I used to come up here with friends all through school," he reminded him. "I learned to snowboard on this hill when I was younger than Charlie."

In high school, his knee injury from soccer had sidelined Logan from everything—except partying and painkillers. That had been the start of a crazy, headlong descent down the wrong path. Then the reality that he'd gotten a girl pregnant had smacked him sober, and he'd put his life back together again. The knee had taken longer to heal, and sometimes still ached, but nothing could keep him from doing sports with his son. He never wanted to be a sideline dad. He wanted to be right in it with Charlie.

He and Karsten led the tour through the hotel, showing off its signature rooms with their tree branch bed frames and birch-clad furnishings. There was a spa at one end of the complex, an oddly appealing combination of Nordic traditions and Asian innovations. It looked like a hunting lodge with gongs in place of the trophy heads.

The bar was called the Powder Room and featured furniture and fixtures made from recycled chairlift parts, the walls decorated with vintage wooden skis. The restaurant offered the kind of food you wanted to stuff yourself with after a day on the slopes—mac and cheese, chili, poutine, hot chocolate.

Logan went out on the deck of the restaurant, which faced an expansive view of the slopes. His father came out with him. "This would be a perfect spot to build the zip line course,"

Logan said. "It would be a big draw in summer and winter both."

"You're determined to do this," said Al.

"Correction. I *am* doing it."

"Son, I applaud your sense of enterprise. The business plan you drew up is an impressive piece of work. But the fact is, resorts are notoriously risky. You're choosing a hard path."

"If it was easy, everyone would do it."

"I just don't understand," his father said. "You've built a rock-solid business in town. You're doing well in the insurance field—"

"Underwriting other people's risks while taking none of my own," said Logan.

"And it's worked out well for you," his father pointed out.

"Has it?" Logan asked. "How so?"

"You've got a beautiful home, your own business to take care of, the respect of the community."

Those were the things that mattered most to his father. Logan knew then he'd never make Al understand. He tried to explain, anyway. "I played it safe. I tried to be responsible. I was a good husband, and the marriage still didn't work out. I'm a good father, and now my son is moving to Japan. I've been a good businessman, and I'm so bored some days I want to hit myself in the head with a hammer."

"It's the ebb and flow of life," said Al, a hint of his Irish heritage coming out.

"Not *my* life. I'm done playing it safe all the time. I've decided to live the way I want to, taking risks, doing something that matters to me, creating something."

"Creating what?" His father seemed genuinely baffled. "A glorified playground?"

"This is a project I'm passionate about. I have big plans for

Saddle Mountain. More mountain-biking in the summer. The zip line. A climbing course. Ice-climbing in winter."

"You'll lose your shirt."

"I've lost more than that and survived."

Al paced the deck, casting dubious glances at the green and gold hills, the grand view of Willow Lake in the valley with the town of Avalon hugging its shore. "I understand that restless feeling," Al said. "I was young once, too. But it's a cockamamie scheme. It's not that I don't trust you or think you're a good businessman. I simply can't give my approval to your financial downfall."

"The plan is to succeed, not fail," Logan said, struggling to keep his voice even. A decade of anger and resentment simmered just beneath the surface. "And I don't need your approval."

"You haven't thought this out," his father said. "You're panicking because Charlie is going to be moving so far away. You miss him and you're trying to fill the void."

Ah, so now Al was the armchair psychologist. "And what if I am?" asked Logan.

"Never make a decision driven by panic. It won't work."

"I'm not panicking, and it's going to work."

"You'll be taking on a terrible burden of debt," his father blustered. "It could be really bad."

"Only if I default." For some reason, Darcy Fitzgerald's words came back to him. When it comes to leaps of faith, I'm a frequent flyer.

PART FOUR

❖◆❖◆❖

There's nothing like starting the holidays with a spirited breakfast…

Eggnog Pancakes
with Whiskey Butter

1½ cups all-purpose flour
1 tablespoon sugar
2½ teaspoons baking powder
½ teaspoon salt
½ teaspoon nutmeg
1 cup eggnog
2 tablespoons oil
1 egg, beaten

Mix the flour, sugar, baking powder, nutmeg and salt. Make a well in the center, and pour in the eggnog, oil and egg. Mix until dry ingredients are evenly moist.

Pour ¼ cup batter onto a medium-hot griddle. When it's bubbly on top, flip with a spatula, and continue cooking until lightly browned on bottom.

Recommended: Spray a metal cookie cutter with cooking spray and pour the batter into it to create shaped pancakes. This will elevate you in the eyes of friends and family.

Serve hot off the griddle with whiskey butter and real maple syrup.

Whiskey Butter

½ cup butter, softened
2 tablespoons bourbon
1 tablespoon maple syrup
½ teaspoon cinnamon
¼ teaspoon nutmeg

Blend everything together. Chill until ready to serve.

[Source: Original; inspired by true events]

CHAPTER FIVE

❖·❖·❖·❖·❖

Sorry, I'm afraid I heard you wrong," Darcy said to her sister Lydia. "Because I think I heard you say Huntley was planning to come to Thanksgiving dinner." Darcy and Lydia had met at a lunch counter on Madison Avenue. She was juggling a big work project, but she'd made time to meet with her sister to talk about the upcoming holidays. She was already regretting the decision.

"No, you heard correctly," Lydia assured her. "You know our families always celebrate the holidays together. It would just be weird if we suddenly stopped."

"You know what would be weird?" Darcy demanded. "Forcing me to endure Thanksgiving within a mile of my ex. *That* would be weird."

"Come on, Darce. There'll be at least twenty people at dinner. You don't even have to talk to him."

I'll have to breathe the same air as Huntley, she thought, seething. "I can't believe you think this could work for me on any level," she stated.

"I'm still married to Huntley's brother, or have you forgotten? This puts Badgley and me in an incredibly awkward position."

"And where does it put me?" Darcy shot back.

"At the far end of the room, eating and drinking with friends and family, the way we've always done."

"The way we've always done no longer works for me." Darcy tried to picture herself spending Thanksgiving the traditional way, pretending all was well as she slowly strangled inside. She pictured the gathering—friends, families, relatives, everyone convivial and excited as they set out the good china and their best recipes for the holiday feast. The gathering would convene at the Fitzgerald place on Long Island, in the house where Darcy had grown up. The big warm kitchen, with its old-fashioned hearth and scrubbed Colonial maple table, would be teeming with chattering women and guys trying to steal a sample of pumpkin pie or toasted sage dressing. Though the image made Darcy nostalgic, she knew she'd end up having a miserable day, trying to pretend that all was well, that the breakup had been so civilized that she could stand to be in the same room with Huntley Collins.

"Lyddie," she said gently, "as much as I love you, I'll break out in hives if I have to see Huntley."

"Come on, your divorce was amicable—"

"News flash—there is no such thing as an amicable divorce."

Darcy struggled with the decision, she really did. Letting down your family simply was not done, not by a Fitzgerald girl. But in the crazy new reality she'd been living since her divorce, letting go had become the more important task. The day before Thanksgiving, she called India. "I've been thinking about your invitation. How does your family feel about having stragglers and rejects at Thanksgiving?"

India didn't miss a beat. "We'd love to have you. You know that."

Thank God. Darcy was determined to make this Thanksgiving different. She grasped at the invitation. India was being incredibly kind and sensitive. One important discovery Darcy had made in the wake of her divorce was that friends were the people who took care of you when your family let you down.

"We're in Florida, you know. Can you get a flight?"

"Sure, I'll get myself down there. It'll probably have to be early morning on Thanksgiving Day. Standby is easy for solo travelers."

Darcy told herself she liked being a solo traveler. She did. Going it alone simplified everything. Thanks to her work schedule, she would have to return before the weekend was up, but the prospect of a couple of days of sunshine filled her with a powerful craving.

She needed this. She needed a festive rendezvous with people who didn't judge her. She needed to sink her toes into the white sand of a Florida beach, far from anything resembling her former life. She needed *escape.* That was what she was after.

True to her word, she caught a flight at the crack of dawn, and emerged into the tropical warmth of Paradise Cove in Florida just as most people were having breakfast and getting their turkeys in the oven on Thanksgiving morning. India had sent her a text message, asking her to pick up some flowers for the table and letting her know the back kitchen door was open, and to let herself in.

At the airport, she rented a car and made a pit stop at a discount liquor store that boasted extended holiday hours. With the help of the navigator on her phone, she found the O'Donnell residence, a luxurious rambler with its own gardens and orange grove, steps away from a glorious sunny beach. The gated neighborhood was old Florida at its finest and most exclusive, a community of broad boulevards hung with Spanish moss, shiny cars parked in wide driveways, manicured lawns and whimsical names for the houses, like "Pirates' Cove" and "Gem of the Ocean." It was all very elite, giving her a glimpse of the wealth and privilege of the O'Donnells.

Darcy decided she could do worse than spend the holiday with people who wanted nothing from her except the pleasure of her company. She just hoped she could be pleasurable enough for them. She had not grown up the way her friend India had. The O'Donnells were vastly wealthy, thanks to Al O'Donnell's successful worldwide shipping company. They enjoyed the best of everything.

The Fitzgeralds, by contrast, were merely comfortable. With five daughters, and both parents working as college professors, the concept of a second home in Florida—or anywhere, for that matter—was considered a wild extravagance. The Fitzgerald girls had grown up on the fringes of the elite. Darcy had often found herself in the role of the less privileged friend brought along on trips with girls whose families took them skiing in Gstaad or yachting in Cape d'Antibes. She was the kind of friend favored by parents—polite, unassuming, unlikely to overshadow their own daughters. This was fine with Darcy. She'd been lucky enough to see some of the world that way. She'd attended college on scholarship, excelled at sports and ultimately found a best friend in India O'Donnell.

Florida opened its sunshiney, welcoming arms to her. It felt good to be away from the cold, hissing sleet of Manhattan, the crowds and exhaust from traffic cramming the dark, wet streets. Juggling her variety case of booze, with a nice Thanksgiving centerpiece perched precariously on top, she backed into the kitchen, determined not to cause a disaster.

"I'm here," she warbled. "India? Did you miss me? I brought enough booze to make me forget Huntley Collins and his rotten, soul-crushing kids, as well."

She maneuvered the cardboard case to a countertop and set it down. Moving the centerpiece aside, she found herself looking at Logan O'Donnell.

Logan O'Donnell, of the big shoulders and red hair and killer smile. Her heart flipped over. She hadn't seen him since the end of summer in Avalon—but that didn't mean she'd stopped thinking about him. Far from it; she thought about him every day.

"Oh God," she said. "Tell me you won't judge me for saying that."

He grinned. Yep, killer smile. "I make it a practice not to judge anyone struggling with substance abuse."

She grinned back at him. She couldn't help herself. "It's use, not abuse. Alcohol is useful to me. Helps me get over my rotten marriage and even rottener divorce."

"So, you were married. To… Huntley Collins? No wonder it didn't work out. No one could stay married to someone named Huntley Collins."

"Good point." Maybe she was being too flippant and dismissive, but it was hard to think clearly around him. At the moment, he was wearing board shorts and flip-flops, and a dusting of sand on his bare chest. She couldn't keep herself from noticing he was a true redhead, with ginger-colored chest hair that came together in an arrow shape, pointing south. She found herself wishing she'd worn more attractive clothes for her flight instead of the usual yoga pants and shapeless top.

He helped her move the bottles from the case to a sideboard bar—vodka, tequila, rum, bourbon. "You're bringing coal to Newcastle," he said. "This is the O'Donnell place. Booze is as plentiful as water."

"It's my contribution to the feast. Along with this amazing centerpiece." It was a crazy arrangement of birds-of-paradise in the shape of a turkey.

"Nice," he said. "Mom will love it."

They finished unloading everything and he stuck out his hand. "Welcome to Sea Breeze. Yes, my parents named their house. I had nothing to do with it."

She looked around the kitchen—granite countertops, stainless-steel appliances, a view of the flat forever of the Atlantic. "It's beautiful. Really nice of your family to have me." She looked around the kitchen again. "Where is everyone?"

"The beach," he said. "We're having a beach day."

"Sounds nice. I've never been to the beach on Thanksgiving."

"I just came back to get the turkey in the oven and get a jump on some of the side dishes."

"Oh, he cooks, too? I'm impressed."

"Just wait until you taste my cooking. I'm awesome in the kitchen."

She thought he'd be awesome in any room of the house. "Wait a minute. I need to alert the media."

"How's that?"

"I need to tell them that hell has frozen over. It's Thanksgiving, and a man is preparing the feast all by himself."

"Not anymore, he's not." He tossed her an apron. "You're going to help me."

"Fair enough. I guess."

"Tell you what," he said. "Get your beach things on and you can give me a hand in the kitchen. Then we'll head down to the beach and join the others."

"Sounds good."

He helped her with her bag and showed her to a guest room, which was airy and bright with white painted plantation shutters and bedding in tropical prints, a stack of fluffy towels in the adjoining bathroom.

"You should find everything you need here," he said. "My mom loves having company."

"This is an amazing room. Better than a five-star hotel."

"If you forgot anything, you'll find stuff in the closet—extra swimsuits, robes, flip-flops, you name it. Just help yourself." As he set her suitcase on the bamboo luggage rack and stepped out, she felt herself, for the first time in forever, feeling happy about the holiday.

She opened her suitcase and studied the contents, feeling a scowl gathering on her forehead. She'd done a lousy job packing, having rushed home from work late the night before. Her swimsuit was old—and admittedly homely, the suit she used for masters swims at the West Village Y.

Of the five Fitzgerald sisters, Darcy was the least stylish, a deficit she freely admitted, and one that usually didn't bother her. The fashion sense chromosome had missed her completely. She should've made her sister Kitty take her shopping for this trip. Kitty was the stylish one; she would have helped Darcy pick out cute sundresses and sandals, maybe a swimsuit that didn't look like a high school swim team practice suit.

"Oh, that's right," she said with a sigh, holding up the seafoam-colored tank suit, "this probably *was* my high school practice suit." What Darcy lacked in style she'd always made up for in athletics. Since she was old enough to walk, she had played sports—swimming, snow sports, water polo, volleyball...if it involved athletics, she was happy to jump right into it.

As she held the suit up to the light, she was appalled to see the fabric had worn through in a couple of key places, including the butt. "Great," she muttered. "Just great." She opened the closet and found a plain black tank suit there. It was several sizes too large, but the only other one she could find was a scandalous wisp of fabric. Some would call it a bikini. Darcy called it ridiculous. In the borrowed bikini, yellow with bows on it, she felt conspicuous, but the thing fit like a glove. An extremely skimpy glove.

She hid beneath her cover-up—a hand-me-down from one of the sisters, several years old, frumpy but serviceable—and a pair of sandals that had seen better days. Then she ran a comb through her hair and put on a big, floppy hat, grabbed her tube of sunscreen and her sunglasses.

"Ready for the beach," she said, joining Logan in the kitchen. "What can I do to help?"

He was putting fresh sprigs of rosemary and sage and pats of butter under the turkey skin while intermittently consulting a video cooking lesson on an iPad.

"Jamie Oliver?" she asked.

"Taught me everything I know," he said without looking away from the screen. "Love this guy."

"Have you always been interested in cooking?"

"It's a relatively new project. I took it up when I became a single dad. I knew I needed to learn how to make something besides quesadillas and microwave burritos. I never wanted to be the dad who raises his kid on takeout and junk food."

"That's nice. I need a job."

"Peel the potatoes?"

"I think I can handle that."

Working alongside him in the kitchen felt strangely...domestic. And freakishly pleasant. In general, she didn't enjoy cooking, and lately she didn't enjoy men, so the pleasantness of the moment startled her.

"You didn't tell me you were divorced," he said.

She thought he might have sounded slightly accusing, as if this was something she had a duty to share with him. But that was ridiculous. She'd only met him the one time, at the end of summer. It wasn't as if she needed to share her life story with him.

But now here she was, in his house—his family's house—and he'd asked her a direct question. He was just being friendly, she told herself. He had no idea that it was her least favorite question. It was like being asked, "So, how'd you get that giant hideous scar?"

"Yes," she said simply, knowing she was now expected to elaborate. "I was married for five years."

He cut an onion into quarters using swift, confident strokes with a sharp knife; then he added the pieces to the roasting pan. "Just asking," he said. "Didn't mean to pry."

"Oh, you weren't prying," she told him hastily. It was comforting in a perverse way, knowing the two of them were both divorced. It was like meeting another shipwreck survivor who understood just what the other had endured.

She remembered seeing Logan's ex at the end of summer, and wondered where he was in the recovery process. She could still picture the look of longing in Logan's eyes when he'd handed his son over to the ex. And why not? The mother of his child was blonde and beautiful, with a glowing smile. Yikes, Logan might even still be in love with her.

"I wanted to make sure the coast was clear," he said to Darcy.

"The coast?"

"For when I start hitting on you."

She swallowed hard. Maybe she was wrong about his ex. "You're going to start hitting on me?"

He plucked a pinch of salt from a small bowl. "Yeah," he said. "I might."

Her chest tightened. She remembered the never-again vow she'd made after her marriage. "How will I know if you're hitting on me?" she asked, her light teasing tone masking apprehension.

He grinned. "You'll be the first to know. Anyway, I'm glad you didn't think I was prying. Prying comes later."

"I can hardly wait," she said.

He hoisted the turkey into the pan. "This," he said, "is going to make you glad I'm single. It's going to be the most delicious turkey you've ever tasted."

"How did you end up with kitchen duty?" she asked.

"I volunteered. Later, everybody will pitch in."

"And all hell will break loose?"

He grinned. "Pretty much."

"So, tell me about the O'Donnell family traditions. Anything unusual?"

"Not unless you consider sibling squabbles, cranky kids and overeating unusual."

"Oh boy. That sounds extremely familiar. Are you sure we're not related?" She and Logan had plenty in common. On the one hand, it was kind of cool, feeling so comfortable with him, so quickly. On the other hand, this likely meant a relationship between them would never work. She and Huntley had had everything in common, yet ultimately they'd fallen apart. "What do you squabble about?"

"It's mainly the kids who squabble these days. Although my old man's not too pleased with me at the moment."

"Why not?"

"I made a kind of impulsive career move. Sold my stable, lucrative, predictable, boring business for a crazy, risky, unstable one."

"Are you talking about that ski resort in your town?"

"Yeah. Cool you remember it."

"I think it sounds incredible. Congratulations."

"My family thinks I've gone off the deep end."

"I know the feeling. The first time I disappointed my parents was the moment I was born."

"What, did you have a tail or something?"

"Ha-ha."

"I've heard those can be removed."

"It's what I *didn't* have that disappointed them."

"What's that?"

"A penis. After four girls, they were desperate for a boy."

"You have four older sisters. And I thought I had it bad, with India and China."

"And how is it your sisters were named after exotic foreign countries while you were named after an airport?"

"Quirky folks. I just feel lucky they didn't call me Madagascar or Sri Lanka."

"Yet another thing we have in common—quirky parents. Mine are English professors. My sisters and I are named after literary figures. I guess that makes them quirky but predictable."

"Darcy. I can't recall a Darcy from college English."

"Hint—it's a surname."

He gave a short laugh. "As in Fitzwilliam Darcy? You're named after Mr. Darcy?"

"It gets worse. My sisters are Mary, Kitty, Lydia and Lizzie. My full name is Darcy Jane." She punctuated the list by plopping chunks of potato into a pot of cold water.

"Don't tell me Lydia is married to a reverend…"

"Worse. A motivational speaker, who happens to be the brother of my ex."

"And suddenly it all comes clear. You came to Florida to escape the dubious pleasures of the family Thanksgiving."

"Exactly. It's so much easier to get along with other people's families."

"Agreed. And can I just say, this dinner is going to be epic." He slid the turkey into the oven. Then he looked around the kitchen and wiped his hands on a tea towel. "We're finished for now. There's nothing more to be done for about three hours. Let's hit the beach."

He flashed that killer smile again. Oh, why did he have to have a killer smile?

CHAPTER SIX

Working alongside Darcy Fitzgerald in the kitchen didn't suck. Logan freely acknowledged that. He kind of liked talking to her. He kind of liked *her,* as much as or maybe more than he had last summer. This was surprising, because he rarely—make that *never*—felt even a spark of interest in a girl who came preapproved by his family.

Yeah, he liked her, but she wasn't his type. Life was simpler without the complication of a divorce survivor. And she didn't even *look* like his type, particularly at the moment, in the floppy hat and shapeless robe. That layered-on style made her look like a human coat tree. Still, she had a fun personality and a cute smile. She was the type of girl to have as a friend, nothing more.

"Time for the beach," he said. "You're going to love it."

"Lead on, Kemosabe."

He walked through the breezeway and held the back door for her. His folks' place had all the perks—an infinity pool and lush gardens, a small grove of orange and calamondin trees, a tennis court, a golf course bordering one side of the yard and on the other side, a scenic path through a bird marsh leading to the beach.

"Not too shabby," she remarked, pausing to get a phone picture of a group of roosting flamingos.

"We spend every Thanksgiving here. The setting is not exactly traditional, though."

"Traditions are overrated," she said.

"Yeah? Which ones?"

"The ones that throw you together with people you don't get along with and force you to pretend to have a good time."

"Ouch."

"Those are the traditions I'm talking about."

"Well, when you put it that way…"

"Sorry." A grin flashed beneath the wide brim of the hat. "Obviously my divorce did a number on me. I'll get over it. I take it you got through yours."

"More or less intact. The hardest part is splitting Charlie's time. Makes me mental." He ground his back teeth, thinking about the past couple of months. "The worst part for me is that he's moving with his mother and stepfather to Japan."

"Whoa, Japan?"

"My ex's husband is in the air force. They're moving right after Christmas, and they'll be away for three years."

"Sounds challenging."

"It's totally screwed up, but I'm going to have to make it work. Charlie has been flying on his own back and forth between his mom and me for the past couple of years, so he's an old hand at it."

Having to shuttle back and forth between parents had

turned Charlie into an independent traveler. But the grin that lit his face each time he saw Logan was all little boy. The fact was, every time Logan saw his little boy walk through the arrivals door at the airport, with his backpack and roll-aboard in tow, travel documents in a packet around his neck, he nearly lost it. Yet for Charlie's sake, he held himself together, told the kid he was proud of him. The Unaccompanied Minor guide could barely keep up with him as Charlie ran to fill his father's arms. Logan never tired of feeling that rush of love and relief washing over him the moment they were reunited.

"If he's an old hand, you've got nothing to worry about."

"But an overseas flight? I'm nervous as hell about how he'll handle it."

"Is Charlie nervous?"

"Good question."

"I bet he'll surprise you. I was a great adventurer as a kid, always up for anything."

Logan found it easy to picture her as a kid, with pigtails and scraped knees. Then he thought about his son. "Charlie's supercautious sometimes. Last summer, there was zip-lining at Camp Kioga, but he wouldn't hear of it. Not even when every other kid went for it."

"I'm no expert, but I bet fear of the unknown is common in kids. Come to think of it, it's common in adults, too."

"You'd love zip-lining," he said.

"How do you know?"

"Just a hunch."

She smiled and ducked her head. Her smile did something funny to his insides. Then, as they reached the end of the path leading to the beach, she said, "Well, this is a great place to come home to. He's a lucky kid."

"That's a nice thing to say. I hope he feels lucky."

"Why wouldn't he? Look where we are." They stepped

onto the sun-warmed sand together. He heard her catch her breath as she clapped a hand atop her head to keep her hat from sailing away in the breeze.

"Amazing," she said, surveying the expanse of brown-sugar sand. The area was bordered by private cabanas. Closer to the surf, the sand was dotted with umbrellas and family groups. Kids played in the waves, and barefoot couples strolled along together. "So this was your childhood playground? It's fantastic here."

Their first stop would be at the O'Donnell cabana—yes, the O'Donnells had been homeowners at Paradise Cove for so long that they had their own cabana, something available only to longtime residents. It bore the traditional canvas stripes and the interior was roomy, like an old-fashioned salon with potted tropical plants and a ceiling fan, upholstered chaises and a small fridge stocked with drinks. On the side, the surfboards were lined up according to size.

In the distance, Charlie and his cousins were boogie-boarding in the waves. "Charlie's the one in the red trunks," he said, pointing him out to Darcy.

"I remember him from last summer."

"Dad!" yelled Charlie. "Yo, Dad!" He jumped up and down, waved his board and rushed into the surf, his cousins surrounding him.

"Looks like he's having a great time."

Logan nodded. Charlie moved with a lithe athleticism that reminded Logan he wasn't a little boy anymore. Every time he saw his son after an absence of any length, he marveled at how much his boy had grown and changed. Not just the inches and pounds, but the attitude, as well. Thanks to the Japanese lessons he'd been taking, he had the rudiments of a new language, a taste for seaweedy snacks and real ramen. He'd told Logan he was excited about living overseas, taking train rides and field trips to pagodas and temples. It's lucky, Logan told himself, his mantra these days. There were perks for Charlie in having two separate families. The chance to experience life in a foreign country with his mom. The chance to go surfing at Thanksgiving with his dad.

Still, the custody arrangement frustrated the hell out of Logan. Even just a couple of months made a difference. Charlie's haircut was different. He wore clothes Logan had never seen.

"He's getting to see the world," Logan said to Darcy. "It's hard, though, feeling like I'm missing out on my son's life."

"You're not missing out now," she said. "He's right here, and he's having the time of his life."

"Good point. Let's go over and say hi to everyone." Around the cabana, his parents, sisters and brothers-in-law were arranged on chaises and canvas sling beach chairs, drinks in hand.

"They look like a fashion layout in a travel magazine," remarked Darcy.

"Yeah? They were, once," he said. "We were."

"Really?"

"*Town & Country,* 2002. My mother's finest moment."

She laughed aloud, as if he was joking. He wasn't joking. Appearing in the pages of a glossy lifestyles magazine had been a peak experience for Marion O'Donnell. More than anything, his parents valued appearances. They wanted the world to see them as the best at everything—a success in business, driving the best cars, sending their kids to the best schools, the unequaled best at being a family.

To this day, they had no idea how much pressure that put on a kid.

Logan was a grown-up now. He was past all that and he'd

never point the finger of blame. But sometimes he admitted there were several unexamined reasons he'd been so screwed up.

"Did that mess with your head?" Darcy asked. "Having to look like a magazine family all the time?"

She was reading his mind. "Hell yeah, it did."

"Why do parents do that?"

"Not sure. I'm trying my best not to repeat the pattern with my own kid." He paused and regarded Charlie, who had abandoned his boogie board and was now staggering around with a red plastic bucket on his head. "I don't think my kid struggles with perfectionism."

"Good for you. And him."

"Come on. Let's let everyone know you're here and then go for a swim. Er, do you like swimming?"

She lit up with a smile. "Yes, I do. I do indeed."

He wasn't sure why she found that funny. "Hey," he called out, approaching the cabana, "Look who I found skulking around the house."

India squealed and jumped up to hug Darcy. Yes, his sister was a squealer. And it didn't seem to matter how old she got, she squealed whenever she was excited. "You made it! I'm so glad."

To his relief, Darcy did not squeal back. "Thanks for having me," she said, addressing Logan's folks. "Your place is beautiful. I really appreciate being here."

"We're so pleased you could come." His mother's smile was a beacon of welcome. She clearly approved of Darcy Fitzgerald, Logan could tell. He always knew when his mom was merely being polite or when she was genuinely pleased. Darcy was the type his mother liked—a girl from a "good" family, whatever that meant—educated, classy. A girl most likely to turn into a woman like Marion O'Donnell.

Logan sometimes took a perverse pleasure in bringing home

women who didn't exactly fit the O'Donnell mold. He'd had one girlfriend with more piercings than a pincushion, and purple hair to boot. Another was multiethnic, with rainbow hair and tribal tattoos, and the most recent was a performance artist who worked in edible paints. He had loved each one, but ultimately, one or the other pulled back. Something wasn't right or didn't match up; somehow their hearts just weren't in sync.

At the moment, there was no one.

It was not for lack of trying. God knew, he loved women. He loved the companionship, the rush of emotion, the sex. He wanted to be in love. Through the years, he'd watched his friends pairing up, moving in together, moving on... And sometimes in the deepest, quietest part of the night, he felt a gaping hollow of loneliness. He tried not to want more than he had—good friends and family, and above all, Charlie.

Still, the biggest lesson he'd learned from being a dad was that he was a family man, through and through. It felt like a special kind of hell sometimes, going it alone, because he wanted to commit himself fully to someone. He wanted a family. More kids, for sure—brothers and sisters for Charlie.

His life wasn't stacking up that way, though. He met women, he dated them, hit it off with them, got laid. And it was fun enough. For a while. Then it would hit him that the fun had gone away, they weren't making each other happy the way he longed to be happy. He'd wake up in the night and realize it wasn't the girlfriend he wanted, but what he thought she could give him.

While Logan was silently bemoaning the barren state of his love life, Darcy was engulfed in greetings. His dad was already fixing her a "morning Mojito," his specialty, made with twenty-three-year-old Cuban rum, an indulgence supplied illegally by one of his shipping clients.

True, she didn't look like his type, but when she let loose

with her easy laugh or dug her bare feet into the warm sand, Logan couldn't take his eyes off her. Whatever it was—loneliness or horniness—it made Darcy Fitzgerald look like a roast turkey leg to him. And he was one hungry pilgrim.

"A toast," said Al O'Donnell. "Welcome to Sea Breeze."

"Thank you." She took a tiny sip of her drink. "I'm thinking of becoming a professional mooch. Al, this is delicious. I didn't think I liked rum."

Logan's dad beamed. "You've been drinking the wrong kind of rum, then." Al O'Donnell loved treating worthy people to fine things.

"I'm going to have to pace myself if you're starting the party this early in the day," said Darcy.

"Thanksgiving is all about overindulging," Marion assured her.

"My parents party harder than we ever did," India said.

"Aunt India says she wouldn't have made it through college without you," said Bernie, Logan's know-it-all niece.

Darcy set her drink on a table. "She's exaggerating."

"Am not," said India. "You coaxed and tutored me through comparative lit *and* advanced calculus."

"You didn't tell me you were a brainiac," Logan said.

"You didn't ask. And if you had, I would have denied it."

"Surf's up," said Logan. "Want to try surfing? Who's up for a ride?"

"I'll join you," said his brother-in-law Bilski. China's husband was a classic guy's guy. He and Logan were buddies.

"So will I," said Darcy.

Logan was startled at her readiness to try it. "Okay. India's board would probably work for you. It's nice and big, for stability."

She nodded, but picked up a small, nimble short board. "This will do."

"It's a thruster," said Logan. "Not a good choice if you're a beginner."

She smiled. "I'll give it a shot. I have pretty good balance."

Logan decided not to argue. She'd find out soon enough whether or not the board would work for her.

"I'm ready," said Bilski. He took a piece of wax from a tub and went to work on his board. After they'd covered their boards with a thick coat of wax, Logan gave the surf's-up sign and waded out into the ocean with his favorite board, a thruster.

He turned back to say something to Bilski, and all the words, along with all coherent thought, drained out of his head. Darcy Fitzgerald was the unexpected cause of his brain damage.

At first he didn't even realize it was her. Then he saw the big floppy hat and shades left by her beach bag. She'd taken off the big shapeless cover-up to reveal the hottest bikini bod he'd seen since…maybe ever. His sister's charming but frumpy friend had suddenly turned into a goddess. He tried not to gawk, but damn. She might not be his type, but she sure as hell was built like his type.

Oblivious of his stare, she bent over to strap the leash of the board around her ankle.

"Oh, sweet mother Mary," whispered Bilski. "Remind me I'm a married man."

"Daddy! Daddy!" Fisher's shrill voice pierced the air. "I made you a wig out of seaweed. Come try it on."

"There's your reminder," said Logan, without taking his eyes off Darcy. She arched her back slightly and shook out her hair. Then in a graceful movement, she bent down again, displaying that perfect ass, and picked up the board. Logan tried not to groan aloud.

This, he realized, was going to go well. Extremely well.

He had been surfing these waters since he was a kid. He knew every wave, every break pattern. She was going to need help. He was the guy to coach her. He'd span his hands across her waist, feel those nice taut abs...

As she approached him, amazing in the yellow bikini, he wondered if he should warn her about her top—or bottom—coming off in the waves.

Naw.

He lowered his board to conceal his excitement.

"Ready?" he asked her.

"As I'll ever be." Her eyes sparkled as she regarded the waves.

India bustled forward with a rash guard. "Put this on," she said, holding out the shirt.

Killjoy, thought Logan. But the rash guard was skintight, concealing nothing. "So, the best breaks are over there," he said, pointing. "If you start in the white water, you'll have fun. The green waves are amazing here, but you might want to work up to them."

"Dad! Check it out!" Charlie splashed toward him through the surf, kicking up a storm of water, spraying both Logan and Darcy. Charlie waved his sand pail. "I caught a mullet!"

"Well, jeez, buddy," Logan said, "you got us both soaked."

"Oh, sorry."

"You remember Darcy?"

"Yeah, from summer. Hi."

"Hey, Charlie."

The kid stared, his mouth slightly open. He was ten years old, just starting to exhibit the signs of female-induced brain damage. He fumbled with the pail. "Want to see my mullet?"

"How could I resist such an invitation?" She leaned over and peered into the bucket. It was all Logan could do to keep his eyes off her tits. "That's pretty cool," she said.

"Yeah," said Charlie. "So, Dad, can I keep him?"

"A mullet? A freaking mullet?"

"I mean, just to watch him, you know."

"You crack me up." Logan tousled his son's damp and salty head.

"You crack me down." Charlie grinned, the exchange a familiar one.

Logan felt a wave of affection for the kid. Charlie wasn't a little boy any longer. Gone were the round apple cheeks and high-pitched voice. In his place was a funny, smart, sometimes cheeky kid—one who was not immune to yellow bikinis.

"Just don't let it drown," he said.

"It's a fish. It's not gonna drown."

"When you keep a fish in a small amount of water, it runs out of oxygen and could suffocate."

Charlie's face fell. "I'm letting him go, then."

"Okay. That's a good decision. Now, I need to give Darcy a surf lesson—"

"Dad."

Logan turned to Darcy, but she was gone. Concern shot through him. Maybe she'd been swamped by a wave, caught in a riptide. He shaded his eyes to check the lifeguard station.

"Dad—"

"Not now, Charlie." Logan's voice was sharp with command. "I need to find Darcy."

"But—"

"Not another word."

At that, Charlie grabbed his arm and pulled him around to face the horizon. He pointed at something out on the water.

Holy crap. Darcy was lying prone on her board, paddling out to the break—completely alone.

Logan bolted into action, rushing through the surf and

jumping on his board to paddle after her. She hadn't even been here an hour. He'd be a lousy host if he drowned his guest.

She had somehow managed to put a good bit of distance between them. She seemed like a strong paddler, using swift, deep strokes, the kind that would give her aching shoulders tonight. When a white wave barreled toward her, Logan called out a warning—having the board swept away could be scary and dangerous.

She surprised him by sinking in front of the wave, then passing the board overhead and coming up on the other side.

Okay, he thought, his worry easing. She knew a little something about how to get out to the surf. Still, he needed to catch up with her before she reached the green water. The waves were not exactly tame today. He paddled full speed but didn't catch her, and the noise of the pounding surf made yelling pointless. She rode up one side of a mounted wave and down the other, disappearing into a trough.

In the distance, a big roller took shape, gathering momentum.

She stopped paddling and turned her board.

No, oh, hell no.

"Darcy!" he yelled, though he knew she couldn't hear. "Wait up." He whistled to get her attention, to no avail.

He imagined the worst—she'd get battered by her surfboard, sucked out to sea, slammed under the force of the wave—and he felt responsible, letting her head blithely out into the open surf alone. "Damn it," he said, paddling furiously in the direction he'd last seen her.

Then a movement flickered in the rise of the wave, and he stopped dead, bobbing on his board. His mouth dropped open as she went surfing past, giving him the cowabunga sign, a grin of delight on her face, her killer body, slick with salt water, flashing past, her hair streaming out behind from the speed, Botticelli's Venus made flesh.

Logan stared like an idiot, mesmerized as she surfed up and down the tube, expertly carving turns, her feet seemingly glued to the board. She rode as if the water were a mountain of glass instead of an undulating tube, skimming one hand into the surface for more control. She flashed momentarily behind and then rose on the other side. At last, the white water caught up with her and she dove headfirst into the surf.

He still couldn't move, riveted by the performance. It had been a long time, way too long, since a woman had taken him by surprise.

Too late, he saw an enormous wave rolling straight at him. Though he bailed over the side of his board, the force of the wave slapped him to the bottom of the ocean.

"This," Logan said, "is what is known as a post-feast stupor." He was slumped on the sofa in his mother's designer living room, his feet propped on her designer coffee table. A football game—the third of the day—was playing on the TV, the crowd noise a low murmur punctuated by cheering. In the next room, Charlie was playing Parcheesi with his cousins. Inez, the housekeeper, was in the kitchen with his sisters, storing away the leftovers and cleaning up after the big meal.

Darcy, equally slumped, turned to him. "You mean you don't want to go surfing again?"

He chuckled, the picture of her surfing like a goddess playing over and over again in his mind. "What, you don't think you schooled me already?"

"I wasn't trying to school you. I just love to surf and don't get to do it often enough."

"Where did you learn to surf like that?"

"Long Island. I was a lifeguard at Cupsogue Beach all

through high school. Then in college, I did a study year abroad in Australia, just a bus ride away from Bondi Beach."

"Very cool." Logan had always sensed a special kind of sexiness in athletic girls. There was something about their confidence that appealed to him. And Darcy had it in spades.

"What about you?" she asked. "You looked pretty good out there yourself."

"I'm surprised I never ran into you at Cupsogue," he confessed. "It was one of my favorite places to go when I was shirking chores in the summer."

"I probably blew the whistle at you when you were a skinny kid getting too close to the jetty," she said.

She was the same age as his older sister, he thought. Four years older than him. "You should have said hi," he pointed out.

"Maybe I did. Or maybe we weren't meant to meet until now."

For some reason, he liked the idea that they'd been circling closer and closer, unaware of each other until now. He'd never felt quite so comfortable around a woman before. She was just easy to be with. And now that he had the indelible image of her in his head—yellow bikini, board glued to her feet, long hair streaming—she was more interesting than ever.

The brothers-in-law perked up when there was a big play in the game. Al pounded his beer bottle on a side table. "Damn, that's sweet," he said. "I always thought you should have gone out for football in high school, son."

Logan chuckled, though he wasn't amused. "As I recall, I stayed so busy with soccer there wasn't time for anything else."

"You make time for what's important to you," said Al.

Logan was determined not to rise to the bait. "Right now I'd like to make time for Mom's pumpkin pie."

"Ah, sounds fantastic," said Bilski.

"I'll go start hovering in the kitchen," said Ethan, the other brother-in-law, rising from the sofa with a groan.

"How about you?" Logan asked Darcy. "Pumpkin pie, or pecan?"

"Pumpkin all the way."

"Hey, I heard a rumor of pie," said Logan's niece, Bernie. The rest of the nieces and nephews, along with Charlie, came charging into the room.

"I have a secret weapon," said Inez as Ethan wheeled out the dessert cart. "I put whipped cream on top and sprinkle it with chopped maple glazed pecans."

"I can't make up my mind," Charlie said.

"Inez, you're killing me," said Logan.

"You're awesome," said Charlie, wedging himself on the sofa between Logan and Darcy.

Thanks, pal, thought Logan. *Thanks a hell of a lot.*

"Arigato," Charlie added.

"He knows lots of words in Japanese," said Fisher.

"Yeah," said Goose. "Charlie speaks Japanese now."

"Are you getting excited about moving to Japan?" Bilski asked him.

"It's gonna be pretty rad." Charlie shoveled in a big bite of pie.

"What are you looking forward to the most?" asked China. She was a teacher, adept at getting kids to talk.

"Dunno," Charlie said. "I'm not there yet. My Japanese teacher said I'm gonna like the food and the culture. What's culture, anyway?"

"It's everything," said Bernie. "Duh. Mom, when can we go to Japan to visit Charlie?"

"We can't," said her older sister, Nan. "He lives with his other family there, and they're the enemy."

"Are not," Charlie snapped.

"He's right," said China. "They are not the enemy. Where in the world did you get that idea?"

"After people split up, they're enemies," said Nan, with firm authority.

"That's just silly. Tell Charlie you're sorry."

"Sorry," she mumbled.

"Sometimes I feel the same way," Charlie admitted, mumbling past another bite of pie.

Logan lost his appetite. He ached for the kid. Was there any way to protect him from feeling torn loyalties? Any way to protect him from the life Logan and Daisy had given him? He hadn't asked to be born to two people who weren't meant to be together. All he wanted was to be part of a family, a regular kid. But Logan wasn't sure it was his job to make the kid feel okay about moving halfway around the globe.

"Hey," he said, "you're in Florida, you stood up on a surfboard today, you had an epic Thanksgiving dinner and pumpkin pie. So life is good."

"Yeah." Charlie nodded agreeably enough.

"We have a lot," said Logan. "A lot to be thankful for."

"Yep."

"Friends and family," China said.

"Full bellies and Florida sunshine," Marion added.

"And pie that makes me forget the whole world," Darcy said. "Marion, I really appreciate being here with you guys."

"I wish you could stay longer," said Logan's mother.

Logan checked his watch. "That reminds me. My shift is about to start."

"How's that? Are we eating in shifts now?" asked Bilski.

"Charlie and I are going to help serve dinner at Ryder House. It's a place for kids who aren't with their families."

"Are they orphans?" asked Bernie.

"Some of them, yes. And some are just there temporarily. They come from lots of different circumstances."

"Can I come?" Bernie asked.

"If you want to help," he said, looking around the room. "Anyone else?"

"I'll join you," Darcy said. "I need to find a way out of this food-induced trance."

The SUV was full, with Charlie and three of his cousins buckled in the backseat and Darcy in the front. The cargo area was loaded with boxed pies Logan had ordered the day before from the Sky High Pie Company, his contribution to the community feast. The afternoon light of South Florida gilded the neighborhood in a dreamy sheen, but as they left Paradise Cove behind, the scenery shed its charm, like the sad aftermath of a parade.

In the backseat, Nan led everyone in a chorus of "Over the River." There were no rivers in sight, no white and drifting snow, just a depressing series of strip centers that all looked virtually the same—nail salons, pawnshops, coin laundries, payday loan outfits.

The Ryder Center was surrounded by chain-link fencing. Although the welcome sign proclaimed it "A Place For Hope," an air of despair hung like Spanish moss from the trees. This was where people brought children they no longer wanted or couldn't care for. The social workers and volunteers were passionate and committed, but sometimes there just wasn't any substitute for family.

"Is this a regular commitment for you?" asked Darcy.

"Yep. I've been bringing Charlie here to help out ever since he was old enough to serve a wedge of pie."

"That's nice," she said.

"Is it?" He pulled in by a small fleet of vans with the Ryder logo on the side, a silhouette of a candle cupped in two hands. "I always find myself wishing I could do more."

"There's always more to do," she murmured.

"I feel sorry for the kids who live here," said Bernie. "I'm kind of bashful about meeting them."

"Kids are kids," said Logan, opening the back of the SUV. "There's usually a pretty good party going on here."

Everyone helped carry the boxed pies to the serving area. The feasting had been going on all day, with a rotating series of kids and volunteers. Some of the children were long-term residents of Ryder House, while others came for the day. People were gathered around tables decorated with flower arrangements, crepe paper turkeys, cornucopia and candles. The buffet line moved slowly along a sideboard laden with a feast with all the trimmings. At one end of the room, a bluegrass ensemble played background music.

"Ready to help out?" Logan asked, handing out aprons to Charlie, the nieces and nephews. "We're on the pie detail."

"Okay." Like his cousin Bernie, Charlie seemed timid around the other kids, though eager to help out. They went to the dessert table and got to work, carefully placing small slices of pie on white china plates and setting them out for people to eat.

There were smiles and subdued thank-yous, although an air of melancholy pervaded the atmosphere. Some of the older kids seemed chastened by the understanding that they were receiving charity. Logan served a slice of berry pie to a boy who looked to be about Charlie's age. His clothes were clean but worn, and he had a peculiar world-weariness that made him seem much older. He furtively took his dessert, mumbled a thank-you and shuffled away to a table.

I will never complain again about my life, thought Logan.

He noticed that Darcy wasn't serving food, but had hunkered down in the play area, supervising a game of Jenga blocks. She seemed so vibrant, surrounded by kids, relaxed in their presence. It made him wonder about her comment last summer, when she'd claimed she was averse to children.

She was something of a puzzle to him. An intriguing puzzle. A puzzle he found far more attractive than he should.

Maybe it was deprivation, plain and simple. He hadn't dated anyone this fall. In the first place, he hadn't met anyone he wanted to date. In the second place, he'd been way too busy with Saddle Mountain. True to his word, he'd created an investor group and they'd acquired the ski area. The transfer was going smoothly, but it was a lot of work. All-consuming work. It left little time for a social life. He'd been working twelve-hour days, seven days a week, since signing the papers, and this holiday was his very first time off. The mountain was slated to open for skiing in a week. It kept him busy to the point of exhaustion. Yet the project fulfilled him in a way his insurance business never, ever had.

The ensemble played some traditional tunes while some of the younger kids ran around, pretending to dance.

"Time for the hokeypokey," announced a guy on the microphone. "Come on, everybody, don't be shy. Let's bust a move!"

Logan scanned the room, and noticed Darcy bearing down on him.

"Oh, hell no," he muttered under his breath, apprehensive about the glint of mischief in her eyes.

"You heard what the guy said," she told him. "Don't be a chicken."

"Yeah, Dad," said Charlie. "Don't be a chicken."

Resigned, Logan took off his apron and set it aside. "You're coming, too, buddy."

"No way." Charlie stuck out his chin. "No w-a-y."

Darcy was having none of it. She grabbed Charlie with one hand and Logan with the other. "Let's go, boys."

Feeling all kinds of foolish, Logan joined the raucous circle and forced himself to do the hokey-freaking-pokey.

Darcy was ridiculously into it, and in spite of himself, he couldn't take his eyes off her when she did the "shake it all about" part. *Damn.*

When Charlie saw his cousins and some of the older kids joining in, he got over his bashfulness and let himself go. Within minutes, he was in the center of the action, laughing and shaking, surrounded by children who seemed to forget, if only for a moment, that they were homeless, neglected, troubled, abused.

Logan caught Darcy looking at him, and she laughed. "Now, that," she said, indicating the mass of squirming, laughing kids, "is what it's all about."

CHAPTER SEVEN

D arcy got up early the day after Thanksgiving. The lovely guest room at Sea Breeze didn't feel like the real world to her. That, at any rate, was something to be thankful for. A quick check of her phone showed that she'd missed a few calls and text messages from her parents and sisters. She shrugged them off; she'd return their calls later, maybe from the airport.

In some respects, being away from her family this Thanksgiving had been unexpectedly painful. She couldn't help resenting Huntley for supplanting her at the Thanksgiving table. Even as she'd toasted and feasted with the O'Donnells, she'd caught herself thinking wistfully of her dad's gentle humor, her mom's perfectly seasoned stuffing, her sisters' gossip and laughter. She missed their chatter and her parents' banter, and the deep, elemental security of being part of a family. But having Huntley there would have put a damper on everything.

The best way to keep from stumbling over the past was to move forward, she reminded herself. That was her whole rationale for braving the holiday travel crowds and coming to Florida in the first place. She got up and went to the window, opening the plantation shutters and looking out over the gardens.

There was a unique sort of beauty in the tropical morning. The air was warm already, and according to the tide chart posted on the wall above the writing desk, the surf was going to be perfect. She slipped into her borrowed swimsuit, cover-up and flip-flops and headed down to the beach.

In the morning quiet of the garden, Darcy woke her mouth up with a calamondin plucked straight from the tree, wincing at the taste of the bittersweet peel and tart center. Then she plucked a couple of oranges and tucked them in her bag.

"Can't stay away from the beach, can you?"

She turned, already blushing. "Oh, hey, Logan."

"Hey yourself. You're up early. It's not even seven."

"I wanted to get a little more beach time in before I have to go. I have to get back to New York this evening."

"Mind if I join you?"

Mind? *Mind?* "That'd be great," she said.

They walked in silence—a silence she found to be quite companionable. For no good reason, she felt very comfortable with Logan. He was easy to be with, easy to talk to. Easy on the eye, though she pretended to look around and not at him. The air was sweet with the smell of magnolias and the sea, and a light breeze brought with it eddies of warmth.

"Your folks have a great spot here," she remarked.

"Yeah. We're really lucky."

"Some would say spoiled."

"Yeah, okay. Spoiled. But in a good way." He flashed a grin.

"True," she said. "That was really nice last night, helping out at the children's center."

"Thanks for coming along. But I thought you were allergic to kids."

"I guess I like them in small doses. Especially when they're at a place like Ryder House. It's nice to help."

"Agreed. I've been really lucky in my life, and I never want to take that for granted. It feels like a special privilege to help out."

"You're right. I've heard it called a 'helper's high.' Otherwise known as doing the hokeypokey."

He chuckled. "You're a good sport."

"I like to think so." She passed through the arch of beach roses and dune grass and stepped onto the sand, which was still slightly cool and damp from the night.

"We practically have it all to ourselves," she said, enchanted by the shifting blue of the water, the slight pink tinge of the morning sky.

A few hundred yards away was a lone jogger, heading up the coast. In the other direction was a woman doing yoga poses. The rest of the beach belonged to the seagulls and sandpipers.

Logan stopped at the cabana and took out two boards, along with a couple of bars of wax. They applied the wax to the already-bumpy surface of each board.

"Okay," he said when they finished. "Surf's up."

She nodded and peeled off her oversize tunic, knowing without looking at him that he was checking her out. His gaze felt like a waft of heat on her bare skin.

He didn't even pretend not to stare. "Sunscreen?" he asked, offering her a tube.

"Thanks." She spread the cream everywhere she could reach while he did the same. Then she donned her rash guard, a tight jersey shirt with three-quarter-length sleeves.

"You missed a spot," said Logan. "Turn around." He went down on one knee and smoothed his hands down the backs of her thighs.

She was startled by the sensation of his bare hands on her skin. It had been so long since a guy had touched her, she'd nearly forgotten what that felt like. And until this moment, she hadn't realized that she missed it.

She was flustered by the time he finished and stood up. "Thanks," she said, hoping her thoughts didn't show on her face. She'd never been good at playing it cool.

"My pleasure." He picked up his board. "Really."

She followed him to the surf. The warm water swirled around her ankles in a rhythm that pulled at her, reminding her of why she loved the ocean—the steady movement, the timeless rhythm, the mysteries beneath, the raw curl of power. "Let's go ride some waves."

"You're going to show me up again," he accused.

She laughed. "Watch and learn."

They waded out together and then mounted their boards to paddle out to the green water. The waves were aggressive, but beyond the first break, the ocean was calm, shifting with a cradling motion.

"Beautiful morning," he said, sitting astraddle and watching the incoming rollers.

"It is. Let's try this one." She indicated a nice glassy mound coming toward them.

"You got it."

They paddled in tandem, and when the momentum took their boards, they both stood up. She laughed aloud, loving the sensation of being propelled by the surge. The first ride of the day made her glad to be alive. She'd taken her stepchildren surfing a few years ago. She couldn't keep herself from remembering that. This morning, though, the memory didn't hurt.

They rode for about an hour. Beyond the break, she caught sight of something out of the corner of her eye. A series of large, dark shapes flurried just under the surface, moving fast, a raft of liquid shadows.

"Hey, Logan!" she yelled, looking around for him. Her heart pounded.

He had seen, too, and seconds later, the dark shapes broke the surface and leaped into the air in a graceful arc. Darcy was transfixed, and then she broke into laughter. "Dolphins," she cried. "I've never been this close to dolphins." The animals leaped again, and she could feel the rush of wind and spray as they passed. It was magical. There was no other word for it.

The animals didn't seem to mind their proximity. They surged past, the muscular undulations of their bodies stirring the water, then causing shower after shower as they breached. She felt both intimidated and reverent, privileged to be part of their world. In that moment, the sense of wonder was so powerful it reminded her of being a child again.

The dolphins leaped several more times, and then disappeared out to sea. Darcy's gaze caught Logan's and she could see that he was every bit as enchanted as she was, sharing the same sense of wordless wonder. The fact that they had witnessed it together bonded them in some intense way. Unforgettable moments had a habit of doing that.

He signaled to her to indicate an incoming wave, and they rode it in together, side by side, to the shallows. She whipped her wet hair out of her face and grinned at him. "Well," she said, "I guess that's something you don't see every day. I'm just… God, it was overwhelming. I have no idea what to say. I'm speechless. I mean, I'm babbling. But really, Logan, I—"

He stopped her with a kiss. It was just that fast. One moment she was attempting to blather on about swimming with the dolphins, and the next, he had cradled her face between his hands and was kissing her with a raw, searing passion that took her breath away. For a second, she went stiff with startlement, and then she melted against him, feeling the unfamiliar shape of him, tasting him for the first time, exploring the texture of his lips, wishing it would go on for a very long time.

"Oh," she said when he finally lifted his mouth from hers. "Oh my." Still at a loss for words, she stared up at him, wanting him to kiss her again, wondering if he wanted to. He tasted delicious, of salt from the sea and his own unique flavor. It was exciting and sexy and wholly unexpected. She had not kissed a man in ages. She was glad the one she was kissing happened to be Logan O'Donnell.

He smiled down at her. "I'm glad we shared that."

She wasn't sure he meant the dolphins or the kiss.

"Me, too," she said, and she knew which one she meant.

"Are you sure you have to leave today?" he asked.

Ah, so tempting. Then she took a deep breath. It was just a kiss, she reminded herself. It was only a kiss. "Yes. I have a work thing." She bent over and unstrapped the ankle tether of her board.

"On a holiday weekend?"

She straightened up and nodded, furrowing a hand through her hair. "It's weather-dependent. There's a photo shoot that needs snow and ice, and that's the prediction for tomorrow and Sunday."

"Sounds awesome. Where's the shoot?"

"Lake Placid," she said. "It's a snow sports shoot."

"Cool. So, do you do photography?"

"No. I'd love to learn one day."

"It's overrated," he said quickly, almost harshly. He caught her quizzical look and added, "My ex is a photographer."

"I don't think it's contagious," she said.

"Yeah, sorry." He passed her a towel. Their hands brushed, and they looked at each other briefly.

Again, she thought. *Let's try kissing again.* To her disappointment, he picked up her beach bag and started back toward the house.

"So, what do you do on the shoot?" he asked. "Stylist, or…?"

"I'm, uh, the subject," she said, suddenly feeling self-conscious.

"Sorry, what?"

"The subject."

"Like, you're a model?"

"I'm one of the athletes," she said, somewhat insulted by his surprise. She knew she wasn't model-pretty, but she wished he thought she was.

"Now I'm confused. I thought you were in advertising."

"I am. I'm in sports marketing," she said. "It's a specialized field. I work with sponsors, and the shoot is set up to show off their gear."

"What do you mean, you work with sponsors?"

"As a sponsored athlete."

"Seriously? What kind of sport?" he asked, holding the back door for her. The kitchen, though deserted, was fragrant with the morning's first pot of coffee.

"Snowboarding is my specialty. I'll be testing gear and apparel, and there will be photos and videos for the sponsors' catalogue and website. Hence the need to shoot when the weather is cooperating." She helped herself to a cup of coffee and poured one for him.

"You snowboard to test and promote your sponsors' gear, and that's your job."

"Yes, some of the time." She started feeling a bit defensive, as if he was judging her. There was a lot more to her job, but this weekend, that was it in a nutshell.

Logan lifted his coffee mug in salute. "That is *made* of awesome."

She laughed. All right, so he wasn't judging her. "The job's not that much fun every day, but I can't complain."

"Coolness. The more I get to know you," he said, "the more I like you." He put a couple of English muffins in the toaster. "Peanut butter, strawberry jam or both?" he asked.

"Be still, my heart."

Oh, this was bad. Because she liked him, too, but he was everything she *wasn't* looking for—a single dad, a man who had said, practically at their first meeting, that he wanted a big family. The idea made her stomach tighten with tension.

"You're going to love hanging out with me," he said, slathering the English muffins with peanut butter and jam, and handing her one.

"What makes you think I'm going to hang out with you?" She took a bite of the warm, gooey muffin. It was almost as delicious as kissing him.

"Because I have a ski resort. I mean, I'm part of the investment group, but I'm the controlling partner and general manager." He paused and watched her savoring the muffin, seeming to focus on her lips. Then he picked up a napkin and gently dabbed at the corner of her mouth. "You inspired me," he said simply.

It was the last thing she expected to hear from him. "Huh?" she said, with peanut butter charmingly stuck to the roof of her mouth.

"Last summer, when you talked about taking risks."

"I can't believe you remember that." She was flustered... but flattered.

"So in the future, if you need a location for doing your gear testing and photo shoots, I can offer you carte blanche at Saddle Mountain. Come check it out some time. Come soon."

"Now, *that,*" she said, "is made of awesome. I'll definitely tell my team. We've got a project going with a new snowboard company, and we'll be doing a shoot sometime in December."

"You ought to come give Saddle Mountain a try. We'll give you VIP privileges."

She polished off the English muffin, unable to recall enjoying a breakfast more. "Wow. I guess knowing the controlling partner is a perk."

"Controlling partner?" Al O'Donnell came into the kitchen. "What the hell are you talking about?"

Darcy sensed it was her cue to leave. "I'd better hit the shower."

"Don't run off," said Al, looking a bit sheepish. "Logan and I can talk about this later."

"Or not," Logan said good-naturedly, pouring coffee for his father. "Actually, I—"

A cell phone on the counter chimed. Logan checked it, and his face changed entirely, turning marble-hard with tension. "Sorry, I have to take this. Excuse me." Grabbing the phone, he stepped out to the backyard.

Darcy took a sip of coffee. She slid the cream pitcher across the counter toward Al. *Your son just kissed me,* she thought. And then: *I liked it.* She hoped she wasn't blushing too much. "Ah," she said, "that awkward moment when one has no idea what to say."

Al chuckled. "Nonsense. I didn't mean… Logan doesn't seem to understand how proud I am of all he's accomplished."

"Have you explained that to him?"

"Maybe not directly, but he knows."

Darcy wasn't so sure of that.

"We talked about that resort," Al said. "That Saddle Mountain place. I was hoping it was just a passing fancy. I didn't think he'd actually go for it. Sounds like a leap off the fiscal cliff to me."

She didn't say anything. This was between the two of them. Yet Al seemed to want to talk. He seemed like a good guy— blustery, bossy, but kindhearted. India adored him. And he was certainly good-looking, big and athletic, his abundant red hair fading at the temples. When she regarded Al, she could picture Logan thirty years from now. Scary thought—she enjoyed picturing Logan thirty years from now.

"He's always been too fond of skiing and snowboarding," Al said, pacing back and forth. "People think that just because they love something, they can make it their life's work."

She laughed. "Al. Listen to yourself."

"Okay, but still. If you saw your kid about to step off a cliff, wouldn't you be concerned?"

"Logan seems pretty sturdy to me. I wouldn't worry."

"Why're you worrying about Dad?" asked Charlie, coming into the kitchen. His face was still sleep-soft, making him look even younger than ten.

Darcy was struck by an urge to reach out to him. Kids needed hugging. *"For somebody who doesn't like kids,"* Logan had said, *"you sure like kids."*

"Should I worry about Dad?" Charlie asked, absently scratching his cheek.

"Of course not," said Al, giving him a kiss on the head. "You have a great dad."

"You can say that again." Logan came back into the kitchen, phone in hand. "I've got a little news, Charlie-my-man."

"Yeah?" His eyebrows shot up.

"Your buddy André?"

"From Camp Kioga, yeah! What about him?"

"He and his sister are going to be spending Christmas with us."

"Cool!"

"What?" asked Al, another thunderous frown darkening his face.

"Christmas at Willow Lake," said Logan. "How does that sound?"

"We always have Christmas here," said Al.

"And now I really *am* hitting the shower," Darcy announced. She truly did not want to be in the middle of this. It sounded like a family matter. It sounded eerily like her own family—the arguing, the affection, the power struggles, the sense of caring, sometimes caring so much that it hurt.

CHAPTER EIGHT

Logan heard the clack of suitcase wheels on the adobe tile of the foyer, and knew Darcy was about to depart. Fresh out of the shower, he leaned toward the mirror to make sure he hadn't missed a spot shaving, then hurried downstairs to tell her goodbye.

He didn't want her to leave. He wanted her to stay. He wanted to kiss her some more, for sure. He wanted to make out with her, run his hands over that amazing, athletic, taut body, inhale the flowery smell of her hair, taste the strawberry jam on her lips…

Not possible, though. She had to rush back to the city and Lake Placid and her work project, while he had to wrap up the holiday here, tell Charlie goodbye until Christmas and get back to Avalon for work. Most of all, he had a project that was going to take all his energy and focus. He had to prepare to look after Maya Martin's children.

It was probably for the best that he and Darcy had been interrupted before they even got started.

But holy crap. It was going to be a long time before he forgot about that kiss.

Darcy was in the foyer with his sisters and mother, doing a final check—phone, boarding pass, rental car key. "This has been such a fantastic stay," she was saying. "Thank you so much for having me."

"Wish you could have stayed longer," said India, who then turned to Logan. "Right, Logan?"

"Of course." He grinned at his sister, wondering if she'd guessed her matchmaking had worked, even just a little. Then he moved past her. "Glad you were here for the holidays," he told Darcy.

"Me, too." She held him with that direct look of hers. "Thanks again for including me at the children's center. Oh, and the surfing. And the dolphins."

"I can't take credit for the dolphins," he said.

"You saw dolphins?" India asked.

"Yep, while surfing," Logan said. "Let's go back with the kids this afternoon, see if we can spot them again."

"It was unforgettable," Darcy said softly, and he noticed a touch of color in her cheeks. Then she said her goodbyes to everyone else.

After she'd gone, Logan decided to bring up the topic of Christmas with his parents and sisters. He hadn't intended to drop two bombs at once, but circumstances made it necessary.

"We're having Christmas here," his mother said. "Just like we always do."

"I've got a different idea," he told her. "Avalon. Everyone's coming to Avalon this year."

"Where will we stay?" his mother asked, uncertainty shadowing her eyes. "There's no way you have room for us all."

"The lodge at Saddle Mountain," he said. "I live there now."

"What?" His mother stared at him. "I don't understand."

"I sold my house and moved up to the mountain."

"And when were you going to tell us about this?"

"It all happened fast. I got a full-price offer as soon as I listed my house—a couple from the city who want a place near Willow Lake. I moved up to the mountain week before last. The residence there is old, but huge. It's been operating as a B and B." He'd sunk his profits from the house sale into the resort, where nearly all his resources went these days.

"What about your insurance business?" his mother asked, her face pale with distress. "Logan, you worked so hard to build it up, and you were doing so well."

"I'm keeping a stake in it as a silent partner, but someone else is running it," Logan said. "I'm putting all my energy into the resort now."

"What?" His mother regarded him, aghast. "You did what?" She turned to her husband. "I thought you said you talked him out of it."

"I believed I had," Logan's father said.

"Look, could we talk about this another time?" Logan said. "How about we discuss Christmas plans?"

"We already have plans," his mother said. "The Costellos are having their usual Christmas Eve party at the Paradise Cove Clubhouse, and I'm cochair of the church breakfast."

"Plans are made to be changed," Logan said. "So I've heard."

"I invited Darcy to spend the holidays with us," India said. "Do you just want to throw her in the mix, as well?"

Darcy of the smoking-hot body and razor-sharp wit? Hell yes, he did.

"I bet she likes snowboarding as much as surfing," he pointed out.

"The kids might like it for a change," said China. "I can't remember the last time they had a white Christmas."

"I can definitely promise you that," Logan said, sending his sister a nod of gratitude. "It's going to be awesome. A perfect Christmas."

PART FIVE

Two unbreakable rules:
 1. Breakfast is the most important meal of the day and should never be skipped.
 2. There is nothing—repeat, *nothing*—that cannot be improved by the addition of bacon.

Maple Bacon Bread Pudding

Nonstick baking spray
1 pound bacon
Maple sugar or brown sugar, to coat bacon slices
1½ cups cream
½ cup pure maple syrup
1 teaspoon pumpkin pie spice
Pinch of salt
6 eggs
8 slices brioche or challah bread

Preheat the oven to 375° F. Coat a 9-inch round or oval pan with baking spray.

Dredge bacon slices in maple or brown sugar. Bake the bacon on a sheet tray between two pieces of parchment paper until crispy, 15 to 20 minutes. Then crumble the bacon.

Mix the cream, maple syrup, pumpkin pie spice, salt and eggs. Line the pan with the bread and pour the egg mixture over it. Sprinkle with bacon crumbles. Cover and refrigerate a couple of hours or overnight. Then bake for 20 to 25 minutes, until eggs are set. Serve with warm syrup.

[Source: Adapted from *Food & Wine* magazine]

CHAPTER NINE

The week after Darcy finished the Lake Placid photo shoot and returned to the city, her sisters took her to lunch. It was their annual pre-Christmas planning-and-strategy lunch during which secret Santa names were drawn, menus and venues were planned and general excitement over the upcoming holiday reached a fever pitch.

Darcy dreaded it.

She used to look forward to the tradition as the kickoff to her favorite time of the year. The five sisters, knowing all their lives that they had more brains and creativity than money, used to delight in coming up with innovative ways to make the holidays merry, and planning things was half the fun. The Collinses, forever known as the "boys next door," always celebrated with the Fitzgeralds, and the tradition was solidified when Lydia married Badgley ten years before. When Huntley was married to his first wife, she'd been included in the joint celebration, as well. After their children—Amy and Orion—had come along, Darcy had happily crocheted them little caps and booties, never dreaming she'd one day be their stepmother. The year the marriage had ended, Darcy had joined her sisters in consoling Huntley. The year after that, she'd become his wife. She'd loved Huntley and his children with all her heart.

She'd loved the combined family holiday, too—the Christmas Eve feast, the caroling trek to midnight services, the Christmas morning breakfast, the opening of the presents, the gift-stealing game and the silly pickle prize, each moment steeped in tradition, becoming part of the cherished fabric of memory. Now that she was divorced, she understood how friable that fabric was, disintegrating at the slightest touch, like a burned veil. The love she'd started out with had simply gone away.

"Thanksgiving wasn't the same without you," said Kitty.

"That's right. We made a new rule. No more going our separate ways at the holidays, no matter what," said Lizzie.

"I don't remember voting on that rule," Darcy said.

"We made it with you in mind. Part Two of the New Rule is that if you're uncomfortable with the guest list, you get to speak up." Lydia eyed the mimosas that came to the table, but settled for orange juice and sparkling water.

"And you'll actually listen? What a concept. So, what brought this about?" Darcy paused. "Oh, wait. Don't tell me. Huntley's kids were horrible." She pictured Amy and Orion at their worst—obnoxious, making a mess, squabbling with each other, fussing about the food. Back when she was married to Huntley, she had known how to take charge of the kids. They complained about her being bossy, but when she was around, they behaved.

"I think they miss you," said Mary.

I miss them, too, Darcy thought. Yes, they'd been impossible the past couple of years, but they were kids, hurting kids.

"However, we decided it's not fair to include Huntley if it means you won't be there for the holidays."

Did they have any idea how small that made her feel? How petty and selfish? She pictured what it might be like, with Huntley and his children barred from the traditional celebration. Would Huntley's parents defect, as well? His brother? And then Lydia? The entire holiday would come apart at the seams, all because Darcy didn't want to be anywhere near Huntley.

"It won't work," she said. "Badgley and Huntley are practically joined at the hip. I can't imagine Badgley would agree to this."

"Badgley doesn't get a vote," Lydia said simply, folding her arms. "Please, Darcy. This is a really important time for us."

"What the heck do you mean, really important?"

"We're…" Lydia's eyes misted. She slowly sipped her mimosa. Her virgin mimosa, made with sparkling water.

"Oh my gosh," Darcy said. "You're pregnant!"

Lydia nodded, her smile soft, aglow with pride and mystery. "Yes. Finally."

Darcy reached over and hugged her so hard they nearly fell off their lunch counter stools. "That's fantastic, Lyddie. I'm so excited for you."

The other sisters squealed and hugged, and Lizzie, always the most emotional of the bunch, teared up.

"You're all the first to know," Lydia said, dabbing at her eyes. "Don't tell Mom and Dad yet. Badgley and I are going to make an announcement on Christmas. That's why it's so important to have everyone present."

Darcy took both her sister's hands and squeezed them tight. "I couldn't be happier for you. I'm completely thrilled for you and Badgley. But I want your announcement to be a wonderful moment for the whole family, one you'll always remember. My being there, having to endure Huntley, would only cast a shadow over your good news."

"Darcy—"

"I'm going to do everyone a favor and make this simple."

"No," said Mary and Kitty simultaneously.

"My friend India invited me to spend the holidays with her and her family, and I've accepted."

"But you did that at Thanksgiving," Lydia pointed out.

"And we all survived." Darcy still thought about that magical weekend, far more than she should. In the middle of Manhattan's freezing rain and winter darkness, she would often catch herself gazing out her office window and conjure up memories of the sunshine warm on her skin, surfing on a private beach, swimming with friendly dolphins, kissing Logan O'Donnell...

"This is different," said Kitty. "This is *Christmas*. Nobody skips out on Christmas."

"I'm not skipping out. I'll just be...elsewhere."

"This is not happening," said Lizzie, doodling with a red pen in her dayrunner. "We have to stick together at Christmas. We *have* to."

"Otherwise the world will come to an end, right?" Darcy touched her sister's arm. "Look, I don't want to make trouble. I'm trying to save everyone the tension and awkwardness of me being in the same room as Huntley."

"Just don't be tense and awkward around him, and all will be well," Mary said simply.

"Sure," Darcy snapped. "I'll just forget that he still shows up for family holidays as if he deserves to be there."

"We don't want him there, either," said Kitty. "We want

you. That's why you should come, and we'll tell Huntley he's not welcome."

Darcy could imagine this conversation going round and round, never finding a conclusion. She was sorely tempted to tell her sisters about the cheating, but that would open yet another avenue of conflict. They would take sides, they'd gang up on Huntley, they'd create a rift between the families, just at the moment Lydia was going to deliver a new Collins baby. Darcy clenched her jaw, unwilling to be the architect of that.

"My mind is made up," she told them. "I'm going away for Christmas. I'm going to have a fantastic time."

"With your friend India? Doesn't she feel guilty, stealing you away from your family? What kind of friend is she?" Mary asked.

"The best sort. The kind who's there when I need her, offering what I need. In this case, I need to do something fun and different, like surfing at Thanksgiving."

"She's got a point," Lizzie said. "Surfing sounds fun."

"Totally fun," Darcy assured her. "They might not be surfing, though. According to India, the O'Donnells are negotiating where they'll be spending Christmas, too."

"What's that supposed to mean?" asked Lydia. "Where are they taking you?"

"They're deciding between sunshine and snow."

"You mean they have more than one fabulous vacation spot?" Kitty nudged Lydia. "Maybe we should all make friends with the O'Donnells."

"Maybe you should," Darcy said. "One faction of the family wants to spend Christmas in the Florida sun. Another wants a white Christmas in the Catskills."

"What sort of place in the Catskills?"

"India's brother, Logan, is a partner in a ski resort in Avalon, up in Ulster County." Darcy knew which location she preferred, but she didn't get a vote.

Lydia gave a low whistle. "There's a *brother.*"

"And this brother," said Lizzie, "does he happen to be single?"

"And does he happen to have red hair and green eyes and a killer smile, not to mention a set of abs like a cheese grater?" asked Mary.

Darcy smacked her. "Hey, you've been snooping."

"I call it research," Mary stated. "Is it a secret?"

"No, but it's...new. It might be nothing. Or it might be a thing." She knew she was blushing furiously now, because she kind of wanted it to be a thing. She'd even scheduled a shoot for a sports gear client at Saddle Mountain next week, hoping she'd run into him.

"Now it all comes clear," Lydia said, laughing at Darcy's flaming cheeks. "We know what Darcy wants for Christmas."

"Hey—"

"And you can't smack me," Lydia said. "No smacking the pregnant sister."

CHAPTER TEN

Logan paced back and forth on the train platform, stomping his feet and swinging his arms across his chest in order to stay warm. A cold front had arrived the night before, and it hovered like an alien spaceship, beaming wintry weather down on Willow Lake. A fresh dumping of new snow blanketed the town, and the sun was trying to break through, offering glimpses of frigid blue sky. The fresh snow was a boon for Saddle Mountain, which had opened with great fanfare the first Saturday of December. The place had been busy ever since, teeming with locals and tourists, visitors from the city, people who loved the bright chill of winter and the exhilaration of a day on the slopes.

He hadn't taken a day—or even more than a few hours— off since the ribbon had been cut by the town mayor at the base of the main chairlift. This day was special, though. In a kind of terrible way. Maya Martin was bringing her kids to stay with him for the next two months.

The cold bit at his earlobes. He tugged his hat down lower and paced a little faster, stimulated by nerves as well as the temperature. He couldn't imagine what Maya must be feeling right now. How did you tell your kids goodbye for two whole months? Sure, he had a similar challenge with Charlie every time he sent him to his mom's, but the circumstances were never as extreme as Maya faced.

They would not be allowed to visit her. She had insisted on this. She didn't want her children brought to the concrete-and-razor-wire-surrounded facility to be frisked and questioned and then ushered into some cheerless, monitored holding room where they would undoubtedly watch her fall apart, only to be escorted away in tears.

After agreeing to take the kids, Logan had gone down to the city a couple of times to see André and to meet Angelica, his younger sister, so she wouldn't feel so completely foisted off on a stranger. He'd submitted to screening questions and a background check by social services, intrusive but understandable. He couldn't imagine what the children were feeling right now.

He checked his phone, scrolling through the photos on the screen to a shot of the little girl. She was aptly named, completely angelic, as beautiful as her mother, though in a tiny, seven-year-old-missing-two-front-teeth way.

The first time he'd met her, she had sung a song to him—her own rendition of Lady Gaga's "Born This Way." Little kids singing and smiling never failed to tug at the heartstrings. Little kids who had to be taken away from their mothers at Christmas didn't just tug at the heart. They yanked until that fragile organ broke.

The train arrived, lumbering into the station with a steamy

hiss and screech of brakes. Logan's heart sped up. He wanted this to go well. He prayed the kids wouldn't cry or worse, burst into hysterics.

He and Maya had a plan. They would drive together up to his new place on the mountain, get the kids settled in and then she'd say goodbye to them there. It seemed the least traumatic way to handle the situation.

The passenger car disgorged an eclectic mix of people—tourists and travelers, everyone bundled up for the cold. He was gratified to see a good number of skiers and snowboarders heading up to Saddle Mountain. The chalet was booked solid through the holidays.

Logan was determined to make not just a success of the resort, but a major success. He wanted to do it for the sake of accomplishing something, and to build something for the future. For Charlie. And yes, he could admit this—to prove to his father that it could be done.

"Well, well," said a bright, cheery voice. "Now I feel like a VIP. It's really nice of you to meet my train."

Logan was amazed to see Darcy Fitzgerald, of all people, pulling a roll-aboard along the platform toward him. What the hell was she doing here?

His heart skipped a beat when she smiled at him. In the space of that one missed heartbeat, everything came back to him—the laughter and fun they'd had last time they were together. Surfing in the Florida sunshine. The beach. The kiss. He had thought about that kiss for days.

He should have called her. But he'd let himself get busy. First there was the process of getting Charlie on his flight to his mom's. Then there was the return to Avalon to oversee the opening of the resort. He also had to work with Maya on the plan to take care of her children. Time had gotten away from him, and eventually, it just seemed awkward to chase Darcy down. She probably didn't want to hear from him, anyway.

And yet here she was, appearing without notice, like a surprise delivery.

She gave him a quick hug, her breath warm on his frozen cheek. Even through the layers of their jackets, he could feel her taut, athletic body. What the hell—? He tried to figure out the meaning of the hug. Was it the hug of his sister's friend… or of a girl who was interested in him?

"I guess India told you I was coming." She spoke rapidly, as if she was nervous. Or maybe just excited.

"Actually, I—" He stopped himself. Okay, this was crazy. She seemed to think he was here at the station for her. Trying to explain the situation with Maya's kids would take more time than he had.

"This week turned out to be perfect timing for one of the firm's clients." Darcy definitely sounded excited now. "We're going to shoot some video and photos of their snowboard gear with a holiday theme. I took your suggestion and organized everyone to come here instead of Gore or Whiteface. You were right about this place being perfect at the holidays." Her eyes sparkled as she pushed back the hood of her parka and looked around the station. It was decked with swags of fresh greenery, lights and shiny ornaments. Carols streamed from hidden speakers.

"Anyway," she said, "the photo crew we've booked is the best. They'll make Saddle Mountain look like a dream, I swear. Everyone else drove up yesterday to get organized for the shoot, but I had some work stuff to take care of. We're all going to rendezvous at the resort. Your assistant's been really helpful in coordinating all this."

Finally Logan put the pieces together. He had extended the invitation to Darcy, never dreaming she'd take him up on it.

His assistant, the superefficient Brandi, had one mission—to deal with everything he didn't have time to deal with, including public relations, which was probably why he hadn't heard anything about Darcy's project.

Suddenly he found himself getting very excited about this new wrinkle. Christmas was coming early this year, it seemed.

"That's great," he said.

"Which way is your car?" She looked toward the exit.

Oh shit. She was expecting him to offer her a ride.

"Uh, yeah. I'm actually meeting someone else today," he said, supremely uncomfortable. "I didn't realize—"

"Oh!" Her cheeks turned red—even redder than they were from the cold. "Oh my gosh, that was totally presumptuous of me, to assume you'd come to give me a ride."

"Any other time, I'd love to offer you a lift." He cast about, trying to figure out when he could get together with her. With the arrival of Maya's kids, it was going to be hard to carve out time to do anything. "It's just that today, someone special is coming."

"Oh." The smile left her eyes, yet stayed frozen on her lips. Those delicious ripe lips. He knew how soft they were, he knew they tasted like berry lip gloss; the memory had haunted him since he'd kissed her. He was an idiot. "I mean, not that you aren't special, but, I mean—"

"Logan," called Maya, waving from down the platform. She came walking toward him, towing her kids along behind her. Her face taut with nervousness, she put her arms around him and gave him a hug. He knew why she clung; he could feel her shuddering intake of breath and sensed she was about to shatter.

"Hey," he said, stepping back. In the realm of awkward moments, this one definitely ranked.

"So," said Maya with forced cheerfulness, "are we going straight to your place or—"

"My place," he said, then stepped farther away from her. It was too late, though. His foot was already planted deep in his mouth. "Er... Maya, this is Darcy."

"Hi," said Darcy; then she shifted her glance at Logan. "Sorry, I'd better be on my way. I've got...you know, that work stuff going on."

"Sure. Of course."

"Good to meet you," she murmured, and hurried away, practically running as she followed signs to the taxi stand.

Logan suppressed a groan of frustration. He couldn't let himself worry about her for the moment. Shifting gears, he focused on the kids, trying to figure out how in God's name to make this easier for them. He couldn't. No one could. "Okay, gang. To the mountaintop. You're going to love it there."

"I've been to your house," said André. "Last summer. Remember? I got to have a sleepover with Charlie before camp started."

"You're right. But that was a different house. The one in town. I sold that house and moved."

"Where do you live now?" asked Angelica.

"On the mountaintop, like I said. There's a big old house up there that will hold everybody who's coming for the holidays. You get to sleep in a bunk room with Charlie and his cousins."

"Cool," said André. "I get the top bunk."

Logan opened the back door of the Jeep and loaded in their luggage. "Buckle up. It takes about half an hour to get to the new place. Even Charlie hasn't seen it yet. He doesn't arrive for two more days."

The kids chattered nonstop on the drive up the mountain. They seemed excited and, to Logan's relief, not terrified that their mother was about to leave them.

"Mama has to go away for a job," said Angelica.

Logan glanced at her in the rearview mirror. The little girl looked guileless. He didn't blame Maya for fudging the details. No point in scaring the kids by telling them their mom was headed for a frightening place. A quick scan of André's face revealed a different story. Logan suspected the boy wasn't fooled for a minute. André's skin was stretched taut across his cheekbones, and his eyes were narrowed as he watched out the window.

"So, Charlie is really excited about having Christmas with you guys," Logan said. "He can't wait to see you. He's coming all the way from Oklahoma."

"He's moving to Japan," said André. "He wrote me an email about it."

"That's cool that you guys email each other." Logan was glad to hear it. He received regular emails from his son, too, filled with briefly stated facts—the world according to Charlie. "I got a haircut today." "There was a field trip to the Vehicle Operations Center." "Sushi was invented in Japan. I ate one sushi roll and it was yucky. When I move to Japan I will not eat sushi."

Logan always wrote back promptly. It was not the same as being with his son, but with the emails and daily video phone calls, they managed to stay connected.

"Why did you move to the mountaintop?" asked André. He kept staring at the winter woods out the window. The black lines of the bare trees etched the hillside.

"It's not exactly the top," said Logan, "but close enough. I live there because it's near my work, a resort called Saddle Mountain."

"What kind of resort?" asked Angelica.

"In winter, it's a place to go skiing or snowboarding, or

sledding. You can also take a nature hike if you bundle up and stick to the trails. We can put on the snowshoes."

"That sounds like fun," said Maya. "Doesn't that sound fun?"

"How will Santa Claus know where we are?" asked the little girl.

"Kids always wonder that," Logan said. "He just does, that's all. It's one of the special things about Christmas."

"Really?"

"When I was your age, my parents took me to Florida at Christmas. And Santa always found me, and I always found what I was wishing for under the tree."

"I don't get how that works," said Angelica.

"It just works," said Maya.

"Your mother is right. Sometimes it takes a miracle. What do you want from Santa?" Logan asked.

"I'm not telling," André said. "I'll only tell Santa."

"Good plan," he said.

"I've heard if you tell too many people, it might not come true," André pointed out.

Logan carefully navigated his way up the winding mountain road. The town fell away, yielding to the fantastic scenery of the winter woods with sunshine peeking through. "Tell you what. We'll put up a special light display to give Santa a landing indicator. Just in case."

"If we live with you while Mom is away, who will take care of us?" asked Angelica.

"I will," said Logan.

"But who'll be the mom?"

"I can do everything a mom can do, except I'm a little better at certain things."

"What things?"

"Singing, for one. Snowboarding."

"Really? What else?"

"Cooking, for sure. Wait until you taste my homemade hot chocolate. You'll be like, Logan, you should make this for everybody on earth. Then there would be world peace. And global warming would end."

A giggle erupted from the backseat. "What else?"

"Armpit farting. I'll teach you how." As they drove past the resort on the way to the house, he pointed out the highlights. "That's the main lodge, where you can get a mean bowl of chili and the best French fries known to man. The ski school is on the end there. All the instructors wear neon lime-green parkas so you can find them. The chalet is like a hotel, and it's got an outdoor pool and two hot tubs."

"Can we use the pool?" asked André.

"Sure. We get special privileges because we run the place," said Logan.

"Sweet."

Logan liked having the kids with him, even though they reminded him of how very much he missed Charlie.

Pulling up in front of the garage of his place, he looked at it as a stranger might, and was struck by how large the residence was. It had been the original resort lodge, later repurposed for the owner's family and a number of resident workers. In recent years, it had served as a rustic B and B. It had the same old-world vibe as the rest of the resort, with shutters on the windows and brown painted railings all around, a chimney on each end of the building and lights glowing in the windows. When he was by himself in the big old place, he felt like a marble in a pinball machine, rolling around aimlessly. Having the kids with him was going to fill a void, for sure.

"Here we are," he said, getting out and gathering their bags. "Come on in, and I'll show you around."

"Who'll look after us when you're at work?" asked Angelica.

"Her name's Chelsea," said Logan. "She's coming up to meet you later this afternoon. You're going to love her." Chelsea was a friend left over from his married days. After the divorce, the friends tended to divvy themselves up: friends of the ex-bride, friends of the ex-groom. Chelsea was one of the few who straddled the line, staying in touch with both Logan and his ex.

"Your house is really big," said Angelica, stepping through the front door. She glanced up at her mother, who nodded reassuringly.

"Lots of room for everybody," Maya said.

Logan gave them a quick tour—the kitchen and great room, TV lounge and boardinghouse-sized dining room with a long table lined with seating for sixteen. He had never eaten at that table, not once. It made him feel ridiculous, one guy in all this space. The second and third stories featured bedrooms and bathrooms of all sizes, including a bunk room for eight.

"Here's where you'll sleep. When Charlie and his cousins get here, there'll be seven kids."

"Cool," said André, climbing like a monkey to a top bunk.

"That's a houseful," said Maya.

"I'm up for it," Logan told her.

She kept checking the screen of her phone. As they walked through the rest of the house, exploring nooks and crannies, dormer windows with views of the snowy woods, she seemed to grow more and more tense. He then gave them a quick tour of the resort.

In the main lodge, he spied Darcy Fitzgerald from afar, but she seemed busy with her friends or work associates, so he steered clear of them. Maya was clearly unraveling, and he needed to focus on getting the kids settled in. He led the way back to the house.

"Doing all right?" he murmured, holding the door for Maya.

"Freaking out," she said. "My doctor gave me something for anxiety, but the pill I took this morning is wearing off."

"Who's hungry?" he asked, turning to the kids.

"Starving," André said.

"Let's go make some sandwiches."

While the kids debated PB&J versus grilled cheese, Maya watched them with her heart in her eyes. Logan hurt for her. He ached all over, imagining how hard this was going to be. "Eye on the prize," he said to her in a low voice. "Keep that February release date in mind."

"It's the only thing keeping me sane," she said, and checked her phone again. "My ride back to the station should be here by now."

Adam Bellamy had volunteered to drive her back down to the station.

"He'll be here soon," Logan assured her.

"I almost want to get it over with."

Logan nodded. "The sooner you get going, the sooner you'll be back."

"Yes. Oh my God, how could I have been so stupid?" she asked, moving to the foyer, where the kids were out of earshot. "So, so stupid?"

"Hey, take it easy. You're only human."

"I thought I loved him. I kept thinking… I wasn't thinking. Love makes us do such stupid things. Why is that?"

"No clue. I've made my share of mistakes." He noticed her watching her kids, devouring them with her eyes. "I swear on my life, I'll take good care of them," he told her.

"I know, Logan. I can't thank you enough."

When her ride pulled up in front of the house, she wobbled a little on her feet, and Logan took her gently by the arm to steady her. "Easy," he murmured. "It's going to be all right."

"Hey, guys," she called to her kids, "I gotta go. Come give me hugs and kisses." Her face was stiff with the battle against tears as she sank down on one knee and opened her arms to them.

Logan's heart felt ripped in two as he watched her tell them goodbye, breathing deeply as though to inhale their essence. The kids clung, but relinquished their hold readily enough, innocent of her true destination.

"Be strong," he told her. "You're going to get through this."

She practically fled to Adam's truck, and she didn't look back. The kids stared after her, stricken.

Logan burst into action. "I've got a surprise for you two."

"What's that?"

"We're going to decorate Christmas cookies. Ever tried it?"

André looked skeptical. "You mean with icing and stuff?"

"Icing and sprinkles and everything good. You should see the stuff I bought. But these aren't just any cookies," Logan warned him.

"Yeah? Then what are they?"

"They're Walking Dead Christmas cookies." Logan went into zombie mode, with a stiff, swaying gait as he growled ominously, taking swipes at both kids.

Angelica squealed and they both ran for cover. Logan herded them into the kitchen, cranked up the music on the stereo and hoped for the best.

CHAPTER ELEVEN

———— ◆ ◆ ◆●◆●◆ ◆ ◆ ————

Darcy was distracted in the worst way when she met up with her team for the video shoot. Everyone bustled around with excitement, and normally she would share that energy, reveling in the sense that they were about to do something very, very cool. There were few things more exciting than being chosen to test gear and show it off for the client.

But today she had something else on her mind—Logan O'Donnell. She'd made a fool of herself over him at the train station. What a boneheaded move, showing up, unannounced, on a transparent pretext. And then to jump to the conclusion that he'd come to meet her at the station... She shuddered in horror and wondered how she was going to smile for the camera.

It was a total bummer to find out that her crush—her very inappropriate crush, as it turned out—was now dating a woman with kids. A woman who happened to look like Sofía Vergara. How nice for him.

Darcy felt like a grade-A idiot, chasing after him even though he hadn't called or sent a text or even a freaking one-line email since Florida. Bringing her team to Avalon for the shoot was hopelessly transparent, the equivalent of a junior high girl riding her bike past the cute boy's house to get his attention.

Come to think of it, she had tried that ploy in seventh grade and it hadn't worked then, either.

No wonder he hadn't called after Florida.

One kiss was hardly an obligation.

Even if it was an amazing kiss.

Even if it happened after a moment of shared magic, like when the dolphins appeared.

Even if it was the kind of kiss she couldn't stop thinking about, long after it was over.

"We're ready for you, Darcy," said the shoot coordinator. "Oh my gosh, you look amazing."

"Two hours of hair and makeup, and I'm a natural beauty," she said, flourishing her fashionably gloved hand.

"Ha-ha."

"Where do you want me?"

"Top of the long chairlift. The light's perfect today. This resort is ideal, by the way. Whose genius idea was it to shoot here instead of Lake Placid?"

"That would be me," Darcy said. *Me and my dumb ideas.*

"It's great. I'll bet we can wrap this up in a day."

That was a relief, Darcy thought as she rode the lift, sharing the ride up with a guy named Jeff, who said he was local and had been skiing Saddle Mountain since he was a kid.

"I like what the new owner's doing," he said, pushing his ski goggles up on his helmet.

I don't, thought Darcy. But to be polite, she said, "What's that?"

"He's keeping what people like about the resort and building on it, instead of changing everything all at once."

At the top of the lift, the crew waited with a woman called Brandi, who was Logan's überefficient assistant. She'd coordinated everything via email. She wore retro stirrup ski pants with a tight sweater, and she was pinup model pretty. She was soon joined by the resort's director of operations, a striking redhead in a green jumpsuit who was causing the videographer to drool. Apparently Logan liked surrounding himself with beautiful women. No wonder he wasn't interested in Darcy. Plain old girl-next-door Darcy.

"Ready?" asked the camera guy.

"Ready," Darcy said.

"Go make our gear look pretty," said the snowboard company rep.

"I'll do my best." Darcy was no supermodel, and she knew it. But when she was on the snow, she felt the same magical rush she felt when surfing. All the beauty of the world flowed through her, and the joy of the ride was a tangible thing, an element that could be seen and photographed. Today there was a bonus—the Christmas season had arrived.

It had always been her favorite time of year, and she was absolutely determined that no one steal the pleasure from her. Even though she'd bowed out of the whole family thing with the Fitzgeralds and the Collinses, the prospect of Christmas buoyed her spirits. Even her realization that Logan was dating someone was actually good news, Darcy decided. Now she didn't even have to decide whether or not she had a crush on him. There was no decision to be made except to remain happily single. It was further proof that she wasn't ready for a relationship of any sort, not at this juncture, and she was particularly not interested in a man with a kid.

Even if that man was wildly attractive and kissed like a dream lover.

So there, she thought, and pushed off the slope into a sunny, powder-dusted glade. It was a day made for floating. The sky was the color of a bluebird's wing. The hill was bejeweled by last night's snowfall, sparkling in the sun.

The joy of the ride overtook her. She could feel it in every movement, in the speed and in her stance. As she wove between the bare maple trees and birches, the cold wind on her face and the sun in her eyes made her feel alive, and full of the special energy of a brilliant winter day.

"Awesome," said Kyle Bohner, the videographer, who was on skis and down the hill from her, draped in camera equipment. "This is going to be rad."

The sunshine today was a rare gift, its rarity making it all the more special. She was able to forget everything as the day progressed. The crew had found her a backcountry run that was untouched, a powdery head wall of snow creating a brilliant natural sculpture on the cheek of the hill, bordered by craggy Catskills granite.

The client's signature gear, from the helmet to the snowboard's colorful underside, would look fantastic in this light, against the dramatic backdrop. They did shot after shot of Darcy floating down the steep terrain, popping up into some trick moves, including her signature Fitz Twist.

By the end of the shoot, the sheer volume of adrenaline pumping through her had chased away the awkward encounter at the train station. The sun was just riding the crest of Saddle Mountain when the shoot coordinator declared it a wrap. They all trooped into the resort lodge for a warm-up before packing up to return to the city. Darcy took off the helmet and was running her fingers through her hair when she spied Logan with his girlfriend and her kids, leaving the lodge. He was holding the door for them as they trooped out.

He looked up and spotted Darcy—how could he miss her, the season's bold color being apple-green—and offered a wave of the hand.

Whatever, she thought, waving back. She'd had a damn good day and she was not about to let him or anyone else ruin it.

She joined the crew in the bar, a rustic spot with Adirondack furniture and a big central river rock fireplace, good music streaming from hidden speakers. She chastised herself for getting her hopes up about Logan O'Donnell. She should've known better.

"Something's on your mind," said Bohner. "What are you thinking?"

"That if you never get your hopes up," she said, taking a sip of hot chocolate, "you'll never be disappointed."

"Ouch," he said. "Not sure I'm down with that."

"Sometimes you need to protect yourself," she said. "No, not sometimes. Always."

"But if you're always protecting yourself, you miss out on the good things as well as the bad."

"At least you're safe," she said.

"Interesting that you're willing to risk life and limb on the ski hill but not emotionally."

"I had no idea you were an armchair psychologist."

He laughed, the movement shaking his shoulder-length dreadlocks. "Just used to looking at people, I guess."

While they were settling the tab, she wondered if this little incident would change her plans for Christmas. She had been totally excited about spending the holidays with the O'Donnells. Fun in the snow, a small-town celebration, good food and good friends. The fact that Logan was apparently hooking up with a superattractive woman should not matter.

Oh, she wished it didn't matter.

Maybe she should change her plans. Maybe she should go overseas and find a country where they'd never heard of Christmas.

Her phone made a glissando sound, signaling an incoming text message.

She checked the screen. Her heart skipped a beat when she saw who the message was from—Logan O'Donnell. She felt very tentative as she touched the screen and read the message: FYI, she's not my girlfriend.

Just that. Nothing more. What the hell was he telling her this for? Was it the truth? Did he think it mattered?

She tapped out a response. FYI, neither am I.

PART SIX

❖◆❖◆❖❖❖

Twisted traditional cookies are always a hit with kids. Also, it makes good use of the broken ones. Everyone knows a broken cookie tastes just as good as a perfect one.

Walking Dead Sugar Cookies

2⅓ cups flour
1 teaspoon baking soda
1 teaspoon ground cinnamon
½ teaspoon ground nutmeg
¼ teaspoon salt
1¼ cups granulated sugar
1 cup (2 sticks) softened butter
1 egg
2 teaspoons vanilla extract
Cookie Icing:
1 cup confectioners' sugar
2 to 3 teaspoons milk
½ teaspoon vanilla extract
3 to 4 drops red food color

Beat granulated sugar and butter in large bowl with electric mixer until light and fluffy. Add egg and vanilla; mix well. Gradually beat in dry ingredients on low speed until well mixed. Refrigerate dough two hours or overnight until firm.

Preheat oven to 375°. Roll out dough on lightly floured surface to ¼-inch thickness. Cut into humanoid shapes with gingerbread-person cookie cutters. Place on parchment-lined baking sheets.

Bake 8 to 10 minutes or until lightly browned. Cool completely.

For the icing, mix all ingredients except food color. Divide white icing into two small cups, and use the red drops to dye one lot blood red.

Use the white icing to create mummy bandages, and the red to create wounds and bloody stumps. Use decorative sprinkles and red hots liberally.

[Source: Freely adapted from McCormick Spice collection.]

CHAPTER TWELVE

Logan was uncharacteristically nervous the day the O'Donnell clan arrived for the holidays. He was on edge, so he worked it off by shoveling the front walkway until he felt himself starting to sweat. The house looked good, he told himself. Not designer-magazine good like his folks' place in Florida, but like a Christmas house, from the icicle-draped roofline of the front porch to the strings of colored lights lining the gables to the fresh tree in the front window, which he and the kids had decorated the day of Charlie's arrival.

It would be the first Christmas he'd hosted for the family, and he wanted it to be just right. The big house at Saddle Mountain had plenty of room for everyone. It would be a relief to fill the upper rooms with guests. The place was just too damn big.

They all pulled into the driveway at once. Three SUVs

disgorged his parents, his sisters and their families, on a frigid day the week before Christmas.

"Come on, Charlie, André, Angelica," Logan called. "Get your coats and boots on, and you can help with the luggage."

"Excellent," said Charlie. "The cousins are here." He was supercharged with excitement. They all tumbled outside into the bright, cold day. There were greetings and hugs all around.

His niece Bernie bounded through the deep snow. "You live in Christmas-land, Uncle Logan."

He grinned and spread his arms wide. "I guess I do. You're going to love it here."

"Are you kidding? I already do." She and her sister Nan toted their pink backpacks up the walk.

His mother took charge the way she always did. Once his parents had agreed to spend the holidays here instead of in Florida, Marion O'Donnell embraced her matriarchal duties. She directed everyone to their rooms and brought tons of decorations in big plastic tubs.

Logan's heart flipped over when he saw Darcy Fitzgerald walking up to his house, toting a big duffel bag. The smile she gave him was guarded.

"Hey," he said.

"Hey yourself. Hope you don't mind taking in a stray for the holidays." She offered a bright smile.

Damn. He liked her smile. "Are you kidding? Some of my best friends are strays. Come on in where it's warm. I've got hot cocoa and spiced cider."

"Two of my favorite things."

He wanted to know about *all* of her favorite things, but he felt his chances slipping away. He hadn't seen or spoken to her since their brief encounter at the train station. Their quick exchange of text messages had left him in a quandary. He had simply wanted her to understand that Maya and he were definitely not an item. The way she was regarding him now was a bit cryptic, just like the text she'd sent him. On second thought, the text wasn't cryptic at all. She didn't want to be his girlfriend.

Once everyone was in the house, chaos ruled. The kids ran around exploring, admiring the tree he had put up, and sorting out the bunk bed situation in the kids' room. André and Angelica seemed to be doing all right so far. It was incredibly gratifying to see them embracing the holidays, far from the city, far from their mom. They each had a part in the annual Christmas pageant at Heart of the Mountains Church. When Maureen and Eddie Haven, the pageant directors, heard Angelica sing, they immediately asked if she'd like to do a solo, "Sleep My Baby," on Christmas morning. The little girl had been practicing nonstop.

They were already taking ski lessons at the resort, too. André was a natural, eagerly learning the new sport. Angelica was more cautious, but happy to try getting down the hill on her skis, making little snowplow turns.

Charlie had arrived a couple days before, and the moment he'd seen his son, Logan's world had felt complete. He was grateful for the ease with which they fell into their roles, like putting on warm, comfortable boots. Having André and Angelica there was great, lending a sense of family energy the house had been missing. Charlie hadn't been out on the slopes yet but was dying to go. Tomorrow morning, Logan had promised.

Dinner was a free-for-all, supervised by the sisters and his mom. Logan's famous chili was the main dish, and he was gratified to see how fast it disappeared.

"I'm proud of your cooking," his mother said. "You're really great at it."

"Hear that, Charlie? I'm a great cook."

"Good to know," replied Charlie.

"Be sure you tell Santa how good I've been."

"Santa," squealed the nieces. "When do we get to see Santa?"

"Tomorrow, after skiing," Logan said. "The big guy has a life-size gingerbread cottage in town, and then there's a Christmas parade."

"I want everything for Christmas," announced his nephew Fisher.

"You can't have everything," said his brother, Goose.

"But I can *want* everything."

Logan chuckled. "Yo, I like the way you think."

"How come your name's Goose?" asked Angelica.

"It's a nickname, on account of Mom's favorite movie."

"*Top Gun*. She watches it at night when she thinks we're asleep, and cries every time Goose crashes his plane," Fisher explained.

"Hey," said India, blushing bright red.

"You are so busted," said Bilski.

"What's your real name?" asked Angelica.

"Reginald, and you can blame my dad. It's *his* dad's name." Goose made a funny face.

"My real name is Emile," Charlie interjected.

Logan touched his chest. "Don't blame me. I didn't get a vote. I'm just glad you have a cool middle name."

"I'm gonna tell them at ski school tomorrow to call you Reginald," said Fisher.

"Are not," Goose retorted.

"Watch me."

"Nobody's doing anything if you kids don't get to bed and simmer down," said India. "I'll take bedtime duty tonight."

Groans erupted, but with impressive efficiency, she herded them all down the hall to the bunk room. In the ensuing quiet, Logan added logs to the fire and put on soft, jazzy music. His father made Irish coffee for everyone, and they all sat around the fire, relaxing.

"Welcome to my new digs," Logan said, raising his mug. "Welcome to my new life."

"Hear, hear!" said Bilski. "Your new life is awesome."

"Thanks." Some days, like today, Logan was absolutely convinced of the awesomeness. Other days, like when Charlie was in a different time zone and Logan rattled around alone in the old, rambling, too-big house, he was not so sure.

"So, how is the resort business going?" his father asked. Of course he would ask. To Al O'Donnell, business was life.

"It's a lot of work, but I have a fantastic team," Logan said. "Karsten's director of mountain operations stayed on. So did most of the senior staff. I get expert advice in all areas." What he wouldn't tell his father was that the financials were precarious. At the end of every day, he felt himself teetering on the fiscal cliff, trying to juggle the overhead with the revenues. Yet somehow he stayed on top of things and made it work. Operations were chugging along. Thanks to a dumping of snow from heaven itself, conditions were great and the daily till kept the cash flow going.

"So, are the revenues just pouring in?" his father persisted.

"Al." Logan's mother sent her husband a warning look. "Now is not the time."

"Pouring in, that's right," said Logan.

"It seems like such a lot of work," China said.

"I'm not afraid of hard work."

"Are you taking care of yourself?" his mother asked. "You look too skinny."

"I'm not skinny, Mom."

"And pale," she added.

"It's the dead of winter," he said. "Everyone is pale."

He tried to keep it light. The dynamics of the family never

changed. Or rarely did. People reverted to the old roles carved out a generation ago. His parents expected him to fail. As a dumb kid, he had cheerfully obliged them, time and time again; right up to getting a girl pregnant in high school.

Now they simply expected him to screw up no matter what he did, no matter how much time had passed.

"It's working out," he said. "Don't worry, I'm not going to lose my shirt. I'd never do that to Charlie."

"Dad thinks owning a ski resort is a guy's fantasy, like owning a sports bar or building hot rods," India explained to Darcy. "Fun to pursue, but no way to make a living."

"Anything that's fun is immediately suspect, right, Dad?" asked China.

"Girls," her mother said. "That's no way to talk to your father."

Logan glanced over at Darcy. "Aren't you glad you're here? Lucky you, getting a ringside seat to our family feud."

She laughed. "Sounds more or less like my own family, except we've got more girls." She turned to Logan's father. "My firm brought one of our biggest clients to Saddle Mountain for a photo shoot. It was fantastic. I can understand why anyone would be suspicious that something so much fun could also be profitable."

"I see," said Al. "And how did the shoot turn out?"

"One of the best we've done all year. The client was thrilled, and Saddle Mountain gets a lot of exposure."

"You should show us the footage," said India. "We'd all like to see."

"I don't know…" Darcy ducked her head.

Logan was intrigued to see her acting reluctant about it. "Come on," he said. "It'll give everybody a preview of the resort."

She hesitated. "It's very commercial, aimed at selling gear."

"But it was filmed right here," said Logan.

"Okay, does your TV have a USB port?" When he nodded, she said, "I'll be right back."

Nice one, thought Logan as she fetched her wallet and pulled out a USB drive. She'd managed to deflect the conversation about resort finance by getting everyone to shift gears.

"All right," she said, "barring any technical difficulties..." She slotted in the thumb drive.

"Did you really bring work with you?" Logan's mother scolded.

"Just a little," said Darcy. "There's a big outdoor retailer trade show in January, so I've got some deadlines." Logan switched on the TV with the remote, and the client's logo came up along with adrenaline-pumped music. "This is a montage with video that will be featured on the client's website and in their retail stores. It's going to go live this weekend."

The opening sequence showed the mountain on a bluebird day, the peaks stark against the crisp sky. The broad panorama narrowed, homing in on a grove of birch trees. There was a panning shot of a deer, its head turned toward the camera, eyes alert with caution, before it turned and fled over the crest of the ridge, tail flipped up to show its white underside. The movement startled a brown-and-white hawk into sudden flight. Almost simultaneously, the scene dissolved into a sequence of a snowboarder exploding straight up into the sky as though shot from a cannon. A trail of sunlit snow sparkled in her wake; then she landed in a spray of knee-deep powder, then floated along through a forest glade.

"That's Darcy, by the way," India told her parents.

"The snowboarder?" her mother asked. "Heavenly days, really?"

"She's good, huh?" India said.

"Good" did not begin to cover it. She was phenomenal,

gliding through the snowy wilderness as if, for her, gravity was optional. She embodied everything a snow sport should be— fun and colorful, graceful and exhilarating. Saddle Mountain had never looked better.

At the conclusion of the presentation, Bilski leaned over to China and said, "Let's take snowboard lessons."

"Better yet," said China, "let's go shopping for all that cool gear."

"My client would love to hear that," Darcy said.

"The resort looks lovely," said Logan's mother. "I'm glad we're here for the holidays. Truly."

"Thanks, Mom. It's going to be great, you'll see," Logan promised her. "It's going to be awesome."

"I hope those weren't my brother's famous last words," said India after the parents had gone to bed.

Darcy, who was with her in the kitchen washing up the Irish coffee mugs, asked, "What, does disaster follow him?"

India chuckled. "I guess we'll find out." She reached for a glass jar and took off the top. "Christmas cookie?"

"Thanks." Darcy helped herself. It was cut out in the shape of a gingerbread man, though it was missing a limb and had only one cinnamon candy eye. The red-and-white icing resembled bloody bandages.

"Those are the Walking Dead Christmas cookies," said Logan, carrying a few more dishes into the kitchen. "The kids and I made them."

Darcy took a bite. "Oh my gosh. This might be the best cookie I ever ate."

"I bet you say that to all the guys."

"I swear, I've never said that to a guy in my life."

"He's good, too, huh?" said India.

Darcy savored another bite. The cookie was tender and

delicately spiced. It tasted exactly like Christmas. "I think he knows it."

"He doesn't mind hearing people say so." Logan dimmed the kitchen lights and switched on the yard lights.

She gazed out the big picture window of the kitchen while polishing off the cookie. "It's snowing again," she whispered.

"He doesn't mind hearing those words, either," he said.

"Everybody loves the phrase 'it's snowing.' There's always been some kind of magic in those words."

"Speaks to the kid in all of us," India said. "Snow days, playing outside. In fact, I'm going to check on the bunk room and make sure lights out really means lights out. Then I'm off to bed. Night, you guys."

"Night, India. Ski tomorrow morning?" Darcy asked.

"Only if you promise not to lead me over a cliff."

"I would never."

Darcy felt so grateful to be where she was tonight, relaxing among friends. But there was also an awkward element. Logan's presence, just a few feet away, tantalized her. She felt confused by him, and full of questions. Maya's kids were here, so where was their mother?

None of your business. She turned her attention to the window again and watched the big flakes gently coming down and settling on the pristine yard. An age-old yearning pressed at her chest; she was a kid again, with her nose pressed to the window. "It's so beautiful."

"Grab your coat and boots," said Logan. "Let's go for a walk."

"Really? You read my mind."

"That's one of my superpowers, didn't you know?"

They bundled up in the mud room off the kitchen—down jackets, mittens, boots, a lantern and a flashlight.

"You'll need these." He handed her a pair of lightweight snowshoes. "Know how to put them on?"

She grinned. "I gear-tested this exact model."

"Man. You'll have to tell me more about being a spon-sored athlete."

"Sometimes it feels like turning work into play. Other times it's more like turning play into work. So I definitely prefer the former."

He handed her a set of poles and donned a backpack.

"What's in the pack?" she asked.

"A project. You can help me with it."

"What kind of project?"

"Come on. I'll show you."

They stepped outside together. The cold air and snow-flakes touched her face, and she welcomed the freshness, tilt-ing back her head.

"When it's clear, you can count the stars," said Logan.

"I feel a million miles away from the city."

To the right and down a snow-covered track was a cluster of lights, the center of the resort. A couple of vehicles were just leaving the parking lot, their taillights making a cautious red line down the road.

"Last call at the Powder Room is at nine o'clock," Logan said. "It gets pretty quiet after that. Let's go this way." They set off in the opposite direction of the resort. The lantern beam shone on a forest glade of striated birch trees. There was a moon, though it was a weak one, its glow diffused by snowfall.

"I love this," she said. "I love the silence and the peace."

"No regrets about not going to my folks' place in Florida?"

"I'm kind of a fan of winter." The snowshoes rode atop the featherlight snow. She savored the cold on her cheeks, the pumping of her heart as they hiked through the shadows.

"I noticed. You were fantastic in that video."

"All in a day's work." She looked over at him. "Kidding. I

have a day like that once in a blue moon. Most days, I'm stuck in meetings or in my cubicle like anybody else."

"No cubicles here," he said.

"You're living the dream," she said. "Maybe that's why your father is so suspicious."

"Yeah, according to him, it's only worth doing if it makes you miserable."

She wondered about his relationship with his father, and why things were strained. She wanted to hear more. She wanted to know everything about him.

The birch grove led to a perfect, unmarked field of white with a tall evergreen. "In the summer," he said, "this is a bird meadow, and there's a sports court over there."

"You'd never know it. This is just beautiful, Logan. It looks like a Christmas card."

"That's what I thought," he said.

A shadow fluttered past. Startled, she clutched his arm. "Hey, look!" It was an owl, swooping through the trees with wings spread wide. She watched, mesmerized, until it disappeared into darkness. "That was amazing," she said.

He nodded. "An owl in winter. First time I ever saw something like that."

"Really?"

"The dolphins were a first for me, too. I have really good luck with wildlife when I'm with you."

For no good reason, she felt ridiculously gratified to hear him say so.

"Warm enough?" he asked her.

"Plenty, thanks."

"So, here's my idea for the project. We're going to string lights all over that big evergreen over there. The one standing all by itself." He pointed out the tree in the middle of the clearing.

"I like it. There's electricity?"

"Yes. In the summer, there are lights for the sports court. There's an outlet at the base of the tree."

"Cool."

"Thought I'd surprise the kids. We could tell them it's Santa's landing strip."

"What else would it be?"

They crossed the meadow, making plate-sized tracks across the powder. Logan left his snowshoes at the base of the tree. "Did you bring a ladder?" Darcy asked. "This thing is, like, twenty feet tall."

"I can climb it."

"You're not serious."

He grinned, unzipping his backpack, and donned a head-lamp. "Watch me."

"You *are* serious. Also crazy."

"The good kind of crazy. I'll climb up and string the lights on the way down. You stand by and keep things untangled and shine the light."

He cleared the lower branches with ease. The upper ones were closer together, bowing with his weight. "Do me a favor and don't fall," she said.

"Not planning on it. Although there's so much new snow, it would be a soft landing."

She positioned herself beneath him, aiming the flashlight beam at the top. He disturbed a snow-laden branch, creating an avalanche that fell on her before she could move out of the way.

"Lovely," she said, rubbing the fresh snow out of her face.

"Sorry," he replied. "Almost there." He climbed until the branches thinned, and reached up to clip the light string close to the top. Then he began his descent, paying out the string of lights from his backpack. "This is what's known as extreme decorating."

"I must say, stringing lights on a tree in the wilderness was not the first thing I thought of when you invited me for a walk."

"You don't mind." It wasn't a question.

"You barely know me. How do you know whether or not I mind?"

"Another one of my superpowers." He worked methodically while she held the beam steady, lighting the way for him. At one point, he went too far out on a limb and it bowed ominously. "Watch it," she said. "That one won't hold you."

There was a loud cracking sound, and he came down like a sack of coal. Her heart leaped to her throat. "Oh my gosh, Logan." She waded through the snow and dropped to her knees beside him. "Are you okay?"

He was practically drowned in the deep snow of the tree well. She could tell he was assessing himself—back, neck, extremities.

"Not a scratch," he informed her, lifting his head. "Superpowers did the trick."

She rose from her knees and held out her hand. "I think there are enough lights on the tree. Let's plug them in and see if they work."

"Sure, they work. I tested them before we came out." He took her hand, but his weight and the soft deep snow unbalanced her, and she fell forward against him, the snow caving in around them.

"Sorry about that," he said. "Damn. This is not going well."

She climbed out of the hole and fetched his snowshoes so he could do the same. If not for the tight cuffs of her sleeves and the muffler around her neck, she would be extremely uncomfortable at this moment.

He found the end of the light string amid the lower branches. "You all right?" he asked as he worked.

"I've survived worse in the snow."

"You'll have to tell me about it one day." He worked quickly, brushing the snow away from a pipe running up the tree trunk with an outlet at the top. "All right. Ready for the lighting?"

"Do you want to do the honors or shall I?"

"You've earned it, putting up with my antics."

"Is that what these are?" she asked. "Antics?"

"I'm good at antics. I excel at antics."

"Okay, I'm connecting the power," she said. She plugged it in and the tree came to life with color. "Success," she exclaimed.

"Hey, how about that?" In the glow of the lights, he looked boyish and wildly attractive. She wished he would tackle her in the snow right now and cover her face with kisses, but he kept his distance. "Glad it worked. Otherwise I risked life and limb for nothing."

"It's been a productive evening," she said, "but I think I need to drink some more."

"Let's go back to the house. I'll make you more of my famous hot chocolate."

"I was talking about a grown-up drink."

"I can put a shot of peppermint schnapps in it."

"Now you're talking."

They crossed the clearing and turned back to admire the tree. It was a winter masterpiece, the lights shimmering through the falling snow.

"It looks like Christmas," she said. "Exactly like a child's dream of Christmas. Good job, Logan."

"Now Santa knows where to land. Let's head back." In a movement that seemed unstudied and natural, he placed his hand at the small of her back and steered her along the path they'd made.

His touch felt good. Too good. She stopped and turned to him. "So, about that text you sent me. She's not your girl-friend."

He hesitated. "Maya, you mean."

"Yes." She hated herself for being the first to bring it up, but she had to know.

"Yeah, I need to explain about her," he stated. "Like I said, we're not... It's like I said in the text."

Oh boy. She wasn't sure what to think of that. If he was in-volved with someone, then she had no dilemma. But if he was available, she would have to admit she was attracted to him. That she wanted to know more about him. That she liked it when he touched her. That she thought about his kiss all the time. That even after the misery of her divorce, she wanted to fall in love again.

A long silence stretched out. It was so quiet she could hear individual snowflakes ever so gently striking the fabric of her parka.

"And the text *you* sent me?" he prompted. "Does it mean you're seeing someone?"

She studied his face, painted in shadows and in the glow from the tree. "I'm seeing you," she whispered, brushing back her hood and looking up at him.

"And I guess I'm seeing you."

"What are we doing, Logan?"

"Getting to know each other."

"Fair enough." A part of her wanted to stay right here in this winter glade with him, kissing him, warming their lips and their bodies together. She forced herself to take a step back. "Let's go inside. You promised me a hot chocolate."

"I'm a man of my word."

They made their way back to the house and took off their snowshoes, jackets and boots. Logan added a couple of logs to the fire and warmed up the hot chocolate. She stood at the window, cupping her hands on the glass to admire the newly lit tree outside. She felt in that moment that life was fresh and new. Coming here was a good idea. Good for her. But was it good for her family? She kept catching herself wondering what her sisters were doing now. Did they miss her? What were they saying about her?

"What are you thinking about?"

"My family."

"Ah. Families." His tone conveyed a deep understanding of the concept. He carefully poured the cocoa into mugs and, true to his word, added a shot of schnapps to hers. "Are you in trouble for ditching them at Christmas?"

"A bit. They'll get over it. It was one thing for me to ditch them at Thanksgiving," she said. "That's a low-stakes holiday. But Christmas is a different story."

"Come here. Have a seat by the fire." They settled into a big cushy Chesterfield sofa with a deep seat and rolled armrests. In front of them, the logs crackled and glowed.

She sank gratefully into its comfort, and he handed her a warm mug.

"Cheers," he said, touching the rim of his cup to hers. "Taste it. You're going to love it so much you'll never let me go."

"You are never serious," she said, though she felt an undeniable thrill at his words. The chocolate was warm and creamy and rich, with just a touch of peppermint. "You're right," she said, savoring the deliciousness. "I want to keep you forever."

"You're never serious, either," he said. "I like that about you."

She took another sip. "I tried serious. It didn't work out so well for me."

"Tell me about your family. What are you missing out on? What did my sister pull you away from?"

"I'm going to miss being present for my sister Lydia's big announcement. She's the first Fitzgerald girl to be expecting a baby."

"Sounds like you already know about the announcement. Congrats to your sister, by the way."

"Thanks."

"So, what else will you miss?"

"A generation of tradition. But after my divorce, those traditions didn't really work so well for me. In a nutshell, my parents and the parents of my ex are best friends."

"Yeah, but blood is thicker than water."

"It gets complicated. My parents and the Collinses considered it one of the great achievements of their life that the two Collins boys married two of the Fitzgerald girls—me and Huntley, and Lydia and Badgley. The marriages were meant to knit our clans together forever."

"And then you and Huntley split up."

"Yes."

"He cheated?"

She did a double take. "How did you know?"

"A hunch," he said. "It's always my first guess. Here's another guess—you didn't tell your family about the cheating."

"And how did you know *that?*"

"Because if you told them, it'd be the end of your knit-together Christmases."

He got it. She felt a sense of relief that finally someone understood. "I couldn't tell my family about the cheating," she said. "I mean, I could have, but it would have been a terrible thing to do to my sister. Lydia's a Collins. They're expecting their first baby, and she wants to make a big announcement at the holidays. I didn't want to ruin anything for her."

SUSAN WIGGS

"You're a martyr."

"No. Just a sister, although in some families, it's the same thing." She drank more of the hot chocolate. It was so delicious she wanted it to last forever.

"And did your breakup cause the world as we know it to end?" he asked.

"I tried not to let that happen. We were supposed to be civil about it all. At first, I did try. But instead, I discovered I couldn't stand to be anywhere near him. I had to break away, and India was nice enough to throw me a life preserver. What about your breakup?" she boldly asked, then regrouped. "Sorry, is it weird that we're sitting here talking about our divorces? Isn't that supposed to be a no-no?"

He shrugged. "I like talking to you. I'll tell you anything you want to know."

She narrowed her eyes. "Was cheating a factor?"

"Nope. She got pregnant our senior year of high school. At that age, we didn't know ourselves, much less each other. Daisy and I, we gave it a shot. For Charlie's sake, we gave it our best shot. But we were never a match. The breakup sucked for me, but made me admit we were both lying to ourselves. Anyway, Charlie's the best thing I ever did, although I could have planned it better."

Kids, she thought. The eternal complication.

"I need to tell you something," he said. "It's kind of personal."

"I can handle personal."

"I'm not the once-burned-twice-shy type. I want to fall in love again. I want to be committed, to create a family. I want Charlie to have that sense of security, maybe even brothers and sisters one day."

You're barking up the wrong tree, then. She didn't say anything, though. When they were getting to know each other, they didn't need to draw a line. Later, she thought. If things progressed, she'd tell him later.

"Ooookay," she said, forcing a smile.

"And just so you know," he said, taking their mugs and setting them on a side table, "your ex is an idiot."

No longer forcing the smile, she wondered how to snuggle closer to him on the sofa without being too obvious about it. He just looked so inviting, with that tousled red hair, those big shoulders. "You, sir, are preaching to the choir."

"I need to tell you about Maya," he said abruptly. "I think you might have questions."

"I might." So much for snuggling. She instantly wondered if they had a past.

"She's just a friend," he stated as if reading her mind. "We met when our kids became friends at summer camp. Charlie and André really hit it off."

"Where is she?" asked Darcy. "Is she coming up for the holidays?" Her stomach curdled. There was a spare twin bed in her room. Was she going to have to share it with Sofía Vergara's twin?

"Unfortunately, no."

Whew, thought Darcy. "That's too bad," she said. *Liar.*

"She had to go away for a while. Until February, actually."

"She's not going to be with her kids at Christmas?"

"She can't. See…" He planted his elbows on his knees and stared into the fire. "She got in some trouble earlier this year. Legal trouble."

"Oh gosh."

"Made a bad decision. Her kids' father is not a good guy. He was running drugs and convinced her to make a delivery for him. It's always just a simple transaction, right? That's what they always say."

"And she got caught holding the bag."

"Yes. She could have been sentenced up to twenty-one months, but she got sixty days instead, so that's a lot better. The bad news is, her sentence spans Christmas."

"So that's what she was doing at the train station. Dropping off her kids."

"Yep. We're trying to make it as easy as possible for them."

"Wow. That's incredible of you to take the kids." What a kind thing to do, she thought. She wondered if, under similar circumstances, she would be that kind.

"I just thought about Charlie. If I were facing a similar situation, I would hope someone would do the same for him."

"How are they doing?"

"Pretty well. They think she went away for work. The little girl, Angelica, does, anyway. André... I think he suspects. Maya's a full-time nanny to a family in New York. She *was*. They've let her go, so she'll have to start over after her release. Anyway, that's the story of Maya and me."

"I am really impressed," she said. "You're incredibly generous."

"Doesn't feel that way. I want to make sure the kids have the best Christmas possible."

"So far so good," she said. "They seem really excited to be here."

"Angelica still believes in Santa Claus, a hundred percent. So when they all go see Santa tomorrow, we need to pay attention to what she wants for Christmas. Because no matter what it is, she's getting it."

"Even if it's a live unicorn or wings that work?"

"Even if. Same goes for André and Charlie. They're true believers, still. I made myself a promise that I'd give them Christmas with all the trimmings."

"That's really cool, Logan." She settled back, enjoying the play of the fire in the grate. "They're lucky kids."

"I'm the lucky one. I'm crazy about Charlie, and the other two are a bonus." He turned to her on the sofa. "That's what you are, too."

"A bonus?"

He gently brushed the hair back from her cheek. "Yeah. I was happy enough that my family came up for the holidays. The fact that you came along... Score."

That was all it took. He kissed her then—at last—warm chocolate and heat from the fire. When he touched his mouth to hers, it felt wonderful—fresh and exhilarating, filling her with the taste of something new, something that might be hope.

"I like kissing you," he said, lifting his mouth from hers. "I like it a lot."

"Then you should do it some more."

There was a part of her—okay, all of her—that wanted to peel all his clothes off and go at it all night long. The rush of desire was powerful and unexpected. She felt a huge sense of relief, because she hadn't felt that burning hot need in so long she had started to worry that it might be gone. A thing of the past. But in Logan's arms, it was alive and well.

She was alive and well. She'd thought she was dead inside, but here was proof that passion could come back to life in the blink of an eye, in the time it took to light a Christmas tree, in the time it took to fall into a well of snow. *Thank God*, she thought. *Thank God*.

He pulled back again and gazed down at her. "That was nice," he said softly. "*You* are nice."

She sighed and stretched, feeling amazed and excited, and surprisingly comfortable with him. "Thank you for saving my Christmas."

"We've got a week to go. Still plenty of time to ruin it. But I'm not planning on that."

"Okay. I trust you."

He leaned in for another kiss. And it was the softest, sweetest kiss imaginable, the kind of kiss that set her on fire. She wanted more, deeper; she put a hand on his chest and was gratified to feel his heart racing even faster than hers. This thing that had initially seemed so impossible now felt exactly right.

She curled her hand into a fist and felt him tighten his arms around her. She wanted the kiss to go on forever, to lead to something more—

"Dad." Charlie's voice shattered the moment.

Darcy and Logan broke apart like a pair of guilty teenagers, leaving a void in the middle of the sofa.

"Hey," said Logan, "what are you doing up?"

"I can't sleep." Charlie looked straight at Darcy. "I have jet lag. It's an hour earlier in Oklahoma."

She knew that look. It was the look of a kid who did not want to share his parent, not with anyone.

"Your dad has the perfect remedy," she said, getting up. "Hot chocolate. Guaranteed to make you sleepy."

"Really?"

She yawned elaborately. "It made me sleepy. I'm heading off to bed right now, as a matter of fact." She shared a look with Logan. He was all silent apology and frustrated desire. "See you guys in the morning," she said.

As she was going up the stairs to her room, she heard Logan say, "Dude."

"It's not my fault I can't sleep, Dad."

"I mean, dude. Really?"

PART SEVEN

————◆◆◆————

Everyone has a favorite hot chocolate recipe. But this one is the best. It has a secret ingredient. No, it's not cinnamon or cayenne pepper or anything weird. It's just cornstarch. Don't judge.

Seductive Hot Chocolate

1½ cups half-and-half
1½ teaspoons cornstarch
Sugar to taste
3 ounces fine-quality dark chocolate, chopped or grated
A shot of peppermint schnapps or espresso (optional)

In a bowl, combine a bit of the half-and-half with the cornstarch, whisking until smooth. Place the remaining half-and-half in a small saucepan over medium heat. Bring to a simmer; don't let it boil. When the half-and-half begins to bubble around the edges, whisk in the sugar. Whisk in the cornstarch mixture until the half-and-half thickens slightly, usually less than a minute. Remove from the heat and quickly whisk in the chocolate until very smooth. Pour into two cups. Add a shot of schnapps or espresso, if desired.

[Source: Adapted from Italian Food Forever (website)]

CHAPTER THIRTEEN

Charlie woke up first, just as it was getting light outside. He lay quietly in his bunk and took stock of his room-mates. There were André and Angelica, spending Christmas here because their mom was away. Then there were his girl cousins, Bernie and Nan, in a bunk they'd already decorated with sparkly beads and a few ornaments.

Fisher and Goose, the twins, were in the double lower bunk under Charlie. Peering over the edge of his bed, Charlie saw that they lay in a tangled heap, as if they'd fought each other and both lost.

It was fun to wake up in a roomful of kids, like being back at camp. At the base in Oklahoma, Charlie had his own room. His mom said he'd have his own room in Japan, too, but she warned that it was going to be kind of small—everything in Japan was smaller—with barely enough space for one kid, let alone seven.

He knew both his mom and his dad would say how lucky he was to have the chance to live in two such different places. Most kids had the same house, same room, same neighborhood all the time. So living in two completely different places was lucky.

Of course, deep down inside, Charlie knew that was something parents said to their kids to help them get over Divorce.

And even deeper down inside, Charlie knew that lucky really meant he didn't get any choice in the matter, so he might as well get used to it.

It meant waking up in the morning and missing his mom, and even his little sister, and knowing they were a zillion miles away. And it meant feeling the same way about his dad when he was with his mom. And it meant knowing things were never going to change, because this was his life whether he liked it or not.

But he felt even more sorry for André and Angelica. Their mom was away, and they had no family at all for Christmas. It must feel awful.

This morning, though, it was not so hard to feel a bubble of happiness about pretty much everything. He could look out the window and see nothing but deep snow and deep woods, the perfect picture for Christmas. And he could look across the room and see his best friend, André, just waking up and blinking in the snow-bright light.

"Psst," whispered Charlie. "Hey."

"Hey," said André, sitting up and rubbing his eyes. His hair looked like a curly mop. André called it nappy hair and said it was on account of him being mixed race. Not biracial like Charlie's aunt Sonnet, but really mixed. He had a grandmother from French Haiti and a grandfather from Mexico, and his other grandma was black. He said he didn't know anything about his other grandpa.

All André had ever said about his dad was that he was white. And mean.

"What's that smell?" André inhaled, his eyes no longer sleepy.

Charlie inhaled, too. Coffee and bacon and something sweet. "That," he said, "is the smell of good news for us. It's the smell of epic breakfast."

"Yeah? What's an epic breakfast?"

"Every kind of good food in the whole world. My dad likes to make epic breakfast before a ski day. Let's go down and I'll show you."

They were both wearing their ninja pajamas, so they fell into their roles as easily as donning their cloaks of invisibility. They sneaked out of their bunks, moving as stealthily as ninja warriors on a mission. The other kids didn't stir, for André and Charlie were as silent as the wind itself. Out the door and down the hall they went, passing the closed doors of the other guestrooms.

Charlie was still getting used to his dad's new place on the mountain. It was definitely the biggest house they had ever lived in, even bigger than his grandparents' place in Florida or their house in Montauk on Long Island. This house, his dad had explained, had been built as the resort's first guest lodge, but it was converted into a house when the bigger hotel had been built.

André motioned for Charlie to crouch down to maintain their stealthy approach. Christmas carols were playing on the radio, and Dad was singing along. Peeking around the corner, Charlie spotted Aunt India and her friend Darcy. Although judging by last night, Darcy was turning into Dad's friend. As in his girlfriend.

His dad had had lots of girlfriends since the divorce. There was Daphne, who had been cool, with pink hair and tattoos, but she and Dad didn't work out because she declared that she was Never Having Kids. Then there was Karma, who taught yoga and was a vegan and had to leave the house whenever Dad cooked bacon. Charlie had liked Tina, who was fun and goofy but she had two bratty daughters who were mean to Charlie behind their mom's back.

After that, Dad got busy with other stuff, like moving up to the mountain and taking over the ski area, and there was no more dating. That was probably about to change. Charlie wasn't sure how he felt about that, but like everything else in the grown-up world, his opinion didn't count.

He and André slithered closer. The smell of bacon lured them down the hallway. "Deck the Halls" came on the radio and all three of them—his dad, India and Darcy—sang along.

Charlie spotted the target—a tray of bacon just off the grill, sitting on a platter lined with paper towels—and they belly-crawled toward it.

"'Don we now our gay apparel,'" sang the radio.

"I love that line," said Darcy.

"But what's gay apparel, anyway?" asked Aunt India.

"I think," said Dad, "it looks like something like this." And without warning, a large hand swooped down, grabbing Charlie around the waist and hoisting him to his feet.

Charlie yelled and started laughing. "We were trying to sneak up on you," he said.

"Because we're starving," added André.

"Then we'd better feed you warriors," said Dad.

They climbed up on a pair of bar stools at the counter and regarded the feast. "See what I mean?" Charlie murmured to André. "Epic."

In addition to the bacon, there was a big dish of berries and a tray of eggnog pancakes, which Dad only made at Christmastime. The maple syrup was warm and served in a pitcher, and there were big glasses of cold milk to drink. There was cereal, fruit, eggs and potatoes, a tray of pastries and bright red berry juice. Charlie was in heaven.

"He said your breakfast is epic," said Darcy.

"He's right," said Dad. "Try this." He fed her a bite of egg-nog pancake, dipped in syrup.

She made a funny face, eyes crossed, hand over heart. "It's like I've seen the face of God," she said.

Darcy was funny. She seemed nice. If she was going to end up being Dad's girlfriend, Charlie figured he was okay with that. Of course if they stayed together, she would become the stepmonster. His friends who had stepmoms called them step-monsters. It was a risk.

At the moment, he wasn't going to worry about it because the breakfast was delicious and the day was shaping up to be a total blast.

"First," Dad said, "we are going to hit the slopes."

"Hit them with what?" asked André.

"Ha-ha," Charlie said. "He means skiing or snowboarding."

"I only had a couple of lessons," said André. "I'm not very good at it."

"I've got you all set up for Powder Hounds. They'll help you out," said Dad.

Finally a sport André didn't dominate. In all other sports, he was the best.

"Later, we're going to town for a little shopping, to watch the tree lighting and the Christmas parade. You're all going to see Santa, too," said Aunt India.

"Do you guys believe in Santa?" Bernie demanded.

The song on the radio switched to "Jingle Bell Rock."

And there it was. The horrible question Charlie did not want to think about. Yet it was the one that pressed like a big invisible weight on his mind.

Here was the thing. There were some kids in his grade who claimed there was no such thing as Santa Claus. And they were always the cool kids, so if you said you did believe, then you were toast because they totally made fun of you and made you feel like a complete idiot.

But Charlie couldn't *not* believe. He knew, deep down in the most secret part of himself, that Santa Claus was real.

Now he and André looked at each other. It was a stare-down. Who would blink first? If Charlie said what he really believed, he risked looking like a fool in front of his friend.

But if he said he didn't believe in Santa, and then it turned out André was a believer, then he would be messing with a kid's true belief, and that just wasn't cool.

They were waiting for an answer. "Well," he said, "um…"

"Are you kidding me?" Darcy burst in. "Why do you even have to ask? Anyone with half a brain believes in Santa. These guys look like between them they have half a brain. Together they probably have a whole one. Hey—'Good King Wences-las,' my favorite carol. Turn up the radio, would you?"

Whew, thought Charlie. He didn't have to answer. He glanced at André, who looked equally relieved, though Charlie wasn't sure why.

"Have you been really good all year?" asked Aunt India.

Charlie stared at the floor.

"What is it, buddy?" asked his dad.

"I got in trouble at school." He'd been hoping he wouldn't have to confess, but his dad had a way of finding stuff out.

Dad frowned. "You've never been a troublemaker at school."

"I brought something for show-and-tell I wasn't supposed to have. This kid Isaiah said they were called Ben Wa eggs. The teacher told me to put them away This Very Instant."

Darcy and Aunt India had a fit. They tried to stay quiet, but he could tell they were dying. Charlie still wasn't a hundred percent sure why the little boxed set of balls was such a problem. His mom had said she'd explain when he was bigger.

"Yeah, uh, it's probably a good idea to check with an adult before you bring something to show-and-tell. When I was a kid I brought in a snake. We practically had to peel the teacher off the ceiling." Dad was grating a chocolate bar into a pot of cream for hot chocolate, which made everyone stop talking about getting in trouble.

While they gorged themselves on breakfast, the other kids and grown-ups showed up, and the kitchen and dining room got very loud with clattering dishes and talking and making plans for the day. André's sister, Angelica, was the last to arrive, still rubbing the sleep from her eyes. She looked really cute in her pink fuzzy slippers, clutching a patched-up stuffed dog she called Patchy Bowwow.

"I bet you're hungry." Dad hoisted her up onto her bar stool.

"Can I have a pancake?"

"You bet." Her face lit up when she saw that the pancakes were shaped like stars and trees. That was Aunt India's doing. She was a professional artist and she couldn't help making things fancy. She had used a metal cookie cutter to pour the pancake batter in.

"We get to see Santa today. What are you going to ask Santa for?" Bernie asked her.

"Oh, that's easy," said Angelica. With all those missing teeth, she didn't really say the letter S right, but she was getting better. "I'm going to tell him I need to see my mom, because I want her to be there when I sing my song at the church on Christmas. Logan's friend Maureen is in charge of the Christmas pageant, and she gave me a song to sing."

Charlie whipped a glance at André. But André was already carrying his dishes to the sink. "Let's go get ready," he said, and went down the hall and up the stairs without waiting to see if Charlie followed.

Alone in the bunk room, they pulled on long johns and snow pants, getting into a suspenders-snapping contest neither of them won, but it made them both giggle like hyenas. Under orders from Grandma Marion, they made their beds. The beds never looked the same as when a professional grown-up did it.

"At least we made the effort," Charlie said, mimicking his grandmother, which made them both laugh again.

"Hey," said André, "can I ask you something?"

"Sure."

"*Do* you believe in Santa Claus?"

And there it was. That question again. Did he say yes and be accused of being uncool? Or did he say no and risk losing his Christmas dream?

"Do *you?*" he asked André.

"The whole world is all about Santa Claus, everywhere you look. Decorations, stockings, songs, school plays, everything. How could the whole world be wrong?" He frowned, then snapped his fingers. "We should figure out a way to prove it, once and for all."

"Yeah!" Charlie said. "Let's do it."

"How? Do we set a trap or something? Or a camera?"

"What's this I hear?" Darcy stuck her head in the doorway. "We're talking about trapping Santa?"

Charlie's cheeks felt hot.

"You know the part of the song that goes, 'You'd better watch out'?"

Charlie and André nodded in unison.

She pursed her lips. "Well, what it means is that you have to be careful. Because if you start questioning his existence, you're already in trouble."

CHAPTER FOURTEEN

Logan had a crush on Darcy. He admitted to himself that it felt good. It was a big crush, maybe the biggest he'd ever felt, one that bounced around inside him as he went through his day. One that made him keep glancing at the clock and wondering what she was doing and wishing he was doing it with her.

Was she snowboarding on the fresh powder that had fallen last night? Having lunch with his sisters at the Powder Room? Sitting in front of her laptop, telecommuting to her job?

At his office in town, he had a meeting with Mason Bellamy, Adam's brother and the finance guy who had organized the investor group for the resort. Logan was supposed to be going over business matters with him, but he had trouble concentrating.

"It's that girl," said Mason, nudging him after about the

third time he drifted off, staring out the window at the snowy afternoon. "The one you were telling me about."

He nodded, reluctantly pulling his attention back to the spreadsheets on the desk in front of him. "I'm having a hard time thinking about anything else."

"Girls will do that to you."

"You know what's weird is that my family likes her."

"How is that weird?"

"All my exes were girls my family disapproved of."

"Maybe that's why they're exes."

"I don't want my family's opinion to matter that much."

"Hey, it does. Get used to it." Mason loosened his shirt collar and spread his arms with a laugh. "I'm a Bellamy. I'm used to family matters." He was only visiting Avalon, having come to town to help his ailing mother. So far, he was not adjusting well to small-town life. But his mother's affairs needed sorting, and Mason, the moneyman, was the one to do it. "So," he said, "you're interested in a girl they all like. What's the problem?"

"I keep thinking there's something wrong with this picture. When I was a kid, I used to actively seek out the wrong kind of girl, just as a kind of f-you to my parents." Logan drummed a pencil on the surface of the desk.

"Yeah, we all did that."

"And then I pulled the ultimate f-you and knocked some girl up."

"And let me guess. They got over it and ended up being awesome grandparents to your boy Charlie."

Logan nodded. "Okay, yeah. They drive me nuts. They always have. But they're the only folks I've got." He settled back and opened a new window on his laptop. "So we've got the year-end board meeting coming up for Saddle Mountain. Tell me something good."

Mason shifted in his chair. Cleared his throat. "The resorts and recreation business is tricky."

"In other words," said Logan, "the finances are in the shitter."

"It's more nuanced than that. There are variables to weigh..." Mason sighed. "Okay. In the shitter, yeah. That about sums it up."

Logan's heart sank. He knew he wouldn't get rich overnight running the mountain resort, but he didn't want to be irresponsible. He had a son to raise.

"The situation is temporary," Mason said. "The cash flow is in good shape, but your reserves are running low."

"What will fix this?" Logan asked. "Besides a Christmas miracle."

"You could use another infusion of cash."

"More investors, you mean."

"Yes. You can do another investor offering, or resolicit your current investors. Or some combination of both."

"How much time do I have?"

"There's a January fifteenth filing date you'll want to keep your eye on."

"Got it." Logan stood and gathered up his papers. "I'll figure something out." And he would, because it was mandatory. He had no alternative. He was not going to let himself fail at this. Still, he couldn't help hearing his father's voice, which was embedded deep inside his head. His father would say he'd made a huge mistake. He had walked away from a stable, thriving insurance business for the sake of a risky enterprise that had equal potential to either make or lose a fortune for him. He'd gambled not just his own future, but that of his son, too. What kind of father was he?

"Want to get a beer?" Mason suggested. "Adam's just winding up his stint as Santa." The firefighters of Avalon took turns donning the red suit each afternoon. "He could meet us at Hilltop Tavern."

"That's okay. I'm meeting my sisters and their husbands and kids. They've just been to see Santa. Adam is under orders to tell us what the kids asked for." He shook hands with Mason and headed out into the wintry afternoon.

"You look superpensive," said Darcy Fitzgerald, approaching him on the frosty sidewalk. "Am I interrupting something?"

He was ridiculously glad to see her. "Just an age-old argument with my father."

They fell in step together. "I assume it's the father in your head," she said.

"He's one of my permanent residents." Logan tapped his temple.

"You, too?" She grinned. "I sometimes have that dad. My mom, too. It's funny how much influence our parents have on us."

"True. I think about that a lot because of Charlie. I want to be the kind of father he actually likes having in his head."

"Is there such a thing?"

"I'm working on it. I'm trying my best to do a good job. For Charlie and for…" He stopped talking. He'd nearly said Charlie and his future siblings. What a boneheaded thing to say. "So," he said, changing the subject, "how was skiing and riding today?"

"Awesome, as I'm sure you knew it would be."

"After the snow last night—yeah." Just the mention of last night made him think about walking with her in the winter woods, kissing her in front of the fire… He shoved his hands in his pockets to keep from grabbing her right then and there. "Where is everyone?"

"India and China are taking everyone to see Santa now,

and then there's apparently some kind of parade. We're supposed to rendezvous in the church parking lot."

He nodded. "There's a parade every Friday evening in December leading up to Christmas. Charlie has never missed a single one. The town kind of goes overboard for Christmas."

She looked around the lavishly decorated and lit village square. "I noticed. I really like it. Can you actually skate on the lake?"

"Can I skate? No. Can the ice hold me? Yeah, probably through February."

"I could teach you to skate."

"I'll hold you to it. So, what does a big-city girl think of Avalon?"

"It's lovely here. You're lucky to live in such a beautiful place." She looked around at the shop windows, the people strolling from place to place, her eyes shining. "I love all the lights and decorations this time of year."

"No regrets about missing out on your family's holiday?"

"No," she said instantly. "Definitely not. If I were back in the city, my sisters and I would be fighting our way along Fifth Avenue, dealing with the crush of holiday shoppers. Then we'd stagger with our parcels to Penn Station for the LIRR and pray we get a seat. It's fun in its own way, but this is definitely more mellow." She watched a kid and his mother crossing the street with a little dog on a leash.

"So, are you a city girl or a small-town girl?" he asked.

"Both. Oh, and a wilderness girl, too. Does that make me hopelessly inconsistent?" She ducked her head and then looked at him again. "I'm still figuring out who I am when I'm single."

"Fair enough." He couldn't quite tell what she was trying to say. That she liked being single and wanted to stay that way? That she was flexible and open to change? That she wanted him to take her to bed and do all the stuff he thought about when he thought about her?

Which was pretty much all the freaking time.

"You must miss something," he said.

"Shopping for the kids, I guess. That was always one of my favorite parts. I mean, it's one thing to pick out the perfect cashmere bathrobe for your mother, or a BugZooka for your dad, but shopping for the kids is the best."

"I've got an idea," he said. "This way."

He took her to the local toy store. It was nice, the way her face lit up when she saw the window display—a model train circling its figure-eight route through the fake snow and trees, and a lit village in the background. There was a robot endlessly lifting hand weights, dolls and boxing gloves, bikes and musketeer swords.

"It's fantastic," Darcy said. "Every kid's dream toy shop."

"Yep." He nodded at the manager, a woman named Guinevere who had been working here since she was a teenager. He drew Darcy over to a display of the latest and greatest. "I'd like to get your help," he said. "We've got a bumper crop of kids this year, and my ever-efficient older sister China sent me a text message with suggestions."

They spent the next hour channeling the kids. What would light them up on Christmas morning? What would make them laugh, excite them, give them warm memories of their Christmas at Saddle Mountain?

"We have to try stuff out," said Darcy.

"That's right, you're all about testing gear, aren't you? Let's steer clear of the things that need to be plugged in," he suggested.

"Are you expecting a power outage?"

"No, but up on the mountain, it happens. Nonelectric toys are more fun, anyway."

"Agreed. Remember Battleship?" She pulled out the classic board game.

"Good one. Everyone's going to want that."

"Then let's get it for the pickle prize."

He scratched his head. "The pickle prize?"

"You don't do the pickle tradition?"

"Never heard of it. But if it involves a pickle, I'm game."

"You need a pickle ornament and you have to hang it in some very arbitrary spot on the tree. And whoever finds the pickle first on Christmas morning gets a prize."

"Gives new meaning to hide the pickle."

She sniffed. "I can't believe you never heard of it. The tradition goes way back. According to Wikipedia, anyway."

"I'll take your word for it."

"Look, they've even got pickles for sale."

They were displayed with the stocking stuffers. They chose one that had eyes and a mouth, a sprinkling of glitter, and a movement activated switch that caused it to yodel.

"How have I managed to live my life without a yodeling pickle?" asked Logan.

"It's a new world order," she said.

Toy-shopping with Darcy, just like cooking with her, snowshoeing with her, surfing with her, did not suck. She was very serious in her deliberations, weighing the merits of the slingshot versus the potato catapult, a xylophone versus a recorder. He couldn't remember laughing with a woman so much. He'd just come from a stressful work meeting and he needed this, needed a change or some shift in perspective.

In the middle of doing a yo-yo trick—an impressive one at that—she looked up at him and grinned.

"What?" he asked, liking the grin.

"Thanks."

"You're welcome. For what?"

She gestured at the toys they picked out. "I thought I'd have to miss out on this."

He paused. "You don't have to miss out on a thing."

"Picking out toys is one of the best things about Christmas. It's part of the magic."

"For somebody who doesn't like kids," he said, "you sure like kids."

"You've got it wrong," she said. "I do like kids—a lot. The whole nieces-and-nephews thing is right up my alley. I'm just not into parenting."

"Aunting, then."

"Yep."

"Sounds good." He changed the subject. "Okay, there's one gift we haven't nailed down yet."

"Angelica," she said. "She's adorable. What should we get her?"

He thought about the conversation at breakfast. Great big round eyes, soft lisping voice. *I want to see my mom.* "The only thing she wants is the one thing we can't give her."

CHAPTER FIFTEEN

Logan O'Donnell was dangerous. Darcy concluded this halfway through the toy store spree. Whenever she was with him, she felt herself getting way too interested in him. That was the dangerous part. Interest led to a deeper crush, which led to passion, which in turn would lead to an emotional entanglement she wasn't ready for.

She said as much to India when they all met for the Christmas parade later that day. It was hugely fun for the kids, waiting for the hometown processional to pass by. Everyone was bundled up, faces aglow in the twinkling lights.

Darcy kept sneaking glances at Logan, who was like a human jungle gym crawling with nieces and nephews. He looked impossibly sexy to her, even covered in small children. At his side, Charlie was a smaller, cherub-faced version of him, reveling in the excitement of the holidays. In his own way,

Charlie was as dangerous to her heart as his father, because when she looked at him, something happened inside her. She yearned to reach out to him, to make him laugh, to gather him into her arms—just as she had done with her ex's kids.

"Remember the definition of insanity?" she asked India, who was taking pictures on her smartphone. "Doing the same thing over and over again, and expecting different results."

"Your point being?" asked India, framing a shot of the glittering pillars of the Avalon Free Library.

"Look, I really like your brother—I think you knew I would. But being with him…it's got disaster written all over it."

"You guys are great together. I'm not seeing how that's crazy."

"He's a single dad—like Huntley. He wants more kids—like Huntley. It's crazy of me to think going down that road again will lead to anywhere but disaster."

"It's not the same. Huntley is a tool," she said simply. "Logan isn't."

"Why does it not make me feel better to know I was married to a tool? I think I was right to swear off any kind of relationship. I'm simply not any good at it."

"Don't be ridiculous. This is not like you, Darce. You don't shy away from things just because they might be difficult."

"I do now." She wondered if she would ever get over the searing pain of betrayal, the sense of loss.

"Look, if you refuse to let yourself go with a guy—a good guy, like my brother—then guess what you're doing?"

"Protecting myself. India, I'm doing the best I can."

"But if you hold back, then you're letting Huntley win. You're letting him walk away with everything he got in the divorce, and he's taking the most vital part of you. He's taking your heart, your soul, your sense of joy and optimism, your belief in love. So ask yourself—do you really want to give him that? Do you really want to surrender and give up on things that used to be so important to you?"

"Jeez, when you put it that way..."

"Don't let him win this one. Don't let him spoil something special."

This, thought Darcy, was what a best friend was for. She told you the truth, even when you didn't want to hear it.

"You know what?" said Darcy. "It's Christmas. I love Christmas. I'm going to enjoy every minute of it, and then I'm going back to the city and to the real world and..."

"And what?"

"And everything will be as it should be," she concluded.

"It's coming," piped Bernie. "The Christmas parade is coming."

A small parade moved down the road. It was headed by a group of carolers—the Heart of the Mountains Church choir, followed by a few community groups and of course, Santa Claus, bringing up the rear.

The short processional was over soon enough. They all walked together to the Heart of the Mountains Church, where they were parked.

It was a cute little traditional church with a brilliantly lit steeple, its slender silhouette looking perfect against the purple sky. In the snowy yard was an elaborate manger scene illuminated by floodlights, and a sign that read O Come All Ye Faithful.

"It's beautiful," India said to Logan, taking more pictures. "The whole day was beautiful—skiing and lunch and Santa. You are one hundred percent forgiven for talking us out of going to Florida."

Darcy was drawn to the PAWS contingent—the town's animal rescue league. Volunteers walked with rescue dogs wearing little jackets with the phrase Rescue Me on the side.

Some of the volunteers were passing out brochures about pet adoptions.

"Oh my gosh, I wish I could take one home," Darcy said, watching a beagle bounding through the snow.

"That can be arranged." Logan came to stand next to her. "I have it on good authority that Santa loves giving away puppies at Christmas."

"My building doesn't allow dogs."

"Maybe you're living in the wrong building, then."

Why did everything he said have a double meaning? It seemed that way to Darcy. "I love my building," she said. "I was on a waiting list forever to live there. It has everything I need."

As the parade disassembled, Santa climbed down from his throne in the back of a fire department utility truck.

Logan gave him a wave. "That's my buddy Adam, behind the beard."

"Aha. So he's telling you what the kids asked for."

"Yep."

"Sneaky."

"Can I tell you a secret?"

Yes. Tell me everything. "Sure," she said.

"Charlie and André wouldn't tell Santa their Christmas wishes. They wrote letters instead."

"Uh-oh. So, what's your best guess?"

"Bad news—I think he wants a dog. He had a dog named Blake, but she was old and passed away."

She gave a low whistle. "That's a tough one."

He nodded. "Not the best timing for me. And of course, when Charlie's with his mom, the dog is all my responsibility."

"So what are you going to do?" she asked.

"I hope he wants something else. I'm considering my options. Like giving him a toy dog. Or making a donation in his name to the animal shelter."

"Dude."

"What?"

"Do you know how lame that sounds? A dog is a *dog*. Not a toy. Not a donation." She indicated the noisy mess in the parking lot as the PAWS volunteers loaded up the animals to take back to the shelter.

He nodded. "I know you're right. Maybe in the summer, then."

"Does Santa give rain checks for summer?"

He laughed. "You're harsh."

"Being the youngest of five, I learned to play hardball at Christmas at an early age."

"I've got a week to figure this out."

She wondered if she should tell him about the Santa trap. Charlie and André were right on the cusp of disbelief. One wrong move, and the myth would be busted.

"Good news," Adam reported, now in his street clothes. "I pried the truth out of Charlie—his Christmas wish. I got him to sing like a canary."

"Yeah?" Logan grinned. "Good work. So, what am I in for?"

"A new snowboard. The kind with flames painted on the bottom. Boots, too."

"Excellent. Much easier than a live animal. I can make that happen."

Darcy felt a twinge of suspicion. That was just too easy. She thought about the conversation she'd overheard between the boys. "What about André?"

Adam shook his head. "That kid's tough as a Kevlar vest. He wouldn't talk. You'll have to figure it out another way."

"Okay," said Logan. "I'm on it."

Adam clapped him on the shoulder. "See you around, buddy. And Darcy."

After he'd gone, Darcy pondered about whether or not to

disclose her suspicions. Not now, she decided. "Can I tell *you* a secret?" she asked.

"What's that?"

"*I* still believe in Santa Claus."

"You probably just like sitting in guys' laps."

"Depends on the guy. Depends on the lap. And how do you know what I like? You don't even know me."

"Then maybe we should work on that some more." He lowered his voice and leaned down toward her. "I know you like kissing me."

"You do, do you?" *Kiss me now,* she thought crazily. *Kiss me now.*

"Yeah, so—sorry, I need to…" He didn't finish, but sprinted across the road toward a tall pile of packed snow. Charlie, André and some other kids were playing on a Bobcat snow mover, which looked like a toy version of a snowplow. The equipment was clearly marked "keep off," but the kids were either blind to that or just ignoring it.

"Hey," Logan called. "Get down off that Bobcat."

"It's cool, Dad," said Charlie. "Check it out."

André was working the levers and making motor sounds with his mouth.

"Damn it, Charlie. It's a week before Christmas. Shouldn't you be on your best behavior?"

"What if that *is* his best behavior?" asked Darcy, coming up behind them. She couldn't decide whether she was grateful for the interruption of her moment with Logan or frustrated.

"Then I've got my work cut out for me," he said.

"You didn't tell anybody, did you?" Back on Saddle Mountain the next day, Charlie and André were making a snow fort.

"Only Santa Claus," said André. "And only in the letter I wrote. A real letter, not an email. You?"

"Same."

"Yeah, but I saw you talking to Santa today. You must have said something," André accused.

"I did. The guy in the Santa hut is my dad's friend Adam. They think I don't know that, but I do. I had to say something because they expect it. So I said I wanted a snowboard, even though that's not what I really want."

"Cool."

"Cool."

They had a stare-down. "So, are we gonna tell each other?"

"Better not."

"Okay." The snow was perfect for packing, just sticky enough but not too heavy. "Hey, I think my dad's going to have a girlfriend," he said. "I think it's gonna be Darcy." He'd already gone over this in his mind. Now he wanted to tell somebody, and André was the perfect choice. A best friend.

"She's cool."

"Yeah. Does your mom have a boyfriend?"

André added another chunk of snow to the wall. "Nope. Sometimes my dad used to come around, but... He's not very nice to her."

"That blows."

"Yeah."

Charlie felt bad for André. Charlie himself had a dad *and* a stepdad and they were both awesome. He looked over at André and frowned. "Wait a second. We can tell each other our Santa wishes. We can take the best-friend oath, and then we can tell each other."

André hesitated, staring down at the snow-covered ground. Then he said, "Okay, but the oath is unbreakable, right?"

Charlie thought about things that broke. Bicycle chains. Thin ice. Christmas bulbs. His parents' marriage. Promises. Sometimes it seemed as if everything was breakable.

Not a friendship, though. Not when you were best friends.

"Right," he said. "Let's go inside the fort to make sure nobody hears."

They crawled through the opening and settled into the icy darkness. Charlie pulled out his flashlight and stuck it in the middle with the beam shining up, lending an eerie bluish glow to the interior of the fort. It felt as if they were the only two kids in the world.

"Okay, do we solemnly swear to keep everything we say and hear a total secret? Forever?"

"I do."

"Me, too."

"A dog," said Charlie. "That's what I want for Christmas. A dog."

André's eyes lit up and a grin broke across his face. "Seriously?"

"Yeah."

"Oh man. That is so rad."

"I know. I used to have a dog named Blake. She died, and I thought I wanted to die, too. I miss her so much. I never believed I would ever be happy again. But then I saw this kid playing with a black Lab, and I started thinking it might be time to get another dog. See, there are other dogs that need me, other dogs that can be my dog. This is the biggest thing I've ever wished for."

"It's big," André admitted. "Really big. What kind of dog?"

"Pretty much any kind, so long as it's friendly and wants to play and likes to sleep with me at night. I don't want to be too picky."

Charlie's heart sped up when he pictured himself with a dog. Playing and feeding, lying around, taking walks, games of fetch. With a dog of his own, he would never be lonely.

"I've been asking and asking," he said. "My mom and stepdad said no after Blake died, on account of we're moving overseas and we move a lot. And my dad said no because he's always busy working and I'm not home enough. Yeah, right. I know deep down in my heart it would be awesome. It would be a dream come true."

"That's totally cool, Charlie. So you think Santa'll actually bring you a dog?"

"If he's real, he has to, right?"

"Yep." They rolled snowball after snowball, and more walls went up. It was awesome, having a best friend, thought Charlie. You could talk, or just be quiet and work side by side. You could tell each other stuff. They finished the shelter, and it was like a dark cave inside, cold and small, a real fort to keep them safe in case of enemy attack.

"What about you?" Charlie asked. "What did you ask for?"

André's smile sank into a line of seriousness. "Remember the promise."

"I remember. I could never forget."

"Good. Because the dog is the biggest thing you ever asked Santa for. My wish is the most *serious* thing I ever asked Santa for."

Charlie tried to imagine what kind of serious thing André was talking about.

"You know how we had to come stay with your dad because my mom went away for work?"

"Yep. That's tough. I miss my mom when I'm away from her."

"Yeah, but you have your dad. It's different. I don't have my dad. And I wouldn't want him. He's mean and he does bad stuff. So it's nice how your dad is letting us come here. But my wish is about my mom."

"You can't ask Santa to bring your mom for Christmas. It doesn't work that way."

"I know. That's not what I asked."

"Then what?"

André drew his knees up to his chest and stared at the flashlight beam. "My mom didn't go away for work," he said in a very quiet voice.

"Then where did she go?" Charlie felt clueless, but he could tell André was building up to something big. Like last summer at Camp Kioga, in the cabin when Leroy Stumpf admitted he was scared of the dark.

Only this was bigger. Charlie could tell.

"She's in jail."

Charlie frowned. "Nuh-uh. You're lying."

"I wish I was."

"Why is she in jail?"

"She got in trouble. My dad was doing something bad, and they both got caught. The judge sent her to a place called Bedford Hills Women's Correctional Facility." André repeated the big words as though he'd memorized them. "She has to stay there until February. It's a jail. Prison. I looked it up online at the library. Angelica doesn't know. No one is supposed to know. But I snooped. I heard her crying at night and I heard her talking on the phone, and I figured it out."

"Oh man. That's bad, André. That's really bad."

"You think I don't know that?"

"Sure you do. And I know it, too."

"I just wish my mom will be okay on Christmas. That's all I wish." André's voice broke then, and he screwed up his face as though he was trying not to cry, and then he just let go and he cried hard, shaking all over.

"It's okay, buddy," said Charlie, patting him on the shoulder the way his dad sometimes did when Charlie was sad. "Maybe it sucks now, but it's going to be okay." The news made his stomach hurt. He wondered if he should send Santa another letter—*Forget the dog. I want the same thing André wants.*

"Do you think Santa will grant my wish?" André asked, dragging a mittened hand across his face.

"If he doesn't, then there really is no Santa."

"But he's really real, right?"

"He's real. So all we gotta do now is not screw up, and we'll get our Christmas wishes."

"Okay, let's make a pact. We have to be good. We have to not screw up."

"So, are we still going to stay up all night on Christmas Eve and wait for Santa?"

"Sure."

"What if he doesn't come?"

Charlie punched a window into the wall of snow. "Then we'll know."

CHAPTER SIXTEEN

O n Christmas Eve, Logan was in his office in town, brooding over the resort accounts. The office was adjacent to the local radio station, and through the wall he could hear the relentlessly cheerful voice of the DJ, Eddie Haven, talking about the town festivities, which would culminate in the Christmas morning pageant at Heart of the Mountains Church.

Logan wished he could scrub the worries out of his brain. He had always been good at numbers. He had always been good at business. That was why the current situation was so frustrating. A looming loan payment and a year-end tax filing weighted the balance sheet heavily into the red. Despite taking a surgeon's scalpel to the budget, he wasn't able to stop the bleeding, not completely.

He glared at the screen and brooded some more, until his eyes glazed over.

The front door opened and shut. His father came in, looking around the small space, the shelves crammed with files and work product.

"So this is where it all happens," said Al.

Logan pushed back from his computer screen, which displayed a spreadsheet with its depressing numbers. "Not exactly O'Donnell Industries," he said.

"How's it going?" asked his father.

There was a world of meaning in the question. What his father really wanted to know was whether or not Logan's crazy enterprise was panning out. Was he making money or losing his shirt?

"I know that look," said Al. "I realize you think I spent your entire boyhood with my nose in a business ledger, but believe it or not, I knew where you were, every minute. Still do."

Logan was startled. "If that's the case, then why did you just stand by and watch me go off the rails?"

"I didn't stand by, and you didn't go off the rails. The things that happened, yeah, some of it was hard, but I watched you turn yourself into a man, same as you're doing for Charlie. A person can get crippled if he doesn't figure things out on his own."

Logan thought about all the dumb mistakes he'd made, the way he'd bumbled through the rough years. But looking back, he realized that despite the trouble and the hurt he'd endured, he wouldn't change a thing. "Tough love?" he asked.

"That's what I've heard it called. Then again, there's no shame in asking for help. Sometimes," said his father, "all you have to do is ask."

"It's Christmas Eve." Darcy came bustling into the office. Her cheeks were bright from the cold, and she looked amazing, outfitted for skating on the lake. "You can't sit here laboring over the books like Bob Marley."

He grinned and pushed back from his desk. She was like a breath of fresh air, especially in the wake of his surprising conversation with his father. "Don't you mean Jacob Marley?"

"Whatever. The point is, it's Christmas Eve and you're working."

He stood up and reached for his jacket. "You're a good influence on me. Where's everybody else?"

"India took the four boys skating on Willow Lake."

"Hope they're staying out of trouble."

"I'm meeting them at the skate house and then we're all heading up the mountain before dark."

"I've got more than work problems," he said, shutting down his computer. "I've got a Santa problem. What the hell are we going to say to Angelica tomorrow when she sings her solo in the Christmas pageant, and her mom's not there to see? I'm planning to film the whole thing, but it's not the same."

Darcy leaned against his desk. "I had an idea about that. I wanted to run it by you."

"You figured out a way to pull off a Christmas miracle?"

"Not quite, but I thought of something that might help. Er, if you don't mind me stepping in."

"Mind? I love that you're stepping in."

She smiled. "You know how I'm a rabid Jezebel fan, right?"

Jezebel, the hip-hop star who had filmed a reality show in Avalon the year before, had become an unlikely local hero. "You and about a million others."

"I watched every episode of *Big Girl, Small Town*. Do you recall that she was doing community service as part of her conditions of parole?"

"I didn't tune in to the series, but yeah, I remember the backstory. The show followed her community service project with inner-city kids at Camp Kioga. That's how the summer program got started."

"Prior to her release, she did time at Bedford Hills."

Now a glimmer of light came on in his work-fogged brain. "The same facility where Maya is."

"Jezebel's filming a Christmas special there, starting tonight and going through tomorrow. I read about it online. I asked if someone could help us set up a video call so Angelica's mom can watch her sing tomorrow." She pulled a tablet device from her bag. "Jezebel is going to provide a device just like this one. There's an app called RealTime. Her friend in Avalon—a woman named Sonnet—do you know her?"

"Oh yeah," he said. "Long story. Remind me to tell you sometime."

"She seems really nice. She and her husband are going to help us out. Tomorrow at ten in the morning, we'll connect, and Angelica and André will get to see their mom. It's not the same as seeing her in person, but it's something."

His heart felt squeezed with emotion. "How did you get to be so awesome?"

"You think I'm awesome?"

He had a lot more thoughts about her. But that conversation would have to wait.

"I'll see you at the house," he said. "I've got a last-minute errand."

He reached for a stack of files. She put her hand on top of them. "Uh-uh," she said. "Christmas Eve, remember?"

"Are you going to be that girlfriend who won't let me get my work done?"

"Who says I'm your girlfriend?"

"Me." In a swift movement, he trapped her between his body and the desk. "I say."

Her eyes and her lips softened. She liked him, he could tell. "Yeah?"

"Yeah." He leaned down, really wanting to kiss her, but instead, he just whispered in her ear. "Tonight," he said. "You and me, tonight."

CHAPTER SEVENTEEN

Skating was lame. Charlie and André both agreed on that. Aunt India told them they could take off their skates and play in the snow if they didn't go far. They found some kids playing king of the mountain on a huge snow mound at the edge of the church parking lot, and that was way more fun.

"Hey, check it out over here," said André, motioning him to the corner of the lot.

Charlie saw the shiny red Bobcat, with its snowplow attachment, parked in the usual spot. He and André climbed up to the scoop-shaped plastic seat, wedging themselves into the small space. They worked the levers and pedals, making motor sounds with their mouths as they fell into their favorite make-believe game, robot wars. Charlie pushed down on a pedal, and to his surprise, the big snowplow blade lifted up. He eased up on the pedal, then pushed it again, and the blade followed his movements.

"Cool," said André. "You got it to work."

"Way cool," Charlie agreed.

André started monkeying with the other controls, reaching across Charlie to work both big levers. "This moves it forward," he said. "This moves it back. I've watched it a million times at construction sites in the city."

"Okay, you be the driver and I'll watch for the enemy," said Charlie.

This year, he decided as he played alongside his best friend, Christmas rocked. There was going to be a feast tonight, and a party and stuff, and then they were going to stay up all night watching for Santa, and in the morning, their wishes would come true. He just knew it. Christmas was like the best thing ever.

André pushed a rubbery green button overhead, and the engine coughed, and then growled, and then turned on.

The two of them looked at each other in shock. The machine vibrated beneath them like a live animal.

"You started the engine," Charlie said, catching a whiff of exhaust.

"I started it." André looked as amazed as Charlie felt. "I bet I can make it work." He pushed one of the hand levers forward, and the machine lurched, then trundled ahead a few feet.

"Holy moly, you're driving it," Charlie said.

"This is so rad." André worked the lever some more, bringing it out into the middle of the empty parking lot. "Look, I can make it go forward and back. And here's how you turn it." He worked the levers with both hands, and the Bobcat turned in a circle.

"Awesome," Charlie said. "Let's see if the snowplow works." He pushed the pedals, and sure enough, the blade went up and down.

"We're working now," said André, his face lit up with excitement. "Let's plow that field down there."

"Yeah," said Charlie. "We can make a path to the manger." He pointed across the smooth white churchyard at the manger scene, which tonight would all be lit up for Christmas Eve.

The yard sloped downward, and the Bobcat leaned like a crazy ride. At first it was really fun, like the coolest ride on a sled, but then it felt as though they were going a little too fast.

"Hey, slow down," Charlie said.

"I can't." André struggled with the levers. "It's not slowing down."

"Then you better turn around, because we're heading straight for—"

"Duck!"

The manger was suddenly right in front of them. The plow blade hooked itself on something and then smashed into the manger.

André's hand flashed up, and he punched a red button overhead. The engine died.

"Holy moly," said Charlie. "We smashed into the manger." He looked at the statues strewn around the snowy yard. "We ran over baby Jesus."

"Oh man, that was not cool," André said. "What should we—"

"What's going on here?" asked a gruff voice.

Charlie's stomach felt as if it had turned into a giant ball of ice. A police cruiser was parked in the lot beside the churchyard. "It's Chief McKnight," he whispered to André.

"We're sunk," André whispered back.

"You boys climb down from that thing." Chief McKnight looked really mad. "Is anybody hurt?"

Charlie eyed the crushed fake baby head down in the snow. He and André scrambled out. "We're okay," Charlie said. "Chief McKnight, we're really sorry."

"We didn't mean to do it," André said.

"You kids are in big trouble," said Chief McKnight.

As if they didn't already know.

"Honest, we were just gonna do some plowing, you know, to help out," André said.

"It was an accident," Charlie said, snatching off his hat.

Chief McKnight leaned down and glared at them. Then his eyebrows shot up. "Charlie? Charlie O'Donnell?"

Chief McKnight had known him ever since Charlie was born. The police chief was married to Jenny, the bakery owner, and they lived in an old-fashioned house on King Street, and when the chief wasn't on duty, Charlie was allowed to call him Rourke.

But right now it was Chief McKnight, all the way. "Y-yes, sir," Charlie replied in a shaking voice. "That's me."

"You stole a piece of equipment. You committed vandalism…on Christmas Eve," said the chief. "Bad timing, guys. *Really* bad timing."

"We're sorry," Charlie said.

"Do we have to go to jail?" André asked in a very quiet, completely horrified voice.

Charlie knew exactly what André was thinking—that he would have to go to jail, like his mom. That was André's deepest, darkest fear. Charlie nearly knocked his friend down, pushing in front of him to stand before Chief McKnight. He stood tall and squared his shoulders the way his dad told him he should do to show respect.

"It was me," he said in a loud, clear voice. "I made André sit next to me, but I was the one who stole the snowplow and ran it into the manger. André didn't have anything to do with it."

"Hey," said André.

"If anybody gets in trouble," Charlie said, "it should be me, not André."

"Is that so?" asked the police chief.

Charlie knew his Christmas wish couldn't possibly come true now. What boy could ever be rewarded on Christmas morning after pulling a prank like this? Santa would never bring him a dog now, not after what they'd just done. So he figured he might as well take the blame, because in one big flash, he realized there was something way more important than his Christmas wish, and that was André. His best friend.

And André's wish—that his mom would be okay—just had to come true.

"Let's go to my car," said Rourke. "I need to call your dad."

Defeated, they followed him up the slope toward the squad car. Normally they would love exploring a police car, but not now.

"Why did you say it was you?" André hissed at Charlie.

"Because we need to make sure your Christmas wish comes true."

"What about *your* wish?"

Charlie's heart sank, but he kept his chin up. "Maybe next year." And in that moment, he felt funny, kind of light and floating. The moment he had stepped up to take the blame, he had felt this terrific sensation whooshing through him like an ocean wave or like the wind through the trees. It felt good. Really good, even though he knew he had just ruined his chances of getting a puppy. He knew why it felt good to throw himself under the bus and he knew the name of the whooshing feeling.

It was the Christmas Spirit. It was the thing all the songs and stories were about—putting somebody's happiness ahead of your own.

Even though it felt good, he still had to deal with Chief McKnight...and with the holy family lying half-buried in the snow. He'd run over baby Jesus. How was he going to fix this?

He was going to need a Christmas miracle.

When they were a few feet from the police car, Charlie

saw Darcy running toward them. "What happened here?" she asked. "Is someone hurt?"

"No visible injuries," said the chief. "And you are?"

"Darcy Fitzgerald," she said. "I'm friends with Charlie's aunt. I was looking for them at the skate house, and his aunt said they came over here to play in the snow." She planted her hands on her hips. "Looks like you had a little too much fun with the snowplow."

"We're sorry," said Charlie. "We didn't mean it."

"I was just going to call Logan," said Chief McKnight, taking out a phone.

Charlie wished he could freeze into an icicle and not feel so terrible. Everything that had happened was bad, but knowing his dad was about to get a call from the police was the worst.

"Wait a moment," Darcy said. "Do you mind if I have a word with you?"

She and the police chief stepped to the other side of the car and had a quick, quiet conversation. A few minutes later, the chief said, "So here's the deal. I'm going to move the snowplow, and you kids are going to rebuild the manger. I'm letting you off with a warning this time, but if you ever pull a stunt like this again—"

"We won't," Charlie said.

"Never, ever, we swear on a stack of Bibles," André added.

The chief drove the snowplow back to its parking spot. Darcy looked at Charlie and then at André.

Charlie shook in his shoes. What if she decided to act like the stepmonster and rat him out to his dad? *Oh man.*

"All right, you two," she said. "Let's get moving. We've got work to do."

Dark came early to the mountain on Christmas Eve, and outside the window, the winter sky brooded with the weight of a coming storm. The airways were filled with warnings of a lake-effect blizzard. Darcy's phone vibrated with messages from her sisters and parents to make sure she was all right.

She was returning a text to Lydia when India handed her a mug redolent of wine and spices. "Glühwein," she said. "Traditional in Tyrolia, I'm told. They made it over at the Powder Room for the overnight guests."

Darcy took a sip. "Oh, that's nice."

India gestured at her phone. "Everything all right?"

"My sister just wanted to make sure we're not going to freeze to death in the storm."

"I heard it was going to hit around midnight."

"It's kind of exciting," said Darcy.

"Let's hope the power stays on." India studied her. "You look good."

"As opposed to…?"

"I thought you might be depressed, missing your family, that sort of thing."

"I'm fine."

"So, you and Logan—"

"Fine," Darcy assured her. "Everything is fine." She wasn't ready to talk about her growing bond with Logan. It was very unexpected, and very fast. And if the encounter with him today was any indication, she was in for a very nice Christmas Eve. She didn't want to spoil things by talking about them too soon. She didn't want to talk herself out of it. He had done nothing specific to win her trust, yet she trusted him. She wanted to take a chance with him.

"I'm going to go say good-night to the kids," she said to India.

"Okay. I think we wore them out sufficiently, and they're exhausted enough to sleep. Charlie practically fell asleep in his Christmas Eve Frito pie."

India had no idea. Darcy had kept the Bobcat mishap to herself on condition that the boys put the manger back in readiness for Christmas morning. She had worked the boys like a pair of rented mules. Fueled by pure repentance and helped by the incredibly understanding chief of police, they had put the manger back in order quickly. They'd managed to swaddle the broken baby Jesus so it would look brand-new. Tonight's layer of fresh snow would cover their tracks.

In the course of repairing the damage with Charlie, she had made two discoveries. Number one, she was falling for the little boy as hard as she was falling for his father. And number two, telling Santa he wanted a snowboard for Christmas was merely a diversion Charlie had set up. As they were finishing up with the manger, André had pulled her aside and whispered the truth. She only hoped there was enough time to do what had to be done.

The process of getting the kids off to bed began with a chorus of groans from the kids. "The sooner you get to bed, the sooner Santa comes," China reminded them.

"And the pickle prize," Darcy reminded them. "Don't forget that." She explained the game to them, and eventually they were all rounded up and sent to bed. Darcy went in to tell them good-night.

"Thank you," said Charlie, "for, um, helping us out today."

"You're welcome." She didn't lecture him. She knew he'd learned his lesson. She'd seen it on his face at the scene of the crime.

"Can I ask you something?"

"Sure."

"Why did you help us?"

"I have four older sisters. I know all about doing something dumb, and getting in trouble, and trying to make it right, and then moving on. And by the way, that's a nugget, Charlie."

"A what?"

"A nugget. Like a nugget of wisdom. Something to remember as you go through life."

"What, like there's a rule that I should never do something dumb?"

"No. Just assume you're going to because you're only human. The important thing is to make it right and move on."

"Okay. I'm really glad you helped us."

"I always help the people I love." It just slipped out. She stared at him, and the little red-cheeked face and bright green eyes stared back at her.

His gaze never wavered. "I love you, too. I hope you stick around."

Oh, boy. This could go so wrong. Charlie was a new love interest for her heart—and also a new risk. If things didn't work out with Logan, her loss would be doubled. She'd been there before and feared going there again. On the other hand, the excitement she felt for Logan was doubled, too. Maybe it was time to quit being afraid.

"Good night, Charlie. I'll see you on Christmas morning, okay?"

CHAPTER EIGHTEEN

T hey're nestled," said Marion O'Donnell, coming down
from the kids' room.

"All snug in their beds," added Al.

"Then Santa had better get to work," said Bilski, nudging
India. "We've got a pair of bikes to put together."

"Humbug," she said. "I'd rather have a hot toddy and go
to bed."

"I'll give you a hand," said China's husband. "But only if
you promise to help me with the dollhouse. All that itty-bitty
furniture. I don't get it."

"We'll put out the milk and cookies," said China.

"You can put them right here," Logan said, indicating the
table next to him. "Santa needs a snack."

Seated on his other side, Darcy felt a warm sense of contentment. She liked this family. She liked the interplay and the

way they cared for one another. It reminded her of her own family, before the trouble with Huntley began.

She felt relaxed and at peace, far from trouble now.

India checked her phone. "Your mother sent a text message," she said to Bilski. "She wants to know how we're making it through the storm."

"Tell her we're suffering." Bilski helped himself to another beer.

The coming storm was making national news because of its predicted size and severity. Currently it was hurling itself across the Great Lakes, gathering strength.

They went over the next day's agenda like a team of battle commanders. "I'm going to get the ham in the oven before we go to church," said Marion.

"We need to leave early," China said. "Midnight service was canceled because of the storm, so the morning celebration is going to be packed."

"Is everything in place for the live feed to Angelica's mom?" Darcy asked.

Logan nodded. "We did a test run. It's all going to come together, blizzard or no blizzard. If the internet service goes down, there's a cellular backup."

Darcy felt a wave of warmth for him. She loved that they were working together on this project. She just hoped it was enough to make Christmas bearable for Angelica and André.

The others peeled off gradually, everyone going to their rooms, until it was just Logan and Darcy and the roaring fire.

"Can I just say, I love this?" He gestured at the roaring fire with an impossible number of stockings hanging from the mantelpiece. "All these stockings. My mom and sisters are serious about stockings." They were different colors, but all the same size so the kids wouldn't bicker over them. There was a photograph of each person pinned to each stocking.

"It's nice," she said.

"I love having a big group like this, a big family. A tribe."

She didn't answer. She'd come from a big family, one that was tribelike. And it hadn't worked out so well for her.

His hand dropped from the back of the sofa to her shoulder, gently caressing. "What are you doing?" she asked.

"Coming on to you."

"That's exciting."

"I think so, too."

It was quiet and warm in the room, with music drifting from the speakers. It was briefly interrupted by a storm update. The new prediction was for up to three feet in Ulster County.

"Are you worried?" she asked him.

"I have a rule," he said. "No worrying on Christmas Eve. Oh, and I have insurance, just in case. I was in the business, so I'm covered. Actually, there is one thing I'm worried about."

"Yeah? What's that?"

"How to get you to spend the night with me."

And there it was. The invitation she had waited for, hoped for, yearned for and at the same time dreaded. Before she opened her mouth she honestly did not know what she would say.

"Sometimes all you have to do is ask."

For Darcy, the biggest surprise of the night was not the blizzard. It was not the power of the wind lashing at the windows.

No, the biggest surprise was that Logan delivered on every single promise he'd made with his kisses. Yes, he really was that tender, that attentive to her. He seemed to know just how to make her want him with a yearning so intense it took her breath away. As stealthy as a pair of teenagers, they crept up the stairs to his room. The only light came from the string of colored bulbs hanging from the eaves outside, casting a rainbow glow across his high, peeled birch bed. The room smelled of woods and soap and some ineffable fragrance she found wildly arousing. He went over to a dresser and lit a tall column of a candle, dimly illuminating an area cluttered with unsorted laundry and a box of gift wrap, curly ribbon and gift bags.

"Sorry about the mess," he murmured. "I wasn't expecting company."

"You weren't?"

"Hoping, maybe. Not expecting." He took her by the hand and brought her over to the bed.

"I'm glad you're here."

She started to reply, but he shushed her with a light brush of his thumb across her lips, and it was all she could do not to moan audibly.

"We're already pretty good at talking," he explained. "We can make conversation, joke around."

"Yes, but—"

"Shh. Let's see how we do at being quiet together." He cupped the side of her head in his hand and kissed her, long and searchingly, his tongue teasing its way into her mouth. She ran her hands over his upper arms and around his shoulders, mapping the terrain of hard muscle under his soft sweater. He felt so good to her. She was so ready for this—another surprise. Before Logan, she'd wanted nothing to do with guys, and relationships. All she thought of was the risk and the emotional pain. Just a few weeks ago, she had been patently unable to imagine being vulnerable again, but suddenly she felt as if someone had let her out of a small, cramped box of her own making. Stepping back, she pulled her top over her head and let it drop to the floor. It felt wonderful, liberating, to finally leave the past behind and step into this unexpected new place—Logan's world.

He took in a sharp breath, then put his hands at her waist

and pulled her close, bending to place a line of kisses along her collarbone, then reaching around to unhook her bra, fumbling a little.

"It's a front clasp," she said, slowly guiding his hands to savor every bit of his touch.

He took it off, and made a wordless sound she found completely gratifying. He peeled his sweater off one-handed and dropped his jeans, and she followed suit. Then he pressed her back on the bed, onto the soft, age-worn quilt. She welcomed the weight of him, feeling amazed at how clear-eyed she was about wanting him. Instead of feeling smothered, she felt untethered, ready for adventure.

He pulled a ribbon of connected packets from a drawer of the bedside table. "Better watch out," he murmured.

"Better not cry," she said.

Then he raised himself above her and held her hands up over her head, sinking down with exquisite timing. "Santa Claus is coming tonight," he whispered.

Time slipped away, the minutes uncounted as they lost themselves in making love. Darcy felt dazed by the storm of pleasure, and in the aftermath, the silence was deep, broken only by their satisfied, tandem breathing. His long, muscular body curved around hers, unfamiliar and exciting.

Her life seemed to be taking an unanticipated turn. She thought she'd come here simply to survive the holidays away from her family. And now here she was with this new thing happening to her. This...romance. Really, there was no other word for it. She was swept into a lovely swirl of emotion, one that freed her heart and filled her with joy, gently unspooling the tension she'd been holding on to from the past. He turned his head and gently kissed her temple. "That was nice," he whispered.

"Yes," she said. "But there's something I don't understand."

"What's that?"

"This is supposed to be awkward," she said. "We're new, it's our first time, so…why isn't this awkward?"

"Because it's the real thing. It's not awkward, because it's real."

"How do you know that? We barely know each other."

"I know stuff." He laughed softly. "I'm smarter than I look."

"What stuff?" she asked. "I mean, you're the first man I've wanted to make love to since my marriage. If you're so smart, you'd realize this is probably rebound sex."

"As opposed to what?"

"The kind of sex you have when you realize you're over your failed marriage and you're ready to move on, and you find someone you click with and you realize you're not reacting to the past but to right now."

"I think you just answered your own question." He trailed his finger along her jawline, then down over her shoulder. "This is not a rebound," he said.

"What makes you so sure of that?"

"Because I'm not letting you go."

Her heart surged with excitement. Happiness. She wished the feeling could go on forever.

And this was unfortunate, because she could not see a way for the situation to sort itself out in the long term. Logan was incredible, but there was a red flag as big and bright as the cape of a matador. He claimed he wanted—he needed—a woman who wanted children, not just Charlie but babies, too. She couldn't promise him that. It just felt too risky, too fraught with pitfalls. She wasn't ready now and couldn't be certain she'd ever be.

"There are things you don't know about me," she confessed. "Things that would make a big difference in the way you feel. Things that would tell you that this might not be the right move for either of us."

"There's plenty we don't know about each other, but it's only a matter of time. I plan to learn everything about you. I'm going to know what makes you laugh, what makes you cry. I'm going to know what makes you mad and what makes you sad. I'm going to learn all about you. And you're going to love every minute of it. Oh, and you're going to learn everything about me, too."

"You sound very sure of yourself."

"Because I *am* sure. And the more you know me, the more you're going to love me."

That word. *Love.* Although her feelings for him were all brand new, she could not convince herself that he was wrong. "You seem to know a lot about us. Do you have a crystal ball?"

"I know what I know." He propped himself up on one elbow and gazed down at her, serious now. In the faint glow of the Christmas lights and the flickering candle flame, his eyes looked deep and intense. "I know what my heart's telling me to do. It's telling me to love you. It's telling me to take you in my arms and never let you go."

A flurry of alarm fluttered in her chest. "But we want such different things. I can never be the person you want me to be."

"Darcy. You already *are* that person."

"You're wrong. I'm not. And I never can be." She suddenly felt overwhelmed by his certainty, by the power in his eyes. She could never live up to what he wanted from her. She could never be the mother he wanted for Charlie, couldn't imagine having his children.

She'd said it a hundred times. She didn't want children. And she was scared. She had emerged from the demise of her marriage more or less intact, but also firmly resolved to be smarter, going forward. She was too young, too hopeful to declare she'd never fall in love again. But now she was wise enough to know that if and when she did, she would do so cautiously, not leaping into something the way she'd just...leaped.

"Why are you so afraid of finding happiness?"

"Because it doesn't last, and it's awful when you lose it."

"You're not going to lose it. When the right thing comes along, it's just going to grow and deepen and get stronger every day, every year until the end of time."

He was a hopeless romantic. She wished she could be that, too, wished she could surrender and not see all the obstacles in the way.

But she couldn't. It was too hard for her. Too scary. She needed time, time to think. Time to see if there was any truth in what he was telling her.

"It's almost Christmas," she said. "Can we just agree to enjoy the holidays?"

"And then?"

"And then I have to go home."

"To the sock warehouse," he said.

"Hey. Don't judge. I searched high and low for my place in the city."

"Yeah? Well, maybe I searched high and low for *you*."

CHAPTER NINETEEN

A t some point in the dead of night, the power went out.
Logan awakened to chilly darkness, and found himself
lying in an empty bed. The Christmas lights were dark and
colorless, and the big candle on the dresser had burned down
to a puddle of white wax. If it was not for warm memories
swirling through him, he might have thought he'd dreamed
the night with Darcy.

He jumped out of bed, pulled on jeans and a sweatshirt and
thick socks and went downstairs. His breath created frozen
clouds. The Christmas tree looked sad and neglected, standing there in the weak light through the window. In the aftermath of the blizzard, the light in the great room was stark
from the deep blanket of snow. Over at the resort, the emer-
gency generator chugged with a distant hum.

Working quickly, he made a fire. A big one. But it would

take more than that to chase away the chill in the air. Suddenly his perfect Christmas wasn't looking so perfect.

His father came into the room, unshaven and bundled up against the frigid weather. "Bad luck on the power," he said.

"Yeah." Logan braced himself, expecting an I-told-you-so and a reminder that they could be enjoying the Florida sunshine today. But the diatribe never came. Al stood in front of the fire, slapping his palms together.

"So much for hot cinnamon buns and coffee this morning," Logan said. "And unless the power company gets right on it, I'm not so sure about Mom's baked ham and all the trimmings." He glared at the dead-looking tree. "There's something totally depressing about an unlit tree by daylight."

"Maybe this will cheer you up." His father handed him a business-sized envelope.

"What's this?"

"A contract. You can read the fine print later. It's an investor's agreement. I'm looking for a stake in Saddle Mountain."

Logan's jaw dropped. "What the—"

"Did he come?" The kids arrived en masse, tumbling into the room, sleep-tousled and still in their pajamas. "Did Santa come?"

Logan put the contract in his back pocket and couldn't keep from grinning at his dad. "Yep," he said. "It appears that he did."

"Yay!"

Al turned to the herd of children. "Well, now, looks like Santa didn't bring any electricity. Better check the stockings."

"Stockings!" There was a mad scramble.

India and China arrived to supervise the first wave of holiday madness. Someone switched on the battery-powered speakers, and lively carols filled the air. Logan's mother went around lighting every candle she could find. The stockings were stuffed with treats and crazy little toys, like windup roaring dinosaurs, stick-on tattoos, nostril-shaped pencil sharpeners, mini whoopee cushions. Charlie was enamored with a set of finger-sized steel drums, and André accompanied him on the harmonica.

"When can we open presents?" Bernie demanded. "We've been waiting *forever.*"

"After everybody gets here," China said.

"Where's Darcy?" Charlie asked, looking around.

Good question, thought Logan. Had last night's conversation freaked her out so much she'd disappeared into the frozen tundra?

"I'll go look in her room." Bernie clambered up the stairs.

Uh-oh, thought Logan.

A few minutes later, Bernie returned, her eyes wide. "She's gone. Her bed is all made up, and she's *gone.*"

Instantly Logan's sisters turned to him with knowledge written clearly in their gazes.

He offered a sheepish grin and a shrug.

"Where'd she go?" Charlie asked. "Should we go look for her?"

A commotion ensued as everyone debated and speculated, but it didn't last long. "Hey, check it out," said André, running to the front door.

There was Darcy in her parka and snowshoes, coming up the front walk, pulling a small sled behind her. She looked like a dream to Logan. Small and bright, a breath of fresh air. Last night had been incredible, and deep down, he felt completely certain this was not a fling or a rebound. They had a lot more talking to do.

Maybe not just talking.

"Hot coffee and hot chocolate from the lodge," Darcy announced, leaving her snowshoes on the porch. Al and Bilski went outside to help her.

"Christmas is saved," Logan's mother declared.

As Logan took her coat and shut the door behind her, he noticed a line of snowshoe tracks leading around to the back of the house.

"Now can we open presents?" Charlie asked.

"Ready, set, go!" India yelled.

The kids rushed toward the Christmas tree. Despite the lack of electricity, their squeals of excitement lit the room. The Santa gifts were a hit—a dollhouse and princess outfits for the girls, sleds and snowball bazookas for the boys, André's baseball mitt, the snowboard for Charlie. Logan saw the boys sharing a knowing look.

"I got a special card," Angelica exclaimed. "Look, it's from Santa!" She opened the card, which featured a sparkly picture of Santa and a simple message. "See you at the church, later."

"I wonder what it means." Bernie turned the card this way and that, squinting at the careful lettering.

Angelica's eyes shone with hope and excitement. "Maybe it means I'm getting my Christmas wish."

"I bet it does," Bernie declared.

Logan was probably the only one who noticed Charlie's smile seemed forced as he inspected the shiny new snowboard. "It's really cool," he said.

"I bet you can't wait to try it out," said Al.

"That's right."

"Just what you wanted?" asked Fisher.

Charlie ducked his head and slid his snowboard along the rug under the tree. Logan could tell something was up. Charlie's cheerfulness was an act, that was apparent.

Logan's gut twisted unpleasantly as he went over to the fireplace mantel, where there was a small stack of Christmas cards.

Among the cards were the notes they had written to themselves last summer at Camp Kioga. True to her word, Sonnet had mailed them to arrive the day before. Logan's message to himself had been succinct: *Make Christmas awesome for Charlie.*

He sensed Darcy beside him, peering over his shoulder. "Remember this?" he asked her.

She nodded. "I filled one out, too. But I wasn't home to get my mail."

"What'd you write on it?"

She hesitated, but smiled up at him. "Maybe I'll tell you someday."

He liked the sound of "someday" coming from her. "I'll hold you to that."

"What did you write?"

He showed her. "I'm not doing so hot."

"Nonsense. Look at this, Logan." She gestured around the room, at his parents and sisters, nieces and nephews, André and Angelica and Charlie. Everyone was laughing or relaxing or playing while outside the window, a soft snow began to fall. His parents were on the sofa, sipping coffee and watching the kids. "Joy to the World" was playing on the stereo. "Look at these happy faces. You did this, Logan. *You.*"

It was exactly what he needed to hear. How had she known? His heart skipped a beat. He was going to love this woman forever. He just knew it. Now he had to figure out if she knew it, too. "Hey—"

"The pickle prize," she said suddenly, turning to Charlie. "Don't forget the pickle prize."

The kids perked up, and there was another mad dash for the tree. Darcy nudged Charlie and pointed at a spot in the tree.

"There it is," Charlie yelled. "I saw it first!" Reaching through the branches, he unhooked the ornament from the

341

tree. The motion sensor went off, and the pickle made a yo-deling sound.

"You won the pickle prize," Darcy declared.

"What's the pickle prize?" he asked, narrowing his eyes.

"I bet it's on that little note," Bernie said, indicating the tiny tag attached to the ornament.

"What's it say?" asked Nan.

"Read it!" Fisher and Goose demanded.

Charlie unfolded the note. "It says pant…pantry. I got it, I'm supposed to look in the pantry." He set down the ornament and made a beeline for the big storage room off the kitchen.

Mystified, Logan shot Darcy a look and followed him. Charlie swung open the door and peered into the dark.

"What'd you find?" asked André, crowding in behind him.

"It's just pantry stuff," Charlie mumbled. "I don't—" He stopped and held very still.

"What?" asked André.

"Shh." Nearly masked by the music and conversation, a tiny noise sounded. Charlie bent down and picked up a wicker basket filled with fleece blankets.

When he turned, his face was lit with wonder. "Dad," he said, his voice hoarse. "Dad, look!" He set down the basket and moved the blankets aside to reveal a fluffy, squirming, squeaking bundle. "A puppy! I got a puppy!" His eyes shone with joy as he carefully lifted it up.

"Charlie got a puppy!" Bernie exclaimed. "Oh my gosh, he's so cute!"

Everyone gathered around to admire the little puppy. It had floppy ears and butterscotch-colored fur, a black button nose and bright eyes. There was a red ribbon around its neck and a tag. Charlie read it aloud. "Please look after this dog. His name is Taffy, and he wants to be your forever friend. Love, Santa."

The pup licked Charlie's face, and the laughter that came

from him was the sweetest sound Logan had ever heard. He looked over at Darcy—clearly, the culprit in this. She looked back, grinning.

"Whaddya know," André said, "Santa really is real."

Logan had told Darcy all the reasons it was a bad time to get a dog—the mess, the noise, the work, the inconvenience. But for now, he simply caught her eye from across the room and mouthed two words: *thank you.*

"How are we going to get to church?" asked Logan's mother, checking her watch. "And will we make it on time?" All the adults in the house were in on the Angelica project. Everyone wanted the live video link to work so Maya Martin could see her kids on Christmas.

"Not to worry," said Logan. "One of the groomers is driving the big plow down the mountain road."

"Then let's get going," said India, rounding everyone up.

The town of Avalon looked as if it had been covered in fluffy white icing, but the church parking lot was full.

The church had power, thanks to a generator. Volunteers were pouring hot chocolate and coffee in the candlelit lobby. Everyone filed inside, breathing a sigh of relief at the warmth. More candles glowed around the altar. Charlie brought his puppy in a portable carrier lined with soft bedding, thoughtfully provided by Santa.

"How'd you pull that off?" Logan murmured.

"A little bird told me," she whispered. "I paid a visit to PAWS yesterday, and they kept the dog at the lodge overnight. I just had to sneak him into the house this morning."

"You've got a lot of tricks up your sleeve."

"I know I put a lot on your plate without asking you, but I've heard it said that it's easier to apologize after the fact than to ask permission in the first place."

"Don't apologize. You're amazing. Charlie and I will never forget what you did."

"It was Santa's doing. I was only following orders."

Eddie and Maureen Haven, the pageant directors, greeted people at the door to the sanctuary. Charlie handed the travel crate to André and approached them, his face pale and serious. "I'm sorry about the manger. I'm really sorry."

"You fixed it just in time," Eddie said. "No harm done." He glanced down at his wife. "Years ago, I made a much bigger mess on Christmas Eve. Took me a long time, but I made amends." They shook hands.

Logan frowned at Darcy. "What was that about?"

"I'll tell you later. Or maybe Charlie will."

Inside the sanctuary, the kids got into their choir robes while the adults filed into their seats. Logan and Darcy found Zach Alger getting the video link ready. He motioned them over. "All set," he said.

Logan brought André and Angelica to look at the setup. "There's someone who wants to say hi," he said. The children's faces lit up when they looked at the small screen. There was Maya, smiling tremulously. She wore a collared blue shirt and had every hair in place. There were rings of sleeplessness around her eyes, but when the kids stood in front of the camera, the tense lines were softened by joy.

"Hey, babies," she said. "Merry Christmas."

"Merry Christmas to you, Mama," said Angelica.

"We miss you," André said. "We can't wait to see you."

"Are you gonna watch the singing?" Angelica asked, toying with the red ribbon of her robe. "I'm gonna sing a special song."

"Yes, I get to watch. And I'm going to be so proud of you. I love you both. I'll see you soon."

"How soon, Mama? Sometimes in the night, I miss you so much that I cry," said Angelica.

"Ah, baby, I'm so sorry I can't be there. I cry, too. But not today. Not on Christmas. I hope you're having fun, up there in the mountains."

"It's really fun!" said Angelica.

"I'm learning to snowboard," André said.

"And Charlie got a puppy from Santa," his sister added. "A real live puppy. Show her, Charlie."

He took the pup from the crate and held it in front of the screen. "His name's Taffy."

"Wow, that's really cute," said Maya. "Santa was good to you this year."

"Yes," Angelica said. "I got what I wanted, Mama. *You* were my Christmas wish. And here you are."

"Yeah," Maya said, her voice rough. "Here I am."

"I really wanted you to see me sing and I didn't think it could come true and it did."

"Are you okay, Mama?" asked André, his voice subdued. He sounded mature beyond his years.

Logan put a hand on the boy's shoulder. Watching Maya on camera, he could see her struggling to keep her smile in place.

"I'm okay now, baby boy," she said. "I swear, I'm okay."

"Christmas wasn't perfect." Logan eased his arm around Darcy as they sat together on the sofa that night, after everyone else had gone to bed. "But it was one of my favorites."

Darcy smiled, snuggling closer. The power hadn't come on until evening, and their Christmas dinner had consisted of hot dogs roasted over the fire. Yet the kids had all had a great day, and they'd gone to bed content.

"Maybe we just have to redefine perfect," she said. She felt nervous and excited. She told herself she'd better have the conversation she was afraid to have. If it didn't go her way, if it scared him off, then at least she could know. She could move on with no lingering doubts. Would she miss him? Of course she would. Would it kill her? No, she'd survived worse.

She finally felt like herself again. After all this time and after all she had been through, her wishes and dreams had stumbled. They'd been downgraded. She had come to believe that shrinking her dreams was better than inflating her hopes. It was the ultimate self-protection against disappointment.

That was the wrong kind of thinking, though. In Logan's arms, she remembered the value of taking a risk. It was better to risk everything for something she believed in than to hide from the best part of life, from love and connection and joy. Now here was this unexpected thing happening, right in the middle of her life, something she had never planned for or dared to imagine for herself.

With Logan, she discovered that the dreams she had set aside actually had a chance of coming true. Almost in spite of her hopes and fears, without even realizing it, something new was forming. She sensed it in the deepest part of her, the way she felt when something clicked into place. It seemed as if her body knew what was happening before her mind accepted the concept. She felt herself relax, a big unwinding of the squeezing tension she didn't know she was holding on to. It was like exhaling at last after holding her breath for a year.

"How is this going to go?" she asked Logan. "Do we get a happy ending or…"

"What if it doesn't end at all?" he asked.

"Meaning?"

He smiled and kissed her temple. "Suppose it's a happy beginning that never has to end?"

She couldn't think straight when he kissed her. "Fair enough. But there are logistics to consider."

"Logistics," he said, his voice prompting.

She shifted on the sofa, turning to face him. "Logan, we want different things."

He looked away. "I always thought my happiness depended on having a family. You know, more kids. Brothers and sisters for Charlie. More babies to raise. That's what I thought would make me happy."

She felt her insides freeze up with apprehension. More babies to raise. Would she? Could she? "I don't—"

"Something occurred to me," he said.

Oh God, she thought. *Oh no.* She teetered. Could a person who never wanted kids be happy with a person who did want kids? There really was no room for compromise.

She pictured a future with him. Pictured being pregnant, her belly growing. The discomfort. The night feedings. The struggles and the joy. With Logan.

This was not a compromise. With all her heart, she yearned to fall in love with him. It was already happening. But could she want the same things he wanted? *Don't be afraid anymore,* she told herself. *When it's right, you don't have to be afraid.* Maybe, she thought, it wasn't the prospect of children that made her feel trapped but the way she approached a relationship and the way her partner treated her. Everything was different now. Everything. "Logan—"

"Let me finish." He stroked her hair. "Listen. Everything I imagined when I thought about the future has changed. And it's because of you. I want you to be my future. Not some image I had, not some concept in my head. You make me happy. You and me together—that's what I want. Us."

"I don't understand. What are you saying?"

"That now when I think of family, I think of you. And Charlie. I don't need any more than that."

Her breath caught, and then for no reason she could fathom, she started to cry. "I feel exactly the same way."

"You do?"

"But I changed my mind about something, too."

"Darcy—"

"No, listen. I've been so scared, for so long. Scared of hurt and disappointment. Then I realized disappointment doesn't kill you. Either it just teaches you not to hope...or it shows you how strong you can be."

"I won't hurt you, Darcy. I won't disappoint you."

She trusted that with all her heart. "I know," she said. "I want the future with you, too. I want the family. I want us." Declaring this to him made her feel both vulnerable and liberated. She put her arms around him, praying she would never have to let him go. "What I don't know is if I can keep from disappointing *you*."

"I've heard you're a true believer. You told me so yourself."

"Yes."

"Then you have to believe wishes can come true."

EPILOGUE

One year later

Saddle Mountain was overrun with children, and Darcy loved it. She reveled in it—the noise, the chaos, the bickering, the laughter, the fun. It was easy to find delight in every moment. Even André and Angelica were present. Following her release, Maya had relocated to Avalon. She had a little rental apartment in town, and she worked at the bridal shop, doing alterations. She was in a safe place with her kids, far from her ex.

Another family had come for the holidays this year—the Fitzgeralds. The parents and sisters, Lydia and Badgley with their new baby. Huntley was nowhere to be found, and no one seemed to miss him.

The past year had been a time of growth and change for

Darcy. It had not always been easy. She still caught herself looking over her shoulder, back at the past—but mostly she faced forward.

Falling in love with Logan was very physical. Not only in the standard sense of the word, with the pounding heart and giddy light-headedness. She felt all that, and it was incredibly beautiful, more wild and exhilarating than any ride on a snowboard or surfboard. But there was more to it than that.

When she was with him, she slept. This was a big change. She had not slept soundly until she found herself in Logan's arms. After her marriage had died, she had tossed and turned, night after night, mulling the situation over and over in her mind, pacing the floor, trying every technique she could think of to sleep, but to no avail.

Now she knew why she hadn't been sleeping. It was because she'd been filled with restlessness, knowing she needed more in her life but not knowing how to get there. Now, finally, with Logan, her heart was at home.

These days, she faced the future with a sense of wonder. This in itself was a miracle, because she had never before realized the possibilities life offered now that she'd found the person she was meant to spend her life with.

It was a love she had never before dared to imagine. A happiness she had never known could exist. It was not perfect. She was not perfect, nor was Logan. Their love was filled with imperfections. Yet it was beyond doubt the best thing that had ever happened to her.

On Christmas morning, Taffy the dog woke everyone up, and the children made a mad scramble for their presents. Darcy sat next to Logan and laughed as she watched them playing with boxing gloves, makeup sets, a xylophone, a karaoke machine.

"Hey, what about the pickle?" Charlie asked suddenly. "Darcy, come help me find it."

The look Charlie shared with his dad made her suspicious, but she went over to the tree and peered through the branches. Charlie moved a swag of tinsel, and she heard the familiar, utterly silly yodeling sound. There it was, dangling in the middle, near the trunk.

"You found the Christmas pickle," Charlie said.

She dangled the ornament for all to see. "The yodeling pickle. That's awesome."

"It means you get a prize," Charlie reminded her.

"Sounds like my lucky day."

"You're going to have to excuse us," Logan told everyone, standing up. "We'll be back."

Darcy's breath caught. She thought about the past year. She and Logan had grown closer and closer, and she hoped with all her heart that they were about to take the next step together. At the moment, his face was unreadable.

They put on parkas and snowshoes and walked out into the woods together. It was a quiet, snowy morning, the air still, the birch trees and evergreens motionless. To Darcy it felt as if the world was holding its breath. They went to the clearing where they'd decorated the tall evergreen tree, both last year and this.

Logan took a flat, oblong package from his pocket. "I actually bought this last year, on Christmas Eve. I knew then, Darcy. I knew I wanted to be with you forever, but we were so new. I wanted you to feel ready. You were still hurting. I didn't want to scare you."

"I don't hurt anymore and I'm not scared," she said. "How's that for a big change?"

He placed the box in her hands. It wasn't a ring box.

She hated the fact that it wasn't a ring box. It was covered in thick, glossy gold paper and tied with a bright golden bow.

"Go ahead," he said. "Open it."

She took off her mittens and removed the paper, then peeked into the slender black box. "A charm bracelet." She smiled, but it felt bittersweet, because her expectations had painted a different scenario. "You got me a charm bracelet." She lifted the silver chain from the box. It was pretty, catching glints of light.

"Check it out," he said. "The first charm is the Camp Kioga flag, because that's where I met you for the first time. Got it from the gift shop there."

"I yelled at India for trying to fix us up."

"I think I did, too," he admitted. "Now I can't thank her enough. Okay, the next two. A surfboard and a dolphin."

"Our Florida Thanksgiving."

"Our first kiss. I was so hot for you I couldn't see straight."

"Yeah?" she teased, liking the bracelet more and more, even though it wasn't what she expected. "I guess you couldn't see the screen on your phone, because you never called. You never wrote…"

"Hey. I made up for it. Here's the snowshoe charm for last Christmas. The heart—that's Valentine's Day, of course."

"We were in New York, taking Maya to lunch to celebrate her release. I loved that day, Logan."

There were charms to mark the milestones through the year—a seashell for the first time she'd taken him to Cupsogue and introduced him to her family, and a tiny lighthouse for the weekend they'd spent in Montauk, where the O'Donnells lived. A maple leaf for their fall weekend in Canada, and a pinecone from Mohonk Mountain House, where he'd taken her for her birthday.

"It's very romantic," she said. "*You're* very romantic."

"Because you're very inspiring."

The last charm was a pickle. "It's a tiny silver pickle," she said stupidly. "Who knew there was such a thing?"

"I had no idea, until you explained it to me last year."

"So the pickle is to commemorate this Christmas?"

"Yep. It means you win the pickle prize."

"Isn't this bracelet the pickle prize?"

"Nope. This is." He opened his hand and, in one smooth motion, slipped a diamond ring on her finger.

Her jaw dropped, even as her heart soared. "Logan…"

"I want forever with you. I'm going to love you until the end of time. Darcy, will you marry me?"

She threw her arms around him, burying her face in his parka. The inevitable tears came, but she was laughing, too. "Oh my gosh. Yes, of course yes. A thousand yeses wouldn't be enough."

There was a sweetness to their kiss that felt brand-new, like something she'd never tasted before. "You had me going," she murmured against his soft mouth. "You made me think I was getting a silver bracelet for Christmas."

"Instead, you get me. And Charlie. And Taffy."

"And forever," she said. "You're my forever person. Ah, Logan. I'm so happy. I was just thinking this morning, I've never felt this kind of happiness. It's amazing. *You're* amazing."

He kissed her lips, and then her hand with the ring on it. "Hold still," he said. "I'll put the bracelet on you."

She admired the collection of charms, a chronicle of their year together. "Let's go back and tell everyone. And I still haven't given you *your* gift."

He leaned over and gave her a kiss, and whispered in her ear, "I haven't opened a single present, but I already have everything I want."

★ ★ ★ ★ ★

Keep reading for a special preview of The Apple Orchard, *from* New York Times *bestselling author Susan Wiggs!*

CHAPTER ONE

San Francisco

Tess Delaney's to-do list was stacked invisibly over her head like the air traffic over O'Hare. She had clients waiting to hear from her, associates hounding her for reports and a make-or-break meeting with the owner of the firm. She pushed back at the pressing anxiety and focused on the task at hand—restoring a treasure to its rightful owner.

The current mission brought her to an overfurnished apartment in Alamo Square. Miss Annelise Winther, still spry at eighty, ushered her into a cozy place with thready lace curtains, dust-ruffled chairs and a glorious scent of something baking. Tess wasted no time in presenting the treasure.

Miss Winther's hands, freckled by age, the joints knotted with arthritis, shook as she held the antique lavaliere. Beneath a pink knitted shawl, her bony shoulders trembled.

"This necklace belonged to my mother," she said, her voice breaking over the word. "I haven't seen it since the spring of 1941." She lifted her gaze to Tess, who sat across the scrubbed pine kitchen table from her. There were stories in the woman's eyes, winking like the facets of a jewel. "I have no words to thank you for bringing this to me."

"It's my pleasure," said Tess. "Moments like this—they're the best part of my job." The sense of pride and accomplishment helped her ignore the insistent buzz of her phone, signaling yet another incoming message.

Annelise Winther was Tess's favorite kind of client. She was unassuming, a woman of modest means, judging by the decrepit condition of her apartment, in one of the city's rambling Victorians that had seen better days. Two cats, whom the woman had introduced as Golden and Prince, lazed in the late-afternoon autumn sunshine spilling through a bumped-out bay window. A homey-looking needlepoint piece hung on the wall, bearing the slogan Live This Day.

Miss Winther took off her glasses, polished them and put them back on. Glancing again at Tess's business card, she said, "Tess Delaney, Provenance Specialist, Sheffield Auction House. Well, Ms. Delaney. I'm extremely glad you found me, too. You've done well for yourself."

Her voice had a subtle tinge of an accent. "I saw that History Channel special about the Kraków Museum. You won an award last month in Poland."

"You saw that?" Tess asked, startled to know the woman had recognized her.

"Indeed I did. You were given a citation for restoring the rosary of Queen Maria Leszczynska. It had been stolen by Nazi looters and was missing for decades."

"It was…a moment." Tess had felt so proud that night. The only trouble was, she'd been in a room full of strangers. No one was present to witness her triumph. Her mother had promised to come but had to cancel at the last minute, so Tess had accepted the accolades in front of a small camera crew and a cultural minister with sweaty hands.

"The very second I saw your face, I knew you would be the one to find my treasure." Miss Winther's words were slightly startling. "And I'm so pleased that it's you. I specifically requested you."

"Why?"

A pause. Miss Winther's face softened. Perhaps she'd lost her train of thought. Then she said, "Because you're the best. Aren't you?"

"I try my best," Tess assured her. She thought the conversation odd, but in this business, she was accustomed to quirky clients. "This piece was with a group of recovered objects from World War II." Tess fell quiet as she thought of the other pieces—jewelry and art and collectibles. The majority of objects remained in limbo, their original owners long gone. She tried not to imagine the terrible sense of violation so many families had suffered, with Nazis invading their homes, plundering their treasures and probably sending many of the family members off to die. Restoring lost treasures seemed a small thing, but the look on Miss Winther's face was its own reward.

"You've made a miracle happen," she declared. "I was just telling a friend on the phone that we're never too old to appreciate a true miracle."

For a miracle, Tess reflected, the task had entailed a lot of hard work. But the expression on the woman's face made all the research, travel and red tape worthwhile. At her own expense, Tess had paid an expert to meticulously clean every link, baguette and facet of the lavaliere. "This is a copy of the provenance report." She slid the document across the table. "It's basically a history of the piece from its creation to the present, as near as I could trace it to its origins in Russia."

"It's amazing that you were able to find this. When I first contacted your firm, I thought..." Her voice trailed off. "How on earth did you do it?"

Working backward through the provenance report, Tess explained the progress of her research. "This piece was found with a collection of treasures seized in Copenhagen. The lavaliere is pink topaz, with gold filigree embellishments. The chain and clasp are original. It was made by a Finnish designer by the name of August Holmstrom. He was the principal jeweler for the house of Fabergé."

Miss Winther's eyebrows lifted. "*The* Fabergé?"

"The very one." Taking out her loupe, Tess pointed out a tiny spot on the piece. "This is Holmstrom's hallmark, right here, his initials between a double-headed Imperial eagle. He designed it specifically to foil counterfeiters. This particular piece was first mentioned in his design catalog of 1916 and produced for a fashionable shop in St. Petersburg. It was bought by a member of the Danish diplomatic corps."

"My father. He brought the necklace home from a business trip to Russia, and my mother was seldom without it. Besides her wedding ring, it was her favorite piece of jewelry. He gave it to her to celebrate my birth. Though she never said so, I suspect she couldn't have more children after me." Her eyes took on a faraway look, and Tess wondered what she was seeing—her handsome father? Her mother, wearing the jewel against her heart?

The stories behind the treasures were always so intriguing, though often bittersweet. The sad ones were particularly hard to bear. There were some cruelties that were simply inconceivable to normal people, some injustices too big to grasp. Miss Winther must have been tiny when her world was ripped apart. How scared she must have been, how confused.

"I wish I could do more than simply restore this object," said Tess. "It wound up with a number of other pieces in a repository in the basement of an abandoned government building. I spent the past year researching the archives. The Gestapo claimed they kept objects for safekeeping. It was a common ploy. The one helpful thing they did was to keep meticulous records of the things they seized."

Here was where things got dicey. How much information did Miss Winther really need? Did she have to know what had likely happened to her parents?

There were facts Tess had no intention of sharing, such as the evidence that Hilde Winther had been seized without authority by a corrupt officer, and probably treated like a sex slave for months before she was put to death. This was the trouble with uncovering the mysteries of the past. Sometimes you ended up discovering things better left buried. Was it preferable to expose the truth at any cost or to protect someone from troubling matters they had no power to change?

"This piece was taken from your mother after she was arrested on suspicion of hiding spies, saboteurs and resistance fighters at Bispebjerg Hospital. According to the arrest report, she was accused of pretending her patients were extremely ill, and she would tend to them until they conveniently disappeared."

Miss Winther caught her breath, then nodded. "That sounds like Mama. She was so very brave. She told me she was a hospital volunteer, but I always knew she was doing something important." Behind her spectacles, the old lady's eyes took on a cold glaze of anger. "My mother was dragged away on a beautiful spring afternoon while I watched."

Tess felt an unbidden shudder of sympathy for the little girl Miss Winther had once been. "I'm so sorry. No child should have to witness that."

Miss Winther held out the necklace, the facets of the large pink topaz catching the light. "Could you...put it on me?" she asked.

"Of course." Tess came around behind her and fastened the clasp of the necklace, feeling the old woman's delicate bone structure. Her hair smelled of lavender, and her dress under the pink shawl was threadbare and faded. Tess felt a surge of emotion. This find was going to change Miss Winther's life.

In a single transaction, the old woman could find herself living in the lap of luxury.

Miss Winther reached up, cradling the jewel between her palms. "She was wearing it that day. Even as they were taking her away, she ordered me to run for my life, and that is just what I did. I was very lucky in that moment, or perhaps there had been a tip-off. A boy who was with the Holger Danske—the Danish resistance—spirited me to safety. Such a hero he was, like the Scarlet Pimpernel in the French Revolution, only he was quite real. I wouldn't be here today if not for him. None of us would."

None of us…? Tess wondered who she was referring to. Ghosts from the woman's sad past, probably. She didn't ask, though; she had other appointments on her schedule and couldn't spare the time. And knowing the human cost of the tragedy made Tess feel vulnerable. Still, she was taken by the old lady's sweetness and the air of nostalgia that softened her features when she touched the reclaimed treasure around her neck.

We're both all alone, we two, thought Tess. Had Miss Winther always been alone? *Will I always be?*

"Well, I'm certainly glad you're here." The old lady's smile was soft and strangely intimate.

"This is the appraisal on the piece. I think you'll be very pleased."

The old lady stared at the document. "It says my mother's lavaliere is worth $800,000."

"It's an estimate. Depending on how the bidding goes, it could vary by about ten percent up or down."

Miss Winther fanned herself. "That's a fortune," she said. "It's more money than I ever dreamed of having."

"And not nearly enough to replace your loss, but it's quite a find. I'm really happy for you." Tess felt a glow of accomplishment and pleasure for Miss Winther. In her frayed shawl, surrounded by old things, she didn't look like a wealthy woman, but soon, she would be.

All the painstaking work of restitution had led to this moment. Tess spread a multipage contract on the table.

"Here's the agreement with Sheffield Auction House, my firm. It's standard, but you'll want to go over it with a contracts expert."

A timer dinged, and Miss Winther got up from the table. "The scones are ready. My favorites—I make them with lavender sugar. It's an old Danish recipe for autumn. You sit tight, dear, and I'll fix the tea."

Tess pressed her teeth together and tried not to seem impatient, though she had more appointments and work to do at the office. Honestly, she didn't want a scone, with or without lavender sugar. She didn't want tea. Coffee and a cigarette were more to her taste and definitely more suited to the pace of her life. She'd been running since she'd rocketed out of grad school five years before, and she was in a hurry now. The quicker she brought the signed agreement to her firm, the quicker she earned her bonus and could move on to the next transaction.

However, the nature of her profession often called for forbearance. People became attached to their things, and sometimes letting go took time. Miss Winther had gone to a lot of trouble to make scones. Knowing what she knew about the Winther family, Tess wondered what the woman felt when she reminisced about the old days—fear and privation? Or happier times, when her family had been intact?

As she bustled around her old-fashioned kitchen, Miss Winther would pause every so often in front of a little framed mirror by the door, gazing at the necklace with a faraway look in her eyes. Tess wondered what she saw there—her pretty, adored mother? An innocent girl who had no idea her entire world was about to be snatched away?

"Tell me about what you do," Miss Winther urged her, pouring tea into a pair of china cups. "I would love to hear about your life."

"I guess you could say finding treasure is in my blood."

Miss Winther gave a soft gasp, as though Tess's statement surprised her. "Really?"

"My mother is a museum acquisitions expert. My grandmother had an antiques salon in Dublin."

"So you come from a line of independent women."

Nicely put, thought Tess. Her gaze skated away. She wasn't one to chat up a client for the sake of making a deal, but she genuinely liked Miss Winther, perhaps because the woman seemed truly interested in her. "Neither my mother nor my grandmother ever married," she explained. "I'll probably carry on that tradition, as well. My life is too busy for a serious relationship." *Gah, Tess, listen to yourself,* she thought. *Say it often enough and you'll believe it.*

"Well. I suspect that's only because the right person hasn't come along…yet. Pretty girl like you, with all that gorgeous red hair. I'm surprised some man hasn't swept you off your feet."

Tess shook her head. "My feet are planted firmly on the ground."

"I never married, either." A wistful expression misted her eyes. "I was in love with a man right after the war, but he married someone else." She paused to admire the stone once again. "It must be so exciting, the work of a treasure hunter."

"It takes a lot of research, which most people would find tedious. So many dead ends and disappointments," said Tess. "Most of my time is spent combing archives and old records and catalogs. It can be frustrating. But so worthwhile when I get to make a restitution like this. And every once in a great while, I might find myself peeling away a worthless canvas to find a Vermeer beneath. Or unearthing a fortune under a shepherd's hut in a field somewhere. Sometimes it's a bit macabre. The plunder might be stashed in a casket."

Miss Winther shuddered. "That's ghoulish."

"When people have something to hide, they tend to put it where no one would want to look. Your piece wasn't stored in a dramatic hiding place. It was tagged and neatly cataloged, along with dozens of other illegally seized pieces."

Miss Winther arranged the scones just so with a crisp linen napkin in a basket, and brought them to the table.

Tess took a warm scone, just to be polite.

"It sounds as though you like your work," Miss Winther said.

"Very much. It's everything to me." As she said the words aloud, Tess felt a wave of excitement. The business was fast-paced and unpredictable, and each day might bring an adrenaline rush—or crushing disappointment. Tess was having a banner year; her accomplishments were bringing her closer to the things she craved like air and water—recognition and security.

"That sounds just wonderful. I'm certain you'll get exactly what you're looking for."

"In this business, I'm not always sure what that is." Tess sneaked another glance at the clock on the stove.

Miss Winther noticed. "You have time to finish your tea."

Tess smiled, liking this woman almost in spite of herself. "All right. Would you like me to leave the contract with you or—"

That's not necessary," the old lady said, touching the faceted pink topaz. "I won't be selling this."

Tess blinked, shook her head a little. "I'm sorry, what?"

"My mother's lavaliere." She pressed the piece against her bosom. "It's not for sale."

Tess's heart plummeted. "With this piece, you could have total security for the rest of your life."

"Every last shred of security was stripped from me forever by the Nazis," Miss Winther pointed out. "And yet I survived. You've given me back my mother's favorite thing."

"As you say, it's a thing. An object you could turn into comfort and peace of mind for the rest of your days."

"I'm comfortable and secure now. And if you don't believe memories are worth more than money, then perhaps you've not made the right kind of memories." She regarded Tess with knowing sympathy.

Tess tried not to dwell on all the hours she'd spent combing through records and poring over research in order to make the restitution. If she thought about it too much, she'd probably tear out her hair in frustration. She tended to protect herself from memories, because memories made a person vulnerable.

"You must think I'm being a sentimental old fool." Miss Winther nodded. "I am. It's a privilege of old age. I have no debt, no responsibilities. Just me and the cats. We like our life exactly as it is."

Tess took a sip of strong tea, nearly wincing at its bitterness.

"Oh! The sugar bowl. I forgot," said Miss Winther. "It's in the pantry, dear. Would you mind getting it?"

The pantry contained a collection of dusty cans and jars, its walls and shelves cluttered with collectibles, many of them still bearing handwritten garage sale stickers.

"It's just to the right there," said Miss Winther. "On the spice shelf."

Tess picked up the small, footed bowl. Almost instantly, a tingle of awareness passed through her. One of the first things she'd learned in her profession was to tune into something known as the "heft" or "feel" of the piece. Something that was real and authentic simply had more substance than a fake or knockoff.

She set the tarnished bowl on the table and tried to keep a poker face as she studied the object. The sweep of the handles and the effortless swell of the bowl were unmistakable. Even the smoky streaks of age couldn't conceal the fact that the piece was sterling, not plate.

"Tell me about this sugar bowl," she said, using the small tongs to pick up a cube. Sugar tongs. They were even more rare than the bowl.

"It's handsome, isn't it?" Miss Winther said. "But the very devil to keep clean. I was not in a terribly practical frame of mind when I picked it up at a church rummage sale long ago. It's been decades. Rummage sales have always been a weakness of mine. I'm afraid I've brought home any number of bright, pretty things that just happened to catch my eye. Once I get something home, though, it's anyone's guess whether or not I'll actually use it."

"This is quite a find," Tess said, holding it up to check the bottom, and seeing the expected hallmark there.

"In what way?"

Could she really not know? "Miss Winther, this bowl is a Tiffany, and it appears to be genuine."

"Goodness, you don't say."

"There's a style known as the Empire set, very rare, produced in a limited edition. I'd have to do more research, but my sense is, this could be extremely valuable." Not that it would matter to the old lady, who preferred her artifacts to cash. "It's a lovely piece, regardless," Tess conceded.

"What a surprising aspect of your job," Miss Winther said, clasping her hands in delight. "Sometimes you stumble across a treasure when you're looking for something else entirely."

Tess watched the sugar cube dissolve in her cup. "It keeps my job interesting."

"Tell me, is this something your firm would sell?" asked Miss Winther.

"It's possible, though even with the sugar tongs, a single piece—"

"I didn't mean just the bowl. I meant the entire set."

Tess dropped her spoon on the table with a clatter. "There's a *set?*"

The Apple Orchard
by New York Times *bestselling author Susan Wiggs,*
available wherever MIRA Books are sold!